The
BLACK
UNICORN

By Terry Brooks

TERRY BROOKS

THE BLACK UNICORN

A Magic Kingdom of Landover Novel

orbit

www.orbitbooks.co.uk

ORBIT

First published in the United States by Ballantine Books, an imprint of
The Random House Publishing Group
First published in Great Britain in 1987 by Macdonald & Co (Publishers) Ltd
Published by Futura in 1988. Reprinted once.
First published by Orbit in 1992. Reprinted fifteen times.
This edition published by Orbit in 2007

condition being imposed on the subsequent purchaser.

A CIP catalogue record for this book
is available from the British Library.

ISBN 978-1-84149-558-3

Papers used by Orbit are natural, recyclable products made from
wood grown in sustainable forests and certified in accordance with
the rules of the Forest Stewardship Council.

Printed in England by Clays Ltd, St Ives plc
Paper supplied by Hellefoss AS, Norway

Orbit
An imprint of
Little, Brown Book Group
Brettenham House
Lancaster Place
London WC2E 7EN

A Member of the Hachette Livre Group of Companies

www.orbitbooks.co.uk

For Amanda
She sees unicorns that are hidden from me . . .

"How do you know she is a unicorn?" Molly demanded. "And why were you afraid to let her touch you? I saw you. You were afraid of her."

"I doubt that I will feel like talking for very long," the cat replied without rancor. "I would not waste time in foolishness if I were you. As to your first question, no cat out of its first fur can ever be deceived by appearances Unlike human beings, who enjoy them. As for your second question—" Here he faltered, and suddenly became very interested in washing; nor would he speak until he had licked himself fluffy and then licked himself smooth again Even then he would not look at Molly, but examined his claws.

"If she had touched me," he said very softly, "I would have been hers and not my own, not ever again."

Peter S. Beagle, The Last Unicorn

Contents

The Black Unicorn

Prologue

The black unicorn stepped from the morning mists, almost as if born of them, and stared out over the kingdom of Landover.

Daybreak hovered at the crest of the eastern horizon, an intruder that peeked from its place of concealment to catch a glimpse of night's swift departure. The silence seemed to deepen further with the appearance of the unicorn—as if that one small event in that one tiny corner was sensed somehow throughout the whole of the valley. Everywhere sleep gave way to waking, dreams to being, and that moment of transition was as close as time ever came to being frozen.

The unicorn stood near the summit of the valley's northern rim, high in the mountains of the Melchor, close to the edge of the world of fairy. Landover spread away before it, forested slopes and bare rock crags dropping toward foothills and grasslands, rivers and lakes, forests and scrub. Color glimmered in hazy patches through the fading dark where streaks of sunlight danced off morning dew. Castles, towns, and cottages were vague, irregular shapes against the symmetry, creatures that hunkered down in rest and breathed smoke from dying embers.

There were tears in the eyes of green fire that swept the valley end to end and glittered with newfound life. It had been so long!

A stream trickled down and collected in a basin of rocks a dozen yards from where the unicorn stood. A tiny gathering of forest creatures crouched at the edge of that pool and stared in awe at the wonder that had materialized before them—a rabbit, a badger, several squirrels and voles, an opossum and young, a solitary toad. A cave wight melted back into the shadows. A bog wump flattened back into its hole. Birds sat motionless upon the branches of the trees. All were stilled. The only sound was the ripple of the stream over mountain rock.

The black unicorn nodded its head in recognition of the homage being paid. Ebony body gleamed in the half light, mane and fetlocks shimmering like silk thrown in the wind. Goat's feet shifted and lion's tail swished, restless movements against the backdrop of the still-life world. The ridged horn knifed the darkness, shining faintly with magic. There had never before been a thing of such grace and beauty in all of creation as the unicorn and never would be again.

Dawn broke sharply over the valley of Landover, and the new day was begun. The black unicorn felt the sun's heat on its face and lifted its head in greeting. But invisible chains still bound it, and the cold of their lingering presence dispelled almost instantly the momentary warmth.

The unicorn shivered. It was immortal and could never be killed by mortal things. But its life could be stolen away all the same. Time was the ally of the enemy who had imprisoned it. And time had begun to move forward again.

The black unicorn slipped like quicksilver through shadows and light in search of its freedom.

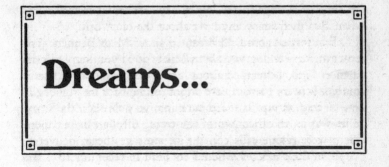

Dreams...

"**I** had a dream last night," Ben Holiday announced to his friends at breakfast that morning.

He might as well have been giving a weather report. The wizard Questor Thews did not appear to hear him, his lean, owlish face furrowed in thought, his gaze directed some twenty feet above the breakfast table at an invisible point in space. The kobolds Bunion and Parsnip barely looked up from eating. The scribe Abernathy managed a look of polite curiosity, but for a shaggy-faced dog whose normal look *was* one of polite curiosity, that was not particularly difficult.

Only the sylph Willow, just come into the dining hall of castle Sterling Silver and seated next to him, showed any real interest—a sudden change of expression that was oddly disquieting.

"I dreamed about home," he continued, determined to pursue the matter. "I dreamed about the old world."

"Excuse me?" Questor was looking at him now, apparently returned from whatever planet he had been visiting. "Excuse me, but did I hear you say something about . . . ?"

"Exactly *what* did you dream about the old world, High Lord?" Abernathy interrupted impatiently, polite curiosity become faint disapproval. He looked at Ben meaningfully over the rims of his eyeglasses. He always looked at him like that when Ben mentioned anything about the old world.

Ben forged ahead. "I dreamed about Miles Bennett. You remember my telling you about Miles, don't you—my old law partner? Well, I dreamed about him. I dreamed that he was in trouble. It wasn't a complete dream; there wasn't a true beginning or end. It was as if I came in halfway through the story. Miles was in his office, working, sorting through these papers. There were phone calls coming in, messages being delivered, people in the shadows where I couldn't see them clearly. But I could see that Miles was practically frantic. He looked terrible. He kept asking for me. He kept wondering where I was, why I wasn't there. I called out to him, but he didn't hear me. Then there was a distortion of some sort, a darkness, a twisting of what I was seeing. Miles kept calling, asking for me. Then something came between us, and I woke up."

He glanced briefly at the faces about him. They all were listening now. "But that doesn't really tell you everything," he added quickly. "There was a sense of . . . some impending disaster lurking behind the whole series of images. There was an intensity that was frightening. It was so . . . real."

"Some dreams are like that, High Lord," Abernathy observed, shrugging. He pushed the eyeglasses back on his nose and folded his forelegs primly across his vested chest. He was a fastidious dog. "Dreams are frequently manifestations of our subconscious fears, I've read."

"Not this dream," Ben insisted. "This was more than your average, garden-variety dream. This was like a premonition."

Abernathy sniffed. "And I suppose the next thing you are going to tell me is that on the strength of this emotionally distressing, but rationally unfounded, dream you feel compelled to return to your old world?" The scribe was making no effort to conceal his distress now, his worst fears about to be realized.

Ben hesitated. It had been more than a year since he had passed into the mists of the fairy world somewhere deep in the forests of the Blue Ridge Mountains twenty miles southwest of Waynesboro, Virginia, and entered the kingdom of Landover. He had paid a million dollars for the privilege, answering an advertisement in a department store catalogue, acting more out of desperation than out of reason. He had come into Land-over as King, but his acceptance as such by the land's inhab-itants had not come easily. Attacks on his claim to the throne had come from every quarter. Creatures whose very existence he had once believed impossible had nearly destroyed him. Magic, the power that governed everything in this strangely compelling world, was the two-edged sword he had been forced to master in order to survive. Reality had been redefined for him since he had made his decision to enter the mists, and the life he had known as a trial lawyer in Chicago, Illinois, seemed far removed from his present existence. Still, that old life was not completely forgotten, and he thought now and then of going back.

His eyes met those of his scribe. He didn't know what answer to give. "I admit that I am worried about Miles," he said finally.

The dining hall was very quiet. The kobolds had stopped eating, their monkey faces frozen in those frightening half grins that showed all their considerable teeth. Abernathy was rigid in his seat. Willow had gone pale, and it appeared that she was about to speak.

But it was Questor Thews who spoke first. "A moment, High Lord," he advised thoughtfully, one bony finger placed to his lips.

He rose from the table, dismissed from the room the serv-ing boys who stood surreptitiously on either side, and closed the doors tightly behind them. The six friends were alone in the cavernous dining hall. That apparently wasn't enough for Questor. The great arched entry at the far end of the room opened through a foyer to the remainder of the castle. Questor walked silently to its mouth and peered about.

Ben watched curiously, wondering why Questor was being so cautious. Admittedly, it wasn't like the old days when there were only the six of them living at Sterling Silver. Now there were retainers of all ages and ranks, soldiers and guardsmen, emissaries and envoys, messengers and assorted others that comprised his court, all stumbling over one another and into his private life when it was least convenient. But it wasn't as if the subject of his going back to the old world hadn't been discussed openly before—and by practically everyone. It wasn't as if the people of Landover didn't know by this time that he wasn't a native Landoverian.

He smiled ruefully. Ah, well—there was no harm in being cautious.

He stretched, loosening muscles still tightened from sleep. He was a man of ordinary appearance, his height and build medium, his weight evenly distributed. His movements were quick and precise; he had been a boxer in his youth and still retained much of his old skill. His face was brown from sun and wind with high cheekbones and forehead, a hawk nose, and a hairline that receded slightly at the corners. Age lines were beginning to show at the corners of his eyes, but the eyes themselves were brilliant blue and icy.

His gaze shifted ceilingward. Morning sunlight streamed through high glass windows and danced off polished wood and stone. The warmth of the castle seeped through him, and he could feel her stir restlessly. She was always listening. He knew that she had heard him speak of the dream and was responding with a measure of discontent. She was the mother who worried for her brash, incautious child. She was the mother who sought always to keep that child safe beside her. She didn't like it when he talked of leaving.

He glanced covertly at his friends: Questor Thews, the wizard whose magic frequently misfired, a ragtag scarecrow of patchwork robes and tangled gestures; Abernathy, the court scribe become a soft-coated Wheaten Terrier through Questor's magic and left that way when the magic couldn't be found to change him back again, a dog in gentleman's clothing; Willow, the beautiful sylph who was half woman, half tree, a creature of the fairy world with magic of her own; and Bunion and Parsnip, the kobolds who looked like big-eared monkeys in knickers, a messenger and a cook. He had found them all so strange in the beginning. A year later, he found them comfortable and reassuring and felt protected in their presence.

He shook his head. He lived in a world of dragons and witches, of gnomes, trolls, and other strange creatures, of living castles and fairy magic. He lived in a fantasy kingdom in which he was King. He was what he had once only dreamed of being. The old world was long past, the old life gone. Odd, then, that he still thought of that world and life so frequently, of Miles Bennett and Chicago, of the law practice, of the responsibilities and obligations he had left behind. Threads from the tapestry of last night's dream entwined within his memory and tugged relentlessly at him. He could not forget easily, it seemed, what had comprised so many years of his life . . .

Questor Thews cleared his throat.

"I had a dream last night as well, High Lord," the wizard declared, returned from his reconnaissance. Ben's eyes snapped up. The tall, robed figure hunched down over his high-backed chair, green eyes clear and distant. The bony fingers of one hand scratched the bearded chin, and the voice was a wary hiss. "My dream was of the missing books of magic!"

Ben understood the other's caution now. Few within Landover knew of the books of magic. The books had belonged to Questor's half-brother, the former court wizard of Landover, a fellow Ben had known in the old world as Meeks. It was Meeks, in league with a disgruntled heir to the throne, who had sold Ben the kingship of Landover for one million dollars—certain that Ben would fall victim to one of any number of traps set to destroy him, certain that when Ben was finally dispatched the kingship would become his to sell again. Meeks had thought to make Questor his ally, the promise of knowledge from the hidden books of magic the carrot used to entice his half-brother to his cause. But Questor and Ben had become allies instead, eluding all the traps that Meeks had set and severing the old wizard's ties with Landover for good.

Ben's eyes fixed Questor's. Yes, Meeks was gone—but the books of magic still remained concealed somewhere within the valley . . .

"Did you hear what I said, High Lord?" Questor's eyes sparkled with excitement. "The missing books—magic gleaned by wizards of Landover since the dawn of her creation! I think I know where they are! I saw where they were in my dream!" The eyes danced. The voice dropped to a whisper. "They are hidden in the catacombs of the ruined fortress of Mirwouk, high in the Melchor! In my dream, I followed after a torch that no hand carried, followed it through the dark, through tunnels and stairways to a door marked with scroll and runes. The door opened; there were blocks of stone flooring and one marked with a special sign. It gave at my touch and the books were there! I remember it all . . . as if it really happened!"

Now it was Ben's turn to look dubious. He started to say something in reply and stopped, not knowing what to say. He felt Willow stir uneasily beside him.

"I did not know whether to speak of my dream or not, to be honest with you," the wizard confided, his words coming in a rush. "I thought maybe I should wait until I was able to discover if the dream was false or true before I said anything. But then you spoke of your dream, and I . . ." He hesitated. "Mine was like yours, High Lord. It was not so much a dream as a premonition. It was strangely intense, compelling in its vividness. It was not frightening like yours; it was . . . exhilarating!"

Abernathy, at least, was not impressed. "All this could be the result of something you ate, wizard," he suggested rather unkindly.

Questor seemed not to hear him. "Do you realize what it would mean if I were to have the books of magic in my possession?" he asked eagerly, hawk face intense. "Do you have any idea of the magic I would command?"

"It seems to me you command quite enough already!" Abernathy snapped. "I would remind you that it was your command—or lack thereof—over magic that reduced me to my present state some years back! There is no telling what damage you might cause if your powers were enhanced further!"

"Damage? What of the good I might accomplish?" Questor wheeled on the other, bending close. "What if I were to find a way to change you back again!"

Abernathy went still. It was one thing to be skeptical—another to be foolishly so. He wanted nothing more in all the world than to be human again.

"Questor, are you sure about this?" Ben asked finally.

"As sure as you, High Lord," the wizard replied. He hesitated. "Odd, though, that on a single night there should be two dreams . . ."

"Three," Willow said suddenly.

They stared at her—Questor, his sentence unfinished; Ben, still trying to grasp the significance of Questor's revelation; Abernathy and the kobolds speechless. Had she said . . . ?

"Three," she repeated. "I, too, had a dream—and it was strange and disturbing and perhaps more vivid than either of yours."

Ben saw the disquieting expression again, more pronounced, more intense. He had been preoccupied before and had not paid close attention. Willow was not given to exaggeration. Something had shaken her. He saw a worry in her eyes that bordered on fear.

"What was it that you dreamed?" he asked.

She did not speak immediately. She seemed to be remembering. "I was on a journey through lands that were both familiar and at the same time foreign. I was in Landover and yet I was somewhere else. I was seeking something. My people were there, dim shadows that whispered urgently to me. There was a need for haste, but I did not understand why. I simply went on, searching."

She paused. "Then daylight passed away into darkness, and moonlight flooded a woods that rose all about me like a wall. I was alone now. I was so frightened I could not call for help even though I felt I must. There was a mist that stirred. Shadows crowded so close that they threatened to smother me." Her hand crept over Ben's and tightened. "I needed you, Ben. I needed you so badly I could not stand the thought of not having you there. A voice seemed to whisper within me that if I did not complete my journey quickly, I would lose you. Forever."

Something in the way Willow spoke that single word chilled Ben Holiday to the bone.

"Then suddenly a creature appeared before me, a wraith come from the mists of the predawn night." The sylph's green eyes glittered. "It was a unicorn, Ben, so dark that it seemed to absorb the white moon's light as a sponge would absorb water. It was a unicorn, but something more. It was not white as the unicorns of old, but ink black. It barred my passage, its horn lowered, hooves pawing at the earth. Its slender body seemed to twist and change shape, and I saw it was more demon than unicorn, more devil than fairy. It was blind in the manner of the great marsh bulls, and it had their fury. It came for me, and I ran. I knew, somehow, that I must not let it touch me— that if it were to touch me I was lost. I was quick, but the black unicorn followed close behind. It wanted me. It meant to have me."

Her breath came quickly, her slender body tense with the emotions that raged within. The room was deathly still. "And then I saw that I held in my hands a bridle of spun gold—real gold threads drawn and woven by the fairies of the old life. I didn't know how I had come to possess that bridle; I only knew that I mustn't lose it. I knew that it was the only thing in the world that could harness the black unicorn."

The hand tightened further. "I ran looking for Ben. The bridle must be taken to him, I sensed, and if I did not reach him with it quickly, the black unicorn would catch me and I would be . . ."

She trailed off, her eyes fastened on Ben's. For an instant, he forgot everything she had just told him, lost in those eyes, in the touch of her hand. For an instant, she was the impossibly beautiful woman he had come upon bathing naked in the waters of the Irrylyn almost a year ago, siren and fairy child both. The vision never left him. He recaptured it each time he saw her, the memory become life all over again

There was an awkward silence. Abernathy cleared his

throat. "It seems to have been quite a night for dreams," he remarked archly. "Everyone in the room but me appears to have had one. Bunion, how about you? Did you dream about friends in trouble or books of magic or black unicorns? Parsnip?"

The kobolds hissed softly and shook their heads in unison. But there was a wary look to their sharp eyes that suggested they did not wish to treat the matter of these dreams as lightly as Abernathy did.

"There was one thing more," Willow said, still looking only at Ben. "I came awake while I ran from the thing that hunted me—black unicorn or devil. I came awake, but I felt certain the dream had not ended—that there was still something more to come."

Ben nodded slowly, his reverie broken. "Sometimes we dream the same dream more than once . . ."

"No, Ben," she whispered, her voice insistent. Her hand released his. "This dream was like yours—more premonition than dream. I was being warned, my High Lord. A fairy creature is closer to the truth of dreams than others. I was being shown something that I am meant to know—and I have not yet been shown all."

"There are stories of sightings of a black unicorn in the histories of Landover," Questor Thews advised suddenly. "I remember reading of them once or twice. They happened long ago, and the reports were vague and unconfirmed. The unicorn was said to be a demon spawn—a thing of such evil that even to gaze once upon it was to become lost . . ."

The food and drink of their breakfast sat cooling on plates and in cups on the table before them, forgotten. The dining hall was still and empty, yet Ben could sense eyes and ears everywhere. It was an unpleasant feeling. He glanced briefly at Questor's somber face and then back at Willow's once more. Had he been told of her dream—and perhaps even of Questor's as well—and not experienced his own, he might have been inclined to dismiss them. He did not put much stock in dreams. But the memory of Miles Bennett in that darkened office, nearly frantic with worry because Ben was not there when he was needed, hung over him like a cloud. It was as real as his own life. He recognized a similar urgency in the narrative of the dreams of his friends, and their insistence simply reinforced a nagging conviction that dreams as vivid and compelling as theirs should not be dismissed as the by-products of last night's dinner or a collection of overactive subconsciousnesses.

"Why are we having these dreams?" he wondered aloud.

"This is a land built on dreams, High Lord," Questor Thews replied. "This is a land where the dreams of fairy world and mortal world come together and are channeled one to the other. Reality in one is fantasy in the other—except here, where they meet." He rose, spectral in his patchwork robes. "There have been instances of such dreams before, frequently in scatterings of up to half a dozen. Kings and wizards and men of power have had such dreams throughout the history of Landover."

"Dreams that are revelations—or even warnings?"

"Dreams that are meant to be acted on, High Lord."

Ben pursed his lips. "Do you intend to act on yours, Questor? Do you intend to go in search of the missing books of magic—just as your dream has advised?"

Questor hesitated, his brow furrowed in thought.

"And should Willow seek out the golden bridle of her dream? Should I return to Chicago and check out Miles Bennett?"

"High Lord, please—a moment!" Abernathy was on his feet, a decidedly harried look about him. "It might be wise to think this matter through a bit more carefully. It could be a very grave mistake for the lot of you to go running off in search of . . . of what may very well turn out to be a collection of gastrically induced falsehoods!"

He faced Ben squarely. "High Lord, you must remember that the wizard Meeks is still your greatest enemy. He cannot reach you as long as you stay in Landover, but I am certain he lives for the day you are foolish enough to venture back into the very world in which you left him trapped! What if he discovers that you have returned? What if the danger that threatens your friend is Meeks himself?"

"There is that chance," Ben agreed.

"Yes, there most certainly is!" Abernathy pushed his glasses firmly back on his nose, his point made.

He glanced now at Questor. "And you should be wise enough to appreciate the dangers inherent in any attempt to harness the power of the missing books of magic—power that was the tool of wizards such as Meeks! There were rumors long before you and I came into being that the books of magic were cast in demon iron and conjured for evil use. How can you be certain that such power will not consume you as quickly as fire would a piece of dried parchment? Such magic is dangerous, Questor Thews!

"As for you—" He turned quickly to Willow, cutting short Questor's attempts at protest. "—yours is the dream that frightens me most. The legend of a black unicorn is a legend of evil—even your dream tells you that much! Questor Thews failed to advise in his recitation of the histories of Landover that all those who claimed to have seen this creature came to a sudden and unpleasant demise. If there is a black unicorn, it is likely a demon strayed from Abaddon—and best left alone!"

He finished with a snap of his jaws, rigid with the strength of his conviction. His friends stared at him. "We are only surmising," Ben said, attempting to sooth his agitated scribe. "We are only considering possible alternatives . . ."

He felt Willow's hand close again about his own. "No, Ben. Abernathy's instincts are correct. We are past considering alternatives."

Ben fell silent. She was right, he knew. Not one of the three had said so, but the decision had been made all the same. They were going on their separate journeys in pursuit of their separate quests. They were resolved to test the truth of their dreams.

"At least one of you is being honest!" Abernathy huffed. "Honest about going if not about the danger of doing so!"

"There are always dangers . . ." Questor began.

"Yes, yes, wizard!" Abernathy cut him short and focused his attention on Ben. "Have you forgotten the projects presently underway, High Lord?" he asked. "What of the work that requires your presence to see it to completion? The judiciary council meets in a week to consider the format you have implemented for hearing grievances. The irrigation and road work at the eastern borders of the Greensward is set to begin, once you have surveyed the stakings. The tax levy requires an immediate accounting. And the Lords of the Greensward are to visit officially three days from now! You cannot just leave all that!"

Ben glanced away, nodding absently. He was thinking all at once of something else. Just when was it he had decided that he would leave? He couldn't remember making the decision. It was almost as if somehow the decision had been made for him. He shook his head. That wasn't possible.

His eyes shifted back to Abernathy. "Don't worry. I won't be gone long," he promised.

"But you cannot know that!" his scribe insisted.

Ben paused, then smiled an entirely unexpected smile. "Abernathy, some things must take precedence over others. Landover's business will keep for the few days it will take me to cross over to the old world and back again." He rose and walked to stand close to his friend. "I can't let this pass. I can't pretend the dream didn't happen and that I'm not worried for Miles. Sooner or later, I would have to go back in any case. I have left too many matters unfinished for too long."

"Such matters will keep better than those of this kingdom, should you fail to return, High Lord," his scribe muttered worriedly.

Ben's smile broadened. "I promise I will be careful. I value the well-being of Landover and her people as much as you."

"Besides, I can manage affairs of state quite nicely in your absence, High Lord," Questor added.

Abernathy groaned. "Why is it that I feel no reassurance whatsoever at such a prospect?"

Ben cut off Questor's response with a cautionary gesture.

"Please, no arguing. We need each other's support." He turned to Willow. "Are you determined in this as well?"

Willow brushed back her waist-length hair and gave him a studied, almost somber look. "You already know the answer to that question."

He nodded. "I suppose I do. Where will you start?"

"The lake country. There are some there who may be able to help me."

"Would you consider waiting for me until I return from my own journey so that I might go with you?"

The sea green eyes were steady. "Would you wait instead for me, Ben?"

He squeezed her hand gently in reply. "No, I guess not. But you are under my care, nevertheless, and I don't wish you to go alone. In fact, I don't wish either Questor or you to go alone. Some sort of protection may prove necessary. Bunion will go with one of you, and Parsnip with the other. No, don't argue with me," he continued quickly, seeing words of protest forming on the lips of the sylph and the wizard both. "Your journeys could prove dangerous."

"And yours as well, High Lord," Questor pointed out.

Ben nodded. "Yes, I realize that. But our circumstances are different. I can take no one with me from this world into the other—at least not without raising more than a few eyebrows—and it is in the other world that such danger as might threaten me awaits. I will have to be my own protector on this outing."

Besides, the medallion he wore about his neck was protection enough, he thought. He let his fingers stray down the front of his tunic to the medallion's hard outline. Ironically, Meeks had given him the medallion when he had sold him the kingship—the key to the magic that was now his. Only the bearer could be recognized as King. Only the bearer could pass through the fairy mists from Landover to the worlds beyond and back again. And only the bearer could summon and command the services of the invincible armored champion known as the Paladin.

He traced the image of the knight-errant riding out from the gates of Sterling Silver against the sunrise. The secret of the Paladin was his alone. Even Meeks had never understood the full extent of the medallion's power or its connection with the Paladin.

He smiled tightly. Meeks had thought himself so clever. He had used the medallion to pass over into Ben's world and then let himself be trapped there. What the old wizard wouldn't give to get that medallion back now!

The smile faded. But that would never happen, of course. No one but the bearer could remove the medallion once it was in place—and Ben never took it off. Meeks was no longer any threat to him.

Yet somewhere at the back of his mind, almost buried in the wall of determination that buttressed everything to which he committed himself, a tiny fragment of doubt tugged in warning.

"Well, it appears that there is nothing I can say on the matter that will change your minds," Abernathy declared to the room at large, drawing Ben's attention back again. The dog peered at him over the rims of his glasses, pushed the spectacles farther up on his nose, and assumed the posture of a rejected prophet. "So be it. When will you depart, High Lord?"

There was an awkward silence. Ben cleared his throat. "The quicker I go, the quicker I can return."

Willow rose and stood before him. Her arms went about his waist, drawing him close. They held each other for a moment as the others watched. Ben could feel something stir in the sylph's slender body—a kind of shiver that whispered of unspoken fears.

"I imagine it would be best if we all got about our business," Questor Thews said quietly.

No one replied. The silence was enough. Dawn was already stretching into midmorning and there was a shared need to make use of the day ahead.

"Come back safe to me, Ben Holiday," Willow spoke into his shoulder.

Abernathy heard the admonishment and glanced away. "Come back safe to us all," he said.

Ben did not waste any time in setting out.

He retired directly to his bedroom after departing the dining hall and packed the duffel he had brought with him from the old world with the few possessions he felt he would need. He changed back into the navy blue sweat suit and Nikes he had worn over. The clothes and shoes felt odd after Landover's apparel, but comfortable and reassuringly familiar. He was going back at last, he thought as he changed. He was finally going to do it.

He went from the bed chamber down a set of back stairs and through a number of private halls to a small courtyard just off the front gates where the others waited. The morning sun shone from a cloudless blue sky against the white stone of the castle, flashing in blinding streaks where it caught the silver trim. Warmth eased from the earth of the island on which Sterling Silver sat and gave the day a lazy feel. Ben breathed the freshness of the day and felt the castle stir in response beneath his feet.

He locked hand to wrist firmly with the kobolds Bunion and Parsnip, returned Abernathy's stiff, formal bow, embraced Questor, and kissed Willow with a passion usually reserved for deepest night. There was not much talking. All the talking had already been done. Abernathy again warned against Meeks, and this time Questor cautioned him as well.

"Be careful, High Lord," the wizard advised, one hand gripping Ben's shoulder as if to hold him back. "Though shut in a foreign world, my half-brother is not entirely shorn of his magic. He is still a dangerous enemy. Watch out for him."

Ben promised he would. He walked with them through the gates, past the sentries stationed on day watch and down to the shore's edge. His horse waited on the far bank, a bay gelding he had named Jurisdiction. It was his private joke that wherever he traveled on horseback, he always had Jurisdiction.

No one other than himself understood what he was talking about.

A squad of mounted soldiers waited there as well. Abernathy had insisted that within the kingdom, at least, Landover's King would not travel without adequate protection.

"Ben." Willow came to him one final time, her hands pressing something into his. "Take this with you."

He glanced down covertly. She had given him a smooth, milky-colored stone intricately marked with runes.

Willow closed his hands back about it quickly. "Keep the stone hidden. It is a talisman often carried by my people. If danger threatens, the stone will heat and turn crimson. That way you will be warned."

She paused, and one hand reached up to stroke his cheek softly. "Remember that I love you. I will always love you."

He smiled reassuringly, but the words bothered him as they always did. He didn't want her to love him—not so completely, not so unconditionally. He was frightened of what that meant. Annie had loved him like that—his wife, Annie, now dead, a part of his old life, his old world, killed in that car accident that sometimes seemed as if it had happened a thousand years ago, but more often seemed to have happened yesterday. He wasn't willing to risk embracing that kind of love and losing it a second time. He couldn't. The prospect terrified him.

A sudden twinge of sadness passed through him. It was strange, but until he met Willow he had never dreamed he might experience again those feelings he had shared with Annie . . .

He gave Willow a brief kiss and shoved the stone deep into his pocket. The touch of her hand lingered on his face as he turned away.

Questor took him across in the lake skimmer and waited until he was mounted. "Keep safe, High Lord," the wizard bade him.

Ben waved back to them all, took a final look at the spires of Sterling Silver, wheeled Jurisdiction about, and galloped away, with the squad of soldiers in tow.

• •

Morning slipped into midday and midday into afternoon as Ben rode westward toward the rim of the valley and the mists that marked the boundaries of the fairy world. Late-year colors carpeted the countryside through which he passed in bright swatches. Meadows were thick with grasses of muted greens, blues, and pinks, and with white clover dotted crimson. Forest vegetation still retained much of its new growth. Bonnie Blues, the trees that were a staple of life within the valley with their offering of drink and food, grew in clusters everywhere—half-grown pin oaks colored a brilliant blue against the various shades of forest green. Two of Landover's eight moons hung low against the northern horizon, visible even in daylight—one peach, the other a pale mauve. Harvesting was underway in the fields of the small farms scattered about the countryside. Winter's week-long stay was still a month distant.

Ben drank in the smell, taste, sight, and feel of the valley as if sampling a fine wine. Gone was the mistiness and wintry gray blight that had marked the land when he had first come over and the magic had been dying. The magic was well now, and the land was whole. The valley and her people were at peace.

Ben was not. He set a steady pace as he traveled, but not a quick one. The need for haste he had felt earlier had given way to a strange anxiety at the thought of actually leaving. This would be his first trip out of Landover since his arrival, and although the idea of leaving had not bothered him before, it was beginning to bother him now. A nagging concern lurked about the edges and corners of his determination—that once he left Landover he would not be able to come back again.

It was ridiculous, of course, and he tried valiantly to beat it down, seeking to convince himself that he was experiencing the same misgivings any traveler encountered at the beginning of a trip away from home. He tried arguing that he was a victim of his friends' repeated warnings and humming "Brigadoon" to lighten the mood.

Nothing helped, however, and he finally gave it up. Some

things you simply had to put up with until they lost their grip on you.

It was midafternoon when his party reached the lower slopes of the valley's western rim. He left the soldiers there with the horses and instructions to set up camp and wait for his return. He might be gone as long as a week, he told them. If he wasn't back by then, they were to return to Sterling Silver and advise Questor. The captain of the squad gave him a funny look, but accepted the orders without argument. He was used to his King going off on strange errands without his guard—although usually he had one of the kobolds or the wizard in tow.

Ben waited for the captain's salute, then slung the duffel bag over one shoulder and began the hike up the valley slope.

It was nearing sunset when he reached the summit and crossed toward the misted forest line that marked the boundaries of the fairy world. Daytime's warmth was slipping rapidly toward evening's cool, and his elongated shadow trailed after him like a grotesque silhouette. There was a deep, pervasive stillness in the air, and he felt a sense of something hidden.

Ben's hand strayed to the medallion that hung about his neck, and his fingers closed about it firmly. Questor had told him what to expect. The fairy world was everywhere and nowhere at the same time, and all of its many doorways to the worlds beyond were settled within. The way back was whatever way he chose to go and it could be found at whatever point he chose to enter. All he need do was fix in his mind his destination and the medallion would see him to the proper passageway.

That was the theory, at least. Questor had never had the opportunity to test it.

The mist swirled and stirred within the great forest trees, its trailers twisting like snakes. The mist had the look of something alive. There's a cheerful thought, Ben chided himself. He stopped before the mist, regarded it warily, took a deep breath to steady himself, and started in.

The mist closed about him instantly and the way back

became as uncertain as the way forward. He pushed on. A moment later, a tunnel opened before him—the same vast, empty, black hole that had brought him across from the old world a year earlier. It burrowed through mist and trees and disappeared into nothingness. There were sounds in the tunnel, distant and uncertain, and shadows dancing at its rim.

Ben's pace slowed. He was remembering what it had been like when he had passed through this tunnel the last time. The demon known as the Mark and his black, winged carrier had come at Ben from out of nowhere; by the time he had decided they were real, they had very nearly finished him. Then he had practically stumbled over that sleeping dragon . . .

Slender shapes darted at the fringes of the darkness within the trees and mist. *Fairies.*

Ben quit remembering and forced himself to walk more quickly. The fairies had helped him once, and he should have felt comfortable among them. But he did not. He felt alien and alone.

Faces materialized and vanished again in the mists, sharp-eyed and angular with hair the consistency of willow moss. Voices whispered, but the words were indistinct. Ben was sweating. He hated being in the tunnel; he wanted out of there. Ahead, the darkness pressed on.

Ben's fingers still clutched the medallion in a death grip, and he thought suddenly of the Paladin.

Then the darkness before him brightened to dusky gray, and the tunnel's length shortened to less than fifty yards. Indefinable shapes swayed unevenly in the half-light, an interlacing of spider webs and bent poles. Voices and movement in the walls of the tunnel gave way to a sharp hissing. A sudden wind rose and howled sharply.

Ben peered ahead into the gloom. The wind whipped at him from the edges of the tunnel's end and carried the hissing sound into his face with a wet, stinging rush.

And there was something else . . .

He stepped from the tunnel's shelter into a blinding rainstorm and found himself face to face with Meeks.

...and Memories

*B*en Holiday froze. Lightning streaked from skies leaden and packed with low-hanging clouds that shed their rain in torrents. Thunder boomed, reverberating across the emptiness, shaking the earth beneath with the force of its passing. Massive oak trees rose all about like the staked walls of some huge fortress, their trunks and leaf-bare limbs glistening blackly. Shorter pine and fir bristled in clumps through the gaps left by their taller sisters, and the rugged slopes of the Blue Ridge Mountains lifted darkly against the nearly invisible horizon.

The spectral figure of Meeks stood pinned against this backdrop. He stood without moving, tall and bent and old, white hair grizzled, craggy face as hard as iron. He looked almost nothing of the man Ben remembered. That man had been human; this man had the look of an enraged animal. Gone were the pressed woolen slacks, corduroy jacket, and loafers—the trappings of civilization that had complemented an urbane, if gruff sales representative of a highly respected department store. Those reassuringly familiar business clothes had been replaced by robes of gunmetal blue that billowed like sailcloth and seemed to absorb the light. A high collar jutted from the shoulders to frame a ghastly, pitted face twisted by fury that bordered on madness. The empty sleeve of his right arm still hung limp. The black leather glove that covered his left hand was yet a claw. But each was more noticeable somehow, as if each were a scar left bare for viewing.

Ben's throat constricted sharply. There was a tension in the old man that was unmistakable—the tension of an attacker poised to strike.

My God, he has been waiting for me, Ben thought in shock. He knew I was coming!

Then Meeks started for him. Ben took one step back, his right hand tightening frantically about the medallion. Meeks was almost on top of him. The wind shifted, and the sounds of the storm echoed through the mountains with renewed sharpness. The rain swept back against his face, forcing him to blink.

When he looked again, Meeks was gone.

Ben stared. Meeks had disappeared as completely as if he had been a ghost. Rain and darkness cloaked the whole of the surrounding forestland in a shroud of gray wetness. Ben glanced about hurriedly, disbelief twisting his face. There was no sign of Meeks.

It took only a moment for Ben to regain his scattered thoughts. He caught sight of the dim outline of a pathway directly before him and started for it. He moved quickly ahead through the trees, following the pathway's curve as it wound down the mountainside and away from the time passage that had brought him back to his old world from Landover. And he was indeed back—of that much he was certain. He was back in the Blue Ridge Mountains of Virginia, deep in the George Washington National Forest. This was the same pathway that had brought him into Landover more than a year ago. If he followed it far enough, it would take him down out of the mountains to Skyline Drive, a turn-around with the black number 13 stenciled on a green sign, a weather shelter, and—most important of all—a courtesy telephone.

He was soaked through in moments, but he kept moving steadily ahead, the duffel clutched tightly under one arm. His mind worked rapidly. That wasn't Meeks he had seen, hadn't even looked like the old Meeks, had been barely recognizable, for Pete's sake! Besides, Meeks wouldn't have just disappeared like that if it had really been him, would he?

Doubt tugged sharply at his mind. Had he simply imagined it all, then? Had it all been some sort of mirage?

Belatedly, he thought of the rune stone that Willow had given him. Slowing, he fished through the pocket of his jacket until he found the stone and brought it out into the light. It was still milky in color and gave off no heat. That meant no magic threatened him. But what did that tell him about the phantom vision of Meeks?

He pushed ahead, slipping on the damp, water-soaked earth, pine boughs slapping at his face and hands. He was aware suddenly of how cold it was in these mountains, the chill settling through him with an icy touch. He had forgotten that late autumn could be unpleasant, even in western Virginia. Illinois could be frigid. It might even be snowing in Chicago . . .

He felt something catch in his throat. Shadows moved through the mist and rain, darting and sliding from view. Each time, he saw Meeks. Each time, he felt the wizard's gloved hand reaching for him.

Just keep moving, he told himself. Just get yourself to that phone.

It seemed to take much longer, but he reached the courtesy phone some thirty minutes later, climbing down from among the trees and crossing the parkway to the weather shelter that housed it. He was soaked to the skin and freezing, but he felt none of it. The entirety of his concentration was focused on the Plexiglas-enclosed black and silver metal box.

Please let it be working, he prayed.

It was. Rain beat down on the shelter roof in a steady thrum, and mist and gloom closed tightly about. He thought he heard footsteps. He rummaged through his duffel for the coins and credit card he still carried in his wallet, rang information for the name of a limo service out of Waynesboro, and called for a car to come up and get him. It was all done in a matter of minutes.

He sat down then to wait on the wooden bench fastened

to the side of the shelter. He was surprised to discover that his hands were shaking.

By the time the limo reached him and he was safely inside, he had regained his composure enough to reason through what had happened to him.

He no longer thought that he had imagined the appearance of Meeks. What he had seen had been real enough. But it hadn't been Meeks he had seen; it had been an image of Meeks. The image had been triggered by his crossing back through the time passage. He had been meant to see the image. It had been placed there at the tunnel's end so that he would see it.

The question was, why?

He hunched down in the backseat of the limo as it sped down the parkway toward Waynesboro and considered the possibilities. He had to assume that Meeks was responsible. No other explanation made any sense. So what was Meeks trying to accomplish? Was he trying to warn Ben off—to chase him back through the time passage? That didn't make any sense. Well, no, the warning part did. Meeks was arrogant enough to want to let Ben know that he was aware of his coming back. But there had to be more to it than that. The image must have been placed there to accomplish something else as well.

He had his answer almost immediately. The image had not only warned Ben of Meeks; it had warned Meeks of Ben! The image was a device to alert the wizard that Ben had come back from Landover!

It made perfect sense. It was only reasonable to expect that Meeks would employ some contrivance—magic or otherwise—to warn him when Landover's failed Kings crossed back into their old world with the medallion. Once alerted, Meeks could then come after them . . .

Or, in this case, after him.

It was late afternoon when the driver deposited him at the front steps of a Holiday Inn in downtown Waynesboro, the rain still falling, the daylight completely gone. Ben told the fellow he was on vacation and had hiked the parkway north from

Staunton until the bad weather forced him to abandon the plan and call for help. The driver looked at him as if he were nuts. The weather had been like this for better than a week, he snapped. Ben shrugged, paid him in cash, and hurried inside.

On his way to the front desk, he paused long enough to check the date on a newspaper someone had left lying on a table in the lobby. It read Friday, December 9. It was ten days more than a year since he had first walked through the time passage from the Blue Ridge Mountains of Virginia into Landover. Time in the two worlds did indeed pass synchronously.

He booked a room for the night, sent out his clothes to be cleaned and dried, took a steaming-hot shower to warm himself, and ordered dinner sent in. While he waited for the meal and his clothes, he called the airport for reservations to Chicago. There was nothing until morning. He would have to fly to Washington, then transfer to Chicago. He booked the reservation, billed it to his credit card, and hung up.

It was while he was eating dinner that it occurred to him that using a credit card to pay for his air fare wasn't exactly the smartest thing he could have done. He was sitting on the edge of his bed in front of the TV, the tray balanced on his lap, a Holiday Inn towel wrapped about him, and the room temperature at about eighty. His clothes were still out. Tom Brokaw was giving the news, and it suddenly struck Ben that in a world of sophisticated communications a computerized credit-card trace was a relatively simple matter. If Meeks had gone to the trouble of placing that image at the opening of the time passage to warn of Ben's return, then he would almost certainly take the matter a step further. He would know that Ben would attempt a visit to Chicago. He would know that Ben would probably elect to fly. A credit-card trace would tell him the airline flight, date of travel, and destination.

He could be waiting when Ben stepped off the plane.

That possibility ruined what was left of the meal. Ben put the tray aside, clicked off the TV, and began to consider more carefully what he was up against. Abernathy had been right. This was turning out to be more dangerous than he had imagined. But he really didn't have any choice. He had to go back to Chicago and see Miles long enough to discover whether there was any truth to his dream. Meeks would probably be waiting for him somewhere along the line. The trick was to avoid bumping into him.

He permitted himself a brief smile. No problem.

He had his clothes back by nine o'clock and was asleep by ten. He awoke early, had breakfast, shouldered the duffel, and caught a cab to the airport. He flew to Washington on the previous night's reservation, then canceled the balance of the ticket, walked over to another airline, booked a seat to Chicago on standby under an assumed name, paid for this ticket with cash, and was airborn before noon.

Let's see Meeks pick up on that one, he thought to himself.

Eyes closed, he leaned back in his seat and reflected on the strange set of circumstances that had taken him away from his home in Chicago to Never-Never Land. The memories made him shake his head reprovingly. Maybe, like Peter Pan, he had just never grown up. He had been a lawyer then, a damn good one, one from whom great things were expected by those who were the movers and shakers in the business. He was in practice with his friend and longtime associate Miles Bennett, a shared partnership in which the two complemented each other like old shoes and work jeans—Ben the outspoken, audacious trial lawyer, Miles the steady, conservative office practitioner. Miles often deplored Ben's judgment in taking cases, but Ben always seemed to land on his feet despite the heights from which he insisted on jumping. He had won more courtroom battles than the average bear—battles in which his corporate opponents had thought to bury him under an avalanche of money-backed rhetoric and paperwork, legal dodges, delays, and gamesmanship of all sorts. He had so surprised Miles after his victory in the Dodge City Express case that his partner had begun referring to him as Doc Holiday, courtroom gunfighter.

He smiled. Those had been good, satisfying times.

But the good times faded when Annie died. The satisfaction disappeared like quicksilver. His wife had died in a car accident, three months pregnant, and he seemed to lose everything after that. He turned reclusive, shunning everyone but Miles. He had always been something of a loner and he sometimes thought that the death of his wife and baby had just reinforced what was always there. He began to drift, the days running together, their events merging indecipherably. He sensed that he was slowly slipping away from himself.

It was difficult to know what might have happened had he not come across the bizarre offering in the Rosen's Department Store Christmas Wishbook for the purchase of the throne of the kingdom of Landover. He had thought it ridiculous at first—a fantasy kingdom with wizards and witches, dragons and damsels, knights and knaves for sale for one million dollars. Who would be foolish enough to believe that? But the desperate dissatisfaction he was experiencing in his life had led him to take the chance that something in this impossible fantasy might be real. Any risk was worth taking if it could bring him back to himself. He had shelved his doubts, packed his bags, and flown to Rosen's New York office to see what was what.

He was required to undergo an interview in order to complete the sale. The interviewer had been Meeks.

The familiar image of Meeks flashed instantly to mind— the tall, old man with the whispered voice and dead eyes, a veteran of wars Ben could only imagine. The interview was the only time they had ever met face to face. Meeks had found him an acceptable candidate to be Landover's King—not to succeed as Ben had believed, but to fail. Meeks had convinced him to make the purchase. Meeks had charmed him like a snake its prey.

Meeks had also underestimated him.

He let his eyes slip open again and he whispered, "That's right, Ben Holiday—he did underestimate you. Now be sure that you don't underestimate him."

The plane touched down at Chicago O'Hare shortly after three, and Ben caught a cab into the city. The driver talked all the way in, mostly about sports: the Cubs' losing season, the Bulls' playoff hopes with Jordan, the Blackhawks' injury problems, the Bears at 13 and 1. The Chicago Bears? Ben listened, replying intermittently, a small voice at the back of his mind telling him there was something wrong with this conversation. He was nearly downtown before he figured out what it was. It was the language. He understood it, even though he had neither heard it nor spoken it for more than a year. In Landover, he heard, spoke, wrote, and thought Landoverian. The magic made it possible for him to do so. Yet here he was, back in his old world, back in good old Chicago, listening to this cab driver speak the English language—or a reasonable facsimile thereof—as if it were the most natural thing in the world.

Well, maybe that's exactly what it was, he thought and smiled.

He had the cab driver deposit him at the Drake, unwilling to return to his old penthouse apartment or to contact any friends or acquaintances just yet. He was being careful now. He was thinking about Meeks. He checked in under an assumed name, paid cash in advance for one night, and let the bellhop guide him to his room. He was increasingly grateful for the fact that he had decided to carry several thousand dollars in cash as a precaution when he had crossed into Landover a year ago. The decision had been almost an afterthought, but it was turning out to be a sound one. The cash was saving him from using the credit card.

Leaving the room with the cash and the billfold in one pocket of his running suit, he took the elevator down, left the hotel, and walked several blocks to Water Tower Place. He shopped, bought a sport coat and slacks, dress shirts, tie, socks and underwear, and a pair of dress loafers, paid cash, and headed back again. There was no point in being conspicuous, and a running suit and Nikes in the middle of the downtown Chicago business district was far too conspicuous. He simply didn't look the type. Sometimes appearances were everything—particularly in the short view. That was exactly why he hadn't brought any of his friends with him. A talking dog, a pair of grinning monkeys, a girl who became a tree, and a wizard whose magic frequently got the better of him would hardly escape notice on Michigan Avenue!

He regretted the superficial characterization of his friends almost immediately. He was being needlessly flip. Odd as they might be, they were genuine friends. They had stood by him when it counted, when it was dangerous to do so, and when their own lives were threatened. That was a whole lot more than you could say for most friends.

He bowed his head against a sudden gust of wind, frowning.

Besides, wasn't he as odd as they?

Wasn't he the Paladin?

He shoved the thought angrily to the darkest corners of his mind and hurried to catch the crossing light.

He bought several newspapers and magazines in the hotel lobby and retired to his room. He ordered room service and killed time waiting for his dinner by skimming the reading material to update himself on what had been happening in the world during his absence. He stopped long enough to catch an hour of world and local news, and by then his meal had arrived. He continued reading through the dinner hour. It was closing in on seven o'clock by this time, and he decided to call Ed Samuelson.

There were two reasons for Ben's return to Chicago. The first was to visit with Miles and discover whether the dream about his friend had been accurate. The second was to set his affairs in order permanently/ He had already decided that the first would have to wait until morning, but there was no reason to put off the second. That meant a call to Ed.

Ed Samuelson was his accountant, a senior partner in the accountancy firm of Haines, Samuelson & Roper, Inc. Ben had entrusted management of his estate—an estate that was considerable in size—to Ed before he had left for Landover. Ed Samuelson was exactly the sort of person one would hope for in an accountant—discreet, dependable, and conscientious. There had been times when he thought Ben clearly mad in his financial judgment, but he respected the fact that it was Ben's

money to do with as he chose. One of those times had been
when Ben decided to purchase the throne of Landover. Ed had
liquidated the assets necessary to collect the one million dollar
purchase price and had been given power of attorney to manage
the balance of Ben's assets while Ben was away. He had done
all this without having the faintest idea what Ben was about.

Ben had not told him then and he had no intention of
telling him now. But he knew Ed would accept that.

Calling Ed Samuelson was something of a risk. He had to
assume that Meeks knew Ed was his accountant and would be
contacted eventually. Anticipating that contact, Meeks might
have tapped the accountant's phone. That was a somewhat para-
noid assumption perhaps, but Meeks was no one to fool with.
Ben only hoped that, if Meeks had decided on a phone tap, he
had opted for one at Ed Samuelson's office and not one at his
home.

He called Ed, found him just finished with his evening
meal, and spent the next ten minutes convincing him that it
really was Ben Holiday who was calling. Once he got that job
done, he warned Ed that no one—and that meant absolutely
no one—was to know about this call. Ed was to pretend that
he had never received it. Ed asked the same question he always
asked when Ben made one of his bizarre requests: Was Ben in
some sort of trouble? No, Ben assured him, he was not. It
simply wasn't convenient for anyone to know he was in town
at the moment. He did plan on seeing Miles, he assured Ed.
He did not think he would have time to see much of anyone
else.

Ed seemed satisfied. He listened patiently while Ben explained what he wanted done. Ben promised he would stop by
the office tomorrow about noon to sign the necessary papers if
Ed could arrange to be there. Ed sighed stoically and said that
would be fine. Ben said good night and placed the phone re-
ceiver back on its cradle.

Twenty minutes in the shower helped wash away the tension and the growing weariness. He came back out of the bath-
room and crawled into his bed, a few of the magazines and

newspapers stacked next to him. He started to read, gave it up, and let his thoughts drift and his eyes close.

Moments later, he was asleep.

He dreamed that night of the Paladin.

He was alone at first, standing on a pine-sheltered bluff looking down over Landover's misted valley. Blues and greens mixed as sky and earth joined, and it was as if he could reach out and touch them. He breathed, and the air was fresh and chill. The clarity of the moment was stunning.

Then shadows deepened and closed down about him like night. Cries and whispers filtered through the pines. He could feel the shape of the medallion pressing against his palm as he clutched at it in anticipation. He had need of it once more, he sensed, and was glad. The being he kept trapped inside could be let loose again!

There was a darting movement to one side and a monstrous black shape surged forward. It was a unicorn, eyes and breath of fire. But it changed almost instantly. It became a devil. Then it changed again.

It was Meeks.

The wizard beckoned, a tall, stooped, menacing form, face scaled over like a lizard's. He came for Ben, growing in size with each step, changing now into something unrecognizable. There was the smell of fear in Ben's nostrils, the smell of death.

But he was the Paladin, the knight-errant whose strayed soul had found a home within his body, the King's champion who had never lost a battle, and nothing could stand against him. He brought that other self to life with a frightening rush of elation. Armor closed about him, and the smell of fear and death gave way to the acrid smells of iron, leather, and oil. He was no longer Ben Holiday, but a creature of some other time and place whose memories were all of battle, of combat and victory, of fighting and dying. Wars raged in his mind, and there were glimpses of struggling behemoths encased in iron, surging back and forth against a haze of red. Metal clanged, and voices huffed and grunted in fury. Bodies fell in death, torn and broken.

He felt himself exhilarated!

Oh, God, he felt himself reborn!

The darkness broke against him, shadows reaching and clawing, and he went to meet them in a rage. The white charger he rode carried him forward like a steam engine driven by fires he could not begin to control. The pines slipped past him in a blur, and the ground disappeared. Meeks became a wraith he could not touch. He raced forward, flying out from the edge of the bluff into nothingness.

The sense of exhilaration vanished. Somewhere in the night, there was a frightening scream. He realized as he fell that the scream was his own.

The dreams left him after that, but he slept poorly for the remainder of the night anyway. He rose shortly after dawn, showered, called room service for breakfast, ate, dressed in the clothes he had bought yesterday, and caught a cab out front of the hotel shortly after nine. He took his duffel bag with him. He did not think he would be returning.

The cab took him south on Michigan Avenue. It was Saturday, but the streets were already beginning to clog with Christmas shoppers anxious to beat the weekend rush. Ben sat back in the relative seclusion of the cab and ignored them. The joys of the approaching holiday were the furthest thing from his mind.

Traces of last night's dream still whispered darkly to him. He had been badly frightened by that dream and by the truths that it contained.

The Paladin was a reality he had not fully come to grips with. He had become the armored knight only once—and then as much by chance as by intention. It had been necessary to become the Paladin in order to survive, and he had therefore done what was necessary. But the transformation had been a frightening thing, a shedding of his own skin, a crawling into someone else's—someone or something. The thoughts of that other being were hard and brutal, a warrior's thoughts, a gladiator's. There was blood and death in those thoughts, an entire history of survival that Ben could only begin to comprehend. It frankly terrified him. He could not control what this other thing was, he sensed—not entirely. He could only *become* what it was and accept what that meant.

He was not sure he could ever do that again. He had not tried and did not wish to try.

And yet a part of him did—just as in the dream. And a part of him whispered that someday he must.

He had the cab take him to the offices of Holiday & Bennett, Ltd. The offices were closed on Saturdays, but he knew Miles Bennett would be there anyway. Miles was always there on Saturdays, working until noon, catching up on all the dictating and research that he hadn't gotten to during the week, taking advantage of the absence of those bothersome interruptions that seemed to dog him during regular business hours.

Ben paid the cab driver to drop him at the end of the block across the street from his destination, then stepped quickly into the doorway of another building. Pedestrians passed him by, oblivious to what he was about, caught up in their own concerns. Traffic moved ahead at a rapid crawl. There were cars parked on the street, but no one seemed to be keeping watch in them.

"Doesn't hurt to be careful," he insisted softly.

He stepped back out of the doorway, crossed the street with the light, moved up the block, and pushed through the storm glass doors to the lobby of his building. He saw nothing out of place, nothing odd.

He hurried to an open elevator, stepped inside, punched the button to floor fifteen, and watched the doors slide closed. The elevator started up. Just a few moments more, he thought. And if Miles wasn't there for some reason, he would simply track him down at his home.

But he hoped he wouldn't have to do that. He sensed that he might not have the time. Maybe it was the dream, maybe it was simply the circumstances of his being here—but something definitely felt wrong.

The elevator slowed and stopped. The doors slid open, and he stepped into the hallway beyond.

His breath caught sharply in his throat. Once again, he was face to face with Meeks.

Questor Thews brushed at the screen of cobwebs that hung across the narrow stone entry of the ruins of the castle tower and pushed inside. He sneezed as dust clogged his nostrils and muttered in distaste at the damp and dark. He should have had the sense to bring a torch . . .

A spark of fire flared next to him, and flames leaped from a brand. Bunion passed the handle of the light to Questor.

"I was just about to use the magic to do that for myself!" the wizard snapped irritably, but the kobold just grinned.

They stood within the failing walls of Mirwouk, the ancient fortress Questor had seen in his dream of the missing books of magic. They were far north of Sterling Silver, high within the Melchor, the wind whipping about the worn stone to howl down empty corridors, the chill settling through stale air like winter's coming. It had taken the wizard and the kobold the better part of three days to get here, and their travel had been quick. The castle had welcomed them with yawning gates and vacant windows. Its rooms and halls stood abandoned.

Questor pushed ahead, searching for something that looked familiar. The late afternoon was settling down about them, and he had no wish to be wandering about this dismal tomb after dark. He was a wizard and could sense things hidden from other folk, and this place had an evil smell about it.

He groped about for a time, then thought he recognized the passageway he had entered. He followed its twist and turn, eyes peering through the gloom. More cobwebs and dust hindered his progress, and there were spiders the size of rats and rats the size of dogs. They scurried and crawled, and he had to watch for them at every step. It was decidedly annoying work.

He was tempted to use his magic to turn the lot of them into dust bunnies and let the wind sweep them away.

The passageway took a downward turn, and the shape of its walls altered noticeably. Questor slowed, peering at the stonework. Abruptly, he straightened.

"I recognize this!" he exclaimed in an agitated whisper. "This is the tunnel I saw in my dreams!"

Bunion took the torch from his hand without comment and led the way down. Questor was too excited to argue the matter and followed quickly after. The passage broadened and cleared, free of webbing, dust, rodents, and insects. There was a new smell to the stone, a kind of sickly-fragrant musk. Bunion kept up a brisk pace, and sometimes all that Questor could see before him was the halo of the torch.

All was just as it had been in the dream!

The tunnel went on, angling deeper into the mountain rock, a coil of hollowed corridors and curving stairs. Bunion stayed in front, eyes sharp. Questor was practically breathing down his neck.

Then the tunnel ended at a stone door marked with scroll and runes. Questor was shaking with excitement by now. He felt along the markings and his hands seemed to know exactly where to go. He touched something and the door swung open with a faint grating sound.

The room beyond was massive, its floor constructed of granite blocks polished smooth. Questor led the way now, following the vision inside his head, the memory of his dream. He walked to the center of the chamber, Bunion at his side, the sound of their footfalls a hollow echo.

They stopped before a piece of granite flooring on which the sign of a unicorn had been carved.

Questor Thews stared. A unicorn? One hand tugged uneasily at his chin. Something was wrong here. He did not recall anything about a unicorn in his dream. There had been a sign cut into the stone, but had the sign been that of a unicorn? It seemed a rather large coincidence . . .

For just an instant, he considered turning about, walking

directly back the way he had come, and abandoning the entire project. A small voice inside whispered that he should. There was danger hidden here; he could sense it, feel it, and it frightened him.

But the lure of the missing books was too strong. He reached down, and his fingers traced the ridges of the creature's horn—again, almost of their own volition. The block stirred and slid aside, fitting into a neatly constructed chute.

Questor Thews peered downward into the hole that was left.

There was something there.

Nightfall draped the lake country in shadows and mist, and the light of colored moons and silver stars was no more than a faint glimmer as it reflected off the still surface of the Irrylyn. Willow stood alone at the shoreline of a tiny inlet ringed in cottonwood and cedar, the waters of the lake lapping at her toes. She was naked, her clothes laid carefully upon the grass behind her. A breeze blew softly against her pale green skin, wove its careless way through the waist-length emerald hair, curled and ribboned, and ruffled the fetlocks that ran the length of her calves and forearms. She shivered with the touch. She was a creature of impossible beauty, half human, half fairy, and she might have been a descendant of the sirens of myth who had lured men to their doom on the rocks of ancient seas.

Night birds called sharply from across the lake, their cries echoing in the stillness. Willow's whistle called back to them.

Her head lifted and she sniffed the air as an animal might. Parsnip was waiting patiently for her in the campsite fifty yards back, the light of his cooking fire screened by the trees. She had come alone to the Irrylyn to bathe and to remember.

She stepped cautiously into the water, the lukewarm liquid sending a delicious tingle through her body. It was here that she had met Ben Holiday, that they had seen each other for the first time, naked as they bathed, stripped of all pretensions. It was here that she had known that he was the one who was meant for her.

Her smile brightened as she thought back on how it had been—the wonder of the moment. She had told him what was to be, and while he had doubted it—still doubted it, in truth—she had never faltered in her certainty. The fates of her birth, told in the fairy way by the manner of entwining of the bedded flowers of her seeding, could never lie.

Oh, but she loved the outlander Ben Holiday!

Her child's face beamed and then clouded. She missed Ben. She worried for him. Something in the dream they had shared troubled her in a way she could not explain. There was a riddle behind these dreams that whispered of danger.

She had said nothing of it to Ben because she had read in his voice when he told her of his dream that he had already decided he would go. She knew then that she could not turn him from his purpose and should not try. He understood the risks and accepted them. The urgency of her concern paled beside the strength of his determination.

Perhaps it was for that reason that in telling him of her dream she had not told him all. Something in her dream was different than in his—or Questor Thews'. It was a subtle thing and difficult to explain, but it was there nevertheless.

She crouched in the shallows, emerald hair fanning out across her shoulders like a shawl. Her finger traced patterns on the still surface, and the memory of the dream returned. The wrong feeling was in the texture of the dream, she thought. It was in the way it played against her mind. The visions had been vivid, the events clear. But the telling was somehow false—as if it were all something that could happen in a dream, but not in waking. It was as if the memory was a mask that hid a face beneath.

She ceased her tracing motion and rose. What face was it, she wondered, that lay concealed beneath that mask?

The frown that clouded her face deepened, and she wished suddenly she had not been so accepting of Ben's decision. She wished she had argued his going after all or that she had insisted that he take her along.

"No, he will be well," she whispered insistently.

Her eyes lifted skyward and she let the moonglow warm her. Tomorrow she would seek the advice of her mother, whose life was so close to that of the fairy creatures in the mists. Her mother would know of the black unicorn and the bridle of spun gold and would guide her; soon she would be back again with Ben.

She stepped further out into the darkened lake, let the waters close about her, and drifted at peace.

Shadows...

*T*he second appearance of Meeks did not elicit in Ben Holiday the panic that the first had. He did not freeze; he did not experience the same sense of confusion. He was surprised, but not stunned. After all, he had a better idea of what to expect this time around. This was just another apparition of the outcast wizard—tall, stooped, cloaked in the robes of gunmetal blue, white hair grizzled, face craggy and sallow, black leather glove lifted like a claw, but an apparition nevertheless.

Wasn't it?

Meeks started for him, and suddenly he wasn't so sure. The pale blue eyes were alive with hatred, and the hard features seemed to twist into something not quite human. Meeks closed on him, gliding down the empty, fluorescent-lit corridor soundlessly, growing huge in the silence. Ben stood his ground with difficulty, one hand searching out the reassuring bulk of the medallion beneath his shirt. But what protection did the medallion offer him here? His mind raced. The rune stone, he thought suddenly! The stone would tell him if he was threatened! His free hand rummaged frantically in his pants pocket, fumbling for the stone as the robed figure loomed closer. Despite his resolve, Ben took a quick step backward. He could not find the stone!

Meeks was directly in front of him, dark and menacing. Ben flinched as the wizard blocked the light . . .

And then he looked up and found himself alone in the deserted corridor, staring into empty space, listening to the silence.

Meeks was gone—another substanceless apparition.

He had found the rune stone, nestled in the corner of his pants pocket, and he pulled it into the light. It was blood red and burned at the touch.

"Damn!" he muttered, angry and frightened both at once.

He took a moment to gather his wits, scanning the hallway swiftly to be certain that he had missed nothing. Then he straightened, finding himself in a sort of defensive half crouch, and stepped away from the elevator doors. Nothing moved about him. It appeared he really was alone.

But what was the reason for this second vision? Was this another warning? Was it a warning *from* Meeks or *to* Meeks?

What was going on?

He hesitated only a moment before turning sharply left toward the glass doors that fronted the offices of Holiday & Bennett, Ltd. Whatever was going on, he felt it wise to keep moving. Meeks had to know that eventually he would come to Miles. That didn't mean that Meeks was there—or even anywhere close. The apparition might be just another signal to warn him of Ben's coming. If Ben were quick enough, he would be there and gone before Meeks could do anything about it.

The lights in the office lobby were off. He pulled at the handle on the entry doors and found them locked. That was normal. Miles never unlocked the front doors or turned on the lights when he worked alone. Ben had come prepared for that. He pulled out his office key and inserted it into the lock. The lock turned easily, and the door opened. Ben stepped inside, pocketed the key, and let the door close behind him.

A radio was playing softly in the silence—Willie Nelson the kind of stuff Miles liked. Ben looked down the inner hallwa. and saw a light shining out of Miles' office. He grinned. The old boy was at home.

Maybe. A new wave of doubt and mistrust washed over him, and the grin faded. Better safe than sorry, he cautioned himself, worrying that old chestnut as if it were a spell to cast out evil spirits. He shook his head. He wished there was some way to be sure about Meeks . . .

He eased his way silently down the hall until he stood before the lighted doorway. Miles Bennett sat alone at his desk, hunched over his law books, a yellow pad crammed with notes open beside him. He had come to work wearing a coat and tie, but the knot in the tie had been pulled loose, and the coat had been shed in favor of rolled-up sleeves and an open collar. He glanced up as he sensed Ben's presence, and his eyes widened.

"Holy Saint Pete!" He started up, then eased back down again. "Doc—is that really you?"

Ben smiled. "It's me all right. How are you doing, buddy?"

"How am I doing? How am I doing?" Miles was incredulous. "What the hell kind of question is that? You go trouping off to Shangri-La or whatever, you're gone better than a year, no one hears a word from you, then one day back you come—right out of nowhere—and you want to know how I am? Pretty damn cheeky, Doc!"

Ben nodded helplessly and groped for something to say. Miles let him struggle with it a moment, then laughed and pushed himself to his feet, a big, rumpled teddy bear in business clothes.

"Well, come on in, Doc! Don't stand out there in the hallway like the prodigal son returned—even if that's what you are! Come on in, have a seat, tell me all about it! Damn, I can't believe it's really you!"

He hastened around the desk, his big hand extended, took Ben's, and pumped it firmly. "I'd just about given up on you, you know that? Just about given up. I thought something had happened to you for certain when I didn't hear anything. You know how your mind works overtime in this business anyway. I began imagining all sorts of things. I even considered calling the police or someone, but I couldn't bring myself to tell anyone my partner was off chasing little people and dragons!''

He was laughing again, laughing so hard his eyes were tearing, and Ben joined in. "They probably get calls like that all the time.''

"Sure, that's what makes Chicago the great little town it is!" Miles wiped his eyes. He wore a rumpled blue shirt and dress pants. He looked a little like a giant Smurf. "Hey, Doc— it's good to see you."

"You, too, Miles." He glanced around. "Doesn't appear that anything has changed since I left.''

"Naw, we keep the place a living shrine to your memory.'' Miles glanced around with him, then shrugged. "Wouldn't know where to start anyway, the place is such a monumental piece of art deco." He smiled, waited a moment for Ben to say something, and, when Ben didn't, cleared his throat nervously. "So, here you are, huh? Care to tell me what happened out there in fairyland, Doc? If it's not too painful to relate, that is. We don't have to discuss it if you'd rather . . ."

"We can discuss it."

"No, we don't have to. Forget I asked. Forget the whole business." Miles was insistent now, embarrassed. "It's just such a surprise to have you come waltzing in like this . . . Hey, look, I've got something for you! Been saving this for when we got together again. Look, got it right here in the drawer." He hastened back around behind the desk and rummaged quickly through the bottom drawer. "Yeah, here we go!"

He pulled out a bottle of Glenlivet, still sealed, and plopped it on the desk. Two glasses followed.

Ben shook his head and smiled with pleasure. His favorite scotch. "It's been a long time, Miles," he admitted.

Miles broke the seal, uncorked the bottle, and poured two fingers into each glass. He pushed one across the desk to Ben, then lifted his own glass in salute. "To crime and other forms of amusement," he said.

Ben touched glasses with him, and both drank. The Glenlivet was smooth and warm going down. The two old friends took seats across the desk. Willie Nelson continued to sing through the momentary silence.

"So you gonna tell me or what?" Miles asked finally, changing his mind once more.

"I don't know."

"Why not? You don't have to be coy with me, you know. You don't have to feel embarrassed if this thing didn't turn out the way you expected."

Memories flooded Ben's thoughts. No, it surely hadn't turned out the way he had expected. But that wasn't the problem. The problem was in deciding how much he should tell Miles. Landover wasn't something that could be easily explained. It was sort of like the way it was when you were a kid and your parents wanted to know about Susie at the freshman sock hop.

It was like telling them that Santa Claus really *did* exist.

"Would it be enough if I told you that I found what I was looking for?" he asked Miles after a moment's thought.

Miles was silent for a moment. "Yeah, if that's that best you can do," he replied finally. He hesitated. "*Is* that the best you can do, Doc?"

Ben nodded. "It is just now."

"I see. Well, what about later? Can you do better later? I'd hate to think that this was the end of it and I'd never learn anything more. Because I don't think I could stand that. You left here in search of dragons and damsels in distress, and I told you you were crazy. You believed all that hype about a kingdom where magic was real and fairy-tale creatures lived, and I told you it was impossible. See, Doc, I need to know which of us was right. I need to know if dreams like yours are still possible. I *have* to know."

Disappointment reflected in the roundish face. Ben felt sorry for his old friend. Miles had been in on this business from the beginning. He was the only one who knew that Ben had spent a million dollars to purchase a fantasy kingdom that sane men knew couldn't possibly exist. He was the only one who knew that Ben had gone off in search of that kingdom. He knew how the story started, but he didn't know how it ended. And it was eating at him.

But there was more to consider here than Miles' discomforting curiosity. There was his safety. Sometimes knowledge was a dangerous thing. Ben still didn't know how great a threat Meeks posed—to either of them. He still didn't know how much truth there was to his dream. Miles appeared to be well, but . . .

"Miles, I promise I'll tell you everything one day," he answered, trying to sound reassuring. "I can't tell you exactly when, but I promise you'll know. It's a difficult thing to talk about—sort of the way it used to be about Annie. I could never talk about her without . . . worrying about what I said. You remember, don't you?"

Miles nodded. "I remember, Doc." He smiled. "Have you made peace with her ghost finally?"

"I have. Finally. But it took a lot of time, and I went through a lot of changes." He paused, remembering when he had stood alone in the mists of the fairy world and come face to face with the fears he had harbored deep within himself that somehow he had failed his dead wife. "I guess talking about where I've been and what I've found there will take a little time and help as well. I still have to work a few things through . . ."

He trailed off, the glass of scotch twirling through his fingers on the desk before him.

"It's all right, Doc," Miles said quickly, shrugging. "It's enough just having you back again and knowing you're all right. The rest will come later. I know that."

Ben stared at the scotch for a moment, then lifted his eyes to Miles. "I'm only here for a short time, buddy. I can't stay."

Miles looked uncertain, then forced a quick grin. "Hey, what are you telling me? You've come back for something, haven't you? So what was it? You missed the Bulls' nosedive last winter, the Cubs' el foldo this spring, the marathon, the elections, all the rest of the vintage Chicago season. You want to catch a Bears game? The monsters of the midway are thirteen and one, you know. And they still serve Bud and nachos at the food stands. What do you say?"

Ben laughed in spite of himself. "I say it sounds pretty good. But that's not what brought me back. I came back because I was worried about you."

Miles stared at him. "What?"

"I was worried about you. Don't make that sound like such an astounding event, damn it. I just wanted to be sure you were all right."

Miles took a long pull on the scotch, then eased back carefully in the padded desk chair. "Why wouldn't I be all right?"

Ben shrugged. "I don't know." He started to continue, then caught himself. "Oh, what the hell—you already think I'm nuts, so what's a few more pecans in the fruitcake. I had this dream. I dreamed you were in real trouble and you needed me. I didn't know what the trouble was, only that it was my fault that you were in it. So I came back to find out if the dream was true."

Miles studied him a moment the way a psychiatrist might study a prize patient, then drained off the rest of his scotch and tipped forward in the chair once more. "You are nuts, Doc—you know that?"

"I know."

"Fact is, your conscience must be working overtime."

"You think so?"

"I do. You're just feeling guilty because you bailed out on me in the middle of the pre–Christmas season court rush, and I was left with all those damn cases! Well, I've got news for you! I took care of those cases, and office routine never skipped a beat!" He paused, then grinned. "Well, maybe half a beat. Proud of me, Doc?'

"Yeah, sure, Miles." Ben frowned. "So there aren't any problems at the office—nothing wrong with you, nothing that needs me back here?"

Miles rose, picked up the Glenlivet, and poured them each another finger. He was smiling broadly. "Doc, I hate to tell you this, but things couldn't be better."

And right then and there, Ben Holiday began to smell a rat.

Fifteen minutes later he was back on the streets. He had visited with Miles just long enough to avoid giving the impression that anything was seriously wrong. He had stayed even when everything inside him was screaming that he ought to run for his life.

Taxis were at a premium Saturday mornings, so he caught a bus south to Ed Samuelson's office for his noon meeting. He sat alone two seats from the back, clutched the duffel to him like a child's security blanket, and tried to shake the feeling that there were eyes everywhere watching him. He sat hunched down in his suit and dress coat and waited for the chill to steal from his body.

Think like a lawyer, he admonished himself! Reason it through!

The dream had been a lie. Miles Bennett was not in trouble and had no need of his assistance. Maybe the dream had only been his sense of guilt at leaving his old friend behind working overtime. Maybe it was only coincidence that Questor and Willow had experienced similar dreams on the same night. He didn't think so. Something had triggered those dreams—something or someone.

Meeks.

But what was his enemy up to?

He left the bus at Madison and walked several doors down to Ed Samuelson's building. The eyes followed after him.

He met with his accountant and signed various powers-of-attorney and trust instruments enabling management of his affairs to continue in his absence for as long as several years. He didn't anticipate being gone that long, but you never knew. He shook Ed's hand, exchanged good-byes, and was back out the door at 12:35 P.M.

This time he waited until he found a taxi. He had the driver take him directly to the airport and caught a 1:30 P.M. flight on Delta to Washington. He was in the nation's capital by 5:00

P.M. and an hour later caught the last flight out that night on Allegheny to Waynesboro. He kept his eyes open for Meeks the whole time. A man in a trench coat kept looking at him on the flight from Chicago. An old woman selling flowers stopped him in the main terminal at National. A sailor with a duffel bumped him as he turned away too quickly from the Allegheny ticket counter. But there was no sign of Meeks.

He checked the rune stone twice on the flight from Washington to Waynesboro. He checked it almost as an afterthought the first time and reluctantly once after. Both times it glowed blood red and burned at the touch.

He did not go any further that night. He was desperate to continue on—the need for haste was so strong he could barely control it—but reason overcame his sense of urgency. Or maybe it was fear. He did not relish venturing into the Blue Ridge in the dark. It was too easy to become lost or hurt. And it was likely that Meeks would be waiting for him at the entrance to the time passage.

He slept poorly, rose at daybreak, dressed in the warm-up suit and Nikes, ate something—he couldn't remember later what it was—and called the limo service to pick him up. He stood in the lobby with his duffel in hand and kept an uneasy watch through the plate glass windows. After a moment, he stepped outside. The day was cold and gray and unfriendly; the fact that it was dry offered what little comfort there was to be found. The air smelled bad and tasted worse, and his eyes burned. Everything had an alien look and feel. He checked the rune stone half-a-dozen times. It still glowed bright red.

The limo arrived a short time later and sped him on his way. By midmorning he was hiking back up into the forested mountains of the George Washington National Park, leaving Chicago, Washington, Waynesboro, Miles Bennett, Ed Samuelson, and everything and everyone else in this world in which he now felt himself a stranger and a fugitive far behind.

He found the mists and oaks that marked the entrance to the time passage without incident. There was no sign of

Meeks—not in the flesh, not as an apparition. The forest was still and empty; the way forward was clear.

Ben Holiday fairly ran to gain the tunnel's entrance.

He stopped running on the other side.

Sunshine streamed down out of lightly clouded skies and warmed the earth with its touch. Brightly colored meadows and fruit orchards spread down valley slopes like a quilt of patchwork swatches. Flowers dotted the landscape. Birds flew in dashes of rainbow silk. The smells were clean and fresh.

Ben breathed deeply, chasing the spots that danced before his eyes, waiting for the strength that had been sapped by his flight to return. Oh, yes, he had run. He had flown! It frightened him that he had allowed himself to panic like that. He breathed, deep and slow, refusing to look back again at the dark and misted forests that rose like a wall behind him. He was safe now. He was home.

The words were a litany that soothed him. He let his eyes lift skyward and pass down again across the length and breadth of Landover, comforted by the unexpected sense of familiarity he experienced. How strange that he should feel this way, he marveled. His passing back was like the passing from winter's slow death to spring's life. Once he would never have believed he could feel this way. Now it seemed the most logical thing in the world.

It was closing on midday. He walked down from the valley's rim to the campsite where he had left his escort. They were waiting for him and accepted his return without surprise. The captain greeted him with a salute, brought Jurisdiction around, got his men mounted, and they were on their way. From a world of jet liners and limousines to a world of walking boots and horses—Ben found himself smiling at how natural the transition seemed.

But the smile was a brief one. His thoughts returned to the dreams that Questor, Willow, and he had shared and the nagging certainty that something was very wrong with those dreams. His had been an outright lie. Had those of Questor and

Willow been lies as well? His was tied in some way to Meeks—
he was almost certain of it. Were those of Questor and Willow
tied to Meeks as well? There were too many questions and no
answers in sight. He had to get back to Sterling Silver quickly
and find his friends.

He reached the castle before nightfall, pressing for a
quicker pace the entire way. He scrambled down from his horse,
gave the escort a hurried word of thanks, called for the lake
skimmer, and crossed quickly to his island home. Silver spires
and glistening white walls beamed down at him, and the
warmth of his home-mother reached out to wrap him close.
But the chill within him persisted.

Abernathy met him just inside the anteway, resplendent
in red silk tunic, breeches and stockings, white polished boots
and gloves, silver-rimmed glasses, and appointment book.
There was irritation in his voice. "You have returned none too
soon, High Lord. I have spent the entire day smoothing over
the ruffled feelings of certain members of the judiciary council
who came here expressly to see you. A number of problems
have arisen with next week's meeting. The irrigation fields
south of Waymark have sprung a leak. Tomorrow the Lords
of the Greensward arrive, and we haven't even looked at the
list of concerns they sent us. Half-a-dozen other representatives
have been sitting about . . ."

"Nice to see you again, too, Abernathy," Ben cut him off
in midsentence. "Are either Questor or Willow back yet?"

"Uh, no, High Lord." Abernathy seemed at a momentary
loss for words. He trailed along silently as Ben moved past him
toward the dining hall. "Did you have a successful trip?" he
asked finally.

"Not very. You're certain neither has returned?"

"Yes, High Lord, I am certain. You are the first one back."

"Any messages from either?"

"No messages, High Lord." Abernathy crowded forward.
"Is something wrong?"

Ben did not slow. "No, everything is fine."

Abernathy looked uncertain. "Yes, well, that is good to

know." He hesitated a moment, then cleared his throat. "About the judiciary council's representatives, High Lord. . . ?"

Ben shook his head firmly. "Not today. I'll see them tomorrow." He turned toward the dining hall and left Abernathy at the door. "Let me know the minute Questor or Willow returns—no matter what I'm doing."

Abernathy pushed his glasses further up his long nose and disappeared back down the passageway without comment.

Ben ate a quick meal and climbed the stairs to the tower that held the Landsview. The Landsview was a part of the magic of Sterling Silver, a device that gave him a quick glimpse into the happenings of Landover by appearing to allow him to fly the valley end to end. It was a circular platform with a silver guard rail that looked out from the tower through an opening in the wall that ran ceiling to floor. A lectern fastened on the guard rail at its midpoint. An aged parchment map of the kingdom was pinned to the lectern.

Ben stepped up onto the platform, fastened both hands firmly to the guard rail, fixed his eyes upon the map, and willed himself northward. The castle disappeared about him an instant later, and he was sailing through space with only the silver railing and the lectern for support. He sped far north to the mountains of Melchor, swept across their heights and down again. He sped south to the lake country and Elderew, the home city of the people of the River Master. He crisscrossed the forests and hills from one end of the lake country to the other. He found neither Questor Thews nor Willow.

An hour later, he gave it up. His body was drenched with sweat from the effort, and his hands were cramped from gripping the railing. He left the tower of the Landsview disappointed and weary.

He tried to soak the weariness and disappointment away in the waters of a steaming bath, but could not come entirely clean. Images of Meeks haunted him. The wizard had lured him back with that dream of Miles; Ben was certain of it and was also certain that the wizard had some plan in mind to gain revenge on him for Meeks' exile. What Ben was not certain about was what part the dreams of his friends played in all this—and what danger they might be in right now because of it.

Night descended, and Ben retired to his study. He had already decided to send out search parties for both his missing friends by morning. Everything else would have to wait until he solved the mystery of the dreams. He was becoming increasingly convinced that something was terribly wrong and that he was running out of time to set it right again.

Evening deepened. He was immersed in catching up on the paperwork that had piled up during his absence when the door to his study flew open, a sudden gust of wind scattered the stacks of documents he had arranged carefully on the work table before him, and the gaunt figure of Questor Thews stalked out of the darkness into the light.

"I have found them, High Lord!" Questor exclaimed with an elaborate flourish of one arm, a canvass-wrapped bundle clutched to his chest with the other. He crossed to where Ben was working and deposited the bundle on the table with a loud thump. "There!"

Ben stared. A rather bedraggled Bunion trudged through the door behind him, clothes torn and muddied. Abernathy appeared as well, nightshirt twisted and nightcap askew. He shoved his glasses in place and blinked.

"It was all just exactly as the dream promised," Questor explained hurriedly, hands working at the canvass wrapping. "Well, not quite as promised. There was the matter of the demon imp hidden in the stonework. A nasty surprise, I can tell you. But Bunion was its equal. Took it by the throat and choked the life out of it. But the rest was just as it was in the dream. We found the passages in Mirwouk and followed them to the door. The door opened, and the room beyond was covered with stonework. One stone had the special markings. It gave at the touch, I reached down and . . ."

"Questor, you found the missing books?" Ben asked incredulously, cutting him short.

The wizard stopped, stared back at him in turn, and frowned. "Of course I found the books, High Lord. What do you think I have been telling you?" He looked put upon. "Anyway, to continue, I was about to reach down for them—I could see them in the shadows—when Bunion pulled me back. He saw the movement of the imp. There was a terrific struggle between them . . . Ah, here we are!"

The last fold of canvass fell back. A pair of massive, aged books nestled amid the wrappings. Each book was bound in a leather covering that was scrolled in runes and drawings, the gilt that had once inscribed each marking worn to bits and tracings. Each book had its corners and bindings layered in tarnished brass, and huge locks held the covers sealed.

Ben reached down to touch the cover of the top book, but Questor quickly seized his hand. "A moment, High Lord, please." The wizard pointed to the book's lock. "Do you see what has happened to the catch?"

Ben peered closer. The catch was gone, the metal about it seared as if by fire. He checked the catch on the second book. It was still securely in place. Yes, there was no doubt about it. Something had been done to the first book to break the lock that sealed it. He looked back at Questor.

"I have no idea, High Lord," the wizard answered the unasked question. "I brought the books to you exactly as I found them. I have not tampered with them; I have not attempted to open them. I know from the markings on the covers that they are the missing books of magic. Beyond that, I know no more than you." He cleared his throat officiously. "I . . . thought it proper that you be present when I opened them."

"You thought it proper, did you?" Abernathy growled, hairy face shoving into view. He looked ridiculous in his nightcap. "What you mean is you thought it *safer*! You wanted the power of the medallion close at hand in case this magic proved to be too much for you!"

Questor stiffened. "I have significant magic of my own, Abernathy, and I assure you that . . ."

"Never mind, Questor," Ben cut him short. "You did the right thing. Can you open the books?"

Questor was rigid with indignation by now. "Of course I can open the books! Here!"

He stepped forward, hands hovering over the first of the aged tomes. Ben moved back, his own hands closing on the medallion. There was no point in taking any chances with this sort of . . .

Questor touched the fastenings, and green fire spit sharply from the metal. Everyone jumped back quickly.

"It would appear that you have underestimated the danger of the situation once again!" Abernathy snapped.

Questor flushed, and his face tightened. His hands came up sharply, sparked, then came alive with a fire of their own—a brilliant crimson fire. He brought his fire down slowly to the metal fastenings, then held it there as it slowly devoured the green fire. Then he brushed his hands together briskly, and both fires were gone.

He gave Abernathy a scornful look. "A rather insignificant measure of danger, wouldn't you say?"

He reached again for the fastenings and pulled the metal clasp free. Slowly he opened the book to the first page. Aging yellow parchment stared back at him. There was nothing there.

Ben, Abernathy, and Bunion pressed forward about him, peering down through the shadows and half-light. The page was still empty. Questor thumbed to the second page. It was empty as well. He thumbed to the third. Empty.

The fourth page was empty, too, but its center was seared slightly as if held too close to a flame.

"I believe it was you who used the word *insignificant*, wizard?" Abernathy goaded.

Questor did not reply. There was a stunned look on his face. Slowly he began to leaf through the book, turning one blank page after another, finding each sheet of yellowed parchment empty, but increasingly seared. Finally pages began to appear that were burned through entirely.

He thumbed impulsively to the very center of the book and stopped.

"High Lord," he said softly.

Ben peered downward at the ruin that lay open before him. A fire had burned the center of the book to ashes, but it was as if the fire had somehow been ignited from within.

High Lord and wizard stared at each other. "Keep going," Ben urged.

Questor paged through the remainder of the book quickly and found nothing. Each sheet of parchment was just like the others—empty save for where the mysterious fire had burned or seared it.

"I do not understand what this means, High Lord," Questor Thews admitted finally.

Abernathy started to comment, then changed his mind. "Perhaps the answers lie in the other book," he suggested wearily.

Ben nodded for Questor to proceed. The wizard closed the first book and set it aside, gloved his hands in the red fire, brought them carefully down, and drew free the green fire that protected the lock on the second book. It took somewhat longer this time to complete the task, for the lock was still intact. Then, the fires extinguished, he released the lock and cautiously opened the book.

The outline of a unicorn stared back at him. The unicorn was drawn on parchment that was neither yellowed nor seared, but pristine white. The unicorn was standing still, its silhouette perfectly formed by dark lines. Questor turned to the second page. There was a second unicorn, this one in motion, but drawn the same way. The third page revealed another unicorn, the fourth still another, and so on. Questor leafed quickly through the entire book and back again. Each page of the book appeared new. Each page held a unicorn, each drawn in a different pose.

There were no writings or markings of any kind other than the drawings of the unicorns.

"I *still* do not understand what this means." Questor sighed, frustration etched into his lean face.

"It means these are not the books of magic you believed them to be," Abernathy offered bluntly.

But Questor shook his head. "No, these are the books. The dream said so, the markings on the bindings say so, and they appear as the old stories described them. These are the missing books, all right."

They were silent for a moment. Ben stared thoughtfully at the books, then glanced about until his eyes found the shadowy figure of Bunion peering from behind Questor. The kobold grinned ominously.

Ben looked back again at the books. "What we have here," he said finally, "is one book with unicorns drawn on every page and another book with no unicorns drawn anywhere, but a burned-out center. That has to mean *something*, for Pete's sake! Questor, what about Willow's dream of a black unicorn? Couldn't the unicorns here have something to do with that?"

Questor considered the possibility for a moment. "I do not see any possible connection, High Lord. The black unicorn is essentially a myth. The unicorns drawn here are not inked in black, but sketched deliberately in white. See how the lines define the features?" He turned a few pages of the second book to illustrate his point. "A black unicorn would be shaded or marked in some way to indicate its color . . ."

He trailed off, brows knitting tightly in thought. His bony fingers traced the seared lock on the first book delicately. "Why has this lock been broken and the other left intact?" he asked softly, speaking to no one in particular.

"There have not been any unicorns in the valley since its inception, according to the histories of the Kings of Landover," Abernathy interjected suddenly. "But there were unicorns once—a whole raft of them. There was a legend about it, as a matter of fact. Now let me think . . . Yes, I remember. Just wait here a moment, please."

He hurried from the room, nails clicking on the stone, nightshirt trailing. He was back a few moments later, a book of the royal histories of Landover cradled in his arms. The book was very old and its covers worn.

"Yes, this is the one," the scribe announced. He placed it next to the books of magic, thumbed through it quickly, and stopped. "Yes, right here." He paused, reading. "It happened hundreds of years ago—very close to the time of the valley's creation. The fairies dispatched a large gathering of unicorns into our valley from out of the mists. They sent them here for a very particular reason. It seems that they were concerned about a growing disbelief in the magic in many of the outlying worlds—worlds such as your own, High Lord—" The scribe extended him a disapproving look. "—and they wished to give some sign to those worlds that the magic did indeed still exist." He paused, frowning as he squinted at the aged writing. "I think I have that right. It is difficult to read this clearly because the language is very old."

"Perhaps it is your *eyes* that are old," Questor suggested, none too kindly, and reached for the book.

Abernathy snatched it away irritably. "My eyes are twice what yours are, wizard!" he snapped. He cleared his throat and went on. "It appears, High Lord, that the fairies sent the unicorns as proof to the disbelieving worlds that the magic was still real. One unicorn was to travel to each of these worlds out of Landover through the time passages." He paused again, read some more, then closed the book with a bang. "But, of course, that never happened."

Ben frowned. "Why not?"

"Because all the unicorns disappeared, High Lord. They were never seen again by anyone."

"Disappeared?"

"I remember that story," Questor declared. "Frankly, it always struck me as a rather strange story."

Ben frowned some more. "So the fairies send a raft of white unicorns into Landover and they all disappear. And that's the last of the unicorns except for a black unicorn that may or may not be real and appears only occasionally from God knows where. Except now we also have the missing books of magic that contain nothing about magic at all—just a lot of drawings of unicorns and some half-burned empty pages."

"One lock broken and one still sealed," Questor added.

"Nothing about Meeks," Ben mused.

"Nothing about changing dogs back into men," Abernathy huffed.

They stared at one another in silence. The books lay open on the table before them—two of magic that didn't seem very magical at all and one of history that told them nothing historically useful. Ben's uneasiness grew. The further they followed the threads of these dreams, the more confused matters got. His dream had been a lie; Questor's had been the truth. The source of their dreams had been different . . .

Apparently.

But maybe not. He was not sure of anything just now. It was growing late. The trip back had been a long one, he was tired, and the fatigue dulled his thinking. There wasn't enough time, and he didn't have enough energy to reason it all through tonight. Tomorrow would be soon enough. When morning came, they would search out Willow; once they found her, they would pursue this matter of the dreams until they understood exactly what was going on.

"Lock up the books, Questor. We're going to bed," he declared.

There was muttered agreement from all quarters. Bunion went off to the kitchen to clean up and eat. Abernathy went with him, carrying the aged history. Questor scooped up the books of magic and carted them out wordlessly.

Ben watched them go, left alone in the shadows and halflight. He almost wished he had asked them to stay while he forced himself to work on this puzzle a bit longer.

But that was foolish. It would all keep.

Reluctantly, he trudged off to sleep.

...and Nightmares

*L*ater, Ben Holiday would remember how ill-conceived his advice to himself had been that night. He would remember the words clearly. It will all keep. Tomorrow will be soon enough. He would remember those words as he ate them. He would reflect bitterly on the undiscerning reassurance he had allowed himself to take from them.

That was the beauty of hindsight, of course. It was always twenty-twenty.

The trouble began almost immediately. He retired directly to his bed chamber from the study, slipped on a nightshirt, and crawled beneath the covers. He was exhausted, but sleep would not come. He was keyed up from the day's events, and the mystery of the dreams played about like a cornered rat in his mind. He chased the rat, but he couldn't catch it. It was a shadow that eluded him effortlessly. He could see its outline, but could not grasp its form.

Its eyes glowed crimson in the darkness.

He blinked and shoved himself up on his elbows. The rune stone that Willow had given him shone fire red on the night-stand where he had placed it. He blinked, aware suddenly that he must have been nearly asleep when the light had brought him back. The color of the stone meant danger threatened—just as it must have threatened during the whole of the trip back.

But where was the danger to be found, damn it?

He rose and walked about the room like a creature stalking prey. There was nothing there. His clothes still lay draped over the chair where he had thrown them; his duffel still occupied its spot on the floor by the dressing room. He stood in the center of the room for a moment and let the warmth of the castle's life reach out to him. Sterling Silver responded with a deep, inner glow that wrapped him from head to foot. She was undisturbed.

He frowned. Perhaps the stone was mistaken.

It was distracting, in any case, so he covered it with a towel and climbed back into his bed. He waited a moment, closed his eyes, opened them again, closed them a second time. The darkness cloaked him and did not tease. The rat was gone. Questions and answers mixed and faded in the night. He began to drift.

He might have dreamed for a time, then. There were images of unicorns, some black, some white, and the slender, timeless faces of the fairies. There were images of his friends, both past and present, and of the dreams he had envisioned for his kingdom and his life. They ran through his subconscious, and their fluid motion lulled him as the rolling of an endless sea.

Then a curious fire flared to sudden life within his mind, disrupting the flow. Hands reached from out of nothingness, and fingers clasped the chain about his neck—his hands, his fingers. What were they doing?

And suddenly there was an image of Meeks!

The image appeared from out of a black mist, the wizard a tall, skeletal form cloaked in gunmetal blue with a face as rough and hard as raw iron. He loomed over Ben as if he were death come for its latest victim, one sleeve empty, the other a black claw that reached down, down . . .

Ben jerked awake with a start, kicking back the bedclothes, sweeping blindly at the dark with one hand. He blinked and squinted. A candle's flame lit one corner of the room, a solitary pinprick of white-gold against a haze of crimson fire given off by Willow's rune stone as it blazed in frantic warning on the nightstand, the towel that had covered it gone. Ben could feel the presence of the danger it signaled. His breath came in sharp gasps, and it was as if a giant hand pressed down upon his chest. He fought to push it off, but his muscles would not obey. His body seemed locked in place.

Something moved in the dark—something huge.

Ben tried to shout, but the sound was no more than a whisper.

A figure materialized, scarlet light covering it like blood. The figure stood there and, in a voice that sounded of nails on slate, whispered, "We meet again, Mr. Holiday."

It was Meeks.

Ben could not speak. He could only stare. It was as if the image that had haunted him during his visit to the old world had somehow managed to follow him back into this one. Except that this was no image. He knew it instantly. This was real!

Meeks smiled thinly. He was quite human in appearance now, the predatory look vanished. "What—no clever words of greeting, no brave admonishments, not even a threat? How unlike you, Mr. Holiday. What seems to be the matter? Cat got your tongue?"

The muscles of Ben's throat and face tightened as he struggled to regain control of himself. He was paralyzed. Meeks' flat, terrifying eyes bound him with cords he could not break.

"Yes, yes, the will is there, isn't it, Mr. Holiday—but the way is so dark! I know that feeling well! Remember how it was when you left me last? Remember? You taunted me in the vision crystal—my sole link with this world—and then you shattered it! You broke my eyes, Mr. Holiday, and you left me blind!" His voice had become a hiss of fury. "Oh, yes, I know what it is like to be paralyzed and alone!"

He moved forward a step further and stopped, his gaunt, craggy face bent against the crimson light of the rune. He seemed impossibly huge. "You are a fool, play-King—do you know that? You thought to play games with me and you did not even bother to understand that it was I who made all the rules. I am the games master, little man, and you are but a novice! I made you King of this land; I gave you all that it had to offer. You took that from me as if you were entitled to it! You took it as if it belonged to you!"

He was shaking with anger, the fingers of his gloved hand knotted in front of his robes in a clawed fist. Ben had never been so terrified in his life. He wanted to shrink down into himself, to crawl beneath the covers once more. He wanted to do anything—*anything*—that would let him escape this terrible old man.

Then Meeks straightened, and abruptly the anger in his face was replaced by cold indifference. He looked away. "Well, it hardly matters now. The game is over. You have lost, Mr. Holiday."

Sweat ran down Ben's rigid back. How could this have possibly happened? Meeks had been trapped in the old world; he had been denied any possible entrance into Landover as long as Ben held the medallion!

"Would you like to know how I got here, Mr. Holiday?" Meeks seemed to have read his mind. The wizard swung slowly back on him. "It was simple, really. I let you bring me." He saw the look in Ben's eyes and laughed. "Yes, Mr. Holiday— that's right. *You* were responsible for bringing me back again. What do you think of that?"

He came forward until he was standing next to the bed. His craggy face bent close. Ben could smell the stench of him. "The dreams were mine, Mr. Holiday. I sent them to you— to you, my half-brother, and the sylph. I sent them. Not all of my powers were lost in the destruction of the crystal! I could still reach you, Mr. Holiday! In your sleep! I could bridge the two worlds through your subconscious! My foolish half-brother forgot to think of that in cautioning you against me. Dreams were the only tools I needed to take control of you again. How vivid the imagination can be! Did you find the dream I sent you compelling, Mr. Holiday? Yes, of course you did. Your dream was sent to bring you to me, and bring you to me it did! I knew you would come if you thought your friend Mr. Bennett needed you. I knew you *must* come. It was simple after that, Mr. Holiday. The image at the end of the time passage was magic that alerted me to your return and let me trace your movements. It settled down within you, and you were never free of me after!"

Ben's heart sank. He should have known that Meeks would use the magic to keep track of him in some way. He should have known the wizard would leave nothing to chance. He had been a fool.

Meeks was smiling like the Cheshire Cat. "The second image was an even more interesting ploy. It diverted you from what I was really about. Oh, yes, I was there with you, Mr. Holiday! I was *behind* you! While you were preoccupied with my image, *I* slipped down into your clothing, a thing no bigger than a tiny insect. I concealed myself upon you and I let you carry me back into Landover. The medallion allows only your passage, Mr. Holiday—yet if I am a part of you, it also allows mine!"

He was hidden within my clothing, Ben thought in despair, with me all the way back, and I never realized it. That was why the rune stone glowed in warning. The threat was always there, but I couldn't see it!

"Ironic, isn't it, Mr. Holiday—you bringing me back as you did?" The skin on Meeks' cheeks and forehead was pulled back with the intensity of his smile, and his face was like a skull. "I had to come back, you know. I had to come back immediately because of your damnable, insistent meddling! Have you any idea of the trouble you have caused me? No—no, of course not. You have no idea. You do not even know what I am talking about. You understand nothing! And, in your ignorance, you have very nearly destroyed what it has taken years to create! You have disrupted everything—you and your campaign to become King of Landover!"

He had worked himself into a rage again, and it was only with great effort that he brought himself back under control. Even so, the words spit from him like bile. "No matter, Mr. Holiday, no matter. This all means nothing to you, so there is no point in belaboring it. I have the books now, and there is no further damage that you can do. I have what I need. Your dream has given me mastery of you, my half-brother's dream has given me mastery of the books, and the sylph's dream will give me . . ."

He stopped sharply, almost as if he had erred. There was a curious uneasiness in the pale, hard eyes. He blinked and it was gone. One hand brushed the empty air in dismissal. "Everything. The dreams will give me everything," he finished.

The medallion, Ben was thinking frantically. If I could only manage to put my hands on the medallion . . .

Meeks laughed sharply. "There is undoubtedly much that you wish to say to me, isn't there, Mr. Holiday? And surely much that you wish to do!" The craggy face shoved close before his own once more. The hard eyes bored into him. "Well, I will give you your chance, play-King. I will give *you* the opportunity that you were so quick to deny *me* when you smashed the crystal and exiled me from my home!"

One bony finger crooked before Ben's frozen eyes. "But first I have something to show you. I have it right here, looped safely about my neck." His hand dipped downward into the robes. "Look closely, Mr. Holiday. Do you see it?"

He withdrew his hand slowly. There was a chain gripped tightly in the fingers. Ben's medallion hung fastened at its end.

Meeks smiled in triumph as he saw the look of desperation that flooded Ben's eyes. "Yes, Mr. Holiday! Yes, play-King! Yes, you poor fool! It *is* your precious medallion! The key to Landover—and it belongs to me now!" He dangled it slowly before Ben, letting it twirl to catch the mixed light of blazing rune stone and candle's flame. His eyes narrowed. "Do you wish to know what happened to separate you from the medallion? You gave it to me in a dream I sent you, Mr. Holiday. You took the medallion off and passed it to me. You gave the medallion to me willingly. I could not take it by force, but you *gave* it to me!"

Meeks was like a giant that threatened to crush Ben—tall, dark, looming out of the shadows. His breath hissed. "I think there is nothing I can tell you that you do not already know, is there, Mr. Holiday?"

He made a quick gesture with his hand, and the invisible chains that held Ben paralyzed dropped away. He could move again and speak. Yet he did neither. He simply waited.

"Reach down within your nightshirt, Mr. Holiday," the wizard whspered.

Ben did as he was told. His fingers closed on a medallion fastened to the end of a chain. Slowly he withdrew it. The medallion was the same shape and size as the one he had once worn—the one Meeks now possessed. But the engraving on the face was changed. Gone was the Paladin, Sterling Silver, and the rising sun. Gone was the polished silver sheen. This medallion was tarnished black as soot and embossed with the robed figure of Meeks.

Ben stared at the medallion in horror, touched it disbelievingly, then let it drop from his fingers as if it had burned him.

Meeks nodded in satisfaction. "I own you, Mr. Holiday. You are mine to do with as I choose. I could simply destroy you, of course—but I won't. That would be too easy an end for you after all the trouble you have caused me!" He paused, the smile returning—hard, ironic. "Instead, Mr. Holiday, I think I will set you free."

He moved back a few steps, waiting. Ben hesitated, then rose from the bed, his mind working frantically to find a way out of this nightmare. There were no weapons close at hand. Meeks stood between him and the bedroom door.

He took a step forward.

"Oh, one thing more." Meeks' voice stopped him as surely as if he had run into a wall of stone. The hard, old face was a mass of gullies and ridges worn by time. "You are free—but you will have to leave the castle. Now. You see, Mr. Holiday, you do not belong here anymore. You are no longer King. You are, in fact, no longer even yourself."

One hand lifted. There was a brief sweep of light and Ben's nightshirt was gone. He was dressed in laborer's clothing—

rough woolen pants and tunic, a woolen cloak, and worn boots. There was dirt on him and the smell of animals.

Meeks studied him dispassionately. "One of the common folk, Mr. Holiday—that is who you will be from this day forward. Work hard and you may find a way to advance yourself. There is opportunity in this land even for such as you. You will not be King again, of course. But you may find some other suitable occupation. I hope so. I would hate to think of you as destitute. I would be most distressed if you were to suffer inconvenience. Life is a long time, you know."

His gaze shifted suddenly to Willow's rune stone. "By the way, you will not be needing that any more, will you?" His hand lifted, and the rune stone flew from the nightstand into his gloved palm. His fingers closed, and the stone shattered into dust, its red glow winking out abruptly.

He looked back again at Ben, his smile cold and hard. "Now where were we? Oh, yes—we were discussing the matter of your future. I can assure you that I will monitor it with great interest. The medallion with which I have supplied you will tell me all I need to know. Be careful you do not try to remove *that* medallion. A certain magic protects against such foolishness—a magic that would shorten your life rather considerably if it were challenged. And I do not want you to die, Mr. Holiday—not for a long, long time."

Ben stared at the other man in disbelief. What sort of game was this? He measured quickly the distance to the bedroom door. He could move and talk again; he was free of whatever it was that had paralyzed him. He had to try to escape.

Then he saw Meeks watching him, studying him as a cat might a cornered mouse, and fear gave way to anger and shame. "This won't work, Meeks," he said quietly, forcing the edge from his voice. "No one will accept this."

"No?" Meeks kept the smile steady. "And why is that, Mr. Holiday?"

Ben took a deep breath and a couple of steps forward for good measure. "Because these old clothes you've slapped on me won't fool anyone! And medallion or no medallion, I'm still me and you're still you!"

Meeks arched his eyebrows quizzically. "Are you certain of that, Mr. Holiday? Are you quite sure?"

There was a tug of doubt at the back of Ben's mind, but he kept it from his eyes. He glanced sideways at the floor-length mirror to catch a glimpse of himself and was relieved to find that physically, at least, he was still the same person he had always been.

But Meeks seemed so certain. Had the wizard changed him in some way that he couldn't see?

"This won't work," he repeated, edging closer to the door as he spoke, trying to figure out what it was that Meeks knew that he didn't—because there most certainly was *something* . . .

Meeks' laughter was sharp and acrid. "Why don't we see what works and what doesn't, Mr. Holiday!"

The gloved hand swept up, the fingers extended, and green fire burst from the tips. Ben sprang forward with a lunge, tumbling past the dark form of the wizard, rolling wildly to dodge the fire, and scrambling back to his feet. He reached the closed door in a rush and had his fingers on the handle when the magic caught up with him. He tried to scream, but couldn't. Shadows wrapped him, smothered him, and the sleep that wouldn't come earlier couldn't now be kept away.

Ben Holiday shuddered helplessly and dropped slowly into blackness.

Stranger

*B*en came awake again in shadows and half-light, eyes squinting through a swirl of images that rocked like the flotsam and jetsam an ocean's waters tossed against a beachhead. He lay on a pallet of some sort, the touch of its leather padding cool and smooth against his face. His first thought was that he was still alive. His second was to wonder why.

He blinked, waiting for the images to stop moving and take definite shape. The memory of what had happened to him recalled itself with painful intensity. He could feel again the anger, frustration, and despair. Meeks had returned to Landover. Meeks had caught him unprepared, smashed the rune stone given him by Willow, stripped him of his clothing, turned the dark magic on him until consciousness was gone, and . . .

Oh, my God!

His fingers groped down the front of his tunic, reached inside, and withdrew the medallion that hung from its chain about his neck. Frantically, he held it up to the twilight, the warnings already whispering urgently in his mind, the certainty of what he would find already taking shape in his thoughts. The carved metal face of the medallion seemed to shimmer. For an instant, he thought he saw the familiar figure of the Paladin riding out of Sterling Silver against the rising sun. Then the Paladin, the castle, and the sun were gone, and there was only the cloaked form of Meeks, black against a surface tarnished with disuse.

Ben swallowed against the dryness he felt in his throat, his worst fears realized. Meeks had stolen the medallion of the Kings of Landover.

A sense of desperation flooded through him, and he tried to push himself to his feet. He was successful for a moment, a small rush of adrenaline giving him renewed strength. He stood, the swirl of images steadying enough that he could recognize something of his surroundings. He was still within Sterling Silver. He recognized the room as a sitting chamber situated at the front of the castle, a room reserved for waiting guests. He recognized the bench on which he had been lying, with its rust-colored leather and carved wooden feet. He knew where he was, but he didn't know why—just as he didn't know why he was still alive . . .

Then his strength gave out again, his legs buckled, and he crumpled back onto the bench. Wood scraped and leather creaked, the sounds alerting someone who waited without. The door opened inward. Gimlet eyes glittered from out of a monkey face to which large ears were appended.

It was Bunion!

Bunion stepped into view and peered down at him.

Ben had never been so happy to see anyone in his entire life. He would have hugged the little kobold if he could have found the strength to do so. As it was, he simply lay there, grinning foolishly and trying to make his mouth work. Bunion helped him back onto the bench and waited for him to get the words out.

"Find Questor," he managed finally. He swallowed again against the dryness, the inside of his mouth like chalk. "Bring him. Don't let anyone know what you're doing. And be careful. Meeks is here in the castle!"

Bunion stared at him a moment longer, an almost puzzled look on his gnarled face, then turned and slipped from the room wordlessly. Ben lay back again, exhausted. Good old Bunion. He didn't know what the kobold was doing there—or even what *he* was doing there, for that matter—but it was exactly the piece of good fortune he needed. If he could find Questor quickly enough, he could rally the guard and put an end to any threat Meeks might pose. Meeks was a powerful wizard, but he was no match for so many. Ben would regain the stolen medallion, and Meeks would regret the day he ever even *thought* about sneaking back into Landover!

He closed his eyes momentarily, marshaling what inner resources he could, then pushed himself upright once more. His eyes swept the room. It was empty. Candlelight from a wall bracket and a table dish chased the shadows. Light from without crept through the crack beneath the closed door. He stood, bracing the backs of his legs against the bench for support. He was still dressed in the peasant garb with which Meeks had clothed him. His hands were black with grime. Cute trick, Ben thought—but it won't work. I'm still me.

He took a dozen deep breaths, his vision steadying, his strength rebuilding. He could feel the warmth of the castle reaching out from the flooring through his battered work boots. He could feel the vibrancy of her life. There was an urgency to her touch that was disturbing. She seemed to sense the danger he was in.

Don't worry; it's going to be all right, he reassured her silently.

Footsteps approached and the door opened. Questor Thews stood there with Bunion. He hesitated, then entered the room wordlessly. The kobold followed, closing the door behind them.

"Questor, thank God you're here!" Ben blurted out. He started forward, hands reaching out in greeting. "We have to act quickly. Meeks is back—here, now, somewhere in the castle. I don't know how he managed it, but he stole the medallion. We have to alert the guard and find him before . . ."

He came to an abrupt stop half-a-dozen feet from his friend, his words trailing off into silence. The wizard's hands were still at his sides—not extended to receive his own. The owlish face was hard, and the bushy eyebrows furrowed.

Questor Thews was looking at Ben as if he had never seen his King before in his life.

Ben stiffened. "Questor, what's the matter?"

The wizard continued to stare at him. "Who are you?"

"Who am I? What do you mean, who am I? It's me, Ben!"

"Ben? You call yourself Ben?"

"Of course, I call myself Ben! What else would I call myself? That's my name, isn't it?"

"Apparently *you* believe so."

"Questor, what are you talking about? I believe so because it *is* so!"

Questor Thews frowned. The lines about his brows furrowed even more deeply. "*You* are Ben Holiday? *You* are Landover's High Lord?"

Ben stared back at him speechlessly. The disbelief in the other's voice was unmistakable. "You don't recognize me, do you?" he ventured.

The wizard shook his head. "I do not."

Ben felt a sharp sinking sensation in the pit of his stomach. "Look, it's just the clothes and the dirt, for Pete's sake! Look at me! Meeks did this—changed the clothes, messed me up a bit. But it's still me!"

"And you are Ben Holiday?"

"Yes, damn it!"

Questor studied him a moment, then took a deep breath. "You may believe yourself to be Ben Holiday. You may even believe yourself to be High King of Landover. But you are not. I know because I have just come from the King—and he was not you! You are an intruder in this castle. You are a spy and possibly even worse. You have entered uninvited, you have listened in on conversations that were private, you have attacked the High Lord in his bedchamber, and now you are claiming to be someone you clearly are not. If the choice were mine, I would have you imprisoned at once! It is only because the High Lord has ordered your release that you are free now. I suggest you go quickly. Seek help for your affliction, whatever it is, and stay far, far away from here!"

Ben was stunned. He could not think of what to do. He heard himself telling Meeks, "Medallion or no medallion, I'm still me and you're still you!" He heard Meeks reply, "Are you certain of that?"

What had been done to him?

He turned quickly to Bunion, searching for some hint of recognition in the kobold's sharp eyes. There was none. He rushed past them both to a mirror that hung upon the wall next to the doorway. He peered through the half-light at his image reflected in the glass. It was his face! He was exactly the same as he had always been! Why couldn't Questor and Bunion see that?

"Listen to me!" He wheeled on them, frantic. "Meeks has come back from the old world, stolen the medallion, and somehow disguised from everyone but myself who I am! I look the same to me, but not to you!"

Questor folded his arms across his chest. "You look different to everyone but yourself?"

It sounded so ridiculous that for a moment Ben just stared at him. "Yes," he replied finally. "And he has made *himself* appear as me! Somehow he has stolen my identity. I didn't attack him in his bedchamber! He attacked me in mine!" He came forward a step, eyes darting from one face to the other. "He sent the dreams, don't you see? He arranged all of this! I don't know why, but he did! This is part of his revenge for what we did to him!"

There was irritation in Questor's eyes, indifference in Bunion's. Ben felt his grip on the situation slipping. "You can't let him do this, damn it! You can't let him get away with this!" His mind raced. "Look, if I'm not who I say I am, how do I know all that I do? How do I know about the dreams—mine of Miles Bennett, yours of the missing books of magic, Willow's of the black unicorn! For God's sake, what about Willow? Someone has to warn her! Listen, damn it! How do I know about the books you brought in last night—the ones with the unicorns? I know about those. I know about the medallion, about . . . Ask me something! Go on, ask me anything! Test me!"

Questor shook his head solemnly. "I do not have time for these games, whoever-you-are. You know what you know because you are a spy and learned these things by spying. You listened to our conversations and you adapted them to your own purposes. You forget that you already confessed all this to the High Lord when he caught you sneaking about his bed-chamber. You admitted everything when pressed. You are fortunate you were not dispatched by the guard when you attempted to flee. You are fortunate you . . ."

"I did not flee anything!" Ben shouted in fury. He tried to reach out to Questor, but Bunion interceded at once and kept him away. "Listen to me! I am Ben Holiday! I am High Lord of Landover! I . . ."

The doors opened and guards appeared, alarmed by the frenzy in his voice. Questor beckoned, and they seized hold of his arms.

"Don't do this!" he screamed. "Give me a chance . . ."

"You have been given that chance!" Questor Thews interjected coldly. "Take advantage of it and leave!"

Ben was dragged from the room struggling, still screaming his identity, still protesting what had been done to him, while his mind spun with anger and frustration. He caught a glimpse of a tall, dark-robed figure standing in the distance, watching. Meeks! He screamed louder, trying to break free. One of the guards cuffed him and he saw stars. His head drooped and his voice trailed away. He had to do something! But what? What?

The robed figure disappeared. Questor and Bunion were left behind. Ben was dragged through the entry to the castle gates and beyond the walls. The bridge he had rebuilt after he had assumed the throne was bright with torchlight. He was dragged across it. When he reached the far side, he was thrown to the ground.

"Good night, your Majesty," one of the guards mocked.

"Come visit again soon," said another.

They walked away laughing. "Next time we'll have his ears," one said.

Ben lay upon the ground momentarily, head spinning. Slowly he pushed himself upright and looked back across the bridge at the castle lights. He stared at the towers and battlements as they glistened silver in the light of Landover's eight moons and listened to the fading sound of voices and the heavy thud of the gates being closed.

Then all was silent.

He still could not believe that this was happening to him.

"Mother!" Willow whispered, and there was excitement and longing in her voice.

Moonlight draped the great forests of the lake country in a mix of rainbow colors, its cool brightness a beacon against the shadows. Parsnip was encamped somewhere far back within those shadows, patiently awaiting her return. Elderew lay distant, the city of the River Master wrapped in silence, her inhabitants asleep. Elderew was Willow's home and the River Master was her father, but it was neither her home nor her father that she had come to see this night.

It was the wood nymph who danced before her like a vision out of fairy.

Willow knelt at the edge of a clearing surrounded by aging pines and watched the magic unfold. Her mother spun and leaped through the night's stillness, light and ephemeral, born of air and blown on the wind. She was a tiny thing, little more than a wisp of life. White gauze clothed her, transparent and weightless, and the pale green skin of her child's body glimmered beneath the covering. Waist-length silver hair rippled and shimmered with each movement she made, a trailer of white fire against the night's dark. Music that she alone could hear swept her on.

Willow watched in rapture. Her mother was a wild thing, so wild that she could not live among humans, even the once-fairy people of the lake country. She had bonded briefly to Willow's father, but that had been long ago. They had bonded once only, her father nearly driven mad with need for the wood nymph he could not have, and then her mother had disappeared back into the forests again. She had never come back. Willow had been born of that brief union, her father's constant reminder of the fairy being he forever wanted and could never have. His impossible longing aroused in him both love and hate. His feelings for Willow had always been ambivalent.

Willow understood. She was a sylph, an elemental. She was the child of both her parents, her constant water sprite father and her mercurial wood nymph mother. Her father's domesticity gave her stability, but she was imbued with her mother's wildness as well. She was a creature of contradictions. Amorphous, she was both flesh and plant. She was human in the greater part of the moon's cycle and plant briefly in the cycle's apex—a single night each twenty-day. Ben had been shocked to see her transformation that first night. She had changed from human to tree in this very clearing, feeding on the energy implanted by her mother in the earth where she danced. Ben had been shocked, but she was what she was, and he had come to accept that. One day he would even love her for it, she believed. It was not so with her father. His love was conditional and always would be. He was still a captive of the insatiable need her mother aroused in him. Willow only seemed to emphasize the weight of the chains that bound him.

So Willow had not come to her father in her effort to understand the dream of the black unicorn. She had come instead to her mother.

Her mother spun closer, whirling and twisting with grace and strength that defied understanding. Although wild and captive in her own way to desires she could not resist, her mother loved her nevertheless—without condition, without measure. She came when Willow needed her, the bond that linked them so strong that they could often sense each other's thoughts. They spoke now in the silence of their minds, trading images of love and want. The bonding grew stronger, an entwining that expanded thoughts into words . . .

"Mother," Willow whispered a second time.

She felt herself dream. Her mother danced, and she saw in the balletic, frenzied movements the vision that had brought her. The black unicorn appeared once more, a creature of exquisite, terrible beauty. It stood before her in the dark wood of which she had first dreamed, slender shape shimmering in moonlight and shadows, in the manner of a wraith. Willow shook to see it so. One moment it was a creature of fairy, the next a demon of Abaddon. Its spiraled horn flared and its hooves pawed the forest earth. Head lowered, it feinted with a quick rush, then backed cautiously away. It seemed trapped with indecision.

What bothers it so? Willow wondered in surprise.

She looked down suddenly and the answer lay cradled in her hands. She was holding again the bridle of spun gold. It was the bridle that kept the unicorn at bay; she knew it instinctively. She caressed it and felt the weave and draw of the threads run smooth against the touch of her fingers. A strange rush of emotions coursed through her. Such power the bridle offered! It could make the unicorn hers, she sensed. There were no unicorns left in all the world, none but in fairy, where she might never go again, none but this one only, and it might be hers if she wished it. All she need do was to stretch out her hand . . .

But, no, she cautioned abruptly, if she were to touch this creature for even the briefest instant, she would be lost to herself. She knew that; she had always known that. She must take the bridle to Ben because it belonged to him . . .

And then the unicorn's head lifted, all beauty and grace. The dark face was perfectly symmetrical, the long mane blown like silk on a whisper of wind. There was fear in its eyes, fear of something other than the sylph and her bridle of spun gold, fear of something beyond her comprehension. Willow was paralyzed with the horror of it. The eyes of the black unicorn threatened to engulf her. The dream closed about. She blinked rapidly to break the spell and caught for just an instant something more than fear in the creature's eyes. She saw an unmistakable plea for help.

Her hands lifted, almost of their own volition, and she held the bridle before her like a talisman.

The black unicorn snorted, an indelicate, frightened sound, and the shadows of the wood seemed to shimmer in response. Abruptly, the dream faded into vapor and the unicorn was gone. Willow's mother danced alone again in the pine-sheltered clearing. The wood nymph spun one final time, a bit of moonlight against the dark, slowed in her pirouette, and flitted soundlessly down to where her daughter knelt.

Willow sank back upon her heels in exhaustion, the strength drained from her by the effort she had given over to the dream. "Oh, Mother," she murmured and clasped the slender, pale green hands. "What have I been shown?" Then she smiled gently and there were tears in her eyes and on her cheeks. "But there is no purpose in asking you, is there? You know no more of this than I. You dance only what you feel, not what you know."

Her mother's delicate features changed in a barely perceptible manner—a lowering of her eyes, a slight twisting of her mouth. She understood, but could not help. Her dance was a conduit to knowledge, but not its source. The magic worked that way with elementals.

"Mother." Willow clasped the pale hands more tightly, drawing strength from their touch. "I must know the reason for these dreams of the unicorn and the bridle of gold. I must know why I am being shown something that both lures and frightens me as this does. Which vision am I to believe?"

The small hands tightened back on her own, and her mother answered in a brief, birdlike sound that echoed of the forest night.

Willow's slender form bent close, and something like a chill made her shiver. "There is one in the lake country who can help me understand?" she asked softly. "There is one who might know?" Her face grew intense. "Mother, I must go to him! Tonight!"

Again her mother responded, quick, eerie. She rose and spun swiftly across the clearing and back again. Her hands beckoned frantically. *Tomorrow*, they said. *Tonight is taken. It is your time.*

Willow's face lifted. "Yes, Mother," she whispered obediently.

She understood. She might wish it otherwise—and indeed had done so more than once before—but she could not deny the fact of it. The twenty-day cycle was at its end; the change was upon her. The need was already so strong that she could barely control herself. She shivered again. She must hurry.

She thought suddenly of Ben and wished he were there with her.

She stood up and walked to the clearing's center. Her arms lifted skyward as if to draw in the colored moonlight. A radiance enveloped her, and she could feel the essence of her mother emanating from the earth upon which she had danced. She began to feed.

"Stay close to me, Mother," she pleaded as her body shimmered. Her feet arched and split into roots that snaked downward into the dark earth, her hands and arms lengthened into branches, and the transformation began.

Moments later it was finished. Willow had disappeared. She had become the tree whose namesake she bore and would stay that way until dawn.

Her mother sank down next to her, a child's ghost slipped from the shadows. She sat motionless for a time. Then her pale, slender arms wrapped about the roughened trunk that harnessed her daughter's life and held it tight.

Dawn was approaching. Landover's moons were fading away, one after the other, and night's shadows were giving ground before a broadening golden hue that edged its way slowly out of the eastern horizon.

Questor Thews stalked the halls of Sterling Silver, a skeletal, ragtag figure in his gray robes with the colored sashes, looking for all the world as if he had lost his best friend. He rounded a corner near the front entry hall and bumped up against Abernathy.

"Taking an early constitutional?" the scribe inquired archly.

Questor grunted and the furrows lining his forehead deepened. "I find I cannot sleep, and I do not for the life of me know why that is. There is reason enough to be tired, heaven knows."

Abernathy's shaggy face revealed nothing of what he thought of that. He shrugged and turned to walk next to the wizard. "I understand someone was caught breaking into the High Lord's bedchamber this evening—someone who claimed to be the King."

Questor grunted a second time. "A madman. He was lucky to be released. But the High Lord ordered it. 'Put him across to the mainland,' he said. I would not have been so generous about the matter had the decision been mine, I assure you."

They walked a bit further. "Odd that the High Lord simply released him," Abernathy remarked finally. His nose twitched. "He usually finds better uses for his enemies."

"Hmmmmmm." Questor didn't seem to hear. He was shaking his head at something. "It bothers me that the man knew so much about the dreams. He knew of the books of magic, of the High Lord's visit back, of the unicorn . . ." He trailed off momentarily. "He seemed to know everything. He seemed so sure of himself."

Neither spoke for a time. Questor led the way up a stairwell to a walk overlooking the outer parapets at the front of the castle. Below, the bridge which connected the island to the mainland stretched out across the lake, misted and empty. Questor peered through the fading gloom to the far shore, scanning the water's edge. His owlish face tightened like a drawn knot.

"The stranger appears to be gone," he said finally.

Abernathy glanced at him curiously. "Did you expect anything else?" he asked.

He waited in vain for an answer to his question. Questor continued to stare out across the lake and said nothing.

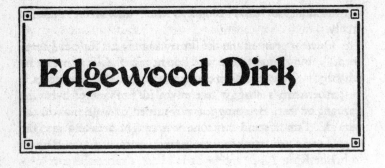

Edgewood Dirk

The new day did not find Ben Holiday standing about the gates of Sterling Silver with his nose pressed up against the timbers as might have been expected. It found him hiking his way south into the lake country. He walked quickly and purposefully. By the time the sun had crested the rim of the valley east above the mists and tree line, he was already half-a-dozen miles into his journey and determined to complete at least a dozen more before the day was finished.

The decision to leave had not been an easy one. It had taken him a long time to make it. He had sat out there in the dark and the chill, staring back at the lights of the castle and wondering what had hit him, so stunned he didn't even move for the first half hour; he just sat there. His emotions ran the gamut from shock to fear to anger and back again. It was like a bad dream from which you are certain you will escape—even after the time for escape is long past. He recounted the events of the night over and over again in his mind, trying to construct some rational explanation for their being, to discover some purpose to their order. He failed. It all came down to the same thing—Meeks was in and he was out.

It was with a sense of desperation that he finally acknowledged that what had happened to him was for real. He had given up a life and a world that were familiar and safe to come into

Landover; he had risked losing everything he had on the chance
that he would find something better. Obstacles had confronted
him at every turn, but he had overcome them. He had gained
in reality what most found only in dreams. Now, just when he
had begun to feel comfortable with what he had, just when it
seemed the worst was past, everything he had struggled so hard
to find had been snatched away from him, and he was faced
with the distinct possibility that he would end up losing it all.

It wasn't possible. It wasn't fair.

But it was a fact, and he hadn't been a successful trial lawyer for all those years in the old world by avoiding the reality
of facts. So he choked down his desperation, got over being
too stunned to move, swept away the anger and the fear, and
forced himself to deal with his situation. His repeated replays
of what had happened to him failed to yield the information he
might have wished. Meeks had tricked him into returning to
the old world, and he had carried the wizard back with him
into Landover. Meeks had done that by sending him a false
dream about Miles. But Meeks had also sent the dreams of the
missing books of magic and the black unicorn to Questor
Thews and Willow. Why had he done that? There had to be a
reason. The dreams were all tied together in some way; Ben
was certain of it. He was certain as well that something had
forced Meeks to choose this particular time to return to Landover. His diatribe in the bedchamber had made that clear. In
some way Ben had messed up his plans—and it was more than
simply the thwarting of the wizard's sale of the throne of Landover to others or the exiling of the wizard from his home
world. It was something else—something of far greater importance to Meeks. The wizard's anger at Ben was fueled by
events and circumstances that Ben hadn't yet uncovered. They
had compelled Meeks to return—almost out of desperation.

But Ben had no idea why.

He did know that, despite what should have been adequate
provocation, Meeks hadn't killed him when he could have. That
was puzzling. Clearly Meeks hated him enough to want him
to suffer awhile as an outcast, but wasn't it a bit risky letting

him wander around loose? Sooner or later someone was going
to see through the deception and recognize the truth of things.
Meeks could not assume his identity and Ben remain a stranger
to everyone indefinitely. There had to be some way to counter
the magic of that vile amulet Meeks had stuck him with, and
he would surely search it out eventually. On the other hand,
maybe what he accomplished in the long run didn't matter.
Perhaps time was something he didn't have. Maybe the game
would be over for him before he understood all the rules.

The possibility terrified him. It meant he had to act quickly
if he didn't want to risk losing the chance of acting at all. But
what should he do? He had stared back across the lake at the
dark shape of the castle and reasoned it through. He was wasting
his time here where he was a stranger to everyone—even to his
closest friends. If neither Questor nor Bunion recognized him,
there was little chance anyone else at Sterling Silver would.
Meeks was King of Landover for the moment; he would have
to concede that much. It grated on him like sand rubbed on
raw flesh, but there was nothing to be done about it. Meeks
was Ben—and Ben himself was some fellow who had slipped
uninvited into the castle and tried to cause trouble. If he attempted to break in a second time, he would undoubtedly wind
up in worse shape than he was in now.

Maybe Meeks was hoping for that. Maybe he was expecting it. Ben did not want to chance it.

Besides, there were better alternatives to choose from. Admittedly he did not know exactly what Meeks was about, but
he knew enough to know how to cause the wizard problems
if he could act fast enough. Meeks had sent three dreams, and
two of them had already served their purposes. Meeks had regained entry into Landover through Ben, and he had used Questor to bring him the missing books of magic. Make no mistake,
Ben admonished himself—Meeks had those books by now as
surely as the sun would rise in the east. That left only the third
dream to be satisfied—the dream sent to Willow of the black
unicorn. Meeks was looking for something from that third
dream as well; he had let a hint of it slip in his anger. He was

looking for the golden bridle that would harness the black unicorn and he fully expected Willow to bring it to him. And why shouldn't she, after all? The dream had warned her that the unicorn was a threat to her, that the bridle was the only thing that would protect her, and that she must bring the bridle to Ben. That was exactly what she would think she was doing, of course, once she found the bridle—except that it would be Meeks disguised as Ben who would be waiting to greet her. But if Ben could reach the sylph first, he could prevent that from happening. He could warn Willow, and perhaps the two of them could discover the importance of the bridle and the unicorn to the wizard and throw a monkey wrench into his plans.

So off Ben went, heading south, the difficult decision made. It meant forgoing his responsibilities as King of Landover and conceding those responsibilities to Meeks. It meant abandoning the problems of the judiciary council, the irrigation fields south of Waymark, the always-impatient Lords of the Greensward, the tax levy, and all the others who still waited for an audience with Landover's High Lord. Meeks could act in his place with impunity in the days ahead—or fail to act, as the case might be. It meant abandoning Sterling Silver and leaving his friends, Questor, Abernathy, and the kobolds. He felt like a traitor and a coward going this way. A part of him demanded that he stay and fight. But Willow came first. He had to find her and warn her. Once that was accomplished, he could turn his attention to exposing Meeks and setting things right.

Unfortunately, finding Willow would not be easy. He was traveling down into the lake country because that was where Willow had said she would go to begin her search for the unicorn and the golden bridle. But Willow had been gone almost a week, and that search might have taken her anywhere by now. Ben would appear a stranger to everyone, so he could not trade on his position as Landover's King to demand help. He might be ignored totally or not even be allowed into the lake country. If that happened, he was in trouble.

On the other hand, it was difficult to imagine being in worse trouble than he was in already.

He walked all that day, feeling better about himself as he went, for no better reason than the fact that he was doing something positive and not simply sitting around. He wound his way southward out of the lightly forested hill country around his island home into the more densely grown woods that comprised the domain of the River Master. The hills smoothed to grasslands, then thickened to woods damp with moisture and heavy with shadow. Lakes began to dot the countryside, some no larger than marshy ponds, some so vast they stretched away into mist. Trees canopied and closed about, and the smell of damp permeated the failing light. A stillness settled down about the land as dusk neared, then began to fill slowly with night sounds.

Ben found a clearing by a stream feeding down out of the distant hills and made his camp. It was a short project. He had no blankets or food, so he had to content himself with the leaves and branches from a stand of Bonnie Blues and the spring water. The fare was filling, but hardly satisfying. He kept thinking that something was moving in the shadows, watching him. Had the lake country people discovered him? But no one showed. He was quite alone.

Being so alone eroded his confidence. He was all but helpless when you got right down to it. He had lost his castle, his knights, his identity, his authority, his title, and his friends. Worst of all, he had lost the medallion. Without the medallion, he did not have the protection of the Paladin. He was left with only himself to rely upon, and that was precious little against the dangers posed by Landover's denizens and their mercurial forms of magic. He had been lucky to survive his arrival in Landover when he had enjoyed the benefit of the medallion's protection. What was he to do now without it?

He stared off into the dark, finding the answers as elusive as the night's shadows. What distressed him most was the fact that he had lost the medallion to Meeks. He could not figure out for the life of him how that could have happened. No one was supposed to be able to take the medallion from him. That meant he must have given it over willingly. But how had Meeks compelled him to do something so stupid?

He finished his meager dinner and was still brooding over the turn of events that had brought him to this sorry state when he saw the cat.

The cat was sitting at the edge of the clearing, perhaps a dozen feet or so away, watching him. Ben had no idea how long the cat had been there. He hadn't seen it until now, but it was keeping perfectly still, so it might have been occupying that same spot for some time. The cat's eyes gleamed emerald in the moonlight. Its coat was silver-gray except for black paws, face, and tail. It was a slender, delicate thing—seemingly out of place in the forest wild. It had the look of a strayed house pet.

"Hello, cat," Ben ventured with a wry smile.

"Hello, yourself," the cat replied.

Ben stared, certain that he must not have heard correctly. Had the cat spoken? He straightened. "Did you say something?" he asked cautiously.

The cat's gleaming eyes blinked once and fixed on him, but the cat said nothing. Ben waited a few moments, then leaned back again on his elbows. It wasn't as if it were surprising to imagine that the cat *might* have said something, he told himself. After all, the dragon Strabo spoke; and if a dragon could speak, why not a cat?

"Too bad you can't talk," he muttered, thinking it would be nice to share his misery with someone.

The night brought a chill with it, and he shivered briefly in the rough work clothes. He wished he had a blanket or a fire to help ward off the damp; or better, that he were back in his own bed at the castle.

He glanced over again at the cat. The cat hadn't moved. It simply sat there, staring back at him. Ben frowned. The cat's steady gaze was a bit unnerving. What was a cat doing out here in the woods alone like this anyway? Didn't it have a home? The emerald eyes gleamed brightly. They were sharp and in-

sistent. Ben shifted his own gaze to the shadowed woods. He
wondered again how he was going to find Willow. He would
need help from the River Master and he hadn't the foggiest idea
as to how he would convince that being of his true identity.
His fingers brushed the tarnished medallion that hung about his
neck, tracing the outline of Meeks. The medallion certainly
wouldn't be of any help.

"Maybe the River Master's magic will help him recognize
me," he thought aloud.

"I wouldn't count on it, if I were you," someone replied.

He started and looked quickly in the direction of the
speaker. There was no one there but the cat.

Ben's eyes narrowed. "I heard you that time!" he snapped,
irritated enough that he didn't care how foolish he sounded.
"You *can* speak, can't you?"

The cat blinked and answered. "I can when it pleases me."

Ben fought to regain his composure. "I see. Well, you
might at least have the courtesy to announce the fact instead of
playing games with people."

"Courtesy has nothing to do with the matter, High Lord
Ben Holiday. Playing games is a way of life with cats. We tease,
we taunt, and we do exactly as we please, not as others would
have us do. Playing games is an integral part of our personae.
Those who wish to have any sort of relationship with us must
expect as much. They must understand that participation in our
games is necessary if they wish communication on any level."

Ben stared at the cat. "How do you know who I am?" he
asked finally.

"Who else would you be but who you are?" the cat replied.

Ben had to stop and think that one through a minute.
"Well, no one," he said finally. "But how is it that *you* can
recognize me when no one else can? Don't I look like someone
else to you?"

The cat lifted one dainty paw and washed it lovingly.
"Who you look like counts for little with me," the cat said.
"Appearances are deceiving, and who you look like might not
be who you really are. I never rely on appearances. Cats can

appear as they choose. Cats are masters of deception and masters of an art cannot be deceived by anyone. I see you for who you really are, not who you appear to be. I have no idea if how you appear just now is how you really are."

"Well, it isn't."

"Whatever you say. I do know that however you might appear, you are in any case Ben Holiday, High Lord of Landover."

Ben was silent a moment, trying to decide just what it was he was dealing with here, wondering where on earth this creature had come from.

"So you know who I am in spite of the magic that disguises me?" he concluded. "The magic doesn't fool you?"

The cat studied him a moment, then cocked its head, reflecting. "The magic wouldn't fool you either, if you didn't let it."

Ben frowned. "What do you mean by that?"

"Much and little. Deception is mostly a game we play with ourselves."

The conversation was turning a bit oblique. Ben sat back wearily. "Who are you, Mr. Cat?" he asked.

The cat stood up and came forward a few feet, then sat back down again, prim and sleek. "I am a great many things, my dear High Lord. I am what you see and what you don't. I am real and imagined. I am something from the life you have known and something from dreams of life you have not yet enjoyed. I am quite an anomaly, really."

"Very insightful," Ben grunted. "Could you be a bit more precise, perhaps?"

The cat blinked. "Certainly. Watch this."

The cat shimmered suddenly in the dark, glowing as if radioactive, and the sleek body seemed to alter shape. Ben squinted until his eyes closed, then looked again. The cat had grown. It was four times the size it had been, and it was no longer just a cat. It had assumed a slightly human face beneath cat's ears, whiskers, nose and fur, and its paws had become fingers. It swished its tail expectantly as it stared at him.

Ben started half-a-dozen questions and gave up. "You must be a fairy creature," he said finally.

The cat grinned—an almost-human grin. "Exactly so! Very well reasoned, High Lord!"

"Thank you so much. Would you mind awfully telling me what sort of fairy creature you are?"

"What sort? Well, um . . . hmmmmm. I am a prism cat."

"And what is that?"

The grin disappeared. "Oh, I don't think I can explain it—not even if I wanted to, which I really don't. It wouldn't help you to know anyway, High Lord. You wouldn't understand, being human. I will tell you this. I am a very old and very rare sort of cat. I am but one of just a few still remaining. We were always a select breed and did not propagate the species in the manner of common animals. It is that way with fairy creatures—you have been told this, haven't you? No? Well, it is that way. Prism cats are rare. We must spread ourselves quite thin to accomplish our purposes."

"And what purpose is it that you are trying to accomplish here?" Ben asked, still trying to make some sense out of all the verbiage.

The cat flicked its tail idly. "That depends."

"Depends on what?"

"Oh you. On your . . . intrinsic self-worth."

Ben stared at the cat wordlessly. Things were becoming a bit too muddled for him to stay with this conversation. He had been assaulted in his own home and bounced out like a stranger. He had lost his identity. He had lost his friends. He was cold and he was hungry. He felt as if any intrinsic self-worth he might possess rated just about zero.

The cat stirred slightly. "I am deciding whether or not I shall be your companion for a time," the creature announced.

Ben grinned faintly. "My companion?"

"Yes. You certainly need one. You don't see yourself to be who you really are. Neither does anyone else, apparently, save for me. This intrigues me. I may decide to stay with you long enough to see how it all turns out for you."

Ben was incredulous. "Well, I'll say one thing for you. You're a different sort—whether cat, human, fairy, or whatever. But maybe you'd better think twice about sticking with me. You might be letting yourself in for more than you can handle."

"Oh, I rather doubt that," the cat replied. "I seldom encounter anything that difficult these days."

"Is that so?" Ben's patience slipped a notch. This cat was insufferable! He hunched closer to the prim creature. "Well, try this on for size, Mr. Cat. What if I were to tell you that there is a wizard named Meeks who has stolen my identity, my throne, and my life and consigned me to exile in my own land? What if I were to tell you that I intend to get all of that back from him, but that to do so I need to find a sylph who in turn searches for a black unicorn? And what if I were to tell you that there is every chance that I—and anyone brash enough to offer to help me in this endeavor—will be disposed of most unpleasantly if found out?"

The cat said nothing. It simply sat there as if considering. Ben leaned back, both satisfied and disgusted with himself. Sure, he could congratulate himself for having laid all of his cards on the table and setting the cat straight. But he had also just destroyed the one chance he might have had of finding someone to help him. You can't have it both ways, he admonished himself.

But the cat seemed unperturbed. "Cats are not easily discouraged once they have decided on something, you know. Cats are quite independent in their behavioral patterns and cannot be cajoled or frightened. I fail to see why you bother trying such tactics with me, High Lord."

Ben sighed. "I apologize. I just thought you ought to know how matters stand."

The cat stood up and arched its back. "I know exactly how matters stand. You are the one who is deceived. But deception needs only to be recognized to be banished. You have that in common with the black unicorn, I think."

Once more, Ben was surprised. He frowned. "You know of the black unicorn? There really is such a creature?"

The cat looked disgusted. "You search for it, don't you?"

"For the sylph more than the unicorn," Ben answered hastily. "She had a dream of the creature and of a bridle of spun gold that would hold it; she left to search for both." He hesitated, then plunged ahead. "The dream of the unicorn was sent by the wizard. He sent other dreams as well—to me and to Questor Thews, another wizard, his half-brother. I think that in some way the dreams are all tied together. I am afraid that Willow—the sylph—is in danger. If I can reach her before the wizard Meeks . . ."

"Certainly, certainly," the cat interrupted rather rudely. There was a bored look on its face. It sat down again. "It appears I had better come with you. Wizards and black unicorns are nothing to be fooling about with."

"I agree," Ben said. "But you don't appear to be any better equipped than I to do what needs to be done. Besides, this isn't your problem. It's mine. I don't think I would feel comfortable risking your life as well as my own."

The cat sneezed. "Such a noble expression of concern!" Ben could have sworn he caught a hint of sarcasm, but the cat's face revealed nothing. The cat circled briefly and sat down again. "What cat is not better equipped than *any* human to do *anything* that needs to be done? Besides, why do you persist in thinking of me as simply a cat?"

Ben shrugged. "Are you something more?"

The cat looked at him for a long time, then began to wash. It licked and worried its fur until it had groomed itself to its satisfaction. All the while, Ben sat watching. When the cat was at last content, it faced him once more. "You are not listening to me, my dear High Lord. It is no wonder that you have lost yourself or that you have become someone other than who you wish to be. It is no wonder that no one but I can recognize you. I begin to question if you are worth my time."

Ben's ears burned at the rebuke, but he said nothing. The cat blinked. "It is cold here in the woods; there is a chill in the air. I prefer the comfort of a hearth and fire. Would you like a fire, High Lord?"

Ben nodded. "I'd love one—but I don't have the tools."

The cat stood and stretched. "Exactly. But I do, you see. Watch."

The cat began to glow again, just as it had before, and its shape within the glow grew indistinct. Then suddenly there was a crystalline glimmer, and the flesh and blood creature of a moment earlier disappeared completely and was replaced by something that looked as if it were a large glass figurine. The figurine still retained the appearance of a cat with human features, but it moved as if liquid. Emerald eyes blazed out of a clear body in which moonlight reflected and refracted off mirrored surfaces that shifted like tiny plates of glass. Then the light seemed to coalesce in the emerald eyes and thrust outward like a laser. It struck a gathering of deadwood a dozen feet away and ignited it instantly into a blazing fire.

Ben shielded his eyes, then watched as the fire diminished until it was manageable—the size of a campfire. The emerald eyes dimmed. The cat shimmered and returned to its former shape. It sat back slowly on its haunches and regarded Ben solemnly. "You will recall now, perhaps, what I told you I was?" it said.

"A prism cat," Ben responded at once, remembering.

"Quite right. I can capture light from any source—even so distant a source as the land's eight moons. I can then transform such light into energy. Basic physics, actually. At any rate, I have abilities somewhat more advanced than your own. You have seen but a small demonstration of those abilities."

Ben nodded slowly, feeling a bit uneasy now. "I'll take your word for it."

The cat moved a bit closer to the fire and sat down again. The night sounds had died into stillness. There was a sudden tension in the air. "I have been places others only dream about and I have seen the things that are hidden there. I know many secrets." The cat's voice became a whisper. "Come closer to the fire, High Lord Ben Holiday. Feel the warmth." Ben did as he was told, the cat watching. The emerald eyes seemed to flare anew. "I know of wizards and missing books of magic. I know of black unicorns and white, some lost, some found. I even know something of the deceptions that make some beings seem other than what they are." Ben started to interrupt, but the cat hissed in warning. "No, High Lord—just listen! I am not disposed to converse so freely on most occasions, so it would behoove you to let me finish! Cats seldom have anything to say, but we always know much! So it is in this instance. I know much that is hidden from you. Some of what I know might be useful, some not. It is all a matter of sorting out. But sorting out takes time, and time requires commitment. I give commitment to things but rarely. You, however, as I said, intrigue me. I am thinking about making an exception. What do you think?"

Ben wasn't sure what he thought. How could this cat know about black unicorns and white? How could he know about missing books of magic? How much of this was just talk in general and how much specific to him? He wanted to ask, but he knew as surely as it was night that the cat was not about to answer him. He felt his questions all jumble together in his throat.

"Will you come with me, then?" he asked finally.

The cat blinked. "I am thinking about it."

Ben nodded slowly. "Do you have a name?"

The cat blinked once more. "I have many names, just as I am many things. The name I favor just now is Edgewood Dirk. But you may call me Dirk."

"I am pleased to make your acquaintance, Dirk," Ben said.

"We shall see," Edgewood Dirk answered vaguely. He turned and moved a step or two closer to the fire. "The night wearies me; I prefer the day. I think I shall sleep now." He circled a patch of grass several times and then settled down, curling up into a ball of fur. The glow enveloped him momentarily, and he was fully cat once more. "Good night, High Lord."

"Good night," Ben replied mechanically. He was still taut

with the emotions that Dirk had aroused in him. He mulled over what the cat had said, trying to decide how much the creature really knew and how much he was generalizing. The fire crackled and snapped against the darkness, and he moved closer to it for warmth. Whatever the case, Edgewood Dirk might have his uses, he reasoned and stretched his hands toward the flames. If only this strange creature were not so mercurial . . .

And suddenly an unexpected possibility occurred to him.

"Dirk, did you come looking for me?" he asked.

"Ah!" the cat replied softly.

"Did you? Did you deliberately seek me out?"

He waited, but Edgewood Dirk said nothing more. The stillness of a few moments earlier began to fill again with night sounds. The tension within him dissipated. Flames licked against the deadwood and chased the forest shadows. Ben stared over at the sleeping cat and experienced an odd sense of serenity. He no longer felt quite so alone.

He breathed deeply the night air and sighed. No longer alone? Who did he think he was kidding?

He was still trying to decide when he finally fell asleep.

Healer Sprite

Ben Holiday awoke at dawn and could not figure out where he was. His disorientation was so complete that for several moments he could remember nothing of the events of the past thirty-six hours. He lay on grasses damp with morning dew in a clearing in a forest and wondered why he wasn't in his own bed at Sterling Silver. He glanced down his body and wondered why he was wearing such shabby clothing. He stared off into the misted trees and wondered what in the hell was going on.

Then he caught sight of Edgewood Dirk perched on a fallen log, sassy and sleek, preening with studied care as he licked himself, all the while studiously ignoring his human company. Ben's situation came back to him then in a rush of unpleasant memories, and he found himself wishing rather ruefully that he had remained ignorant.

He rose, brushed himself off, drank a bit of spring water, and ate a stalk from the Bonnie Blues. The fruit taste was sweet and welcome, but his hunger for more substantial fare was to go unassuaged for yet another meal. He glanced once or twice in Dirk's direction, but the cat went on about the business of washing himself without noticing. Some things obviously took precedence over others.

When Dirk was finally finished, he rose from his sitting

position, stretched, and said, "I have decided to come with you."

Ben refrained from saying what he was tempted to say and simply nodded.

"For a while, at least," Dirk added pointedly.

Ben nodded a second time. "Do you know where it is that I intend to go?" he asked.

Dirk gave him one of those patented "must you be such an idiot?" looks and replied, "Why? Don't you?"

They departed the campsite and walked in silence through the early morning hours. The skies were gray and oppressive. A heavily clouded sun lifted sluggishly from out of the tree line, its mist-diffused light sufficiently bright to permit small patches of dull silver to chase the shadows and dot the pathway ahead like stepping stones across a pond. Ben led, Dirk picking his way carefully a yard or two behind. There were no forest sounds to keep them company; the woods seemed empty of life.

They reached the Irrylyn at midmorning and followed its shoreline south along a narrow footpath that wound through forest trees and deadwood. Like the woods surrounding, the lake seemed lifeless. Clouds hung low across its waters, and there was no wind. Ben's thoughts drifted. He found himself reliving his first meeting with Willow. He had come to the lake country seeking the support of the River Master in his effort to claim Landover's throne. Willow and Ben had chanced upon each other bathing naked at night in the warm, spring-fed waters of this lake. He had never seen anyone as beautiful as the sylph. She had given back to him feelings he had thought dead and gone.

He shook his head. The memory left him oddly sad, as if it were an unpleasant reminder of something forever lost. He stared out across the gray, flat surface of the Irrylyn and tried to recapture the moment. But all he found were ghosts at play in the mists.

They broke away from the lake at its southern end and moved back into the forest. It was beginning to spit rain. The

small patches of gray sunlight disappeared and shadows closed
about. The character of the woods underwent a sudden and
distinct change. The trees turned gnarled and damp, monstrous
sentinels for a surreal world of imaginary wraiths that slipped
like smoke through a mist that shrouded everything. Sounds
returned, but they were more haunting than comforting, bits
and pieces of life that sprinkled the gloom with hints of what
lay hidden. Ben slowed, blinking his eyes, wiping the water
from his face. He had made the trip down into the lake country
on several occasions since that first meeting with Willow, but
each time it had been in the company of the sylph or Questor
Thews, and one of the fairy people had always met them. He
could find his way as far as the Irrylyn by himself, but he could
not find his way much farther than that. If he expected to find
the River Master and his people, he was going to have to have
some help—and he might not get it. The lake country people
lived in Elderew, their home city, hidden somewhere in these
forests. No one could find Elderew without help. The River
Master could either bring you in or he could leave you out—
the choice was his.

   He walked a bit farther, saw the path before him disappear
completely, and stopped. There was no indication of where to
go next. There was no sign of a guide. The forest about him
was a sullen wall of damp and gloom.

   "Is there a problem of some sort?"

   Edgewood Dirk appeared next to him and sat down gingerly, flinching as the rain struck him. Ben had forgotten the
cat momentarily. "I'm not sure which way to go," he admitted
reluctantly.

   "Oh?" Dirk looked at him, and Ben could have sworn the
cat shrugged. "Well, I suggest we trust to our instincts."

   The cat stood up and padded silently ahead, moving
slightly left into the mist. Ben stared after the beast momentarily, then followed. Who knew? Maybe the cat's instincts were
worth trusting, he thought. They certainly couldn't be any
worse than his own.

   They picked their way slowly ahead, slipping through the

massive trees, ducking low-hanging branches with mossy
trailers, stepping over rotting logs, and skirting marshy patches
of black ooze. The rain quickened, and Ben felt his clothing
grow damp and heavy. The forest and the mist thickened and
wrapped about him like a cloak; everything disappeared outside
a ten-foot sweep. Ben heard things moving all about him, but
saw nothing. Dirk kept padding steadily on, seemingly
oblivious.

Then abruptly a shadow detached itself from the gloom
and brought them to a halt. It was a wood sprite, lean and wiry,
small as a child, his skin browned and grainy, his hair thick and
dark, grown like a mane down the back of his neck and arms.
Dressed in nondescript, earth-colored clothing, he seemed as
much a part of the forest as the trees and, had he wished, might
have disappeared as quickly as he had come. He said nothing
as he glanced first at Ben, then at Dirk. He hesitated as he caught
sight of the cat, seemed to consider something, then beckoned
them forward.

Ben sighed. Halfway home, he thought.

They walked ahead silently, following a narrow trail that
wound snakelike through vast, empty stretches of swamp. Fog
rolled over the still surface of the water, clouds of impenetrable
gray. A thin sheet of rain continued to fall. Shapes darted and
glided wraithlike through the gloom, some with faces that were
almost human, some with the look of forest creatures. Eyes
blinked and peered out at him, then were gone—sprites,
nymphs, kelpies, naiads, pixies, elementals of all forms. The
fairy worlds of dozens of childhood stories came suddenly to
life, an impossible mix of fantasy and truth. As always, it left
Ben filled with wonder—and slightly afraid.

The path he followed was unfamiliar to him. It was like
that whenever he came to Elderew; the River Master always
brought him in a different way. Sometimes he passed through
water that rose to his waist; sometimes he passed along marshy
earth that sucked eagerly at his boots. Whichever way he came,
the swamp was always close about, and he knew that to stray
from any of the paths would bring a quick end to him. It always

bothered him that not only could he not find his way in, but he could not find his way out again either. That meant he was trapped here if the River Master did not choose to release him. That would not have been a consideration in the past. After all, he had been Landover's King and he had possessed the power of the medallion. But all that was changed now. He had lost both his identity and the medallion. He was just a stranger. The River Master could do as he chose with a stranger.

He was still thinking about his dilemma when they entered a great stand of cyprus, brushed aside curtains of damp moss trailers, wove past massive gnarled roots, and emerged at last from the marsh. Ben's boots found firmer ground, and he began a short climb up a gentle slope. The mist and gloom thinned, cyprus gave way to oak and elm, fetid smells dissipated, and the sweeter scent of open woodlands filled the morning air. Colors reappeared as garlands of rain-soaked flowers strung along hedges and roped from sway bars lined the path. Ben felt a tinge of relief. The way forward was familiar again. He quickened his pace, anxious that the journey be done.

Then the slope crested, the trees parted at the path's end, and there he was. Elderew stretched away before him, the city of the lake country fairies. The great, open-air amphitheater where the people held their festivals stood in the foreground, gray and empty in the rainfall. Massive trees framed its walls, the lower branches connected by sawn logs to form seats, the whole ringing an arena of grasses and wild flowers. Branches interlaced overhead to create a leafy roof, the rain water dripping from its eaves in a steady trickle. Beyond, trees twice the size of California's giant redwoods rose over the amphitheater against the clouded horizon and cradled in their branches the city proper—a broad cluster of cottages and shops interconnected by an intricate network of tree lanes and stairways that stretched from forest earth to treetop and down again.

Ben stopped, stared, and blinked away the rain that ran down his forehead into his eyes. He realized suddenly that he was gaping like the country boy come to the city for the first time. It reminded him of how much a stranger he really was in this land—even after having lived in it for over a year, even though he was its King. It underlined in bold strokes the precariousness of his situation. He had lost even the small recognition he had enjoyed. He was an outsider stripped of friends and means, almost completely reliant on the charity of others.

The River Master appeared from a small stand of trees to one side, flanked by half-a-dozen guards. Tall and lean, his strange scaled skin gleaming with a silver cast where it shone beneath his forest green clothing, the lord of the lake country fairies stalked forward determinedly. His hard, chiseled face did not evidence much in the way of charity. His demeanor, normally calm and unhurried, seemed brusque. He said something to the guide in a dialect Ben did not recognize, but there was no mistaking the tone. The guide stepped back quickly, his small frame rigid, his eyes turned away.

The River Master faced Ben. The silver diadem about his forehead flashed dully with rain water as he tilted his head up. Coarse, black hair rippled along the back of his neck and forearms. There were to be no preliminaries. "Who are you?" he demanded. "What are you doing here?"

Ben had anticipated some resistance, but nothing like this. He had expected that the River Master wouldn't recognize him, and, sure enough, he hadn't. But that didn't explain why the ruler of the once-fairy people was being so deliberately unfriendly. The River Master was surrounded by guards, and they were armed. He had left the members of his family behind where always before he had gathered them about him to receive visitors. He had not waited for Ben to reach the amphitheater, the traditional greeting place for visitors. And his voice reflected undisguised anger and suspicion. Something was dreadfully wrong.

Ben took a deep breath. "River Master, it's me, Ben Holiday," he announced and waited. There wasn't even a hint of recognition in the other's dark eyes. He forged ahead. "I know I don't look like myself, but that's because something has been done to me. A magic has been used to change my appearance. The wizard who served the old King's son, the one who abandoned Landover—he calls himself Meeks in my world—has returned and stolen both my identity and the throne. It's a long story. What's important is that I need your help. I have to find Willow."

The River Master stared, obviously surprised. "*You* are Ben Holiday?"

Ben nodded quickly. "I am—even though I don't appear to be. I'll try to explain. I traveled back to . . ."

"No!" The River Master cut him short with an irritated chop of one hand. "There is only one explanation I wish to hear from you—whoever you are. I wish to know why you brought the cat."

Now it was Ben's turn to stare. Rain water tricked steadily down his face, and he blinked it from his eyes. "The cat?"

"Yes, the cat! The prism cat, the fairy creature who sits next to you—why did you bring it here?" The River Master was a water sprite and there were gills directly below his chin at either side of his throat. He was so agitated now that the gills fluttered uncontrollably.

Surprised, Ben glanced at Dirk, who sat a dozen paces away and washed his paws with what appeared to be total disinterest in the conversation taking place. "I don't understand," he replied finally, looking back again at the River Master. "What's the problem with . . . ?"

"Am I not making myself clear to you?" the River Master interrupted once more, rigid with anger now.

"Well, no, not . . ."

"The cat, I asked you—what is the cat doing here?"

Ben gave up trying to be diplomatic. "Now look. I didn't bring the cat; the cat chose to come. We have a nice working arrangement—I don't tell him where to go or what to do, and he doesn't tell me. So why don't you quit being difficult and tell me what's going on. The only thing I know about prism cats is that they can start campfires and change shape. Obviously you know something more."

The River Master's face tightened. "I do. And I would think that the High Lord of Landover would make it *his* business to know as well!" He came forward a step. "You still claim that you *are* the High Lord, don't you?"

"I most certainly do."

"Even though you look nothing like Ben Holiday at all, you wear a workman's clothing, and you travel without retainers or standard?"

"I explained all that . . ."

"Yes, yes, yes!" The River Master shook his head. "You certainly have the High Lord's boldness, if nothing else."

He seemed to consider the matter for a moment, saying nothing. The guards about him and the chastened guide were like statues. Ben waited impatiently. A handful of faces appeared from behind the trunks of surrounding trees, materializing through the rain and gloom. The River Master's people were growing curious.

Finally, the River Master cleared his throat. "Very well I don't accept that you are Landover's High Lord, but whoever you are, allow me to explain a few things about the creature with whom you travel. First, prism cats are fairy creatures—true fairy creatures, not exiles and emigrants like the people of the lake country. Prism cats are almost never seen beyond the mists. Second, they do not normally keep company with humans. Third, they are uniformly unpredictable; no one pretends to understand fully what they are about. And fourth, wherever they journey, they bring trouble. You are fortunate that you were allowed into Elderew at all in the company of a prism cat. Had I known that you traveled with one, I would almost certainly have kept you out."

Ben sighed wearily, then nodded. Apparently superstitions about cats weren't confined to just his world. "Okay, I promise to keep all that in mind in the future," he replied, fighting to keep the irritation from his voice. "But the fact remains you did *not* keep me or the cat out, so here we are and whether you believe that I am High Lord of Landover or not doesn't really matter a rat's whiskers. I still need your help if I . . ."

A sudden gust of rain blew into his face, and he choked on what he was about to say next. He paused, shivering within the cold and damp of his clothing. "Do you suppose that we could continue this discussion somewhere dry?" he asked quietly.

The other man studied him silently, his expression unchanged.

"River Master, your daughter may be in great danger," Ben whispered. "Please!"

The River Master continued to study him a moment longer, then beckoned him to follow. A wave of one hand dismissed the guide. The faces of the watching villagers disappeared just as quickly. They walked a short distance through the trees to a gazebolike shelter formed of sculpted spruce, the guards trailing watchfully. A pair of benches sat within the shelter facing each other over a broad, hollowed stump converted to a planter of flowers. The River Master seated himself on one bench, and Ben took the other. The rain continued to fall all about them, a soft, steady patter on the forest trees and earth, but it was dry within the shelter.

Dirk appeared, jumped up beside Ben, settled down with all four paws tucked away, and closed his eyes sleepily.

The River Master glanced at the cat with renewed irritation, then squared around to Ben once more. "Say what you would," he advised.

Ben told him the whole story. He felt he had nothing to lose in doing so. He told him about the dreams, the journeys embarked upon by Questor, Willow, and himself, the discovery of the missing books of magic, the unexpected appearance of Meeks, the theft of both his identity and the medallion, and his exile from Sterling Silver. The River Master listened without comment. He sat there as if he had been carved from stone, unmoving, his eyes fastened on Ben's. Ben finished, and the lord of the lake country people remained a statue.

"I don't know what else I can say to you," Ben said finally.

The River Master responded with a barely perceptible nod, but still said nothing.

"Listen to me," Ben pleaded. "I have to find Willow and warn her that this dream of the black unicorn was sent by Meeks and I don't think I can do that without your help." He paused, suddenly reminded of a truth that he still had difficulty acknowledging—even to himself. "Willow means a great deal to me, River Master. I care for her; you must know that. Now tell me—has she been here?"

The River Master pulled his forest cloak closer about him. The look in his eyes was distant. "I think perhaps you are who you claim to be," he said softly. "I think perhaps you are the High Lord. Perhaps."

He rose, glanced from his shelter at the guards who ringed them, motioned all but one of them away, and came over to stand next to Ben. He bent down, his strange, wooden face right next to Ben's. "High Lord or fraud, tell me the truth now—how is it that you come to travel with this cat?"

Ben forced himself to stay calm. "It was a matter of chance. The cat found me at the edge of the lake country last night and suggested his company might be useful. I'm still waiting to find out if that's true."

He looked down at Dirk momentarily, half expecting the cat to confirm what he had said. But Dirk sat there with his eyes closed and said nothing. It occurred to Ben suddenly that the cat hadn't said a word since they had arrived in Elderew. He wondered why.

"Give me your hand," the River Master said suddenly. He reached down with his own and clasped Ben's tightly. "There is one way in which I may be able to test the truth of your claim. Do you remember when you first came to Elderew and we walked alone through the village and talked of the magic of the lake country people?" Ben nodded. "Do you remember what I showed you of the magic?"

The pressure of his grip was like an iron bar. Ben winced, but did not try to pull away. "You touched a bush stricken with wilt and healed it," he replied, his eyes locked on those of the other man. "You were attempting to show me why the lake country people could manage on their own. Later, you refused to give your pledge to the throne." He paused deliberately. "But you have given it since, River Master—and you have given it to me."

The River Master studied him a moment, then pulled him effortlessly to his feet. "I have said that you could be Ben Holiday," he whispered, his hard face bent close. "I believe it possible." He placed both of Ben's hands in his own. "I do not know how your appearance was altered, but if magic changed you to what you are, then magic can be used to change you back again. I possess the power to heal much that is sickened and distressed. I will use that power to help you if I can." The scaled hands tightened harder about Ben's. "Stand where you are and do not move."

Ben took a quick breath. The River Master's grip warmed his own, and the chiseled features lowered into shadow. Ben waited. The other's breathing slowed and a sudden flush spread through Ben's body. He shivered at the feeling, but remained stationary.

Finally the River Master stepped back. There was a hint of confusion in the dark eyes. "I am sorry, but I cannot help you," he said finally. "Magic has indeed been used to alter your appearance. But the magic is not of another's making—it is of your own."

Ben stared. "What?"

"You have made yourself who and what you are," the other said. "You must be the one to change yourself back again."

"But that doesn't make any sense!" Ben exploded. "I haven't done a thing to change what I look like—it was Meeks! I watched him do it! He stole the medallion of the Kings of Landover and gave me . . . this!"

He yanked the tarnished image of Meeks from his tunic and thrust it out angrily, almost as if to snap it from its chain. The River Master studied it a moment, touched it experimentally, then shook his head. "The image graven here is clouded in the same manner as your appearance. The magic at work is again of your own making."

Ben's jaw tightened, and he snatched the medallion back

again. The River Master was talking in riddles. Whatever magic was at work was most assuredly not of Ben's making. The River Master was either mistaken or misled—or he was deliberately trying to confuse Ben because he still didn't trust him.

The River Master seemed to read his mind. He shrugged. "Believe me or don't—the choice is yours. What I tell you is what I see." He paused. "If this new medallion you wear was given to you by your enemy, perhaps you should discard it. Is there a reason you keep it?"

Ben sighed. "Meeks told me that the medallion would let him know what I was about. He warned that a certain magic protects against trying to remove it—a magic that could kill me."

"But is that so?" the other asked. "Perhaps the wizard lied."

Ben hesitated before replying. He had considered that possibility before. After all, why should he believe anything Meeks told him? The problem was that there was no way to test the truth of the matter without risking his life.

He lifted the tarnished medallion before him experimentally. "I have given it some thought . . ." he began.

Then out of the corner of his eye, he saw Edgewood Dirk stir. The cat's head lifted, and the green eyes snapped open. It was almost as if the cat had roused himself from his near-comatose state for the express purpose of seeing what Ben would do. The strange eyes were fixed and staring. Ben hesitated, then slowly lowered the medallion back inside his tunic. "I think maybe I need to give it some more thought," he finished.

Dirk's eyes slipped closed again. The black face lowered. Rain beat down steadily in the momentary stillness, and a long peal of thunder rolled across the lake country from somewhere east. Ben experienced a strange mix of frustration and anger. What sort of game was the cat playing now?

The River Master moved back to the other bench and remained standing. "It appears I cannot help you after all," he advised. "I think that you had better go—you and the cat."

Ben saw his chance for any help slipping away. He rose

quickly. "At least tell me where to find Willow," he begged.
"She said she was coming here to the lake country to learn the
meaning of her dream. Surely she would come to you for help."

The River Master studied him silently for a moment, considering in his own mind things hidden from Ben, then shook
his head slowly. "No, High Lord or pretender—whichever you
are—she would not."

He came partway around the stump once more, then
stopped. Wind blew sharply at his cloak, and he pulled it close
to ward away the chill of the rain. "I am her father, but not
the parent from whom she would seek help when it was needed.
I was never that. I have many children by many wives. Some
I am closer to than others. Willow has never been close to me.
She is too much like her mother—a wild thing who seeks only
to sever ties, not to bind them. Neither seeks companionship
from me; neither ever did. The mother came to me only once,
then was gone again, back into the forest . . ."

He trailed off, distracted. "I never even knew her name,"
he continued after a moment. "A wood nymph, no more than
a tiny bit of silk and light, she dazzled me so that names were
of no consequence for that one night. I lost her without ever
really having had her. I lost Willow, I think, because of what
that did to me. I begrudged the mother her freedom, and Willow was forced to live with my anger and resentment. That
caused her to slip gradually from me, and there was no help
for it. I loved her mother so much that I could neither forgive
nor forget what she had done to me. When I gave Willow per-
mission to live at Sterling Silver, I severed the only tie that still
bound us. She became forever her own woman and my daughter no longer. Now she sees me as a man who has more children
than he can ever truly be father to. She chooses not to be one
of those."

He turned away, lost perhaps in memories. His confession
was a strange one, Ben thought—told simply and directly, but
without a trace of emotion. There had been no inflection in the
River Master's voice, no expression in his face. Willow meant
much to him, and yet he could demonstrate nothing of it—he

could only relate the fact of its being. It made Ben wonder suddenly about his own feelings for the sylph and question what they were.

The River Master stared out into the rain for a time, motionless, silent, and then he shrugged. "I could heal so much, but not that," he said quietly. "I did not know how." Suddenly he looked back again at Ben—and it was as if he were seeing him for the first time. "Why is it that I tell this to *you*?" he whispered in surprise.

Ben had no idea. He kept silent as the River Master stared at him as if mystified by his even being there. Then the lord of the lake country people seemed simply to dismiss the matter. His voice was flat and cold. "You waste your time with me. Willow will go to her mother. She will go to the old pines and dance."

"Then I will search for her there," Ben said. He rose to his feet. The River Master watched him, silent. Ben hesitated. "You need not send a guide with me. I know the way."

The River Master nodded, still silent. Ben started away, walked a dozen paces from the shelter, stopped, and turned. The single remaining guard had faded back into the trees. The two men were alone. "Would you like to come with me?" Ben asked impulsively.

But the River Master was staring out into the rain again, lost in its dull silver glitter, lost in its patter. The gills on his neck slowed to a barely perceptible flutter. The hard, chiseled face seemed emptied of life.

"He doesn't hear you," Edgewood Dirk said suddenly. Ben glanced down in surprise and found the cat at his feet. "He has gone inside of himself to discover where he's been. It happens like that sometimes after revealing something so carefully guarded for so long."

Ben frowned. "Carefully guarded? Do you mean what he said about Willow? About her mother?" The frown deepened as he knelt next to the cat. "Dirk, why *did* he tell me all that? He's not even sure who I am."

Dirk looked over at him. "There are many forms of magic

in this world, High Lord. Some come in large packages, some
in small. Some work with fire and strength of body and heart
. . . and some work with revelation."

"Yes, but why . . . ?"

"Listen to me, High Lord! Listen!" Dirk's voice was a hiss.
"So few humans listen to anything a cat has to say. Most only
talk to us. They talk to us because we are such good listeners,
you see. They find comfort in our presence. We do not question
and we do not judge. We simply listen. They talk, and we listen.
They tell us everything! They tell us their innermost thoughts
and dreams, things they would tell no other. Sometimes, High
Lord, they do all this without even understanding why!"

He was still again, and suddenly it occurred to Ben that
Dirk wasn't speaking in general terms, but in very specific ones.
He wasn't talking about just everyone, but about someone defi-
nite. His eyes lifted to find the solitary figure of the River
Master.

And then he thought suddenly about himself.

"Dirk, what . . . ?"

"Shhhhhh!" The cat hushed him into silence. "Let the stillness be, High Lord. Do not disturb it. If you are able, listen to
its voice—but let it be."

The cat moved slowly off into the trees, picking his way
gingerly over the damp, water-soaked forest earth. Rain fell in
steady sheets out of skies clouded over from horizon to horizon,
a gray ceiling canopied above the trees. Silence filled the gaps
left by the sound of the rain, cloaking the city of Elderew, the
houses and tree lanes, the walkways and parks, and the vast,
empty amphitheater that loomed behind the still-motionless figure of the River Master. Ben listened as Dirk had said he should
and he could almost hear the silence speak.

But what was it saying to him? What was it that he was
supposed to learn? He shook his head hopelessly. He didn't
know.

Dirk had disappeared into the haze ahead of him, a pale
gray shadow. Abandoning his efforts to listen further, Ben hurried after.

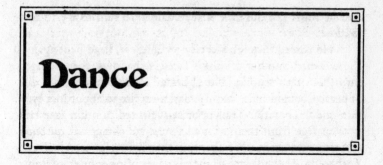

Dance

*T*hat there was something inordinately peculiar about Edgewood Dirk was no longer a matter for debate with Ben Holiday.
You might have argued that *all* cats were somewhat peculiar
and that it should come as no surprise therefore that a cat out
of the fairy world would turn out to be even *more* peculiar than
your average feline, but Ben would have disagreed. The sort
of peculiar exhibited by Dirk went far beyond anything encountered in—oh, say—*Alice in Wonderland* or *Dick Whittington*.
Dirk lent a whole new meaning to the word, and the most
aggravating part of all was the fact that, try as Ben might, he
could not decipher what it was that the beast was about!

In short, who was this cat, and what was he doing here
with Ben?

He would have loved to find immediate answers to his
questions, but time did not permit it. The cat was leading the
way once more—presumptuous beast that it was—and he was
forced once again to hurry after. Rain pelted his face in a quick-
ening downpour, and the wind gusted in chill swipes. Nightfall
was approaching and the weather was growing worse. Ben was
drenched, cold, hungry, and discouraged, despite his resolve to
continue, and he found himself wishing fondly for a warm bed
and dry clothes. But he was unlikely to find either just now.
The River Master was barely tolerating his presence as it was,

and he must use the time that remained to him to try to find Willow.

He passed through the city of Elderew, head bent against the weather, another of dusk's faceless shadows, then plunged into the forest beyond. The lights of cottages and homes disappeared behind him, and the darkness closed about in a wet, rain-sodden curtain. Trailers of mist floated past like kite tails broken free from their winged flyers, touching and rubbing, forming into gradually thickening sheets. Ben ignored it all and pushed on. He had gone to the old pines often enough to know the way blindfolded.

He arrived at the clearing moments later—several steps behind Edgewood Dirk. He glanced about expectantly, but there was nothing to be found. The clearing sat empty, ringed by the old pines, ancient sentinels of the forest, as damp and cold as the rest of the land. He cast about briefly for tracks or other signs of Willow's passing, but there was nothing to indicate whether the sylph had been there or not.

Edgewood Dirk paced the clearing once, sniffing at the earth, then retreated to the shelter of a pine's spreading boughs and sat down daintily. "She was here two nights ago, High Lord," he announced. "She was seated close to where you stand while her mother danced, then let the change take her. She left at dawn."

Ben stared at the cat. "How do you know all this?"

"A good nose," Dirk advised disdainfully. "You should cultivate one. It can tell you all sorts of things you would miss otherwise. My nose tells me what your eyes cannot tell you."

Ben moved over and hunched down in front of the cat, ignoring the water that dripped off the pine's branches and ran down his face in steady streams. "Does your nose tell you where she has gone now?" he asked quietly.

"No," the cat answered.

"No?"

"You are repeating me without need," Dirk sniffed.

"But if your nose told you all the rest, why can't it tell you that?" Ben demanded. "Is your nose always this selective?"

"Sarcasm does not become you, High Lord," Dirk admonished, head cocking slightly. "Besides, I deserve better than that. I am, after all, your sole companion and supporter in this venture."

"Which needs some explaining, I might point out," Ben snapped. "You persist in taunting me with what you know, then tell me only what you wish. I realize that you have a perfectly good excuse for this behavior, being a cat, but I hope I can impress on you how aggravating it is to me!" His temper was getting the better of him, and his voice was rising. "I simply asked how you could determine that Willow was here, that her mother danced, that she transformed, and yet not be able to tell me where . . ."

"I don't know."

". . . she might have gone after leaving . . . What? You don't know? You don't know what?"

"I don't know why I don't know."

Ben stared once more.

"I should be able to read her passing from the clearing, but I can't," Dirk finished calmly. "It is almost as if it was deliberately hidden."

Ben took a moment to consider this new piece of information, then shook his head. "But why would she hide where she was going?"

Dirk did not answer. Instead. he hissed softly in warning and rose to his feet once more. Ben stood up with him and turned. The River Master's dark figure reappeared from out of the mist, striding the length of the clearing to where Ben waited. He was alone.

"Has Willow been here?" he asked abruptly.

Ben hesitated, then nodded. "Been and gone. The cat says her mother danced for her two nights ago."

There was anger reflected in the eyes of the water sprite, but he smoothed it away quickly. "She would appear to her daughter, of course," he murmured. "They share that bond. The dance would reveal truth in the fairy way, would show what was sought . . ." He trailed off, as if thinking of something else, then straightened. "Have you determined where she has gone, High Lord?"

Again Ben hesitated, this time as much in surprise as out of caution. The River Master had called him High Lord. Had he now decided to accept Ben's claim? Ben met his steady gaze. "Her trail has been concealed from us," he said. "Hidden deliberately, the cat thinks."

The River Master glanced briefly at Dirk, frowning. "Perhaps." His chiseled face swung back on Ben. "But my daughter lacks the guile and her mother the means. The concealment, if there be one, comes from another source. There are some who would help her and not tell me. There are some." The anger in his eyes flared anew, then was gone. "Still, it hardly matters. I have the means to find her anyway. And anything else I wish."

Abruptly he turned, muttering. "Time slips away. The rain and the dark will hamper my efforts as it is. I must act quickly if I am to be effective." There was an urgency in his voice—and a determination. "I will not have these games played behind my back. I will know the meaning of the dream of the black unicorn and the golden bridle and I will know it whether Willow and her mother wish me to or not!"

He disappeared back into the forest in a rush, not bothering to see if Ben was following. He needn't have worried. Ben was right on his heels.

Edgewood Dirk stayed beneath the pine boughs and watched them go. After a moment, he began to clean himself.

The River Master had undergone such a complete transformation that Ben could scarcely believe it. One moment he was disinterested in the matter of his daughter and the black unicorn, the next he could not find out about them quickly enough. He strode back through the forest to the edge of the city, calling his guard to him as he went. Retainers appeared from everywhere, hanging at his side momentarily for their instructions, then disappearing back into the night. Like shadows, they came and disappeared again, a smattering of sprites, kelpies, naiads, and others—voiceless, momentary appendages to the dark figure of their lord. The River Master spoke rapidly and precisely, then turned away from each, his pace never slowing. He skirted almost furtively the boundaries of Elderew proper and turned back into the forest. Ben trailed after, all but forgotten.

The moments slipped by as they passed deeper into the forest trees, east and north of the city now. Nightfall had closed down so tightly that nothing beyond a dozen feet was visible. The rain washed over both of them in sheets, a steady downpour that showed little sign of abating. Thunder rolled out of the skies in long peals, and lightning split the clouds from somewhere distant. The worst of the storm had not reached them yet. It was still coming.

The River Master seemed oblivious. His concentration was absolute. Ben began to wonder what was going on and to grow uneasy.

Then they emerged from the trees onto a broad hillside clearing that stretched downward to a vast lake into which a pair of rivers fed at opposite ends. The rivers, swollen with rain water, cascaded down through rocky gorges that fell away from heights anchored by massive clusters of the giant redwoodlike trees. The lake roiled with the pumping action, and the flare of new lightning danced and glimmered with a mix of torchlight from stanchions that ran the length and breadth of the hills in widening arcs and lit the whole of the slope. Ben slowed and stared out into the black. The lake country people seemed to be everywhere—or were there simply a few amid the vast number of torches? Wind whipped the rain into his eyes, and he could not tell.

The River Master turned, saw he was still there, and beckoned him forward to a shelf of rock that jutted out from the hillside and overlooked the rivers, the lake, and the weaving lines of torchlight. The fury of the storm broke over them as they stood on the unsheltered platform, pressed close against each other, their words almost lost in the howl of the wind.

"Watch now, High Lord!" the River Master shouted, his strange, chiseled face inches from Ben's. "I cannot command Willow's mother to dance for me as she danced for her daughter, but I can command her kindred! I will know what secrets are kept from me!"

Ben nodded mutely. There was a frenzy in the other's eyes that he had never seen before—a frenzy that hinted of passion.

The River Master signaled, and a sticklike being approached from out of the night, a creature so thin that it appeared to have been fashioned of deadwood. Rough woolen clothing hung about its body, whipped by the wind, and green cornsilk hair ran from the crown of its head to the nape of its neck and along its spine and the backs of its arms and legs. Its features were formed of what looked to be a series of slits cut into the wood of its face. It carried a set of music pipes in one hand.

"Play!" the River Master commanded, one hand sweeping the valley slope. "Call them!"

The stick creature hunched down against the sodden earth, settled itself with its legs crossed before it, and brought the pipes to its lips. The music began softly, a sweet, lilting cadence that rocked in the troughs of momentary stillness left by lulls in the wind's deep howl. It meshed and blended with the sounds of the storm, weaving its way through the fabric like thread hand-sewn. It had the texture of silk, smooth and quiet, and it wrapped itself about the listeners like a blanket. Downward along the slope it carried, and there was the sense of something changing in the air.

"Hear it!" the River Master said in Ben's ear, exultant.

The player of the pipes lifted the pitch gradually, and the song rose higher into the fury of the storm. Slowly it transcended the dark and the wet and the chill, and the whole of their surroundings began to alter. The howl of the storm diminished as if blanketed away, the chill gave way to warmth, and the night brightened as if dawn had come already. Ben felt himself lifted as on a cushion of air. He blinked, disbelieving. Everything about him was changing—shape, substance, time, everything. There was a magic in the music that was greater than any he had ever encountered, a power that could alter even nature's great force.

Torchlight brightened as if the fires had been given new life, and the slope was lit with their glow. But there was a new glow as well, a glow that hung on the night air like incandescence. It radiated out across the slope and downward to the waters of the lake. The waters had gone still, the churning smoothed away as a mother's hand would smooth a sleeping child's ruffled hair. The glow danced at the water's edge, a living thing.

"There, High Lord—look!" the River Master urged.

Ben stared. Bits and pieces of the glow had begun to take shape. Dancing, whirling, lifting against the torchlight, they had begun to assume the forms of fairy creatures. Slight, airy things, they gathered strength from the glow and from the music of the pipes and took life. Ben knew them instantly. They were wood nymphs, the same as Willow's mother—childlike creatures as insubstantial as smoke. Limbs flashed and glistened nut-brown, hair tumbled waist-length, tiny faces lifted skyward. Dozens of them appeared as if from nowhere and danced and flitted at the shores of the mirrored lake in a kaleidoscope of movement.

The music heightened. The glow radiated the warmth of a summer's day, and colors began to appear in its brightness—rainbow shades that mixed and spread like an artist's brush strokes on canvass. Shape and form began to alter, and Ben felt himself transported to another time and place. He was young again, and the world was all new. The lifting sensation he had experienced earlier intensified, and he was floating free of the earth, free of gravity's pull. The River Master and the player of the pipes floated with him, birdlike in the sweep of sound and color. Still the wood nymphs danced below him, whirling with a new exhilaration into the glow, into the air. They spun outward from the shore's edge, skipping weightless across the waters of the still lake, their tiny forms barely touching the mirrored surface. Slowly they came together at the lake's center, forming intricate patterns as they linked briefly and broke away again, linked and broke away.

Above them, an image began to take shape in the air.

"Now it comes!" the River Master breathed from somewhere so distant that Ben could barely hear him.

The image came clear, and it was Willow. She stood alone
at the edge of a lake—this lake—and held in her hand the bridle
of spun gold that was the vision of her dream. She was clothed
in white silk, and her beauty was a radiance that outshone even
that created by the music of the player and the dance of the
wood nymphs. Flushed with life, her face lifted against the
colors that spun about her, and her long green tresses fanned
out in the whisper of the wind. She held the bridle out from
her as if it were a gift and she waited.

Beware! a voice warned suddenly, a voice so tiny as to be
almost lost in the whirl of the vision.

Ben wrenched his eyes momentarily from Willow. From
what seemed an impossible distance below, Edgewood Dirk
stared up at him.

"What's wrong?" Ben managed to ask.

But the question was irretrievably lost in what happened
next. The music had reached a fever pitch, so intense that it
locked away everything. The world was gone. There was only
the lake, the whirl of the wood nymphs, and the vision of Willow. Colors flooded Ben's vision with impossibly bright hues,
and there were tears in his eyes. He had never known such
happiness. He felt as if he were breaking apart inside and had
been transformed.

Then something new appeared at the edge of the lake,
beyond the nymphs and the vision of Willow—something at
once both impossibly lovely and terrifying. Ben heard the muf-
fled cry of the River Master. It was a cry of fulfillment. The
whirl of sound and color shimmered and bent like fabric
stretched, and the intrusion from without stepped gingerly into
its weave.

It was the black unicorn.

Ben felt his breath catch in his throat. There was a burning
in his eyes and a sudden, impossible sense of need. He had never
seen anything as beautiful as the unicorn. Even Willow in the
vision of the wood nymphs was but a pale shadow next to the

fairy creature. Its delicate body seemed to sway with the music and the dance as it emerged from the dark into the sweep of color, and its horn glowed white with the magic of its being.

Then Dirk's warning came again, no more than a memory this time. *Beware!*

"What is happening?" Ben whispered.

The River Master turned back to him now, head swinging about in slow motion. The hard face was alive with feelings that danced across its chiseled surface in waves of light and color. He spoke, yet the words seemed to come not from his mouth, but from his mind. "I will have him, High Lord! I will have his magic for my own, and it will become a part of my land and my people! He must belong to me! He must!"

And Ben saw suddenly, through the blanket of pleasant feelings and through the music and the dance, the truth of what the River Master was about. The River Master had not summoned the piper and the wood nymphs for the purpose of discovering anything of Willow or her mother. His ambition was much greater than that. He had summoned piper and nymphs to bring him the black unicorn. He had used music and dance to create the illusion of his daughter and her bridle of spun gold to draw the unicorn to the lakeside where it might be taken. The River Master had believed Ben's story all right—but he had decided that the black unicorn would better serve his own purposes than the purposes of a dethroned and powerless King. He had taken Willow's dream and made it his own. This whole business was an elaborate charade—the piper and the wood nymphs the instruments used to create it.

And, oh, God, it had worked! The black unicorn had come!

He watched the unicorn now in fascination, unable to turn away, knowing he must do something to prevent what was about to happen, but frozen by the beauty and intensity of the vision. The unicorn shone like a bit of flawless night against the sweep of colors that had drawn it in. It nodded its slender head to the call of the music and cried once to the vision of the girl with her golden bridle. It was a fairy-tale rendering brought to life, and the loveliness of it was compelling. Goat's feet pranced and lion's tail swished, and the unicorn stepped further into the trap.

I have to stop it! Ben felt himself trying to scream.

And then the fabric through which the black unicorn had passed so easily seemed to shred at its center point high above the vision and the wood nymphs, and a nightmare born of other minds and needs thrust its way into view. It was a loathsome thing, a creature of scales and spikes, of teeth and claws, winged and coated in a black ooze that steamed at the warmth of the air. A cross between a serpent and a wolf, it forced its way in from the night and the storm and plummeted toward the lake, shrieking.

Ben went cold. He had seen this being before. It was a demon out of the netherworld of Abaddon—a twin to the monster once ridden in battle by the Iron Mark.

It came for them in a fury, then veered sharply as it caught sight of the black unicorn. The unicorn saw the demon as well and screamed a terrifying, high-pitched cry. The ridged horn glowed white-hot with magic, and the unicorn leaped sideways as the demon swept by it, talons raking the empty air. Then the unicorn was gone, fled back into the night, having disappeared as suddenly as it had come.

The River Master cried out in anguish and fury. The demon swung back around, and fire lanced from its open maw. The flames engulfed the piper and turned the sticklike figure to ash. Sound and color dissipated into mist, and the night returned. Darkness flooded inward as the vision of Willow and the golden bridle collapsed. Ben stood once more on the shelf of rock beside the River Master, and the fury of the storm washed over them anew.

But the wood nymphs whirled on, still caught up in the frenzy of their dance. It was as if they could not stop. All about the lake's shores they spun, tiny bits of glowing light in the black and the wet. Torches fizzled and went dark, blown out by the rain and the wind, and only the light of the wood nymphs was left against the night. It drew the demon like a hunter to its prey. The monster swung back and down, sweeping the lake end to end, fire bursting from its throat and turning the helpless dancers to ash. The screams as they died were tiny shrieks that lacked real substance, and they disappeared as if candles snuffed. The River Master howled in despair, but could not save them. One by one they died, burned away by the demon as it passed back and forth across the night like death's shadow.

Ben was beside himself. He could not bear the destruction. But he could not turn away. He acted finally because the horror was too much to stand further. He acted without thinking, yanking the tarnished medallion from beneath his tunic as he would have in the old days, thrusting it out against the night, shouting in fury at the winged demon.

He had forgotten momentarily what medallion it was he wore.

The demon turned and glided toward him. Ben was suddenly conscious of Dirk at his feet, sitting motionless next to him. He was conscious now, too, of the fact that by drawing attention to himself he had just signed his own death warrant.

Then lightning flashed, and the demon saw clearly the medallion, Ben Holiday, and Edgewood Dirk. The beast hissed with the fury of steam released through a fissure in the earth, and swung abruptly away. It flew back into the night and was gone.

Ben was shaking. He didn't know what had happened. He only knew that for some unexplainable reason he was still alive. Below, the last of the wood nymphs had ceased finally to dance and disappeared back into forest, the loss of light from their passing leaving dark the whole of the lake and hills. Wind and rain lashed the emptiness that remained.

Ben stilled his hands. Slowly he placed the medallion back within his tunic. It burned against his skin.

The River Master had sunk to one knee. His eyes were fixed on Ben. "That thing knew you!" he cried in anger.

"No, it couldn't have . . ." Ben began.

"The medallion!" the other cut him short. "It knew the medallion! There is a tie between you that you cannot explain away!" He rose to his feet, his breath a sharp hiss. "You have made me lose everything! You have cost me the unicorn! You have caused the destruction of my piper and my wood nymphs. You and that cat! I warned you about that cat! Trouble follows a prism cat everywhere! Look what you have done! Look what you have caused!"

Ben recoiled. "I haven't . . ."

But the River Master cut him short once more. "I want you gone! I am no longer sure who you are and I no longer care! I want you gone from my country now—and the cat as well! If I find you here come morning, I will put you into the swamp in a place from which you will never escape! Now go!"

The fury in his voice defied argument. The River Master had been cheated of something he had wanted very badly and he had made up his mind that Ben was at fault. It made no difference that his wants had been selfish ones or that he had been deprived of something to which he had not been entitled in the first place. It was of no importance that he had misused Ben. All he could see was the loss.

Ben felt an odd emptiness within him. He had expected better of the River Master.

He turned without a word and walked away into the night.

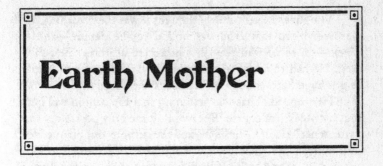

Earth Mother

The rain and the chill turned Ben Holiday into a sodden, disheveled mess as he trudged back through the forest trees from the empty hillside and the angry River Master, and his appearance became an accurate reflection of his mood. The mix of emotions he had experienced from the music of the pipes, the dance of the wood nymphs, the vision of Willow and what followed was still tearing at him with all the savagery and persistence of a wolf pack. He could still feel twinges of the ecstacy and freedom of self that the music and dance had brought, but the predominant feelings were of dismay and horror.

The images played out in the dark solitude of his mind: the River Master, anxious to seize the black unicorn so that its magic might be his alone; that winged demon, burning the frail wood nymphs to ash as they whirled helplessly at the water's edge; Ben himself, instinctively holding forth the blackened image of Meeks as if it were a talisman that would somehow be recognized . . .

And perhaps it was.

Damn, what had happened there? What was it that had happened? The winged creature had come for him to destroy him, then turned aside as if it had flown into a wall! Had it been the medallion, Ben, Edgewood Dirk, or perhaps something else entirely?

The River Master clearly thought it was the medallion. He was convinced that Ben was bound to the demon—and to Meeks—in some foul way that protected all three. Ben shivered. He had to admit to the possibility. The image of Meeks might have been enough to turn back the demon . . .

He stopped. That was assuming that the demon had been sent by Meeks, of course. But wasn't it the only possibility that made sense? Hadn't Meeks invited the demons out of Abaddon in the first place when the old King died? Ben started walking again. Yes, it had to be Meeks. He must have sent the demon because he knew the River Master was close to capturing the black unicorn, and he wanted the unicorn for himself—for whatever reason. But that meant he must have had some way of knowing that the River Master was about to capture the unicorn, and that in turn meant that Ben's medallion might have provided such a way. Meeks had warned that the medallion would let him know what Ben was about. The medallion might have done exactly that. Ben might indeed have been responsible for the destruction of the wood nymphs.

The screams of the dying fairy creatures still echoed in the dark corners of his mind, a savage reminder. Until they died, he had not even thought of them as real—just bits and pieces of light with human images cast upon the glow; slender, lyrical figurines that would shatter like glass if dropped . . .

The whole mixed and teased in his mind until at last he shoved all the pieces aside violently. His questions bred more questions, and there seemed to be answers for none of them. The rain beat down in a wet staccato, drumming, puddling in mud and grasses, and running across the pathway he followed in small rivers. He could feel the cold and the dark pressing in about him and he wished faintly for a moment's warmth and a spark of light. He walked; yet he was not really aware of where it was he was going. Away, he decided. Away from the River Master and the lake country, away from the one good chance he had of finding Willow before Meeks.

His boots slapped at the mud and damp. But where was he to go?

He cast about suddenly for Edgewood Dirk. Where was that confounded cat? It was always there when he didn't need it; where was it now that he did? Dirk always seemed to know which way to go. The cat seemed to know everything.

Dirk had even known what the River Master was trying to do with the music of the piper and the dance of the wood nymphs, Ben thought as he reflected on the events that had just taken place.

Beware, the cat had warned.

Convenient, that.

His thoughts twisted, and he found himself thinking again of the medallion. Had it really brought the demon? Had it really been responsible for the destruction of the wood nymphs and the piper? He couldn't live with that. Perhaps he ought simply to get rid of the thing. After all, what if it actually did work to the benefit of the wizard if Ben kept it on? Maybe that was exactly what Meeks wanted. The warning against trying to remove it might be a ruse. If he took it off, maybe he would be free of the wizard.

He stopped once more and reached down into his tunic. He placed his fingers about the chain from which the medallion hung and slowly lifted it free. Staring at it in the dark, seeing its muted, tarnished image glimmer in the brief flashes of lightning that streaked the forest skies, he had an incredibly strong urge to fling the unsettling piece of metal from him. If he did so, he might set himself free, redeem himself in part at least for the destruction of the wood nymphs. He might begin anew . . .

"Ah, my dear High Lord, there you are—wandering about in the dark like some blind 'possum. I thought I had lost you completely."

Edgewood Dirk stepped delicately from the trees, his immaculate coat glistening with rain water, his whiskers drooping slightly with the damp. He walked over to a fallen log and sat down on the dampened bark with studied care.

"Where have *you* been?" Ben snapped irritably. He hesitated, then let the medallion drop back into his tunic.

"Looking for you, of course," Dirk replied calmly. "It seems that you need a great deal of looking after."

"Is that so?" Ben was steamed. He was weary, frightened, disgusted, and a dozen other unpleasant things, but most of all he was sick and tired of being treated like a lost puppy by this damn cat. "Well, if ever there was someone suited to the task of looking after people, it's you, isn't it? Edgewood Dirk, caretaker of lost souls. Who else possesses such marvelous insight into human character? Who else discerns the truth of things with such remarkable consistency? Tell me again, Dirk—how is it that you know so much? Come on, tell me! How did you know what the River Master was doing back there before I did? How did you know he was summoning the unicorn? Why did you let me just stand there and be part of it? Those wood nymphs probably died because of me! Why did you let that happen?"

The cat stared at him pointedly for a moment, then began to wash. Ben waited. Dirk seemed oblivious to his presence.

"Well?" Ben said finally.

The cat looked up. "You do have a lot of questions, don't you, High Lord?" The pink tongue licked out. "Why is it that you keep looking to me for the answers?"

"Because you seem to have them, damn it!"

"What seems to be and what actually is are quite different, High Lord—a lesson you have yet to learn. I have instinct and I have common sense; sometimes I can discern things more easily than humans. I am not, however, a vast reservoir of answers to questions. There is a difference." He sneezed. "Besides, you mistake the nature of our relationship yet again. I am a cat and I don't have to tell you anything. I am your companion in this adventure, not your mentor. I am here at my own sufferance and I can leave when I choose. I need answer to no one— least of all you. If you desire answers to your questions, I suggest you find them yourself. The answers are all there if you would make the necessary effort to look for them."

"You could have warned me!"

"You could have warned yourself. You simply didn't bother. Be grateful that I chose to intervene at all."

"But the wood nymphs . . ."

"Why is it," the cat cut him short, "that you continually insist on asking for things to which you are not entitled? I am not your *deus ex machina*!"

Ben choked back whatever he was about to say next and stared. *Deus ex machina!* "You speak Latin?" he asked in disbelief.

"And I read Greek," Dirk answered.

Ben nodded, wishing as he did that he might solve even a small part of the mystery of the cat. "Did you know ahead of time that the wood nymphs were going to be destroyed?" he asked finally.

The cat took its time answering. "I knew that the demon would not destroy you."

"Because ?"

"Because you are the High Lord."

"A High Lord no one recognizes, however."

"A High Lord who won't recognize himself."

Ben hesitated. He wanted to say, "I do, but my appearance has been changed and my medallion has been stolen, and so on and so forth." But he didn't because this was a road they had traveled down already. He simply said, "If the demon couldn't recognize me, then how did you know he wouldn't destroy me?"

Dirk almost seemed to shrug. "The medallion."

Ben nodded. "Then I think I should get rid of the medallion. I think the medallion caused what happened back there— the appearance of the demon, the destruction of the wood nymphs, all of it. I think I should chuck it as far away as I can, Dirk."

Dirk rose and stretched. "I think you should see what the mud puppy wants first," he said.

His gaze shifted and Ben's followed. Rain and gloom almost hid the small, dark shape that crouched a dozen feet away on a scattering of pine needles. It was an odd-looking creature, vaguely reminiscent of a beaver with long ears. It stared back at him with eyes that glowed bright yellow in the dark.

"What is it?" he asked Dirk.

"A wight that scavenges and cleans up after other creatures—a sort of four-legged housekeeper."

"What does it want?"

Dirk managed to look put upon. "Why ask me? Why not ask the mud puppy?"

Ben sighed. Why not, indeed? "Can I do something for you?" he asked the motionless shape.

The mud puppy dropped back down on all fours and started away, turned back momentarily, started away, and turned back again.

"Don't tell me," Ben advised Dirk. "It wants us to follow."

"Very well, I won't tell you," Dirk promised.

They followed the mud puppy through the forest, angling north once more away from the city of Elderew and the people of the lake country. The rain lessened to a slow drizzle, and the clouds began to break, allowing some light to seep through to the forestland. The chill continued to hang in the air, but Ben was so numb with cold already that he no longer noticed. He plodded after the mud puppy in silence, wondering vaguely how the creature got its name, wondering where they were going and why, what he should do about the medallion, and most of all what he should do about Dirk. The cat trailed after him, picking its way with cautious steps and graceful leaps, avoiding the mud and the puddles, and working very hard at keeping itself clean.

Just like your typical cat, Ben thought.

Except that Edgewood Dirk was anything but a typical cat, of course, and it didn't matter how long or how hard he protested otherwise. The real question was, what was Ben going to do about him? Traveling with Dirk was like traveling with that older person who always made you feel like a child and kept telling you not to be one. Dirk was obviously there for a reason, but Ben was beginning to wonder if it was a reason that would serve any useful purpose.

The hardwood trees of the high forest began to give way

to swamp as they approached the far north boundary of Elderew. The land began to slope away, and mist to appear in long,
winding trailers. The gloom thickened and the chill dampness
turned to a clinging warmth. Ben was not comforted.

The mud puppy continued on without slowing.

"Do these creatures do this sort of thing often?" Ben whispered at last to Dirk. "Ask you to follow them, I mean?"

"Never," Dirk responded and sneezed.

Ben scowled back at the cat. I hope you catch pneumonia,
he thought darkly.

They passed down into the murk, into stands of cypress
and willow and thickets of swamp growth that defied descrip-
tion or identification. Mud sucked at his boots and water oozed
into the impressions they left. The rain abated completely, and
there was a sullen stillness. Ben wondered what it felt like to
be dry. His clothing felt as if it were weighted with lead. The
mist was quite heavy now, and his vision was reduced to a
distance of no more than a few feet. Maybe we've been brought
here to die, he decided. Maybe this is it.

But it wasn't "it" or anything else of immediate concern;
it was simply a trek through the swamp that ended at a vast
mudhole. The mud puppy brought Ben and Dirk to the mudhole, waited until they were at its edge, and then disappeared
into the dark. The mudhole stretched away into the mist and
dark for better than fifty feet, a vast, placid sinkhole that belched
air bubbles from time to time and evidenced no interest in much
else. Ben stared out at the mudhole, glanced down at Dirk, and
wondered what was supposed to happen next.

He found out a moment later. The mudhole seemed to
heave upward at its centermost point, and a woman rose from
the depths to stand upon its surface.

"Good morning, High Lord," she greeted.

She was naked, it appeared, although it was hard to be
certain because she was plastered from head to foot with mud,
and it clung to her as if it were a covering. There was a glimmer
of light from her eyes as they fastened on him; but, except for
the eyes, there was only the shape of her beneath the mud. She

rested on the surface of the sinkhole as if weightless, relaxed and quite at home.

"Good morning," he replied uncertainly.

"I see that you have a prism cat traveling with you," she said, her voice oddly flat and resonant. "Quite a stroke of good fortune. A prism cat can be a very valuable companion."

Ben was not sure he agreed with that assessment, but held his tongue. Dirk said nothing.

"I am known as the Earth Mother, High Lord," the woman continued. "The name was given to me some centuries ago by the people of the lake country. Like them, I am a fairy creature bound to this world. Unlike them, the choice to come was mine, and it was made at the time of the beginning of the land when there was need for me. I am the soul and spirit of the earth. I am Landover's gardener, you might say. I keep watch over her soil and the things that grow upon it. The province of protection and care of the land is not mine alone, because those who live upon its surface must share responsibility for its care—but I am an integral part of the process. I give possibility from beneath and others see that possibility to fruition." She paused. "Do you understand, High Lord?"

Ben nodded. "I think I do."

"Well, some understanding is necessary. The earth and I are inseparable; it is part of my composition, and I am one with it. Because we are joined, most of what happens within Landover is known to me. I know of you especially, because your magic is also a part of me. There is a bond between Landover's High Lord and the land that is inseparable. You understand that as well, don't you?"

Ben nodded again. "I have learned as much. Is that how you know me now, even with my appearance altered?"

"I know you as the prism cat knows you, High Lord; I never rely on appearances." There was the vaguest hint of laughter, not unkind. "I watched you arrive in Landover and I have followed you since. You possess courage and determination; you lack only knowledge. But knowledge will come in time. This is a land not easily understood."

"It is a bit confusing just now," Ben agreed. Already he liked the Earth Mother a whole lot better than he liked Edge-wood Dirk.

"Confusing, yes. But less so than you believe." She shifted slightly within the swirl of mist, her opaque form featureless and immutable. Her eyes glistened wetly. "I had the mud puppy bring you to me so that I could give you some information about Willow."

"You've seen her?" Ben demanded.

"I have. Her mother brought her to me. Her mother and I are close in the manner of true fairy creatures and the earth. We share the magic. Her mother is ill-used by the River Master, who thinks only to possess her and not to accept her for what she is. The River Master seeks to dominate in the manner of humans, High Lord—a great failing that I hope he will come to recognize in time. Possession of the land and her gifts is not meant to be. The land is a trust to be shared by all of finite lives and never to be taken for private use. But that has never been the way of things—not in Landover, not in all the worlds beyond. The higher orders seek to dominate the lower; all seek to dominate the land. An Earth Mother's heart is often broken in that way."

She paused. "The River Master tries, and he is better than some. Still, he, too, seeks domination in other, less obvious ways. He would use his magic to turn the land pure without understanding that his vision is not necessarily true. Healing is needed, High Lord, but not all healing is advisable. Sometimes the process of dying and regeneration is intrinsic to develop-ment. A recycling of life is a part of being. No one can predict the whole of the cycle, and a tampering with any period can be harmful. The River Master fails to see this—just as he fails to see why Willow's mother cannot belong to him. He only sees what needs are immediately before him."

"Such as his need for the black unicorn?" Ben interjected impulsively.

The Earth Mother studied him closely. "Yes, High Lord—the black unicorn. *There* is a need that none can resist—not even

you, perhaps." She was silent a moment. "I digress. I brought
you here to tell you of Willow. I have felt you with her, and
the feeling is good. There is a special bond between you that
promises something I have long waited for. I wish to do what
I may to preserve that bond."

One dark arm lifted. "Listen, then, High Lord. Willow's
mother brought her to me two days ago at dawn. Willow would
not go to her father for help, and her mother could not give
her what she needed. She hoped that I could. Willow has
dreamed twice now of the black unicorn—once when she was
with you, once after. The dreams are a mix of truth and lies,
and she cannot separate the one from the other. I could not help
her with that; dreams are not a province of the earth. Dreams
live in the air and in the mind. She asked then if I knew whether
the black unicorn was a thing of good or evil. I told her that
it would be both until the truth of it was clearly understood.
She asked if I could show her that truth. I told her that truth
was not mine to give. She asked me then if I knew of a bridle
of spun gold. I told her that I did. She has gone to find it."

"Where?" Ben asked at once.

The Earth Mother was silent again for a moment, as if
debating something with herself. "High Lord, you must promise me something," she said finally. "I know you are troubled.
I know you are afraid. Perhaps you will even become desperate.
The road you travel now is a difficult one. But you must promise me that whatever befalls you and however overwhelming
your feelings because of it, your first concern will always be
for Willow. You must promise that you will do whatever it
lies within your power to do to keep her safe."

Ben hesitated a moment before replying, puzzled. "I don't
understand. Why do you ask this?"

The Earth Mother's arms folded into her body. "Because
I must, High Lord. Because of who I am. That has to be answer
enough for you."

Ben frowned. "What if I cannot keep this promise? What
if I choose *not* to keep it?"

"Once the promise is given, it must be kept. You will

keep it because you have no choice." The Earth Mother's eyes blinked once. "You give it to me, remember, and a promise given to me by you cannot be broken. The magic binds us in that way."

Ben weighed the matter carefully for several long moments, undecided. It wasn't so much the idea of committing himself to Willow that bothered him; it was the fact of the promise itself. It was a foreclosure of all other options without knowing yet what those options might be, a blind vow that lacked future sight.

But then again, that was how life often worked. You didn't always get the choices offered to you up front. "I promise," he said, and the lawyer part of him winced.

"Willow has gone north," the Earth Mother said. "Probably to the Deep Fell."

Ben stiffened. "The Deep Fell? Probably?"

"The bridle was a fairy magic woven long, long ago by the land's wizards. It has passed through many hands over the years and been all but forgotten. In the recent past, it has been the possession of the witch Nightshade. The witch stole it and hid it with her other treasures. She hordes the things she finds beautiful and brings them out to view when she wishes. But Nightshade has had the bridle stolen from her several times by the dragon Strabo, who also covets such treasures. The theft of the bridle has become something of a contest between the two. It was last in the possession of the witch."

A lot of unpleasant memories surged to the fore at the mention of Nightshade and the Deep Fell. There were a good many places that Ben did not care to visit again soon in the Kingdom of Landover, but the home of the witch was right at the top of the list.

But, then, Nightshade was gone, wasn't she, into the fairy world . . . ?

"Willow left when I told her of the golden bridle, High Lord," the Earth Mother interrupted his thoughts. "That was two days ago. You must hurry if you are to catch her."

Ben nodded absently, already aware of a lightening of the

sky beyond the swamp's unchanging murk. Dawn was almost upon them.

"I wish you well, High Lord," the Earth Mother called. She had begun to sink back into the swamp, her shape changing rapidly as she descended. "Find Willow and help her. Remember your promise."

Ben started to call back to her, a dozen unanswered questions on his lips, but she was gone almost at once. She simply sank back into the mudhole and disappeared. Ben was left staring at the empty, placid surface.

"Well, at least I know which way Willow's gone," he said to himself. "Now all I have to do is find my way out of this swamp."

As if by magic, the mud puppy reappeared, slipping from beneath a gathering of fronds. It regarded him solemnly, started away, turned back again, and waited.

Ben sighed. Too bad all of his wishes weren't granted so readily. He glanced down at Dirk. Dirk stared back at him.

"Want to walk north for a while?" he asked the cat.

The cat, predictably, said nothing.

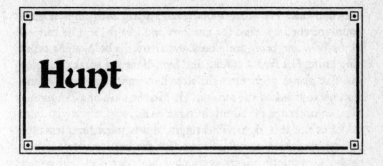

Hunt

*T*hey were four days gone from Elderew, east and slightly south of Rhyndweir in the heart of the Greensward, when they came upon the hunter.

"Black it was, like the coal brought down out of the north mines, like some shadow that hasn't ever seen the daylight. Sweet mother! It came right past me, so close that it seemed I might reach out and touch it. It was all grace and beauty, leaping as if the earth couldn't hold it to her, speeding past us all like a bit of wind that you can feel and sometimes see, but never touch. Oh, I didn't want to touch it, mind. I didn't want to touch something that . . . pure. It was like watching fire—clean, but it burns you if you come too close. I didn't want to come too close."

The hunter's voice was quick and husky with emotions that lay all too close to the surface of the man. He sat with Ben and Dirk in the early evening hours about a small campfire built in the shelter of an oak grove and a ridgeline. Sunset scattered red and purple across the western horizon, and blue-gray dusk hovered east. The close of the day was still and warm, the rain clouds of four nights past a memory. Birds sang their evening songs in the trees, and the smell of flowers was in the air.

Ben watched the hunter closely. The hunter was a big, rawboned man with sun-browned, weathered skin and cal-

loused hands. He wore woodsman's garb with high leather
boots softened by hand for comfort and stealth, and he carried
a crossbow and bolts, long bow and arrows, a bolo, and a skin-
ning knife. His face was long and high-boned, a mask of angles
and flat planes with the skin stretched tightly across and the
features strained by the tension. He had the look of a dangerous
man; in other times, he might have been.

But not this night. This night he was something less.

"I'm getting ahead of myself," the man muttered suddenly, an admonishment as much as a declaration. He wiped
at his forehead with one big hand and hunkered down closer
to the flames of the campfire as if to draw their warmth. "I
almost wasn't there at all, you know. I was almost gone to the
Melchor hunting bighorn. Had my gear all packed and ready
when Dain found me. He caught up with me at the crossroads
out, running like his woman had found out the worst, calling
after me like some fool. I slowed and waited, and that made
me the real fool. 'There's a hunt being organized,' he said. 'The
King himself has called it. His people are out everywhere, drawing the best and the quickest to net something you won't believe. A black unicorn! Yea, it's so,' he says. 'A black unicorn
that's to be hunted down if it takes all month, and we have to
chase the beast from valley's end to valley's end. You got to
come,' he says. 'They're giving each man twenty pieces a day
and food and, if you're the one who snares him, another five
thousand!'"

The hunter laughed sullenly. "Five thousand pieces.
Seemed like the best chance I'd ever get at the time—more
money than I'd see in ten years work any other way. I looked
at Dain and wondered if he'd lost his mind, then saw the way
his eyes were lit and knew if was all real, that there was a hunt,
that there was a bounty of five thousand, that some fool—King
or otherwise—believed there was a black unicorn out there to
be caught."

Ben glanced momentarily at Dirk. The cat sat a few feet
from him, eyes fixed intently on the speaker, paws curled up
underneath so that they didn't show. He hadn't moved or spo-

ken since the hunter had come across their tiny camp and asked
if he might share their meal. Dirk was to all outward appearances a normal cat. Ben couldn't help wondering what he might
be thinking.

"So we went, Dain and me—us and another two thousand
of the same mind. We went to Rhyndweir where the hunt was
to begin. The whole plain between the split in the rivers was
packed tight with hunters camped and waiting. There was beaters and drivers, there was the Lord Kallendbor and all the other
high-and-mighty landsmen with all their knights in armor and
foot soldiers. There was horses and mules, wagons loaded down
with provisions, carriers and retainers, a whole sea of moving
parts and sounds that would have frightened any other prey
from ten miles distant! Mother's blood, it was a mess! But I
stayed on anyway, still thinking about the money, but thinking
about something else now, too—thinking about that black unicorn. There wasn't any such creature, I knew—but what if
there was? What if it was out there? I might not catch it, but,
Lord, just to see it!

"That same evening we were all called before the castle
gates. The King wasn't there; his wizard was—the one they call
Questor Thews. He was a sight! Patchwork robe and sashes
made him look like a scarecrow! And there was this dog with
him that dressed like you and me and walked on his hind legs.
Some said he could talk, but I never heard it. They stood up
there with the Lord Kallendbor and whispered to him things
no one else could hear. The wizard had a face like chalk—looked
scared to death. Not Kallendbor, though—not him. He never
looks afraid of anything, that one! Sure as death itself and ready
to pronounce judgment. He called out to us in that big,
booming voice you could hear for a mile on those plains. He
called out and told us that this unicorn was a real live beast and
it could be tracked and caught like any other beast. There were
enough of us and we would have it or know the reason why!
He gave us our places and the line of sweep and sent us off to
sleep. The hunt was to begin at dawn."

The hunter paused, remembering. His eyes looked past

Ben in the growing darkness to some point distant in time and place from where they sat now. "It was exciting, you know. All those men gathered together like that—a hunt greater than any I had ever heard tell. There were to be Trolls north along the Melchor and a number of the fairy tribes south above the lake country. They didn't seem to think the unicorn would be south of there—don't know why. But the plan was to start on the eastern border and drive west, closing the ends north and south like a huge net. Beaters and horsemen would work from the east; hunters and snares would set up west in moving pockets. It was a good plan."

He smiled faintly. "It started right on schedule. The line east began to move west, clearing out everything in its path. Hunters like myself set up in the hill country where we could see everything that moved in the grasslands and beyond. Some rode chaser all along the front and ends, flushing whatever was hidden there. It was something, all those men, all that equipment. Looked like the whole valley was gathered in that one huge hunt. Looked like the whole world. The line came west all that day from the wastelands to Rhyndweir and beyond— beaters and chasers, horsemen and foot soldiers, wagonloads of provisions going back and forth from castles and towns. Don't know how they got it organized so fast and still made it work— but they did. Never saw a thing, though. Camped that night in a line that stretched from the Melchor down to Sterling Silver. Campfires burned north to south like a big, winding snake. You could see it from the hills where Dain and I were set up with the other hunters. We stayed out of the main camps. We're more at home up there anyway—can see as well at night as in day and had to keep watch so that nothing sneaked past in the dark.

"The second day went the same. We got to the western foothills at the edge of the grasslands, but saw nothing. Camped again and waited. Watched all that night."

Ben was thinking of the time he had wasted since leaving Elderew just to get this far north. Four days. The weather had slowed his travel in the lake country, and he had been forced to skirt east of Sterling Silver to avoid an encounter with the guard—his guard—because they might recognize him as the stranger that the King had ordered out of the country. He had been forced to travel afoot the entire way, because he had no money for horses and was not yet reduced to stealing. He must have missed the hunt by less than twenty-four hours. He was beginning to wonder what that had cost him.

The hunter cleared his throat and continued. "There was some unpleasantness by now among the men," he advised solemnly. "Some felt this was a waste of time. Twenty pieces a day or not, no one wants to be part of something foolish. The Lords were having their say, too, griping that we weren't doing our share, that we weren't watching as close as we should, that something might have sneaked through. We knew that wasn't the case, but that wasn't something they wanted to hear. So we said we'd try harder, keep looking. But we wondered among ourselves if there was anything out there to look for.

"The third day we closed the line west to the mountains, and that's when we found it." The hunter's eyes had suddenly come alive, bright in the firelight with excitement. "It was late afternoon, the sun screened away by the mountains and the mist, and the patches of forest we searched in that hill country were thick with shadows. It was the time of day when everything seems a little unclear, when you see movement where there is none. We were working a heavy pine grove surrounded by hardwood and thick with scrub and brush. There were six of us, I think, and you could hear dozens more all about, and the lines of beaters shouting and calling from just east where the line was closing. It was hot in the hills—odd for the time of day. But we were all worn down to the bone and weary of chasing ghosts. There was a feeling that this hunt had come down to nothing. Sweat and insects made the work unpleasant now; aches and pains slowed us. We had shoved away thoughts of the unicorn beyond completing the hunt and getting home again. The whole business was a joke."

He paused. "Then suddenly there was movement in the pine—just a shadow of something, nothing more than that. I remember thinking that my eyes were playing tricks on me yet another time. I was going to say something to Dain; he was working just off to my left. But I held my tongue—too tired, maybe, to want to say anything. I just sort of stopped what I was doing there in the brush and the heat and I watched the place of the movement to see if there was going to be any more."

He took a deep breath, and his jaw tightened down. "There was this darkening of the little sunlight that remained then— as if clouds had screened it away for a moment. I remember how it felt. The air was all hot and still; the wind had died down into nothing. I was looking, and the brush came apart and there it was—the unicorn, all black and fluid like water. It seemed so tiny. It stood there staring at me—I don't know how long. I could see the goat's feet, the lion's tail, the mane that ran down its neck and back, the fetlocks, that ridged horn. It was just as the old stories described it—but more beautiful than they could ever make it. Sweet mother, it was glorious! The others saw it, too, a few of them anyway. Dain caught a glimpse; another two said they saw it close up. But not as close as me, Lord! No, I was right next to it, it seemed! I was right there!

"Then it bolted. No, not bolted—it didn't flee like that. It bounded up and seemed to fly right past me; all that motion and grace, like the shadow of some bird in flight cast down on the earth by the sun passing. It came by me in the blink of an eye—*whisk!*—and it was gone. I stood there looking after it, wondering if I'd really seen it, knowing I had, thinking how marvelous it was to view, thinking it truly was real . . ."

He choked on the words as they tumbled out one after the other, released from his throat in a rush of strange emotion. His hands were raised before him, knotting with the intensity of the telling of his story. Ben quit breathing momentarily, awed by what he was seeing, not wanting to break the spell.

The hunter's eyes lowered then, and the hands followed. "I heard later that it flew right into the teeth of the chase. I heard it went past the whole mess of them like wind through a forest of rooted trees. Dozens saw it. There was a chance to hold it, maybe—but I kind of wonder. It came right over the nets. There was a chase, but . . . but you know what?" The eyes lifted again. "The unicorn came right up against the Lords of the Greensward and the King's men—right up against them, sweet mother! And the wizard—the very one that organized all this—conjured up some nonsense and it rained flowers and butterflies all over everything. The chase broke up in the confusion, and the unicorn was gone before you could spit!" He smiled suddenly. "Flowers and butterflies—can you imagine that?"

Ben smiled with him. He could.

The hunter drew up his knees then and hugged them. The smile disappeared. "That was it, then. That was all she wrote. The hunt was done. Everyone sort of broke up and went away after that. There was some talk of continuing, of taking the whole line back east again, but it never came to anything. No one wanted any part of that. It was like the heart had gone out of the chase. It was like everyone was glad the unicorn got away. Or maybe it was just that no one thought it could ever be caught anyway."

The hard eyes lifted. "Strange times we live in. The King sacked the wizard and the dog, I hear. Threw them out the minute he heard what had happened. Just dismissed them out of hand for what the wizard had done—or what he thought he'd done. I don't think the wizard could have done much one way or the other anyway. Not with that creature, not with it. No one could have. It was too much a ghost for anything mortal, too much a dream . . ."

There were sudden tears in the hunter's eyes. "I think I touched it, you know, when it went past me. I think I touched it. Sweet mother, I can still feel the silk of its skin brushing me, like fire, like . . . a woman's touch, maybe. I had a woman touch me once that way, long ago. The unicorn felt like that. Now I can't forget it. I try to think of other things, try to be reasonable about the fact of it having happened at all, but the sense of it stays with me." He tightened his face against what he was feeling. "I been looking for it on my own since I left, thinking maybe one man could have better luck than a whole hunting party. I don't want to catch it exactly; I don't think I could. I just want to see it again. I just want to maybe touch it one more time—just once, just for a moment . . ."

He trailed off again. The campfire sparked suddenly in the stillness, a sharp crackling. No one moved. Darkness had settled down across the valley, and the last daylight had dropped from view. Stars and moons had appeared, their light faint and distant, their colors muted. Ben glanced down at Edgewood Dirk. The cat had his eyes closed.

"I just want to touch it once more," the hunter repeated softly. "Just for a moment."

He stared vacantly at Ben. The ghost of who and what he had been was swallowed in the silence that followed.

That same night Willow dreamed again of the black unicorn. She slept huddled close to the faithful Parsnip in a gathering of pine at the edge of the Deep Fell, concealed within a covering of boughs and shadows. Her journey north from Elderew was five days gone. She was now only hours ahead of Ben Holiday. The hunt for the black unicorn had delayed her for almost a day as it swept the hill country west of the Greensward and turned her east. She had no idea what the hunt was about. She had no idea that Ben was searching for her.

The dream came at midnight, stealing into her sleep like a mother to her slumbering child's room, a presence that was warm and comforting. There was no fear this time, only sadness. Willow moved through forest trees and grassland spaces, and the black unicorn watched, as if a ghost come from some nether region to trail the living. It appeared and faded like sunshine from behind a cloud, now in the shade of a massive old maple, now in the lea of a copse of fir. It was never all visible, but only in part. It was black and featureless save for its eyes—and its eyes were a mirror of all the sadness that ever was and would ever be.

The eyes made Willow cry, and her tears stained her cheeks as she slept. The eyes were troubled, filled with pain she could only imagine, haunted beyond anything she had believed possible. The black unicorn of this dream was no demon spawn; it was a delicate, wondrous creature that somehow had been terribly misused . . .

She came awake with a start, the image of the unicorn clearly etched in her mind, its eyes fixed and staring. Parsnip slept next to her, undisturbed. Dawn was still hours away, and she shivered with the night's chill. Her slim body trembled at the whisper of the dream's words in her memory, and she felt the magic of their presence in her fairy way.

This dream was real, she realized suddenly. This dream was the truth.

She straightened back against the pine's roughened trunk, swallowed the dryness in her throat, and forced herself to consider what the dream had shown her. Something required it— the eyes of the unicorn, perhaps. They sought something from her. It was no longer enough to think simply of retrieving the golden bridle and carrying it to Ben. That was the command of her first dream, the dream that had brought her on this quest—but the truth of that dream was now in doubt. The unicorn of that dream was entirely different than the unicorn of this. One was demon, the other victim. One was pursuer, the other . . . hunted? She thought perhaps so. There was a need for help in the unicorn's eyes. It was almost as if it was begging her for that help.

And she knew she must give it.

She shuddered violently. What was she thinking? If she even came close to the unicorn, she could be lost. She should forget this madness! She should go to Ben . . .

She let the unfinished thought trail off, huddled down against the night and the stillness, and wrestled with her indecision. She wished her mother were there to comfort her or that she could seek again the counsel of the Earth Mother.

She wished most of all for Ben.

But none of them was there. Except for Parsnip, she was alone.

The moments slipped by. Suddenly she rose, a soundless shadow, left Parsnip asleep in the gathering of pines, and disappeared silently into the Deep Fell. She went not on reason, but on instinct, without doubt or fear, but with certainty that all would be well and she would be kept safe.

By dawn, she had returned. She did not have the golden bridle in her possession, but she knew now where it was. Her fairy senses had told her what even the Earth Mother could not. The bridle had been stolen yet again.

She woke Parsnip, gathered together her few things, cast a brief glance back at the dark bowl of the hollows, and started walking east.

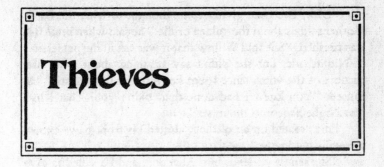

Thieves

*W*hen Ben Holiday and Edgewood Dirk awoke the following morning, the hunter was gone. Neither had heard him leave. He had departed without a word, disappearing so completely that it was almost as if he had never been. Even his face was just a vague memory for Ben. It was only his story of the hunt for the black unicorn that lingered on, still vivid, still haunting.

Breakfast was a solemn affair. "I hope he finds what he's looking for," Ben muttered at one point.

"He can't," Dirk replied softly. "It doesn't exist."

Ben was beginning to wonder about that. The black unicorn seemed as elusive as smoke and about as substantive. The unicorn was seen, but never for more than a few moments and never as more than a fleeting shadow. It was a legend that had assumed a scant few of the trappings of reality, but which remained for all intents and purposes little more than a vision. It was altogether possible that a vision was all the unicorn was— some strayed bit of magic that took form but never body. In Landover, you never knew.

He thought about asking Dirk, but then decided against it. Dirk wouldn't give him a straight answer if he knew one, and he was tired of playing word games with the cat.

He decided to change the subject.

"Dirk, I've been giving some thought to what the Earth Mother told us about the golden bridle," he said when breakfast was finished. "She told Willow that it was last in the possession of Nightshade, but she didn't say anything about what had become of the witch since I sent her into the fairy mists." He paused. "You knew I had done that, didn't you? That I had sent Nightshade into the mists?"

Dirk, seated on an old log, shifted his front paws experimentally. "I knew."

"She sent my friends into Abaddon, and I decided to give her a taste of her own medicine," he went on by way of explanation. "I was given Io Dust by the fairies, a powder that, if breathed, made you subject to the commands of the one who fed you the Dust. I used it later on the dragon Strabo, too, as a matter of fact. At any rate, I used it on Nightshade first and caused her to change herself into a crow and fly off into the mists." Again he paused. "But I never knew what happened to her after that."

"This rather boring recapitulation is leading somewhere, I trust?" Dirk sniffed.

Ben flushed. "I was wondering whether or not Nightshade had found her way out of the mists and back into the Deep Fell. It might help if we knew that before we waltzed blindly on in."

Dirk took a long moment to clean his face, causing Ben's flush to heighten further with impatience. At last the cat looked up again. "I have not been down into the Deep Fell myself in quite some time, High Lord. But I understand that Nightshade might well be back."

Ben took a moment to let the news sink in. The last thing he needed just now was an encounter with Nightshade. He no longer had the medallion to protect him—if indeed it could protect him anyway from a creature as evil as the witch. If she recognized him, he was dead. Even if she didn't, she was hardly likely to welcome him with open arms. And she was hardly likely to welcome Willow either—especially once she learned what the sylph was after. She wasn't about to hand over the golden bridle, however convincing the arguments Willow might offer. She would probably turn Willow into a toad—and turn *him* into a toad. He thought wistfully of the Io Dust and wished he had just a single handful. That would even the odds considerably.

His eyes fixed intently on Dirk. "What do you think about a quick trip back into the fairy world?" he asked abruptly. "I did it once; I could do it again. The fairies would recognize me, magic or no magic. Maybe they could help me change back again. At the very least, they could give me another pod of the Io Dust to use on Nightshade. After all, I promised the Earth Mother I would do my best to look after Willow, and I can't look after her if I can't look after myself."

Dirk studied him a moment, blinked and yawned. "Your problem is not one anyone else can help you with—least of all the fairies."

"Why not?" Ben snapped, irritated with the cat's insufferable smugness.

"Because, in the first place, the magic that has changed you is your own—as you have been told at least half-a-dozen times now. And in the second place, the fairies won't necessarily help you just because you ask. The fairies involve themselves in people's lives when and where they choose and not otherwise." The prim muzzle wrinkled distastefully. "You knew that before you asked the question, High Lord."

Ben fumed silently. The cat was right, of course—he had known. The fairies hadn't interceded in Landover's problems when he had first come into the valley and the tarnish and the Iron Mark had threatened, and they were unlikely to do so now. He was King, and the problems facing him were his.

So how was he going to solve them?

"C'mon," he ordered suddenly, springing to his feet. "I have an idea that might work." He pulled on his boots, straightened his clothing, and waited for Dirk to ask what the idea was. The cat didn't. Finally, he said, "Don't you want to know the details?"

The cat stretched and jumped down from its perch to stand next to him. "No."

Ben ground his teeth and silently swore that, all right then, it would be a cold day somewhere damn hot before *he* would say another word about it!

They walked north through the early morning, skirting the grasslands of the Greensward, veering slightly east toward the foothills that lay below the Melchor. Ben led, but as usual Dirk seemed to know where they were going anyway and often traveled a parallel course, picking his way through the high grasses, seemingly oblivious to what Ben was about. Dirk continued to be a mystery without a solution, but Ben forced himself to concentrate on the task at hand rather than dwell on Dirk, because dwelling on Dirk just made him nuts. It was easier to accept the cat the way one accepted changes in the weather.

The grasslands were still marked from the passing of the hunt. Booted feet had flattened portions of the tall grass and broken down the scrub. Debris from the provision wagons littered the plains, and the ashes of huge campfires scarred the multicolored meadows. The Greensward had the look of a giant picnic ground at the close of July fourth. Ben wrinkled his nose in distaste. Meeks was already using the land selfishly again.

There were other signs of misuse as well. Signs of the wilt that had marked the valley in his early days in Landover had returned to the plants and trees—signs that could only have been brought about by a lessening of the power of the King's magic. When there was no King in Landover, the land lost strength; he had learned that on his first visit. Meeks was not the true King, despite any outward appearance, and Landover was beginning to show the effects. The signs were tiny yet, but they would grow worse. Eventually, the tarnish would return to Sterling Silver and the whole valley would begin to sicken. Ben pressed ahead at a quicker pace, as if somehow speed might help.

A caravan of traders traveling north into the Melchor to obtain metal implements and weapons from the Trolls crossed their path around midday, and they shared lunch. The gossip was all connected with the hunt for the black unicorn and the strange events of the past few days. The King had gone into seclusion, refusing to see anyone, even the Lords of the Greensward. Public works projects had been put on hold, judicial and grievance councils had been dismissed, envoys had been sent home from Sterling Silver, and everything in general had come to a dead halt. No one knew what was happening. There were rumors of demons flying the night skies, monstrous things that carried off livestock and stray children in the manner that the dragons once had. There were even rumors that the King himself was responsible, that he had made some devil's bargain to give the demons of Abaddon their way in Landover if they in turn would bring him the unicorn.

Everything seemed to revolve around the unicorn. The King had let it be known in no uncertain terms that he meant to have the creature, and the one who brought it to him would be hugely rewarded.

"If you can catch smoke, you're a rich man," one trader joked, and the others all laughed.

Ben didn't laugh. He took his leave hastily and continued north at an even quicker pace. Things were getting out of hand, and a good part of that was clearly his fault.

By midafternoon, he was in the country of the G'home Gnomes.

The G'home Gnomes were a burrow people he had encountered during his early days as Landover's King. They were small, furry, grimy creatures that looked something like overgrown moles. They were scavengers and thieves and they couldn't be trusted any farther than your pet dog could be with the evening roast. As a matter of fact, they couldn't be trusted *with* your pet dog, because they considered dogs, cats, and other small domesticated animals quite a delicacy. Abernathy considered the G'home Gnomes cannibals. Questor Thews considered them trouble. Everyone considered them a nuisance. The appellation "G'home Gnome" came from the almost universally expressed demand of those who had the misfortune to come in contact with them: "Go home, gnome!" Two of these gnomes, Fillip and Sot, had made a pilgrimage to Sterling Silver to seek Ben's aid in freeing some of their people from Crag Trolls after the Trolls had carted the unfortunates away for stealing and eating a number of their pet tree sloths. Ben had almost lost his life in that venture, but the G'home Gnomes had proven to be among the most loyal of his subjects—if not the most reformed.

And Fillip and Sot had once confided to him that they knew the Deep Fell as they knew the backs of their hands.

"That's exactly the kind of help we need," Ben told Dirk, despite his vow not to tell the cat anything. "Nightshade will never be persuaded to give up the bridle willingly. Willow has to know that, too—but that won't stop her from trying. She'll probably be direct rather than circumspect; she's too honest for her own good. Whatever the case, if she's gone into the Deep Fell, she's likely in trouble. She'll need help. Fillip and Sot can let us know. They can sneak down without being seen. If Willow or Nightshade is there, they can tell us. If the bridle is there, perhaps they can steal it for us. Don't you see? They can go where we can't."

"Speak for yourself," Dirk replied.

"Do you have a better plan?" Ben snapped back immediately.

Dirk was oblivious to his anger. "I have no plan," he answered. "This is your problem, not mine."

"Thank you very much. I gather you wouldn't consider undertaking this reconnaissance and theft yourself then?"

"Hardly. I am your companion, not your lackey."

"You are a pain, Dirk."

"I am a cat, High Lord."

Ben terminated the discussion with a scowl and stalked off toward the burrow community. The G'home Gnomes lived in towns in the same manner as prairie dogs, and sentinels warned of his approach long before he could see anything. By the time he reached the town, there wasn't a G'home Gnome anywhere—just a lot of empty-looking holes. Ben walked to the center of the town, seated himself on a stump and waited. He had been here a number of times since becoming King, and he knew how the game was played.

A few minutes later, Dirk joined him. The cat curled up beside him without a word and closed its eyes against the late afternoon sun.

Shortly after that, a furry face poked up from one of the burrows. Eyes squinted weakly against the daylight, and a wrinkled nose sniffed the air tentatively.

"Good day, sir," the gnome addressed Ben and tipped his battered leather cap with its single red feather.

"Good day," Ben replied.

"Out for a walk, are you, sir?"

"Out for a healthy dose of fresh air and sunshine. Good for what ails you."

"Yes, oh yes indeed, good for what ails you. Must be careful of colds that settle in the throat and chest during the passing of fall."

"Certainly must. Colds can be tricky." They were dancing on eggshells, and Ben let the music play itself out. The G'home Gnomes were like this with strangers—scared to death. One always tested you. If you posed no threat, the rest came out. If any menace was sensed, you never saw more than the one. "I hope your family is well?" Ben went on, trying to sound casual. "And your community?"

"Oh, quite well, thank you, sir. All quite well."

"That's good to hear."

"Yes, good to hear." The gnome glanced about furtively, looking to see if Ben was alone, looking to see if he was hiding anything. "You must have walked quite a distance north from the Greensward, sir. Are you a craftsman?"

"Not exactly."

"A trader, then?"

Ben hesitated a moment and then nodded. "On occasion, I am."

"Oh?" The gnome's squint seemed to deepen. "But you do not appear to have any wares with you this trip, sir."

"Ah! Well, sometimes appearances are deceiving. Some trading wares can be quite small, you know." He patted his tunic. "Pocket-sized."

The gnome's front teeth flashed nervously out of its grimy face. "Yes, of course—that is so. Could it be that you are interested in trading here, sir?"

"Could be." Ben set the hook and waited.

The gnome did not disappoint him. "With someone in particular?"

Ben shrugged. "I have done some business in the past with two members of your community—Fillip and Sot. Do you know them?"

The gnome blinked. "Yes, Fillip and Sot live here."

Ben smiled his most disarming smile. "Are they about?"

The gnome smiled back. "Perhaps. Yes, perhaps. Would you wait a moment, please? Just a moment?"

He ducked back into his burrow and was gone. Ben waited. The minutes slipped past and no one appeared. Ben kept his place on the stump and tried to look as if he were enjoying himself. He could feel eyes watching him from everywhere. Doubts began to creep into his mind. What if Fillip and Sot took a look at him and decided he was no one they had ever seen? After all, he wasn't the Ben Holiday they knew any longer. He was a stranger—and not a particularly well-dressed one either. He glanced down at his clothing, reminded of his sorry state. He made a rather shabby-looking trader, he thought ruefully. Fillip and Sot might decide he wasn't worth their bother. They might decide to stay right where they were. And if he couldn't get close enough to talk to them, he wasn't about to have any success obtaining their help.

The afternoon shadows lengthened. Ben's patience simmered like hot water over an open fire. He glanced irritably at Edgewood Dirk. No help was there. Eyes closed, paws tucked under, breathing slowed to nothing, the cat might have been sleeping or it might have been stuffed.

The burrow holes continued to yawn back at him in empty disinterest. The sun continued to slip into the western hills. No one appeared.

Ben had just about decided to throw in the towel when a furry, dirt-lined face poked up suddenly from a burrow opening not a dozen yards away, closely followed by a second directly beside it. Two snouts sniffed the late afternoon air warily. Two pairs of weakened eyes peered cautiously about.

Ben heaved a sigh of relief. They were Fillip and Sot.

The squinting eyes fixed on him.

"Good day, sir," said Fillip.

"Good day, sir," said Sot.

"Good day, indeed." Ben beamed, sitting up straight again on the stump.

"You wish to trade, sir?" asked Fillip.

"You wish to trade with us?" asked Sot.

"Yes. Yes, I most certainly do." Ben paused. "Would you gentlemen mind coming over here? That way I can be certain you understand what it is that I have to trade."

The G'home Gnomes glanced at each other, then emerged into the fading sunlight. Stout, hairy bodies were clothed in what looked like Salvation Army rejects. Bearded, ferretlike faces with tiny, squinted eyes and wrinkled noses tested the air like weather vanes directed by the wind. Dirt and grime covered them from head to foot.

Fillip and Sot without a doubt.

Ben waited until they had stopped just a few feet in front of him, beckoned them closer still, then said, "I want you to listen to me very closely, do you understand? Just listen. I'm Ben Holiday. I'm High Lord of Landover. A magic has been used to change my appearance, but that's only temporary. I'll change myself back sooner or later. When I do, I'll remember who helped me and who didn't. And I need your help right now."

He glanced from one furry face to the other. The gnomes were staring at him voicelessly, eyes squinting, noses testing. They looked for a moment at each other, then back again at Ben.

"You are not the High Lord," said Fillip.

"No, you are not," agreed Sot.

"Yes, I am," Ben insisted.

"The High Lord would not be here alone," said Fillip.

"The High Lord would come with his friends, the wizard, the talking dog, the kobolds, and the girl Willow—the pretty sylph," said Sot.

"The High Lord would come with his guards and retainers," said Fillip.

"The High Lord would come with his standards of office," said Sot.

"You are not the High Lord," repeated Fillip.

"No, you are not," repeated Sot.

Ben took a deep breath. "I lost all those things to a bad wizard—the wizard who brought me into Landover in the first place, the wizard we saw in the crystal after we freed ourselves from the Crag Trolls—remember? You were the ones who came to Sterling Silver to ask my help in the first place. I went with you to help you free your people from the Trolls—the same gnomes who had eaten the furry tree sloths that were the Trolls' favorite pets. Now if I'm not the High Lord, how do I know all this?"

Fillip and Sot looked at each other again. They looked a bit uncertain this time.

"We don't know," admitted Fillip.

"No, we have no idea," agreed Sot.

"But you are not the High Lord," repeated Fillip.

"No, you are not," agreed Sot.

Ben took another deep breath. "I smashed the crystal against some rocks after we discovered its purpose. Questor Thews admitted his part in its use. You were there, Abernathy and Willow were there, the kobolds Bunion and Parsnip were there. Then we went down into the Deep Fell. You took Willow and me in. Remember? We used Io Dust to turn Nightshade back into a crow and fly her into the fairy mists. Then we went after the dragon Strabo. Remember? How could I know this if I'm not the High Lord?"

The gnomes were shifting their feet as if fire ants had crawled into their ruined boots.

"We don't know," Fillip said again.

"No, we don't," Sot agreed.

"Nevertheless, you are not the High Lord," repeated Fillip.

"No, you are not," repeated Sot.

Ben's patience slipped several notches despite his resolve. "How do you *know* that I'm not the High Lord?" he asked tightly.

Fillip and Sot fidgeted nervously. Their small hands wrung together, and their eyes shifted here and there and back again.

"You don't smell like him," said Fillip finally.

"No, you smell like us," said Sot.

Ben stared, then flushed, then lost whatever control he had managed to exercise up to this point. "Now you listen to me! I *am* the High Lord, I *am* Ben Holiday, I *am* exactly who I said I was, and you had better accept that *right now* or you are going to be in the biggest trouble of your entire lives, bigger even than when you stole and ate that pet dog at the celebration banquet after the defeat of the Iron Mark! I'll see you hung out to dry, damn it! Look at me!" He wrenched the medallion from his tunic, covering the face and the image of Meeks with his palm, and thrust it forward like a weapon. "Would you like to see what I can do to you with this?"

Fillip and Sot collapsed prone upon the earth, tiny bodies shaking from head to foot. They went down so fast it looked as if their feet had been yanked from beneath them.

"Great High Lord!" cried Fillip.

"Mighty High Lord!" wailed Sot.

"Our lives are yours!" sobbed Fillip.

"Yours!" sniffled Sot.

"Forgive us, High Lord!" pleaded Fillip.

"Forgive us!" echoed Sot.

Now that's much better, Ben thought, more than slightly astonished at the rapid turnabout. A little intimidation seemed to go a whole lot further than a reasonable explanation with the G'home Gnomes. He was a bit ashamed of himself for having had to resort to such tactics, but he was more desperate than anything.

"Get up," he told them. They climbed to their feet and

stood looking at him fearfully. "It's all right," he assured them
gently. "I understand why this is confusing, so let's just put it
all behind us. All right?" Two ferretlike faces nodded as one.
"Fine. Now we have a problem. Willow—the pretty sylph—
may be in a lot of trouble, and we have to help her the same
way she helped us when the Crag Trolls had us in their pens.
Remember?" He was using that word "remember" a lot, but
dealing with gnomes was like dealing with small children.
"She's gone down into the Deep Fell in search of something,
and we have to find her to be certain that she's all right."

"I do not like the Deep Fell, High Lord," complained Fillip
hesitantly.

"Nor I," agreed Sot.

"I know you don't," Ben acknowledged. "I don't like it
either. But you two have told me before that you can go down
there without beeing seen. I can't do that. All I want you to do
is to go down there long enough to look around and see if
Willow is there—and to look for something that I need that's
hidden down there. Fair enough? Just look around. No one has
to know you're even there."

"Nightshade came back to the Deep Fell, High Lord,"
announced Fillip softly, confirming Ben's worst fears.

"We have seen her, High Lord," agreed Sot.

"She hates everything now," said Fillip.

"But you most," added Sot.

There was a period of silence. Ben tried to imagine for a
moment the extent of Nightshade's hatred for him and could
not. It was probably just as well.

He bent close to the gnomes. "You've been back to the
Deep Fell, then?" Fillip and Sot nodded miserably. "And you
weren't seen, were you?" Again, the nods. "Then you can do
this favor for me, can't you? You can do it for me and for
Willow. It will be a favor that I won't forget, I can promise
you that."

There was another long moment of silence as Fillip and
Sot looked at him, then at each other. They bent their heads

close and whispered. Their nervousness had been transformed into agitation.

Finally they looked back at him again, eyes glinting.

"If we do this, High Lord, can we have the cat?" asked Fillip.

"Yes, can we have the cat?" echoed Sot.

Ben stared. He had forgotten Dirk momentarily. He glanced down at the cat, and then back at the gnomes. "Don't even think about it," he advised. "That cat is not what it seems."

Fillip and Sot nodded reluctantly, but their eyes remained locked on Dirk.

"I'm warning you," Ben said pointedly.

Again the gnomes nodded, but Ben had the distinct feeling that he was addressing a brick wall.

He shook his head helplessly. "Okay. We'll sleep here tonight and leave at daylight." He took an extra moment to draw their attention. "Try to remember what I just said about the cat. All right?"

A third time the gnomes nodded. But their eyes never left Dirk.

Ben ate another Spartan meal of Bonnie Blues, drank spring water, and watched the sun sink into the horizon and night settle over the valley. He thought of the old world and the old life and wondered for the first time in a long time whether he might have been better off staying where he was instead of coming here. Then he pushed his maudlin thoughts aside, wrapped himself in his travel cloak, and settled down against the base of the stump for an uncomfortable night's rest.

Dirk hadn't moved from the stump top. Dirk looked dead.

Sometime during the night there was a shriek so dreadful and so prolonged that it brought Ben right up off the ground. It sounded as if it were almost on top of him; but when he finally got his bearings and peered bleary-eyed about the campsite, all he found was Dirk crouched down atop the stump with his hackles up and a sort of steam rising from his back.

In the distance, something—or someone—whimpered.

"Those gnomes are persistent to the point of stupidity," Dirk commented softly before settling back down again, eyes glistening in the night like emerald fire.

The whimpering faded and Ben lay back down as well. So much for his well-intentioned advice to Fillip and Sot. Some lessons had to be learned the hard way.

That same night found an altogether different scene unfolding some miles south of Rhyndweir at an abandoned stock pen and line shack perched on a ridgeline that overlooked the eastern expanse of the Greensward. A sagging roof and shutterless windows marked the line shack as a derelict, and the stock pen was missing rails in half-a-dozen spots. Shadows draped the whole in a web of black lace. A white-bearded scarecrow and an Ozian shaggy dog, both decidedly unkempt, bracketed a brightly burning campfire built a dozen yards or so from the line shack and hurtled accusations at each other with a vehemence that seemed to refute utterly the fact that they had ever been best friends. A wiry, monkey-faced creature with elephant ears and big teeth watched the dispute in bemused silence.

"Do not attempt to ask my understanding of what you have done!" the shaggy dog was saying to the scarecrow. "I hold you directly responsible for our predicament and am not inclined to be in the least forgiving!"

"Your lack of compassion is matched only by your lack of character!" the scarecrow replied. "Another man—or dog—would be more charitable, I am sure!"

"Ha! Another man—or dog—would have bidden farewell to you long ago! Another man—or dog—would have found decent company in which to share his exile!"

"I see! Well, it is not too late for you to find other company—decent or not—if such is your inclination!"

"Rest assured, it is under consideration right now!"

The two glowered at each other through the red haze of the campfire, their thoughts as black as the ashes of the crumbling wood. The monkey-faced watcher remained a mute spec-

tator. Night hung about all three like a mourner's shroud, and
the ridgeline was spectral and still.

Abernathy shoved his glasses further back on his nose and
picked up the argument once more, his tone of voice a shade
softer. "What I find difficult to understand is why you let the
unicorn get away, wizard. You had the creature before you,
you knew the words that would snare it, and what did you do?
You called down a thunderburst of butterflies and flowers.
What kind of nonsense was that?"

Questor Thews tightened his jaw defiantly. "The kind of
nonsense that you, of all people, should understand."

"I am inclined to think that you simply panicked. I am
compelled to believe that you simply failed to master the magic
when you needed to. And what do you mean, 'the kind of
nonsense that *I* should understand'?"

"I mean, the kind of nonsense that gives all creatures the
chance to be what they should be, despite what others think
best for them!"

The scribe frowned. "One moment. Are you telling me
that you *intentionally* let the unicorn escape? That the butterflies
and the flowers were not accidental?"

The wizard pulled on his chin whiskers irritably. "Con-
gratulations on your astute, if belated, grasp of the obvious!
That is exactly what I am telling you!"

There was a long silence between them as they studied
each other. They had been traveling together since daybreak,
inwardly seething at the turn of events that had brought them
to this end, outwardly distanced from each other by their anger.
This was the first time that the subject of the unicorn's escape
had been discussed openly.

The moment of testing passed. Questor looked away first,
sighed, and pulled his patchwork robes closer about him to
ward off the deepening night chill. His face was worn and lined
from worry. His clothing was dusty and torn. Abernathy
looked no better. They had been stripped of everything. Their
dismissal had come immediately after the High Lord had learned
of their failure to capture the black unicorn. The High Lord had

given them no chance to explain their actions nor had he offered any explanation for his. They had been met on their return to Sterling Silver by a messenger, who had delivered a curt hand-written directive. They were relieved of their positions. They could go henceforth where they chose—but they were never to return to the court.

Bunion, apparently given his choice in the matter, went with them. He had offered no reason.

"It was not my intention when we began the hunt to allow the unicorn to escape," Questor continued softly. "It was my intention that it be captured and delivered to the High Lord just as he had ordered. I believed it a dangerous undertaking because the black unicorn has long been reported a thing of ill fortune. But, then again, the High Lord has shown an extraordinary capacity for turning ill fortune to his advantage." He paused. "I admit I was bothered by his insistence on the unicorn's im-mediate capture and by his refusal to explain that insistence to us. Yet I still intended that the unicorn be taken." He took a deep breath. "But when I saw the beast before me in that wood, standing there—when I saw what it was . . . I could not allow it to be taken. I don't know why, I just couldn't. No, that is not true—I do know why. It wasn't right. I could feel inside me that it wasn't right. Didn't you sense it, too, Abernathy? The unicorn was not meant to belong to the High Lord. It was not meant to belong to anyone." He glanced up again uncer-tainly. "So I used the magic to see that it wouldn't. I let it escape."

Abernathy snapped at something that flew past him, then shoved his dust-encrusted glasses back on his nose and sneezed. "Well, you should have said so sooner, wizard, instead of letting me think that your magic had simply bested you once again. This, at least, I can understand."

"Can you?" Questor shook his head doubtfully. "I wish I could. I have acted against the wishes of the High Lord when I am sworn to his service, and the only reason I can give is that serving him in this instance felt wrong. He was right to dismiss me from the court."

"And me also, I suppose?"

"No, he should not have dismissed you. You had no part in what happened."

"The fact of the matter is, he was wrong to dismiss either of us!"

Questor shrugged helplessly. "He is the High Lord. Who are we to question his judgment?"

"Humph!" Abernathy snorted derisively. "The hunt was an ill-advised exercise of judgment, if ever there was one. He knew the history of the black unicorn. We told him the beast would not be trapped in a hunt, and he completely ignored us. He has never done that before, wizard. I tell you, he is obsessed with this beast. He thinks of nothing else. He has spoken of Willow only once—and that a tirade over her failure to return to him with the golden bridle. He ignores his duties, he keeps to his rooms, and he confides in no one. Not a single mention has been made of the books of magic since you returned them to him. I had hoped that the High Lord might give at least some *brief* consideration into looking for a way to use them to return me to my former self. Once, the High Lord would have done so without even having to think about it . . ."

The scribe trailed off self-consciously, glowering at the flames of the little fire. "Well, no matter. The point is, he is not himself these days, Questor Thews. He is not himself."

The wizard's owlish face twisted thoughtfully. "No." He glanced momentarily at Bunion and was surprised to find the kobold nodding in agreement. "No, he most certainly is not."

"Hasn't been since . . ."

"Since we discovered that impostor in his bed chamber?"

"Since then, yes. Since that night."

They were silent again for a moment. Then their eyes met, and they were startled by what they found mirrored there. "Is it possible that . . ." Abernathy began uncertainly.

"That the impostor *was* the High Lord?" Questor finished. He frowned his deepest frown. "I would not have thought so before, but now . . ."

"There is no way we can be certain, of course," Abernathy interrupted quickly.

"No, no way," Questor agreed.

The fire crackled and spit, the smoke blew across them with a shift in the wind, and sparks danced into the ashes. From somewhere far away, a night bird sounded a long, mournful cry that brought shivers down Questor's spine. He exchanged quick glances with Abernathy and Bunion.

"I hate sleeping out-of-doors," Abernathy muttered. "I don't like fleas and ticks and crawly things trying to assume occupancy of my fur."

"I have a plan," Questor said suddenly.

Abernathy gave him a long, hard look, the kind he always gave when confronted with a pronouncement he would just as soon live without. "I am almost afraid to ask what it is, wizard," he responded finally.

"We will go to the dragon. We will go to Strabo."

Bunion's teeth gleamed in a frightening grin. "That is a plan?" demanded Abernathy, horrified.

Questor leaned forward eagerly. "But it makes perfect sense that we should go to Strabo. Who knows more about unicorns than dragons? Once they were the greatest of enemies—the oldest adversaries in the world of fairy. Now the black unicorn is the last of his kind, and Strabo the last of his. They share a common cause, a natural affinity! Surely we can learn something of the unicorn from the dragon—enough perhaps to unravel its mystery and to discover its purpose in coming to Landover!"

Abernathy stared in disbelief. "But the dragon doesn't like us, Questor Thews! Have you forgotten that? He will roast us for a midday snack!" He paused. "Besides, what good will it do to learn anything more about the unicorn? The beast has caused us trouble enough as it is."

"But if we understand its purpose, we might discover a reason for the High Lord's obsession," Questor replied quickly. "We might even find a way to reinstate ourselves at court. It is not inconceivable. And the dragon will not cause us harm. He will be happy to visit with us once he has learned our purpose in coming. Do not forget, Abernathy, that dragons and wizards share a common background as well. The nature and duration of our professional relationship has always dictated a certain degree of mutual respect."

Abernathy's lip curled. "What a lot of nonsense!"

Questor barely seemed to hear him. There was a faraway look in his eye. "There were games played between wizards and dragons in the old days that would challenge the faint of heart, I can tell you. Games of magic and games of skill." He cocked his head slightly. "A game or two might be necessary here if Strabo chooses to be obdurate. Theft of knowledge is a skill I have mastered well, and it would be fun to test myself once more . . . "

"You are mad!" Abernathy was appalled.

But Questor's enthusiasm was not to be dampened. He came to his feet, excitement in his eyes as he paced the circle of the fire. "Well, no matter. What is necessary must be done. I have made my decision. I shall go to the dragon." He paused. "Bunion will go with me, won't you, Bunion?" The kobold nodded, grinning ear to ear. The wizard's hands fluttered. "There, it is settled. I am going. Bunion is going. And you must come with us, Abernathy." He stopped, hands lowering, tall form stooping slightly as if from the weight of his sudden frown. "We must go, you know. After all, what else is there for us to do?"

He stared questioningly at the scribe. Abernathy stared back, sharing the look. There was a long silence while doubt and uncertainty waged a silent war with self-esteem in the old friends' eyes. There were shadows of times they had believed past come back to haunt their present, and they felt those shadows closing inexorably about. They could not permit that. Anything was better than waiting for such suffocating darkness.

The ridgeline was still again, a dark spine against a sky of stars and moons that seemed cold and distant. The line shack and the stock pen were the bones of an aging earth.

"Very well," Abernathy agreed, sighing his most grievous sigh. "We will all be fools together."

No one spoke up to dispute him.

Mask

Sunrise found Fillip and Sot present and accounted for as promised. They were standing a good twenty yards away when Ben came awake, a pair of motionless, squat shadows in the fading dark, their travel packs strapped to their backs, their caps with solitary red feathers set firmly in place. They appeared bushes at first glance; but after Ben rose to stretch muscles cramped from the chill and the hard earth, they came forward a few tentative steps and gave anxious greetings. They seemed more nervous than usual and kept peering past him as if they expected an onslaught of Crag Trolls at any moment.

It took Ben a moment to realize that they were not on guard against Trolls, but against Edgewood Dirk.

Dirk, for his part, ignored them. He was sitting on the tree stump washing when Ben thought to look for him, his silky coat smooth and glistening as if damp from morning dew. He did not glance up or respond to Ben's good morning. He went on about the business of cleaning himself until he was satisfied that the job was properly completed, then settled down to the contents of a bowl of spring water that Ben had provided. Ben hadn't thought about it before, but Dirk never seemed to eat much. What he survived on was something of a mystery, but it was a mystery that Ben chose to leave unsolved. He had enough puzzles to deal with without adding another.

They departed shortly after waking, Ben and Dirk leading—depending on how you defined the word "leading," for
once again Dirk seemed to know where Ben was going almost
before he did. The gnomes trailed. Fillip and Sot clearly wanted
no part of Edgewood Dirk. They stayed well back of the cat
and watched him the way you would a snake. Fillip was limping
noticeably and Sot appeared to have burned a good portion of
the fur off his wrists and the backs of his hands. Neither had
anything to say about their injuries, and Ben let them be.

They traveled through the morning at a steady pace, the
sun shining brightly from out of a cloudless sky, the smell of
wild flowers and fruit trees scenting the air. Signs of the wilt
prevailed. They remained small but noticeable, and Ben thought
again of Meeks in his guise, of the demons come back out of
Abaddon at his bidding, of the lessening of magic in the land,
and the stealing of its life. There was a renewed urgency tugging
him along, a sense that time was slipping from him too quickly.
He was no closer than he had ever been to discovering what
had been done to him. He still had no idea why the black unicorn
had come back into Landover or what its importance was to
Meeks. He knew only that there was a tie connecting all that
had happened and he had to unknot it if he were ever to
straighten this mess out.

Thinking of that led him to think once again about Edgewood Dirk. It continued to grate on him that the cat chose to
remain such an enigma when he could obviously explain himself. Ben was reasonably sure by now that Dirk had not simply
stumbled across him that first night in the lake country, but
had deliberately sought him out. He was also reasonably sure
that Dirk was staying with him for a reason and not simply out
of curiosity. But Dirk was not about to explain himself to Ben
until he felt like it; and given the cat's peculiar nature, that
explanation was likely to be offered along about the twelfth of
never. Still, it seemed abhorrent to Ben simply to accept the
beast's presence without making any further effort whatsoever
to learn something of what had brought it to him in the first
place.

As morning lengthened toward noon and the shadow of
the Deep Fell began to grow visible, he decided to take another
crack at the cat. He had been busy during the trek, mulling over
the possibility of a common link between the various unicorns
he had encountered since his dream. There were, after all, quite
a number of them. There was the black unicorn. There were
the sketched unicorns contained in the missing books of
magic—correction, one of the missing books of magic; the
other was burned-out shell. And there were the fairy unicorns
that had disappeared centuries ago on their journey through
Landover to the mortal worlds. It was the legend of the fairy
unicorns that concerned him just now. He already believed that
there must be a link between the black unicorn and the drawings
contained in the books of magic. Otherwise, why had Meeks
sent dreams of both? Why did he want them both so badly?
The real question was whether they also had some connection
with the missing fairy unicorns. He realized that it would be
something of a coincidence if there actually were a connection
among the three, but he was beginning to wonder if it wouldn't
be an even bigger coincidence if there weren't. Magic tied all
three in a single bond, and he would have bet his life that it
was some sort of control over the magic that Meeks was after.

So. Enough debate. Maybe solving one of the little puzzles
would aid in solving the big one. And maybe—just maybe—
Edgewood Dirk would be less reticent to help . . .

"Dirk, you've been a lot of places and seen a lot of things."
He opened the conversation as casually as he could manage, not
giving himself a chance to dwell further on it. "What do you
think about this legend of the missing fairy unicorns?"

The cat didn't even look at him. "I don't think about it at
all."

"No? Well what if you did think about it? You said you
knew something of the missing white unicorns when we first
met, didn't you?"

"I did."

"About the unicorns the fairy people sent into the other
worlds? The ones who somehow disappeared?"

"The very same." Dirk sounded bored.

"So what do you think happened to them? How did they disappear?"

"How?" The cat sniffed. "They were stolen, of course."

Ben was so astonished at getting a straight answer for a change that he failed to follow up on it for a moment. "But . . . stolen by whom?" he managed finally.

"By someone who wanted them, High Lord—who else? By someone who had the ability and means to capture them and hold them fast."

"And who would that have been?"

Dirk sounded irritated. "Now who do you think that would have been?"

Ben hesitated, considering. "A wizard?"

"Not *a* wizard—*wizards*! There were many in those days, not simply one or two as there are now. They had their own guild, their own association—loosely formed, but effective when it chose to be. The magic was stronger then in Landover, and the wizards hired out to anyone who needed their skills most and could best afford it. They were powerful men for a time—until they chose to challenge the King himself."

"What happened?"

"The King summoned the Paladin, and the Paladin destroyed them. After that, there was only one real wizard permitted—and he served the King."

Ben frowned. "But if the unicorns were stolen by the wizards, what happened to them after the wizards were . . . disposed of? Why weren't they set free?"

"No one knew where they were."

"But shouldn't someone have looked for them? Shouldn't they have been found?"

"Yes and yes."

"Then why weren't they?"

Dirk slowed, stopped, and blinked sleepily. "The question no one asked then is the one you fail to ask now, High Lord. Why were the unicorns stolen in the first place?"

Ben stopped as well, thought momentarily, and shrugged.

"They were beautiful creatures. The wizards wanted them for themselves, I suppose."

"Yes, yes, yes! Is that the best you can do?"

"Well, uh . . ." He paused again, feeling very much a fool. "Why can't you just explain it to me, damn it?" he demanded, exasperated.

Dirk eyed him steadily. "Because I don't choose to," he said softly. "Because you have to learn how to see things clearly again."

Ben stared at him momentarily, glanced back at the G'home Gnomes who were watching from a safe distance back, and folded his arms across his chest wearily. He had no idea what Dirk was talking about, but it didn't do any good to argue with the cat.

"All right," he said finally. "Let me try again. The wizards discovered that the fairies were sending unicorns through Landover into the mortal worlds. They stole the unicorns for themselves instead. They stole them because . . ." He stopped, remembering suddenly the missing books and the drawings. "They stole the unicorns because they wanted their magic! That's what the drawings in that book mean! They have something to do with the missing unicorns!"

Edgewood Dirk cocked his head. "Do you really think so, High Lord?"

He was so genuinely curious that Ben was left not knowing what to think. He had expected the cat to agree with him, but the cat looked as surprised as he!

"Yes, I really think so," he declared at last, wondering nevertheless. "I think the missing unicorns and the missing books are tied together and the black unicorn has something to do with both."

"That does stand to reason," Dirk agreed.

"But how were the unicorns stolen? And how could the wizards steal their magic? Weren't the unicorns as powerful as the wizards?"

"I am told so," Dirk agreed once more.

"Then what happened to them? Where are they hidden?"

"Perhaps they wear masks."

"Masks?" Ben was confused.

"Like your own. Perhaps they wear masks, and we cannot see them."

"Like my own?"

"Would you mind not repeating everything I say?"

"But what are you talking about, for Pete's sake?"

Dirk gave him a "Why bother asking me?" look and sniffed the late morning air as if the answers he sought might be found there. The black tail twitched. "I find I am quite thirsty, High Lord. Would you care to join me for a drink?"

Without waiting for a response, he stood and trotted off into the trees to one side. Ben stared after him a moment, then followed. They walked a short distance to a pool fed from a small rapids and bent to drink. Ben drank rapidly, more thirsty than he had expected. Dirk took his time, dainty to the point of annoyance—lapping gently, pausing frequently, carefully keeping the water from his paws. Ben was conscious of Fillip and Sot in the background watching, but paid them no mind. His attention was given over entirely to the cat and to what Dirk was going to say next—because he most certainly was going to say something or Ben was as mistaken as he had ever been in his life!

Ben was not mistaken. A moment later, Dirk sat back on his haunches and glanced over. "Look at yourself in the water, High Lord," he ordered. Ben did and saw a dilapidated version of himself, but himself nevertheless. "Now look at yourself out of the water," Dirk continued. Ben did and saw ragged clothes and cracked boots, dirt and grime, an unshaved, unkempt, unwashed body. He could see nothing of his face. "Now look at yourself in the water again—look closely."

Ben did, and this time he saw the image of himself shimmer and change into the image of someone he did not recognize, a stranger whose clothes were the same ones he wore.

He looked up sharply. "I don't look like me anymore—not even to myself!" There was a hint of fear in his voice that he could not disguise, even though he tried.

"And that, my dear High Lord, is because you are beginning to *lose* yourself," Edgewood Dirk said softly. "The mask
you wear is becoming you!" The black face dipped closer. "Find
yourself, Ben Holiday, before that happens. Take off your
mask, and perhaps then you can find a way to unmask the
unicorns as well."

Ben looked back hurriedly at the pool of water and to his
relief found his old face back again in the reflection of the waters.
But the definition of his features seemed weak. It was almost
as if he were fading away.

He looked up again for Dirk, but the cat was already trot-
ting away, scattering the fearful gnomes before him. "Best
hurry, High Lord," he called back. "The Deep Fell is no place
to be looking for oneself after nightfall."

Ben climbed slowly to his feet, not only more confused
than ever but also frightened now as well. "Why do I ask that
damn cat anything?" he muttered in frustration.

But he already knew the answer to that question, of course.
He shook his head at matters in general and hastened after.

By midafternoon, they had reached the Deep Fell.

It was unchanged and unchanging—a dark, impenetrable
smudge on an otherwise brightly sunlit expanse of forestland,
hunched down against the earth in the manner of a creature in
hiding, tensed to flee or strike. Shadows and mist played hide
and seek in its sprawling depths, crawling with slow, irregular
movements over trees and swamp and murk. Nothing else
could be seen. What life forms there were lay in wait, pawns
in a hard and vicious game of survival that rewarded only the
quick and the strong. Sounds were muted and colors shaded
gray. Only death was at home within the Deep Fell, and only
death was immutable. Ben and his companions could sense that
truth. Standing at the hollows rim, they stared downward into
its darkness and thought their separate thoughts.

"Well, we might as well get at it," Ben muttered finally.
He was remembering the last time he had come into the Deep
Fell and the terrifying illusions that Nightshade had created to

keep him out—the illusions of endless swamp, lizards, and worse. He was thinking of his encounter with the witch—an encounter that had almost cost him his life. He was not looking forward to a repeat performance.

"Well," he said again, the word trailing off into silence.

No one was paying any attention to him. Dirk sat next to him, eyes lidded and sleepy-looking as he basked in a small patch of sunlight and watched the movement of the mists in the Deep Fell. Fillip and Sot stood a good dozen yards left, well away from the cat and the hollows. They were whispering in small, anxious voices.

He shook his head. "Fillip. Sot."

The G'home Gnomes cringed away, pretending not to hear him.

"Get over here!" he snapped irritably, his patience with gnomes and cats in general exhausted.

The gnomes came sheepishly, tentatively, edging forward with uneasy looks at Dirk, who as usual paid them no heed. When they were as close as they were going to get without being dragged, Ben knelt down to face them, his eyes finding theirs.

"Are you certain that Nightshade is down there?" he asked quietly.

"Yes, High Lord."

"She is, High Lord."

Ben nodded. "Then I want you to be careful," he told them quietly. This was no time for impatience or anger, and he suppressed both. "I want you to be very careful, all right? I don't want you to do anything that will place you in any real danger. Just go down there and look around. I need to know if Willow is there—or even if she's been there earlier. That's first. Find out any way you can."

He paused, and the wide brown eyes of the gnomes shifted uneasily. He waited a moment, captured them again with his own. "There is a bridle made out of spun gold," he continued. "Nightshade has it hidden down there somewhere. I need that bridle. I want you to see if you can find it. If you can, I want you to steal it."

The brown eyes widened suddenly to the size of saucers. "No, it's all right, don't be afraid," Ben soothed quickly. "You don't have to steal it if the witch is anywhere about—only if she's not or if you can take it without her knowing. Just do what you can. I'll protect you."

That was probably the worst lie he had told in his entire life; he didn't really have any way to protect them. But he had to do something to reassure them or they would simply bolt at the first opportunity. They might do that anyway, but he was hoping the majesty of his office would hold them in thrall just long enough to get this job done.

"High Lord, the witch will hurt us!" Fillip declared.

"Hurt us badly!" Sot agreed.

"No, she won't," Ben insisted. "If you're careful, she won't even know you're down there. You've been down there before, haven't you?" Two heads nodded as one. "She didn't see you then, did she?" Two heads nodded again. "Then there's no reason she will see you this time either, is there? Just do as I told you and be careful."

Fillip and Sot looked at each other long and hard. There was enough doubt in their eyes to float a battleship. Finally, they looked back again at Ben.

"Just go down once," said Fillip.

"Just once," echoed Sot.

"All right, all right, just once," Ben agreed, casting an anxious glance at the fading afternoon sun. "But hurry, will you?"

The gnomes disappeared reluctantly into the hollows gloom. Ben watched them until they were out of sight, then sat back to wait.

As he waited, he found himself thinking about Edgewood Dirk's repeated references to masks. He wore a mask. The missing unicorns wore masks. That's what the cat had said, but what did the cat mean? He propped himself up against the base of a tree trunk some dozen yards from where Dirk basked in the sunlight and tried to reason it through. It was, after all, about time he reasoned *something* through. Lawyers were supposed to be able to do that; it was indigenous to their profession. King or no in Landover, he was still a lawyer with a lawyer's habits and a lawyer's way of thinking. So think, he exhorted himself! Think!

He thought. Nothing came. Masks were worn by actors and bandits. You wore them to disguise yourself. You put them on and then you took them off when you were done with the disguise. But what did that have to do with him? Or the unicorns? None of us are trying to disguise ourselves, he thought. Meeks is trying to disguise me. Who's trying to disguise the unicorns?

The wizards who took them, that's who.

The answer came instantly to him. He shifted upright. The wizards stole the unicorns and then hid them by disguising them. He nodded. It made sense. So how did they disguise them? With masks? What, turned them into cows or trees or something? No. He frowned. Start over again. The wizards took the unicorns—how did they do that—so they could steal their magic. The wizards wanted the magic for their own. But what would they do with it? What use would they find for it? Where was the magic now?

His eyes widened. There were no longer any other true wizards besides Meeks. The source of his power was in the missing but now found books of magic, the books that were supposedly a compilation of the magics acquired by wizards down through the years—the books with the drawing of the unicorns! Sure, the unicorns in the books—or the one book, at least—were drawings of the missing unicorns!

But why make drawings?

Or are they the unicorns themselves?

"Yes!" he whispered in surprise.

It was so impossible that he hadn't seen it before—but impossible only in his own world, not in Landover where magic was the norm! The missing unicorns, the unicorns no one had seen for centuries, their magic intact, were trapped in the wizards' books! And the reason that there was nothing else in the books but the drawings of the unicorns was that the magic of the books was entirely that of the unicorns—magic that the wizards had stolen!

And harnessed to their own use?

He didn't know. He started to say something to Dirk, then checked himself. There was no point in asking the cat if he was right; the cat would simply find a way to confuse him all over again. Figure it out for yourself, he admonished! The unicorns had been transformed by wizard magic into the drawings in the missing books—that would explain the disappearance of the unicorns for all these years, the reason that Meeks had sent the dream of the books to Questor, and the need Meeks had for the books. It would even explain Dirk's reference to masks.

Or was he just reaching now?

He paused. There were a few other matters still lacking explanation, he realized. What about the black unicorn? Was it simply a white unicorn that had escaped from the books—the first book, perhaps, the one with the burned-out core? Why was it black now if it had been white before? Ash or soot? Ridiculous! Why had it appeared and then disappeared again at other times over the years if it were a prisoner in the wizards' books? Why was Meeks so desperate to get it back now?

His hands twisted in knots. If one unicorn could break free, why couldn't the rest?

His confusion began to compound. Meeks had hinted that Ben had done something to wreck his plans, but hadn't said what. If that was so, it had to have something to do with the unicorns, black and white. But Ben hadn't the foggiest idea what that something was.

He sat puzzling matters through without success as afternoon stretched toward nightfall and the sun disappeared westward. Shadows lengthened almost imperceptibly across the forest. Slowly, the darkness and mist of the Deep Fell crept out of their daytime confinement to link hands with those shadows and close about Ben and Dirk. The day's warmth faded into evening chill.

Ben ceased his musings and concentrated on the slope of the hollows. Where were Fillip and Sot? Shouldn't they have been back by now? He climbed to his feet and stalked to the edge of the pit. There was nothing to be seen. He walked its rim for several hundred yards in both directions, through patches of scrub and brush, peering into the gloom. No luck. A growing uneasiness settled through him. He hadn't really believed the little gnomes were in any danger or he wouldn't have sent them down alone. Maybe he had been mistaken. Maybe that was the way he had wanted to see it and not the way it was.

He stalked back to his starting point and stood staring at the smudge of the Deep Fell helplessly. The dangers of the hollows had never bothered the gnomes before. Had something changed that? Damn it, he should have gone with them!

He glanced over at Dirk. Dirk appeared to be sleeping.

Ben waited some more because he didn't have much choice. The minutes dragged interminably. It was growing darker. It was becoming difficult to distinguish things clearly as the twilight deepened.

Then suddenly there was movement at the hollows rim. Ben straightened, came forward a step, and stopped. A mass of brush parted, and Fillip and Sot pushed their way into view.

"Thank heavens you're all . . ." Ben started and trailed off.

The G'home Gnomes were rigid with fear. Paralyzed. Their furry faces were twisted into masks of foreboding, their eyes bright and fixed. They looked neither right nor left nor even at Ben. They stared straight ahead and saw nothing. They stood with their backs to the mass of brush and held hands in the manner of small children.

Ben rushed forward, frightened now. Something was dreadfully wrong. "Fillip! Sot!" He knelt down before them, trying to break whatever spell it was that held them fast. "Look at me. What happened?"

"*I* happened, play-King!" an unpleasantly familiar voice whispered.

Ben looked up, past the frozen gnomes, at the tall, black shape that had materialized behind them as if by magic and found himself face-to-face with Nightshade.

Witch and Dragon, Dragon and Witch

*B*en stared voicelessly into the cold green eyes of the witch and, if there had been some place to run, he would have been halfway there already. But there was no running away from Nightshade. She held him fast simply by the force of her presence. She was a wall that he could neither scale nor get around. She was his prison.

Her voice was a whisper. "I never believed it possible that you would be so foolish as to come back here."

Foolish, indeed, he agreed silently. He forced himself to reach out to the terrified gnomes and draw them to him, away from the witch. They fell into him like rag dolls, shaking with relief, burying their furry faces in his tunic.

"Please help us, High Lord!" was the best Fillip could manage, his own voice a whisper.

"Yes, please!" echoed Sot.

"It's all right," Ben lied.

Nightshade laughed softly. She was just as Ben remember-
er ner—tall and sharp-featured, her skin as pale and smooth as marble, her hair jet black, save for a single streak of white down its center, her lean, angular frame cloaked all in black. She was beautiful in her way, ageless in appearance, a creature who had somehow come to terms with her mortality. Yet her face failed to reflect the emotions that would have made her

complete. Her eyes were depthless and empty. They looked ready to swallow him.

Well, I asked for this, he thought.

Nightshade's laughter died away then, and there was the barest hint of uncertainty in her eyes. She came forward a step, peering at him. "What is this?" she asked softly. "You are not the same . . ." She trailed off, confused. "But you must be; the gnomes have named you High Lord . . . Here, let me see your face in the light."

She reached out. Ben was powerless to resist. Fingers as cold as icicles fastened on his chin and tilted his head to the moonlight. She held him there a moment, muttering. "You *are* different—yet the same, too. What has been done to you, play-King? Or is this some new game you seek to play with me? Are you not Holiday?" Ben could feel Fillip and Sot shivering against his body, tiny hands digging into him. "Ah, there is *magic* at work here," Nightshade whispered harshly, fingers releasing his face with a twist. "Whose magic is it? Tell me, now—quickly!"

Ben fought back an urge to scream, fought to keep his voice steady. "Meeks. He's come back. He's made himself King and changed me into . . . this."

"Meeks?" The green eyes narrowed. "That pathetic charlatan? How has he found magic enough to accomplish this?" Her mouth twisted with disdain. "He lacks the means to tie his own shoes! How could he manage to do this to you?"

Ben said nothing. He didn't have an answer to give her.

There was a long moment of silence as the witch studied him. Finally, she said, "Where is the medallion? Let me see it!"

When he didn't immediately respond, she made a quick motion with her fingers. Despite his resolve, he found himself withdrawing the tarnished emblem from his tunic for her inspection. She stared at it a moment, then stared again at his face, then slowly smiled the smile of a predator eyeing dinner.

"So," she whispered.

That was all she said. It was enough. Ben knew instantly that she had figured out what had been done to him. He knew

that she understood the nature of the magic that had changed
him. Her realization of it was infuriating to him. It was worse
than being held like this. He wanted to scream. He *had* to know
what she had learned, and there was no way in the world that
she was going to tell him.

"You are pathetic, play-King," she went on, her voice still
soft but insinuating now as well. "You have always been lucky,
but never smart. Your luck has run out. I am almost tempted
to leave you as you are. Almost. But I cannot forget what you
did to me. I want to be the one to make you suffer for that!
Are you surprised to see me again? I think perhaps you are.
You thought me gone forever, I imagine—gone into the world
of fairy to perish. How foolish of you."

She knelt down before him so that her eyes were level with
his. There was such hate that he flinched from it. "I flew into
the mists, play-King—just as you commanded that I must, just
as I was bidden. The Io Dust held me bound to your command,
and I could not refuse. How I despised you then! But I could
do nothing. So I flew into the mists—but I flew slowly, play-
King, slowly! I fought to break the spell of the Io Dust as I
flew; I fought with all the power that I could summon!"

The smile returned again, slow and hard. "And I *did* break
the spell finally. I shattered it and turned back again. Too late,
though, play-King, much too late—for I was already within
the fairy mists and there was damage done to me! I hurt as never
before; I was scarred by the pain of it! I escaped with my life
and little else. It took me months to regain even the smallest
part of my magic. I lay within the swamp, a creature in hiding,
as helpless as the smallest reptile! I was broken! But I would
not give in to the pain and the fear; I thought only of you. I
thought only of what I would do to you once I had you in my
hands again. And I knew that one day I would find a way to
bring you back to me . . ."

She paused. "But I never dreamed it would happen so
soon, my foolish High Lord. What great good fortune! It was
the change that brought you to me, wasn't it? Something about

the change—but what? Tell me, play-King. I will have it from you anyway."

Ben knew this was so. There was no sense in trying to keep anything from the witch. He could see in the empty green eyes what was in store for him. Talking was the only thing that was keeping him alive, and as long as he was alive he had a chance. Chances at this point were not to be tossed aside lightly.

"I came looking for Willow," he answered, pushing the gnomes behind him now. He wanted them out of the way—just in case. He had to keep his eyes open for the right opportunity. The gnomes, however, continued to cling to him like Velcro.

"The River Master's daughter? The sylph?" Nightshade's look was questioning. "Why would she come here?"

"You haven't seen her?" Ben asked, surprised.

Nightshade smiled unpleasantly. "No, play-King. I have seen no one but you—you and your foolish burrow people. What would the sylph want with me?"

He hesitated, then took a deep breath. "The golden bridle."

There, it was out. Better to tell her and see if he could learn anything than to play it cute. Fencing with Nightshade was too dangerous.

Nightshade looked genuinely surprised. "The bridle? But why?"

"Because Meeks wants it. Because he sent Willow a dream about the bridle and a black unicorn." Quickly he told the witch the story of Willow's dream and of the sylph's decision to try to learn what she could of the bridle. "She was told that the bridle was here in the Deep Fell." He paused. "She should have arrived here ahead of me."

"A pity she didn't," Nightshade replied. "I like her little better than I like you. Destroying her would have given me almost as much satisfaction as destroying you." She paused, thinking. "The black unicorn, is it? Back again? How interesting. And the bridle can hold it fast, the dream says? Yes, that could be possible. After all, it was created by wizard magic. And it was a wizard I stole it from years back . . ."

Nightshade laughed. She studied him, a cunning look creeping into her eyes. "These pathetic burrow people who belong to you—were they sent to steal the bridle from me?"

Fillip and Sot were trying to crawl inside Ben's skin, but Ben was barely aware of them. He was thinking of something else altogether. If Meeks had once possessed the bridle, then that meant the wizard probably once used it—might even have used it to hold captive the black unicorn. Had the unicorn somehow escaped then? Was the dream Meeks had sent to Willow designed to regain possession of the bridle so that the unicorn could be recaptured? If so, what did the unicorns in the missing books of magic have to do with . . .

"Do not bother answering, play-King," Nightshade interrupted his thoughts. "The answer is in your eyes. These foolish rodents crept into the Deep Fell for just that reason, didn't they? Crept into my home like the thieves they are? Crept down on their little cat's paws?"

The mention of cat's paws reminded him suddenly of Edgewood Dirk. Where was the prism cat? He glanced around before he could think better of it, but Dirk was nowhere to be seen.

"Looking for someone?" Nightshade demanded at once. Her eyes swept the darkened forest behind Ben like knives. "I see no one," she muttered after a moment. "Whoever it is you look for must have abandoned you."

Nevertheless, she took a moment to make certain that she was right before turning back to him. "Your thieves are as pathetic as you, play-King," she resumed her attack. "They think themselves invisible, but they remain unseen only when I do not *wish* to see them. They were so obvious in their efforts on this misadventure that I could not fail to see them. The minute they were mine, they called for you. 'Great High Lord; mighty High Lord!' How foolish! They gave you up without my even having to ask!"

Fillip and Sot were shaking so hard Ben was in danger of

being toppled. He put a hand on each to try to offer some sort of reassurance. He felt genuinely sorry for the little fellows. After all, they were in this mess because of him.

"Since you have me, why not let the gnomes go?" he asked the witch suddenly. "They're foolish creatures, as you say. I tricked them into helping me. They really didn't have a choice. They don't even know why they're here."

"Worse luck for them." Nightshade dismissed the plea out of hand. "No one goes free who stands with you, play-King." Her face lifted, black hair sweeping back. Her eyes scanned the darkness once more. "I no longer like it here. Come."

She rose, a black shadow that gained in size as she spread her arms. Her robes billowed out like sailcloth. There was a sudden wind through the trees, cold and sharp, and mist from the Deep Fell lifted to wrap them all. Moons and stars vanished into its murk, and there was a sudden sense of lifting free, of floating. The G'home Gnomes clutched Ben tighter than ever, and he in turn held them for lack of something better to hold. There was a *whoosh*ing sound and then silence.

Ben blinked against the cold and the mist, and slowly the light returned. Nightshade stood before him, smiling coldly. The smells of swamp and mist hung thick on the air. Torchlight revealed a row of stanchions and the bones of tables and benches scattered across an empty court.

They were somewhere within the Deep Fell, down in Nightshade's home.

"Do you know what is to happen to you now, play-King?" she asked softly.

He had a pretty good idea. His imagination was working overtime on the possibilities despite his efforts to restrain it. His chances appeared to have run out. He wondered fleetingly why it was that Willow hadn't gotten here before him. Wasn't this where the Earth Mother had told her to go? If she wasn't here, where was she?

He wondered what had become of Edgewood Dirk.

Nightshade's sudden hiss jarred him free of his thoughts. "Shall I hang you to dry like a piece of old meat? Or shall I play games with you awhile first? We must take our time with this, mustn't we?"

She started to say something more, then paused as a new thought struck her. "But, no—I have a much better idea! I have a much grander and more fitting demise in mind for you!"

She bent into him. "Do you know that I no longer have the golden bridle, play-King? No? I thought not. It was stolen from me. It was stolen while I was too weak to prevent it, still recovering from the hurt that *you* caused me! Do you know who has the bridle now? Strabo, play-King! The dragon has the fairy bridle, the bridle that rightfully belongs to me. How ironic! You come to the Deep Fell in search of something that isn't even here! You come to your doom pointlessly!"

Her face was only inches from his own, skin drawn tight against the bones, the streak in her black hair a silver slash. "Ah, but you give me a chance to do something I could not otherwise do! Strabo dotes on things made of gold, though he has no use for them except as baubles! He has no true appreciation of their worth—especially the bridle with its magic! He would never give it back to me, and I cannot take it from him while he keeps it hidden within the Fire Springs. But he would trade it, play-King. He most certainly would trade it for something he values more."

Her smile was ferocious. "And what does he value more in all the world than a chance to gain his revenge against you?"

Ben couldn't imagine. Strabo had been a victim of the Io Dust as well, and he had left Ben with the promise that one day he would repay him. Ben felt the bottom drop out of his stomach. This was like being *pushed* from the frying pan into the fire. He tried to keep the witch from seeing what he was feeling and failed.

Nightshade's smile broadened in satisfaction. "Yes, play-King—I will be most content to leave the means of your destruction to the dragon!"

She brought her hands up in a sharp swirl of motion, mists rising as if bidden, chill wind returning in a rush. "Let us see what fun Strabo will have with you!" she cried, and her voice was a hiss.

The G'home Gnomes whimpered and fastened once again on his pant legs. Ben felt himself floating and watched the hollows begin to disappear . . .

The eastern wastelands lay empty and desolate in the fading afternoon light as Questor Thews, Abernathy, and Bunion worked their way steadily ahead through tangled brush and deadwood, over ridgelines and down ravines, across brief stretches of desert, and around swamp and bog. They had walked all day, pushing aside fatigue and uneasiness in equal measure, determined to reach the home of the dragon by nightfall.

It was going to be close.

Nothing lived in the wastelands of Landover—nothing but the dragon. He had adopted the wastelands as his home when driven from the mists of fairy centuries ago. The wastelands suited the dragon fine. He liked it there. His disposition found proper solace in the devastation wrought by nature's whims, and he kept the whole of the vast expanse his own. Shunned by the other inhabitants of the valley, he was an entirely solitary being. He was the only creature in the valley—with the exception of Ben Holiday—who could cross back and forth between Landover and the mortal worlds. He could even venture a short distance into the fairy mists. He was unique—the last of his kind and quite proud to be so.

He was not particularly fond of company—a fact not lost on Questor, Abernathy, and Bunion as they hurried now to reach the beast before it got any darker.

It was dusk nevertheless by the time they finally arrived at their destination. They climbed to the crest of a ridgeline that was silhouetted against the coming night by a brightness that flickered and danced as if alive and found themselves staring down into the Fire Springs. The Springs were the dragon's lair. They were settled within a deep, misshapen ravine, a cluster of craters that burned steadily with blue and yellow fire amid tangled thickets and mounds of rock and earth. Fed by a liquid pooled within the craters, their flames filled the air with smoke, ash, and the raw stench of burning fuel. A constant haze hung across the ravine and the hills surrounding, and geysers lifted periodically against the darkness with booming coughs.

They saw the dragon right off. It slouched down within the center of the ravine, head resting on a crater's edge, long tongue licking placidly at a scattering of flames.

Strabo didn't move. He lay sprawled across a mound of earth, his monstrous body a mass of scales, spikes, and plates that seemed almost a part of the landscape. When he breathed, small jets of steam exhaled into the night. His tail was wrapped around a rock formation that rose behind him, and his wings lay back against his body. His claws and teeth were blackened and bent, grown from leathered skin and gums at odd angles and twists. Dust and grime covered him like a blanket.

One red eye swiveled in its socket. "What do you want?" the dragon asked irritably.

It had always amazed Ben Holiday that a dragon could talk, but Ben was an outlander and didn't understand the nature of these things. It seemed perfectly normal to Questor and Bunion that the dragon should talk, and even more so to Abernathy, being a soft-coated Wheaten Terrier who himself talked.

"We wish to speak with you a moment," Questor advised. Abernathy managed an affirming nod, but found himself wondering at the same time why anyone in his right mind would wish to speak with something as awful as Strabo.

"I care nothing for what you wish," the dragon said with a huff of steam from both nostrils. "I care only for what I wish. Go away."

"This will only take a moment," Questor persisted.

"I don't have a moment. Go away before I eat you."

Questor flushed. "I would remind you to whom you are speaking! There is some courtesy owed me, given our long association! Now, please be civil!"

As if to emphasize his demand, he took a meaningful step forward, a scarecrow figure in tattered sashes that looked like nothing so much as a bundle of loosely joined sticks silhouetted against the light. Bunion showed all his teeth in a frightening grin. Abernathy pushed his glasses further up on his nose and tried to calculate how quickly he could reach the safety of the darkened brush at the base of the ravine behind him.

Strabo blinked and lifted his head from the crater fire. "Questor Thews, is that you?"

Questor puffed out. "It most certainly is."

Strabo sighed. "How boring. If you were someone of consequence, you might at least prove a brief source of amusement. But you are not worth the effort it would take me to rise and devour you. Go away."

Questor stiffened. Ignoring Abernathy's paw on his shoulder, he came forward another step. "My friends and I have journeyed a long way to speak with you—and speak with you we will! If you choose to ignore the long and honorable association between wizards and dragons, that is your loss! But you do us both a great disservice!"

"You seem rather ill-tempered tonight," the dragon replied. His voice reverberated in a long hiss, and the serpentine body shifted lazily against the rocks and craters, tail splashing liquid fire from a pool. "I might point out that wizards have done nothing for dragons in centuries, so I see little reason to dwell on any association that might once have existed. Such nonsense! I might also point out that while there is no question about my status as a dragon, there is certainly some question about yours as a wizard."

"I will not be drawn into an argument!" Questor snapped, rather too irritably. "Nor will I depart until you have heard me out!"

Strabo spit at the sulfurous air. "I ought simply to eat you, Questor Thews—you and the dog and that other thing, whatever it is. A kobold, isn't it? I ought to breath a bit of fire on you, cook you up nicely, and eat you. But I am in a charitable mood tonight. Leave me and I will forgive your unwelcome intrusion into my home."

"Perhaps we should reconsider . . ." Abernathy began, but Questor shushed him at once.

"Did the dog say something?" the dragon asked softly.

"No—and no one is leaving!" Questor announced, planting his feet firmly.

Strabo blinked. "No?"

His crusted head swung abruptly about and flame jetted from his maw. The fire exploded directly beneath Questor Thews and sent him flying skyward with a yelp. Bunion and Abernathy sprang aside, scrambling to get clear of flying rocks, earth, and bits of flame. Questor came down again in a tangled heap of robes and sashes, his bones jarred with the impact.

Strabo chuckled, crooked tongue licking the air. "Very entertaining, wizard. Very amusing."

Questor climbed to his feet, dusted himself off, spit out a mouthful of dirt, and faced the dragon once more. "That was entirely uncalled for!" he declared, struggling to regain his lost dignity. "I can play such games, too!"

His hands clapped sharply, pointed and spread. He tried to do something with his feet as well, but he lost his footing on the loose rock, slipped, and sat down with a grunt. Light exploded above the craters and a shower of dry leaves tumbled down over Strabo, bursting instantly into flames from the heat.

The dragon was in stitches. "Am I to be smothered in leaves?" he roared, shaking with mirth. "Please, wizard—spare me!"

Questor went rigid, owlish face flushed with anger.

"Maybe we should come back another time," Abernathy ventured in a low growl from his position behind a protective mound of earth.

But Questor Thews was having none of it. Again, he brushed himself off and got back to his feet. "Laugh at me, will you, dragon?" he snapped. "Laugh at a master practitioner of the magic arts? Very well then—laugh this off!"

Both hands lifted and wove rapidly through the air. Strabo was preparing to send forth another jet of flame when a cloudburst broke immediately overhead and torrents of rain cascaded over him. "Now, stop that!" he howled, but in seconds he was drenched snout to tail. His flame fizzled into steam, and he ducked his head into one of the pools of fire to escape the downpour. When he came up again for air, Questor made a second gesture and the rain ceased.

"There, you see?" the wizard said to Abernathy, nodding in satisfaction. "He won't be quite so quick to laugh next time!" Then he turned back once more to the dragon. "Rather amusing yourself!" he called over.

Strabo flapped his leathered wings, shook himself off, and glared. "It appears that you will continue to make a nuisance of yourself, Questor Thews, until I either put an end to you or listen to whatever it is that you feel compelled to say. I repeat, I am in a charitable mood tonight. So say what it is you feel you must and be done with it."

"Thank you very much!" Questor replied. "May we come down?"

The dragon plopped his head back on the edge of the crater and stretched out again. "Do what you please."

Questor beckoned to his companions. Slowly, they made their way down the side of the ravine and through the maze of craters and rocks until they were twenty yards or so from where the dragon reposed. Strabo ignored them, eyes lidded, snout inhaling the fumes and fires of the crater on which he rested.

"You know I hate water, Questor Thews," he muttered.

"We have come here to learn something about unicorns," Questor announced, ignoring him.

Strabo belched. "Read a book."

"As a matter of fact, I did. Several. But they lack the information about unicorns that you possess. Everyone knows that unicorns and dragons are the oldest of fairy creatures and the oldest of enemies. Each of you knows more of the other than anyone else, fairy or human. I need to know something of unicorns that no one else would."

"Whatever for?" Strabo sounded bored again. "Besides, why should I help you? You serve that detestable human who tricked me into inhaling Io Dust and then made me pledge never to hunt the valley or its people so long as he remained King! He is still King, isn't he? Bah! Of course he is—I would have heard otherwise! Ben Holiday, Landover's High Lord! I would make a quick meal of him, if he were ever to set foot in the springs again!"

"Well, it is highly unlikely that he will. Besides, we are here about unicorns, not about the High Lord." Questor thought it prudent not to dwell on the subject of Ben Holiday. Strabo had taken great pleasure in ravaging the crops and livestock of the valley before the High Lord had put a stop to it. It was a pleasure the dragon would dearly love to enjoy again— and well might one day the way Holiday was behaving lately. But there was no reason to give the dragon any encouragement.

He cleared his throat officiously. "I assume that you have heard about the black unicorn?"

The dragon's eyes snapped open and his head lifted. "The black unicorn? Of course. Is it back again, wizard?"

Questor nodded sagely. "For some time now. I am surprised that you didn't know. There was quite an effort put forth to capture it."

"Capture it? A unicorn?" Strabo laughed, a series of rough coughs and hisses. His massive body shook with mirth. "The humans would capture a unicorn? How pitiful! No one captures a unicorn, wizard—even you must know that! Unicorns are untouchable!"

"Some think not."

The dragon's lip curled. "Some are fools!"

"Then the unicorn is safe? There is nothing that can ensnare it, nothing that can cause it to be held?"

"Nothing!"

"Not maidens of certain virtue nor silver moonlight captured in a fairy net?"

"Old wives' tales!"

"Not magic of any sort?"

"Magic? Well . . ." Strabo seemed to hesitate.

Questor took a chance. "Not bridles of spun gold?"

The dragon stared at the wizard voicelessly. There was,

Questor Thews realized in surprise, a look of disbelief on the creature's face.

He cleared his throat. "I said, 'Not bridles of spun gold?'"

And it was at that moment that Nightshade, the stranger who believed himself Ben Holiday, and two sorry-looking G'home Gnomes appeared abruptly out of a swirl of mist not a dozen feet away.

Fire and Spun Gold

*T*here was an endlessly long moment in which everyone stared at everyone else. It was impossible to tell who was most surprised. Eyes shifted, fixed, and shifted again. Tall forms crouched and robes billowed. The dragon's hiss of warning mingled with that of the witch. Abernathy growled in spite of himself. Night had closed down upon the little still life in a black mantle that threatened to engulf them all. In the silence, there was only the crackle and spit of the flames as they danced across the cratered pools of blue liquid.

"You are not welcome here, Nightshade," Strabo whispered finally, his rough voice a rasp of iron. He rose up from the edge of the crater on which he had been resting in a guarded crouch, claws digging into the stone until it cracked and broke. "You are *never* welcome."

Nightshade laughed mirthlessly, her pale face streaked with shadow. "I might be welcome this time, dragon," she replied. "I have brought you something."

Questor Thews realized suddenly that the two G'home Gnomes standing next to the witch and the stranger who thought himself Ben Holiday were none other than Fillip and Sot! "Abernathy . . . !" he exclaimed softly, but the dog was already saying, "I know, wizard! But what are they doing here?"

Questor had no idea at all. Questor had no idea about any of what was happening.

Strabo's massive head lifted and the long tongue licked out. "Why would you bother to bring me anything, witch?"

Nightshade straightened gracefully, her arms folding in about her once more. "Ask me first what it is that I bring," she whispered.

"There is nothing you could bring me that I would wish. There is no point in asking."

"Ah, even if what I bring is that which you most desire in all the world? Even if it is that dear to you?"

Ben Holiday was frantically trying to decide how he was going to get out of this mess. There were no friends to be found in this bunch. Questor, Abernathy, and Bunion believed him an impostor and a fool. Fillip and Sot, if they still believed anything about him at all, were interested by this time only in escaping with their hides intact. Nightshade had kept him alive this long strictly for the purpose of striking a bargain with Strabo, who would be only too happy to do away with him for her. He cast about desperately, looking for a way out that apparently didn't exist.

Strabo's tail thrashed within a pool of fire and sent a shower of liquid flames skyward against the dark. Ben flinched. "I tire of games this night," the dragon snapped. "Get to the point!"

Nightshade's eyes glimmered crimson. "What if I were to offer you Landover's High Lord, the one they call Holiday? What if I were to offer you that, dragon?"

Strabo's snout curled and the crusted face tightened. "I would accept that gift gladly!" the dragon hissed.

Ben took a tentative step backward and found he could not. The G'home Gnomes were still fastened to him like leg irons. They were shaking and mumbling incoherently and preventing him quite effectively from making any quick moves. When he tried surreptitiously to pry them free, they just clung to him all the tighter.

"The High Lord is at Sterling Silver!" Questor Thews declared suddenly, anger showing in his owlish face. "You have no power over him there, Nightshade! Besides, he would rid the valley of you in a moment if you were to show yourself!"

"Really?" Nightshade drew the word out lovingly, teasingly. Then she came forward a step, one long finger impaling Questor on its shadow. "When I have finished my business here, wizard—when your precious High Lord is no more—then will I deal with you!"

Ben fixed a pleading gaze on his friends. *Get out of here!* he tried to tell them.

Nightshade swung back again to Strabo. One clawed hand fastened on Ben's arm and dragged him forward. "Here is the one the foolish wizard believes so safe from me, Strabo! Ben Holiday, High Lord of Landover! Look closely now! Magic has been used! Look beneath the exterior of what you first see!"

Strabo snorted derisively, belched a quick burst of flame, and laughed. "This one? This is Holiday? Nightshade, you are mad!" He leaned closer, the ooze dripping from his snout. "This one doesn't even begin to look like . . . No, wait—you are right, there is magic at work here. What has been done . . ." The massive head dipped and raised, and the eyes blinked. "Can this be so?"

"Look closely!" Nightshade repeated once again, thrusting Ben before her so hard his head snapped back.

Everyone was looking at Ben now, but only Strabo saw the truth. "Yes!" he hissed, and the massive tail thrashed once more in satisfaction. "Yes, it is Holiday!" The jaws parted and the blackened teeth snapped. "But why is it that only you and I . . . ?"

"Because only we are older than the magic that does this!" Nightshade anticipated and answered the question before the dragon could complete it. "Do you understand how it has been done?"

Ben, prize exhibit that he was, wanted nothing more than to hear the answer to that question. He had accepted the fact that he was not going to get out of this in one piece, but he hated to think he was going to die without ever knowing how he had been undone.

"But . . . but that's *not* the High Lord!" Questor Thews declared angrily, sounding suddenly as if he were trying to convince himself as much as anyone else. "That *cannot* be the High Lord! If this is . . . is . . . then, the High Lord is . . ."

He trailed off, a strange look of understanding crossing his face, a look of disbelief shredded by horror, a look that screamed soundlessly a single name—Meeks! Bunion was hissing and pulling at his arm, and Abernathy was muttering frantically about how all this could explain someone-or-other's odd behavior.

All three were pointedly ignored by the dragon and the witch.

"Why would you give him to me?" Strabo was demanding of Nightshade, wary now of what was being offered.

"I said nothing of 'giving' you anything, dragon," Nightshade replied softly. "I wish to trade him."

"Trade him, witch? You hate him more than I! He sent you into the fairy world and almost destroyed you. He marked you with the magic! Why would you trade him? What could I possess that you would want more than Holiday?"

Nightshade smiled coldly. "Oh, yes, I hate him. And I wish him destroyed. But the pleasure shall be yours, Strabo. You need only give me one thing. Give me back the bridle of spun gold."

"The bridle?" Strabo's response came with a hiss of disbelief. He coughed. "What bridle?"

"The bridle!" Nightshade snapped. "The bridle that you stole from me while I was helpless to prevent it. The bridle that is rightfully mine!"

"Bah! Nothing you possess is rightfully yours—least of all the bridle! You yourself stole it from that old wizard!"

"Be that as it may, dragon, the bridle is what I wish!"

"Ah, well, of course, if that is what you wish . . ." The dragon seemed to be hedging. "But surely, Nightshade, there are other treasures that I possess that would serve you better than such a simple toy! Suggest something else, something of greater worth!"

The witch's eyes narrowed. "Now who is it that plays games? I have decided on the bridle and it is the bridle that I shall have!"

Ben had been momentarily forgotten. Nightshade had released him and he had slipped back behind her again, the gnomes still clinging to his legs. As he listened to the bartering, he caught Questor Thews studying him with renewed interest. Abernathy peered over the magician's shoulder through smoke-streaked glasses, and Bunion peered from behind a fold of robe. All were clearly trying to decide how he could be someone other than what he appeared. Ben gritted his teeth and motioned them frantically away with a shake of his head. For crying out loud, they were all going to end up fried!

"It is simply that I fail to see why the bridle is of such interest to you," Strabo was saying, neck curving upward into the dark so that he loomed over the witch.

"And I fail to see what difference it makes!" Nightshade snapped, straightening up a bit further herself. Firelight danced across her marble face. "I fail to see why you make such an issue of returning what is mine to begin with!"

Strabo sniffed. "I need explain nothing to you!"

"Indeed, you need not! Just give me the bridle!"

"I think not. You wish it too badly."

"And you wish Holiday not enough!"

"Oh, but I do! Why not accept a chest of gold or a fairy scepter that changes moonbeams into silver coins? Why not take a gemstone marked with runes that belonged to the Trolls when the power of magic was theirs as well—a gemstone that can give truth to the holder?"

"I don't want truth! I don't want gold or scepters or anything else you hold, you fat lizard!" Nightshade was genuinely mad now, her voice rising to a near scream. "I want the bridle! Give it to me or Holiday will never be yours!"

She edged forward threateningly, leaving Holiday and the G'home Gnomes half-a-dozen paces behind her. It was the closest to freedom that Ben had been since his capture at the Deep Fell. As the voices of the witch and dragon grew more strident, he began to think that maybe—just maybe—there might be a way out of this yet.

He pried Fillip forcibly from his right leg, held him dangling from the crook of his arm, and began to work Sot free from his left.

"One last time, dragon," Nightshade was saying. "Will you trade me the bridle for Holiday or not?"

Strabo gave a long sigh of disappointment. "I am afraid, dear witch, that I cannot."

Nightshade stared at him wordlessly for a moment, then her lips peeled back from her teeth in a snarl. "You don't have the bridle anymore, do you? That is why you won't trade it to me! You don't have it!"

Strabo sniffed. "Alas, quite true."

"You bloated mass of scales!" The witch was shaking with fury. "What have you done with it?"

"What I have done with it is my concern!" Strabo snapped in reply, looking more than a bit put upon. He sighed again. "Well, if you must know, I gave it away."

"You gave it away?" The witch was aghast.

Strabo breathed a long, delicate stream of fire into the night air and followed it with a trail of ashy vapor. The lidded eyes blinked and seemed momentarily distant. "I gave it to a fairy girl who sang to me of beauty and light and things a dragon longs to hear. No maiden has sung to me in many centuries, you know, and I would have given much more than the bridle for a chance to become lost again in such sweet music."

"You gave the bridle away for a song?" Nightshade spoke the words as if trying to convince herself that they had meaning.

"A memory means more than any tangible treasure." The dragon sighed once more. "Dragons have always had a weakness for beautiful women, maidens of certain virtue, girls of grace and sweet smiles. There is a bond that joins us. A bond stronger than that of dragons and wizards, I might add," he addressed Questor Thews in a quick aside. "She sang to me, this girl, and asked me in return for the bridle of spun gold. I gave it to her gladly." He actually seemed to smile. "She was quite beautiful, this sylph."

Ben started. A sylph? *Willow!*

The dragon's head dipped solemnly toward Ben. "I helped give her back her life once," he intoned. "Remember? You commanded it, Holiday. I flew her out of Abaddon to her home in the lake country where she could be healed. I didn't mind that so much—the saving of her life. I hated you, of course— you forced me to submit to you. But I rather enjoyed saving the sylph. It reminded me of the old days when saving maidens was routine work for a dragon."

He paused. "Or was it devouring them? I can never re-member which."

"You are a fool!" Nightshade spat.

Strabo cocked his head as if thinking it over. Then his snout split wide to reveal all of his considerable teeth. "Do you really think so? A fool? Me? A bigger fool than you, witch? So big a fool as to venture unprotected into the lair of my worst enemy?"

The silence was palpable. Nightshade was a statue. "I am never unprotected, dragon. Beware."

"Beware? How quaint." Strabo suddenly coiled like a spring. "I have endured patiently your venomous assault on my character; I have allowed you to speak what you wished. Now it is my turn. You are a skinny, pathetic excuse for witchhood who believes herself far more powerful than she is. You come into my home as if you belong here, order me about, call me names, demand things you have no right to demand, and think you can go right out again. You mistake yourself, Nightshade. I might, had I the chance to do it over again, keep the bridle of spun gold so that I could trade it to you for Holiday. I might. But I regret nothing that I have ever done, and this least of all. The bridle is gone, and I do not wish it back again."

He bent forward slowly. The rough voice changed to a slow hiss. "But look—Holiday is still here, witch! And since you brought him expressly for me, I rather think I ought to keep him! Don't you?"

Nightshade's fingers were like claws as they lifted before her lean face. "You will take nothing more from me, dragon—not now, not ever!"

"Ah, but you have only yourself to blame. You have made the prospect of destroying Holiday so tempting that I cannot resist your lure! I must have him! He is mine to destroy, bridle or no! I think you had best give him to me—now!"

Flames burst from the maw of the dragon and engulfed Nightshade. At the same moment, Ben ripped Sot free at last of his left leg and flung himself sideways to escape the backlash of heat and fire. Questor Thews was moving as well, all arms and legs as he galloped toward Ben. Bunion sprinted past him, ears flattened back. Abernathy went down on all fours and scurried for the safety of the bushes.

Ben surged back to his feet, still carrying the wailing gnomes. Strabo's fire exploded skyward into the black, filling the air with a shower of sparks and rock. Nightshade stood unharmed in their center, black robes flying like drying bedclothes caught in the wind, pale face lifted, arms gesturing. Fire burst from her fingers and hammered into a surprised Strabo. The dragon flew backward, tumbling into a cratered pool.

"High Lord!" Questor Thews cried out in warning.

Nightshade whirled just in time to be caught by the full force of a magical gesture from the magician that swept the witch up in a blinding flurry of snowflakes. Nightshade swatted at them angrily, screamed, and threw fire back at him. Shards of flame hissed past Ben as he flung himself down again, smothering the gnomes. The fur on Abernathy's hind end caught fire, and the scribe disappeared up the slope of the Fire Springs with a yelp.

Then Strabo surfaced once more from the crater into which he had fallen, roaring in fury. Uncoiling his serpentine body with a lunge, he sprayed the whole of the Springs with fire. Nightshade swung back on him, shrieking with equal fury, spraying fire of her own. Ben was on his feet and running for

his life. The fire swept over him, a wall of heat and red pain.
But Questor was there now, hands gesturing desperately, and
a shield of some impenetrable plastic substance appeared out of
nowhere to slow the fire down. Ben kept his arms locked about
the struggling, whimpering G'home Gnomes and scrambled
desperately to escape the pursuing flames. Bunion's tough arms
closed about his waist and helped haul all three toward the lip
of the cratered valley. Questor followed, calling out in
encouragement.

Moments later, they reached the rim of the Fire Springs
and stumbled from the heat and smoke into the cooling scrub.
Coughing and gasping, they collapsed in a tangled knot. Abernathy joined them from out of the dark.

Behind them, the witch and the dragon continued their
private battle uninterrupted, their shrieks and roars filling the
night. They hadn't even realized yet that the object of their
struggle had escaped.

Ben glanced hurriedly at his companions. White eyes
blinked back at him through the dark. No sense in resting now,
they all seemed to agree. It wouldn't take long for the witch
and the dragon to realize what had happened.

Stumbling to their feet once again, they disappeared
swiftly into the night.

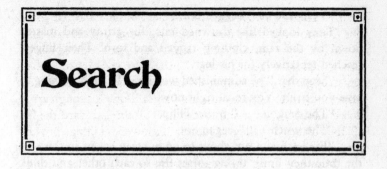

Search

*I*t was sometime after midnight when Ben and his companions finally broke off their flight. The skies had gone black with thunderheads that rolled eastward out of the grasslands. Moons and stars disappeared as if blown from the heavens by the sudden winds, thunder rumbled in long booming peals, and lightning laced the skies. The rains came swiftly, hard and chill, sweeping broomlike across the wastelands. There was barely time to find shelter in a thick copse of fir before the whole of the land surrounding had turned invisible in a wash of impenetrable mist and damp.

The company sat beneath the massive boughs of the centermost fir and peered out through the curtain of needles at the downpour. Wind rushed in stinging swipes through the trees and scrub, and water cascaded down. Everything faded away amid the steady sounds, and the stand of trees became an island in the gloom.

Ben sat back against the fir's massive trunk after a while and stared at the others, eyes shifting from one face to the next. "I am Ben Holiday, you know," he said finally. "I really am."

They looked questioningly at one another and back again at him.

"Save us, mighty High Lord," said Fillip after a moment, the words a toneless whimper.

"Yes, save us," begged Sot.

They looked like drowned rats, fur grimy and matted down by the rain, clothing ragged and torn. Their fingers reached tentatively for his legs.

"Stop that," he admonished wearily. "There is nothing to save you from. You're all right now."

"The dragon . . ." began Fillip.

"The witch . . ." began Sot.

"Far back and not about to go hunting for us in this. By the time they finish trying to set fire to each other and think to wonder what happened to us, the rain will have washed away any trace of where we went." He tried to sound more confident than he felt. "Don't worry. We'll be fine."

Bunion showed all his teeth and hissed. He looked at Ben as he might an errant bog wump. Abernathy didn't seem to want to look at Ben at all.

Questor Thews cleared his throat. Ben glanced expectantly at him, and the wizard seemed suddenly uncertain of what to say. "This is rather difficult," he said finally. He squinted at Ben. "You say you are indeed the High Lord? The witch and the dragon were correct in believing you so?"

Ben nodded slowly.

"And the story you told us at Sterling Silver—that was all true? You were changed somehow by magic? You have lost the protection of the medallion?"

Ben nodded a second time.

"And Meeks *has* returned and taken your place—and made himself appear as you?"

Ben nodded a third time.

Questor's lean features squinched down so hard against each other he appeared to be in danger of causing permanent damage. "But how?" he demanded finally. "How did all this happen?"

Ben sighed. "That is the sixty-four thousand dollar question, I'm afraid."

Briefly he recounted again his confrontation with Meeks in his bedchamber and his transformation into the stranger he appeared to them to be. He took them to the moment of his decision to travel south in search of Willow. "I've been hunting for her ever since," he concluded.

"See—I told you!" Abernathy snapped.

Questor stiffened and he peered down his long nose at the scribe. "Told me *what*?" he demanded, owlish face tightening even further.

"That the High Lord wasn't acting like the High Lord!" Abernathy fairly barked. "That something was definitely wrong! That nothing was what it should be! In fact, wizard, I told you a good deal more than that, if you would bother taking time enough to remember any of it!" He shoved his rain-streaked glasses back on his nose. "I told you that these dreams would bring nothing but trouble. I told you to forget about chasing after them!" He wheeled suddenly on Ben, a prophet whose visions had come to pass. "I warned you as well, didn't I? I told you to stay in Landover where you belonged! I told you Meeks was too dangerous! But you wouldn't listen, would you? Neither of you would listen! Now look where we are!"

He sneezed, shook himself furiously, and showered everyone with water. "Sorry," he muttered, sounding not the least so.

Questor sniffed. "I trust you feel better now?"

Ben decided to head off any further squabbling. "Abernathy is right. We should have listened to him. But we didn't, and what's done is done. We have to put all that behind us. At least we're back together again."

"A lot of good that's going to do us!" Abernathy snapped, still miffed.

"Well, it might do us some good." Ben tried his best to sound positive. "The six of us together might be able to accomplish something more than I could alone."

"The *six* of us?" Abernathy eyed the G'home Gnomes with disdain. "You count two more than I, High Lord. In any case, I am still not convinced that you really are the High Lord. Questor Thews is much too quick to believe. We have already been fooled once; it is possible that we are being fooled again. How do we know that this isn't just another charade? How do we know that this isn't another of Meeks' tricks?"

Ben thought about it a moment. "You don't, I guess. You have to take my word for it. You have to trust me—and trust your instincts." He sighed. "Do you think Meeks could fool both Strabo and Nightshade that badly? Do you think I would be hanging about claiming to be High Lord if I really weren't?" He paused. "Do you think I would still be wearing this?"

He reached down inside his tunic front and produced the tarnished medallion. The image of Meeks gleamed wetly, caught in a flash of distant lightning.

"Why *are* you still wearing it?" Questor asked quietly.

Ben shook his head. "I'm afraid to get rid of it. If Meeks is right and throwing off the medallion will finish me, then who would be left to warn Willow? She doesn't know any of what's happened. She doesn't know that the dreams were sent by Meeks or the danger she's in. I care too much for her, Questor. I can't abandon her. I can't take the chance that she'll fall into the same trap I did and have no one to help her out."

They were all silent for a moment, studying him.

"No, High Lord—you can't," Questor agreed finally. The wizard looked over at Abernathy. "The real Ben Holiday wouldn't even think of such a thing, would he?" he asked pointedly. "Not the real Ben Holiday."

Abernathy considered the possibility silently for a moment, then sighed. "No, I suppose he wouldn't." He glanced at Bunion, who nodded his monkey face approvingly. "Very well. The others accept you as High Lord; I shall do so as well."

"I appreciate that," Ben assured his scribe.

"But I still think that you are no better off with four of us . . ." He glanced once more at the G'home Gnomes. " . . . or six of us—or however many of us can be counted on—than you were by yourself! What is it that six of us are supposed to do that you could not do alone?"

The others looked at him expectantly. He stared past them into the haze of rain and darkness, drew his legs up to his chest to ward off the growing chill, and tried to come up with something. "Find Willow," he said finally. "Protect her."

They stared at him voicelessly.

"Look. The third dream is the key to everything that's happened, and the bridle is the key to the dream. Willow has the bridle now—we know that. Strabo gave it to her. She has it, but what will she do with it?"

"What, Mighty High Lord?" asked Fillip eagerly.

"Yes, what?" echoed Sot.

"She will take it to you, High Lord," Questor answered quickly. Then he paused. "Or at least to the one she believes to be you."

"That's right, Questor," Ben whispered. "That's what the dream told her she must do and that's what she'll do. She'll take the bridle to me. But I won't be me. I'll be Meeks. Or *he'll* be Meeks—the one she'll run to. And then what happens to her?"

"We have to reach her first," Questor insisted quietly.

"As soon as it stops raining," Abernathy added.

Ben nodded. "Six of us will have a better chance than one."

"Bunion will have a better chance than ten times six," Abernathy interjected, sneezing again. "I think I am catching cold," he muttered.

"For once, Abernathy is right!" Questor exclaimed, ignoring the reproving look the dog gave him. "A kobold can track faster and farther than any human. If there is any sign of the girl, Bunion will find it." He looked over at the kobold, who showed all of his teeth in response. "Indeed, Bunion will find her for us—you may depend upon it." He shrugged. "As soon as it stops raining, of course".

Ben shook his head. "We can't wait that long. We don't have . . ."

"But we have to," the wizard interrupted gently.

"But we can't . . ."

"We must." Questor took his arm and held it. "There can be no tracking done in a storm such as this one, High Lord. There would be no signs to follow." His owlish face bent close

and there was sudden warmth in his eyes. "High Lord, you
have come a long way since Sterling Silver. You have clearly
suffered much. Your physical appearance, however distorted it
might be, does not lie. Look at yourself. You are worn to the
bone. You are exhausted. I have seen beggars who looked
healthier than you. Abernathy?"

"You look a wreck," the dog agreed.

"Well, bad enough, at any rate." The wizard tempered the
other's assessment with a smile. "You need to rest. Sleep now.
There will be time enough later to begin the hunt."

Ben shook his head vigorously. "Questor, I'm not tired.
I can't . . ."

"I think you must," the wizard said softly. A boney hand
passed briefly before Ben's face, and his eyes grew suddenly
heavy. He could barely keep them open. He felt a pervasive
weariness slip within his body and weigh him down. "Rest,
High Lord," Questor whispered.

Ben fought the command, struggled to rise, and found he
could not. For once, the wizard's magic was working right on
the first try. Ben was slipping back against the rough trunk of
the fir, downward into a bed of needles. His companions drew
close. Abernathy's furry, bespeckled face peered at him through
a gathering of shadows. Bunion's teeth gleamed like daggers.
Fillip and Sot were vague images that wavered and voices that
murmured and seemed to draw steadily farther away. He found
comfort in their presence, strength, and reassurance—his
friends, all there with him except Parsnip—and Willow!

"Willow," he whispered.

He spoke her name once and was asleep.

He dreamed of Willow while he slept, and the dream was a
revelation that shocked him, even in his slumber. He searched
for the sylph through the forests, hills, and plains of Landover,
a solitary quest that drew him on as a magnet would iron. The
country through which he traveled was familiar and yet foreign,
too, a mix of sunshine and shadows that shimmered with the
inconsistency of an image reflected on water. There were things

that moved all about him, but they lacked face and form. He hunted alone, his search a seemingly endless one that took him from one end of the valley and back again, swift and certain in its pace but fruitless nevertheless.

He was driven by an urgency that surprised him. There was a need to find the sylph that defied explanation. He was frightened for her without understanding the reason for his fear. He was desperate to be with her, yet his desperation lacked cause. It was as if he were captive to his emotions and they determined his course where reason could not. He could sense Willow's presence as he searched, a closeness that teased him. It was as if she waited behind each tree and beyond each hill, and he need only journey a bit further to find her. Weariness did not slow him as he traveled; strength of purpose carried him on.

After a time, he began to hear voices. They whispered to him from all about, some in warning, some in admonishment. He heard the River Master, distrustful yet of who Ben was, strangely anxious that the daughter he could not quite love and who could not quite love him be found. He heard the Earth Mother, asking him to repeat again the promise he had made to her to find and protect Willow, insistent that he honor it. He heard that solitary, defeated hunter speak once more in hollow tones of the black unicorn, of the touch that had stolen away his soul. He heard Meeks, his voice a dark and vengeful hiss that promised ruin if the girl and the golden bridle should escape him.

Still he went on.

And then he heard Edgewood Dirk.

It was the voice of the prism cat that slowed him, aware suddenly of how frantic his search for Willow had become. He stopped, his breath ragged in his ears, his chest pounding. He stood within a forest glade that was cool and solitary, a mix of shadows and light, of boughs canopied overhead and moss grown thick underfoot. Dirk sat upon a knoll within that glade, prim and sleek and inscrutable.

"Why do you run so, High Lord Ben Holiday?" Dirk asked quietly.

"I must find Willow," he replied.

"Why must you find her?" Dirk pressed.

"Because danger threatens her," he answered.

"And is that all?"

He paused. "Because she needs me."

"And is that all?"

"Because there is no one else."

"And is that all?"

"Because . . ."

But the words he searched for would not come, as elusive as the sylph herself. There were words to be spoken, he sensed. What were those words?

"You work so hard to orchestrate your life," Dirk declared almost sadly. "You work so hard to fit all the pieces together, a vast puzzle you must master. But you fail to understand the reason for your need to do so. Life is not simply form, High Lord; life is feeling, too."

"I feel," he said.

"You govern," Dirk corrected. "You govern your king-dom, your subjects, your work, and your life. You organize—here as you once organized there. You command. You com-mand as King as you commanded as lawyer. Court-of-law stagecraft or royal-court politics—you are no different now than you were then. You act and you react with quickness and skill. But you do not feel."

"I try."

"The heart of the magic lies in feeling, High Lord. Life is born of feeling, and the magic is born of life. How can you understand either life or magic if you do not feel? You search for Willow, but how can you recognize her when you fail to understand what she is? You search with your eyes for some-thing they cannot see. You search with your senses and your body for what they cannot find. You must search instead with your heart. Try now. Try, and tell me what you see."

He did, but there was a darkness all about him that would

not let him see. He drew deep inside himself and found passages through which he could not travel. Obstructions blocked his way, shapeless things that lacked clear definition. He tried furiously to push past them, groping, reaching . . .

Then Willow was before him, a misty vision suddenly remembered. She was lithe and quicksilver as she passed, her face stunning in its beauty, her body a whisper of his need. Forest green hair tumbled down about her slender shoulders and fell to her waist. White silk draped and clung like a second skin. Her eyes met his, and he found his breath drawn from him with a sharpness that hurt. She smiled, warm and tender, and her whisper was soundless in his mind. There was no danger that threatened her, no sense of urgency about her. She was at peace with herself. She was at rest.

"Why do you run so, High Lord Ben Holiday?" Dirk repeated from somewhere within the shadows.

"I must find Willow," he answered again.

"Why must you find her?"

"Because . . ."

Again, he could not find the words. The shadows began to tighten. Willow began to fade back into them.

"Because . . ."

She faded further, a memory disappearing. He struggled frantically to find the words he needed to say, but they eluded him still. The sense of urgency returned, quick and hard. The danger to the sylph became real once more, as if somehow resurrected by his indecision. He tried to reach out to her with his hands, but she was too far away, and he was too rooted in place.

"Because . . ."

The shadows were all about, cloaking him now in their blackness, smothering him in their endless dark. He was drawing back out of himself. Dirk was gone. Willow was little more than a patch of light and color against the black, fading, fading . . .

"Because . . ."

Willow!

He came awake with a start, jerking upright from his place of rest, his underarms and back damp with sweat. Night shrouded the eastern wastelands in silence. Clouds masked the skies, though the rain had ceased to fall. Ben's companions slept undisturbed all about him—all except Bunion. Bunion was already gone, his search for Willow begun.

Ben took a deep breath to steady himself. His dream of Willow was still sharp and certain in his mind. He exhaled.

"Because . . . I love her," he finished.

Those were the words he had searched for. And he knew with frightening certainty that the words were true.

He was awake for a time after that, alone with his thoughts in the dark silence of the night. After a while, though, he tired and dropped back off to sleep. When he awoke again, it was nearing dawn, the eastern sky behind the valley rim brightening with faint streaks of gray and gold. Bunion had not returned. The others still slept.

He rolled over on his back, glanced about the storm-dampened campsite, and then blinked in surprise. Edgewood Dirk rested comfortably on a thick bough of the fir just a few feet above his head, paws tucked under his sleek body, eyes squinched closed against the light.

The eyes slipped open as Ben stared. "Good morning, High Lord," the cat offered.

Ben pushed himself up on his elbows. "Good morning, nothing. Where have you been?"

"Oh, here and there."

"More there than here, it seems!" Ben snapped, a great deal of pent-up anger coming quickly to the fore. "I could have used a little help back there in the Deep Fell when you so conveniently disappeared! I was lucky the witch didn't do away with me on the spot! And then I was dragged off to Strabo's den and offered to him as a snack! But all that made precious little difference to you, did it? Thanks for nothing!"

"You are quite welcome," Dirk replied calmly. "I would remind you once again, however, that I signed on as a companion, not as a protector. Besides, it appears you have suffered no harm in my absence."

"But I might have, damn it!" Ben couldn't help himself. He was sick of the cat appearing and disappearing like some wraith. "I might have been fried in dragon oil for all the good you'd have done me!"

"Might have, could have, may have, should have—the haves and the have nots reduced to pointless possibilities." Dirk yawned. "You would do better to forget flogging dead horses and try rounding up a few live ones."

Ben glared. "Meaning?"

"Meaning you have something more important on your mind that chastising me for imagined wrongs."

Ben paused, remembering suddenly his dream, the search he had undertaken, the golden bridle, the black unicorn, Meeks, and all the rest of the puzzle he still didn't understand. Ah, and Willow! Thoughts of the sylph pushed all others aside. I love her, he told himself, trying the words on for size. He found them unexpectedly comfortable.

"There are those who theorize that our dreams are simply manifestations of our subconscious thoughts and desires," Dirk mused, as if delivering an offhand dissertation. "Dreams do not often portray accurately the events upon which those thoughts and desires are formed, but they do demonstrate quite vividly the emotions behind them. We find ourselves involved in bizarre situations and disjointed events, and our tendency is often to dismiss the dream out-of-hand—a self-conscious response. But hidden within the thrashings of our subconscious is a kernel of truth about ourselves that needs to be understood—truth that sometimes we have refused to recognize while awake and now demands recognition while we sleep."

He paused for dramatic effect. "Love is sometimes such a truth."

Ben pushed himself upright, stared at this cat turned philosopher a moment, and then shook his head. "Is all this in reference to Willow?" he asked.

Dirk blinked. "Of course, sometimes dreams lie and the truth can be found only in waking."

"Like with my dream of Miles?" Ben found the cat's conversation needlessly convoluted. "Why don't you just say what you mean for once?"

Dirk blinked again. "Because I am a cat."

"Oh. Sure." The standard answer again.

"Because some things you simply have to figure out for yourself."

"Right."

"Something you have not proven very adept at doing, I'm afraid."

"Certainly not."

"Despite my continuing efforts."

"Hmmmmm." Ben experienced an almost uncontrollable urge to throttle the beast. To suppress the feeling, he glanced about instead at his still sleeping companions. "Why isn't anyone but me awake yet?" he demanded.

Dirk glanced about with him. "Perhaps they are simply very tired," the cat suggested amiably.

Ben gave him a hard look. "What did you do—employ a bit of magic? Fairy magic? As Questor did with me? You did, didn't you?"

"A bit."

"But why? I mean, why bother?"

Dirk rose, stretched, and jumped down next to Ben, pointedly ignoring him. He began to wash himself and continued to do so until he had cleaned himself thoroughly, fur carefully ruffled and smoothed back in place again.

Then he faced Ben, emerald eyes gleaming in the faint dawn light. "The problem is, you do not listen. I tell you everything you need to know, but you do not seem to hear any of it. It really is distressing." He sighed deeply. "I let your companions sleep to demonstrate to you one final lesson about dreams. So much of your understanding of what has happened depends on your understanding of how dreams work. Watch, now, what occurs when your friends awake. And try to pay attention this time, will you? My patience wears exceedingly thin."

Ben grimaced. Edgewood Dirk settled back on his haunches. Together they waited for something to happen. After a moment, Questor Thews stirred, then Abernathy, and finally the gnomes. One by one, they blinked the sleep from their eyes and sat up.

Then they saw Ben, and more especially, Dirk.

"Ah, good morning, High Lord. Good morning, Dirk," Questor greeted brightly. "Slept well the both of you, I hope?"

Abernathy muttered something about all cats being night creatures and not needing sleep anyway, even prism cats, and how it was a waste of time to worry about any of them.

Fillip and Sot eyed Dirk as they would a long-awaited dinner and showed not the slightest trace of fear.

Ben stared in bewilderment, the conversation continuing on about him as if the cat's presence were perfectly normal. No one seemed surprised that the cat was there. Questor and Abernathy were behaving as if his appearance was entirely expected. The gnomes were behaving the way they had at their first encounter with Dirk; neither seemed to remember what their eagerness to make Dirk a meal had cost them.

Ben listened a moment as the others talked and bustled about, then glanced in confusion at the cat. "What . . . ?"

"Their dreams, High Lord," Dirk whispered, interrupting. "I let them discover me in their dreams. I was real to them there, so I am real to them here. Don't you see? Truth is sometimes simply what we perceive it to be—in waking or in dreams."

Ben didn't see. He had paid close attention, he had listened as instructed, and he still didn't see. What was the point of all this and what did it have to do with him?

But there was no more time to consider the matter. A shout from Abernathy—or rather a sort of bark—captured the attention of all. The boughs at the edge of the grove of fir parted and who should appear but Parsnip! Bunion had him in tow, both of them soaked though by the storm, both grimacing ear to ear those wicked, toothy grins. Ben froze. Parsnip was supposed to be guarding Willow! Shaking off his paralysis, he hastened forward with Questor and Abernathy to greet the wiry little creatures, stopped short at the hard, suspicious look directed at him by Parsnip—who, after all, had no idea yet who he was—and finally backed off a step at Questor's urging. Questor and Bunion conversed briefly back and forth in the rough, guttural language of the kobolds with occasional interjections by Parsnip, and then Questor turned hurriedly to Ben.

"Parsnip has kept watch over Willow since she left Sterling Silver, High Lord—just as you commanded—until yesterday. She dismissed him without reason. When he wouldn't leave her, she used the fairy magic and slipped away. Even a kobold can't stay with a sylph when she doesn't wish it. She has the golden bridle, and . . . and she searches for the black unicorn." He shook his owlish features at the look on Ben's face and tugged worriedly at his white beard. "I know. I don't understand this last either, High Lord, and neither does Parsnip. Apparently she has decided *not* to take the bridle to you as her dream instructed!"

Ben fought off the sudden lurch in his stomach. What did this mean, he wondered? "Where is she now?" he asked instead.

Questor shook his head. "Her trail leads north into the Melchor." He hesitated. "Bunion says she appears to be traveling toward Mirwouk!"

Mirwouk? Where the missing books of magic had been hidden? Why would she go there? Ben felt his frustration increase.

"There is more, High Lord," Abernathy interjected solemnly, ignoring the warning tug on his tunic sleeve from Questor. "Strabo and Nightshade are at hunt—presumably for you, Willow, and the bridle. And a demon—a huge, flying thing, a thing that answers to no one, it seems—is rumored to scour the whole of the valley. Bunion saw it last night."

"Meeks' pet," Ben whispered, remembering suddenly the monster that had appeared at the dance of the River Master's nymphs and destroyed them. His face tightened. Edgewood

Dirk and the matter of dreams were forgotten. He thought now only of Willow. "We have to reach her before they do," he announced, his voice sounding hollow in his ears as he fought down the fear that raced through him. "We have to. We're all she has."

Everyone reacted. Abernathy barked sharply at the G'home Gnomes and turned the kobolds about once more. Questor put a reassuring hand on Ben's arm. "We will find her, High Lord. You can depend upon it."

Quickly they departed into the wastelands, the stranger who was High Lord, the wizard and the scribe, the kobolds and the gnomes.

Edgewood Dirk sat quietly and watched them go.

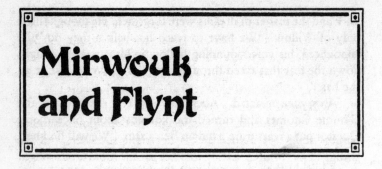

Mirwouk
and Flynt

*W*illow felt the glare of the midday heat on her face through breaks in the forest trees and was suddenly thirsty. She made her way gingerly around an outcropping of rock that jutted from the ever-steepening slope, climbed to a shelf of tall grass and brush that disappeared ahead into a grove of deeply shaded fir, and paused to look back. Landover spread away below, an irregular checkerboard of fields and forests, hills and plains, rivers and lakes, swatches of blues and greens with brush strokes of pastel interspersed like webbing. Sunlight poured down over the valley from a cloudless blue sky and deepened the colors until they blinded with their brilliance.

Willow sighed. It seemed impossible that anything could be wrong on a day such as this.

She was deep within the Melchor now, past the threshold of hardwood forests, past the higher plateau of pine-wooded foothills, a fair distance up into the main peaks. The sun was sharp and hot this day where the shade failed to screen away its light, and the climb was thirsty work. Willow carried no water with her; she relied on her instincts to find what she needed. Her instincts had failed her these past few hours since leaving the foothills, but now she sensed water to be close again.

Nevertheless, she stayed where she was a moment longer and looked out across the valley in silent contemplation. Far,

far distant to the south she could just catch a glimpse of the misted island that was Sterling Silver, and she thought of Ben. She wished he were here with her or that she understood why it was that she wasn't there with him. She looked out across the valley and felt as if she were all alone in the world.

What was she doing here?

She felt burdened by the weight of the woolen-bundled harness she wore draped across her right shoulder, and she shrugged it off and let it drop into her hands. A burst of sunlight flashed sharply from a stray bit of trapping that slipped from beneath the covering folds. The bridle of spun gold clinked softly. She covered it over and shifted it to her other shoulder. The bridle was heavy, the woven threads and fastenings more cumbersome than she would have believed. She adjusted it carefully and straightened. She had been fortunate that the dragon had agreed to give it to her. All the fairy songs, music, tears, and laughter had been potent magic indeed. Strabo had been charmed. She was still surprised that the ploy had been successful. She was still mystified that she had known somehow that it would be. Dreams, visions, and hunches—such were the vicissitudes that had driven her these past few days, a stray leaf blown by the wind.

Last night it had been a dream again. She frowned at its memory, her smooth, lovely face lined with worry. Last night, the dream had been of Ben.

A breath of wind swept back her waist-length hair and cooled her skin. She remembered her need to drink, but stayed yet another moment to think of her High Lord. The dream had been strange again, a mix of real and surreal, a jumble of fears and hopes. She had come upon the black unicorn once more, the creature hidden in woods and shadows, no demon this time but a hunted thing, frightened and alone. She had feared it, but wept at its terror. What frightened it was uncertain, but the look it spared her was unmistakable. Come to me, it had whispered. Put aside your plan to carry back the bridle of spun gold to Sterling Silver and your High Lord. Forego your race from the demon you fear me to be and seek instead the truth of what I am. Willow, come to me.

A single look had said all that, so clear, so certain—a dream, and yet real. So she had come, trusting to her fairy instincts as she had always trusted, believing that they alone of all her senses could not be deceived. She had abandoned the call of the first dream that would have taken her to Ben and gone instead in search of . . .

Of what? Truth?

"Why are the dreams so different?" she questioned softly. "Why am I made so confused?"

Sunlight sparkled off distant waters and forest leaves rippled in the passing wind, but no answers came. She breathed the air deeply and turned away. The shadows of the forest drew her to them, and she let herself be swallowed. Mirwouk was near, she realized in surprise—not more than several miles distant, just beyond the peak she climbed. The fact registered briefly and was forgotten. The broad swath of midday sunlight faded into a scattering of narrow bands, and the shade was cool on her heated skin. She worked her way back into the forest trees, massive fir and pine, seeking the water she knew was hidden there. She found it quickly, a small stream trickling down out of the rocks into a pool and meandering from there to a series of shallows and runs. She laid the bridle carefully on the ground next to her and bent to drink. The water was sweet and welcome to her dry throat. She knelt a long time in the stillness.

The seconds slipped away into minutes. When she lifted her head again, the black unicorn stood across from her.

Her breath caught in her throat and she froze. The unicorn was no more than a dozen paces off, half within shadow, half within pale, filtered sunlight. It was a vision of grace and wonder, slender body as ephemeral as a reflection of love remembered, presence as glorious as a rainbow's sweep. It did not move, but simply regarded her. Ebony body with goat's feet and lion's tail, eyes of green fire, immortal life—all the songs of all the bards through all the ages of the world could not begin to express what the unicorn truly was.

Willow felt a rush of emotion tear through her, stripping bare her soul. She felt her heart begin to break with the ecstasy of it. She had never seen a unicorn and never thought it would be like this. There were tears in her eyes, and she swallowed uncontrollably against what she was feeling.

"Oh, you beautiful thing," she whispered.

Her voice was so soft that she believed only she could hear her words. But the unicorn nodded in response, and the ridged horn shone brightly with magic. The green eyes fixed upon her with new intensity and flared from some inner well of being. Willow felt something seize hold within her. Her hand groped blindly the earth next to her and came to rest at last upon the bridle.

Oh, I must have you, she thought. I must make you mine!

But the eyes held her and she could not move to act upon her need. The eyes held her, and they whispered of something remembered from the dream.

Come to me, they said. Seek me.

She felt herself flush with the heat of that memory and then go cool. She saw the memory reflected in her eyes, in her mind, and in her heart. She looked across the tiny stream of water as it rushed and gurgled over the rocks in the forest stillness, and the stream was a river she could not bridge. She listened to the singing of birds in the trees, a mingling of songs that cheered and heartened, and the sound became the voice of all her secrets revealed.

She felt magic rage within her in waves of insistence she had never known could exist. She no longer belonged to herself; she belonged now to the unicorn. She would have done anything for it. Anything.

Then, in the next instant, it was gone, disappearing so suddenly and so completely that it might never have been. Indeed, she wondered—had it? Willow stared at the space the black unicorn had occupied, an emptiness of mingled light and shadow, and she fought against the sharpness of her pain.

Had she seen the unicorn? Truly seen it? Had it been real?

The questions left her dazed. She could not move. Then, slowly, purposefully, she rose to her feet, shouldered again the golden bridle, and moved with quiet determination in search of her answers.

She searched all that day. Yet she did not search so much as follow, for there was a sense of being led that she could not explain. She climbed through the tangle of rocks and trees and scrub that carpeted the uneven heights of the Melchor and sought a thing that might not even be. She thought she saw the black unicorn several times more, brief flashes only—an ebony flank, an emerald eye, a ridged horn shining with magic. It did not occur to her that her efforts might be misdirected. She chased quite deliriously and without regret. She knew that the unicorn was there, just beyond her reach. She could feel it waiting for her; she could sense it watching. She did not know its purpose, but she was certain of its need.

Nightfall found her less than a mile west of Mirwouk, exhausted, still alone. She had traversed the forest all about the aging, crumbling fortress. She had retraced her own steps several times. She was no nearer the black unicorn than she had been when she had first spied it, but she was as determined as ever that she would catch up to it. At dawn, she would try again.

She lay down within a sheltering of birch, hugged the bridle of spun gold within its woolen covering close against her breast, and let the cool night air wash over her. Slowly the heat of the day faded, and her exhaustion slipped away. She slept undisturbed and dreamed once more.

Her dream this night was of dozens of white unicorns chained and fettered and begging to be set free. The dream was like a fever that would not break.

From shadows close at hand, eyes of green fire kept watch through the night.

Ben Holiday and his companions spent that night within the

Melchor as well, although they were still some distance from
Mirwouk and Willow. They were camped just above the foothills leading into the mountains and lucky to be that far. It had
taken them the better part of the day just to get out of the
wastelands, and they had trekked on through the late afternoon
and evening to reach the base of the mountains. Ben had insisted. The kobolds had found Willow's tracks near sundown,
and Ben thought they might catch up to her yet that day. It
was only after complete darkness had set in and Questor had
pleaded with Ben to be reasonable that the search was tem-
porarily abandoned.

It resumed at daybreak, and the little company found itself
less than a mile below Mirwouk by midmorning. It was then
that matters began to grow confusing.

The confusion was manifold. In the first place, Willow's
trail was leading toward Mirwouk. Since she wasn't carrying
the golden bridle to Ben—or Meeks disguised as Ben—it was
somewhat uncertain what it was that she was doing with it.
Possibly she was searching for the black unicorn, although that
didn't make much sense, since in her dream the black unicorn
had been a demon creature that threatened her, and she still
didn't know that the dream had been sent by Meeks. Whatever
she was doing, she was definitely going toward Mirwouk, and
Mirwouk was where Questor's dream had taken him in search
of the missing books of wizard magic and where, in fact, the
missing books had been found.

In the second place, the kobolds had discovered that twice
already Willow's tracks had retraced themselves. Sylphs were
fairy creatures and not in the habit of getting lost, so that meant
either she was searching for something or following something.
But there was no indication at all of what that might be.

In the third place, Edgewood Dirk was still among the
missing. No one had seen the cat since they had departed their
shelter of two nights earlier, following Bunion's return with
Parsnip and the news of Willow's tracks. Ben hadn't paid much
attention to Dirk's absence until now, too caught up in his
search for Willow really to notice. But confronting these other

puzzles had led him almost without thinking to look around for Dirk, perhaps in the vain hope of getting a straight answer from the beast for once; but Dirk was nowhere to be found.

Ben took it all in stride. There wasn't much any of them could do to clear up the confusion just now, so he simply ordered them to press on.

They crossed Willow's tracks a third time within a stone's throw of Mirwouk, and this time the kobolds hesitated. The new trail was fresher than the old. Should they follow it?

Ben nodded and they did.

By midday, they had circled Mirwouk almost completely and crossed Willow's tracks yet a fourth time. Now she was moving *away* from the aged fortress. Bunion studied the tracks for several minutes, his face almost pressed up against the earth in his effort to read the markings. He announced finally that he couldn't tell which tracks were more recent. All seemed quite fresh.

The members of the little company stood staring at each other for a moment, undecided. Sweat lay in a thin sheen across the faces of Ben and Questor, and the G'home Gnomes were whining that they were thirsty. Abernathy was panting. Dust covered all of them like a mist. Eyes squinted against the glaring light of the sun, and faces grimaced and tightened with discomfort. They were all weary and cross and they were all sick and tired of running around in circles.

Though anxious to continue, Ben was nevertheless reluctantly considering the idea of a lunch break and a brief rest when a crashing sound brought him sharply about. The crashing sound was of stone breaking and falling. It was coming from the direction of Mirwouk.

He looked at the others questioningly, but no one seemed anxious to venture an opinion.

"Couldn't hurt to check it out at least," Ben declared and resolutely started off to investigate, the others trailing with various degrees of enthusiasm.

They picked their way upward through the tangle of scrub and trees, watching the crumbling walls and towers of Mir-

wouk appear through breaks in the branches and rise up before
them. Parapets loomed against the skyline, ragged and broken,
and shutterless windows gaped emptily. Bats darted past in
shadowy bursts and cried out sharply. Ahead, the crashing
sounds continued—almost as if something was trapped and
trying to break free. The minutes slipped away. The little company approached the sagging gates of the fortress and drew to
a halt, listening.

The crashing sounds had stopped.

"I don't like this one bit," Abernathy announced darkly.

"High Lord, perhaps we ought to . . ." Questor Thews
began, then stopped as he saw a look of disapproval cross Ben's
face.

"Perhaps we ought to have a look," Ben finished.

So they did, Ben leading, the kobolds a step behind, the
others trailing. They passed through the gates, crossed the
broad outer courtyard beyond, and slipped into the passageway
that ran from the secondary wall to the inner courtyard and the
main buildings. The passageway was long and dark and it
smelled of rot. Ben wrinkled his nose in distaste and hurried
ahead. There was still only silence.

Ben reached the end of the tunnel a dozen steps ahead of
everyone and was thinking to himself that he might have been
smarter to send Bunion ahead to look things over when he
caught sight of the stone giant. It was huge and ugly, a featureless, rough-hewn monstrosity that looked like the beginning stages of some novice sculptor's efforts at a tribute to Her-
cules. It appeared to be just a grotesque statue at first, standing
there in the middle of the inner courtyard amid a pile of stone
rubble. But then the statue moved, turning with a ponderous
effort that sounded of rock grating on rock, and it became immediately apparent that this particular statue was very much
alive.

Ben stared in bewilderment, not quite certain yet what to
do. A sudden tumult rose from the tunnel behind him, and the
others of the company emerged in a rush and practically ran
over him in their haste to get clear. The G'home Gnomes were

no longer whining; they were howling like injured cats. Abernathy and Questor were both yelling at once, and the kobolds were hissing and showing all their teeth in an unmistakable display of hostility. It took Ben a moment to realize that they weren't responding to anything they saw at *this* end of the tunnel but to something they had seen at the *other*.

Ben peered hurriedly past the frenzied group, neck craning. A second stone giant had entered the passageway and was lumbering toward them.

Questor grasped his elbow as if he might strangle it. "High Lord, that is a Flynt! It will smash us to dust if we let it get close enough . . . ! Ecchhh!" He saw the second one now, as it, too, lumbered forward. "Two of them! Run, High Lord—this way!"

The kobolds were already moving, leading the pack of them across the courtyard to an entryway that disappeared into the fortress proper. The first Flynt had joined the second and both were in pursuit, shambling giants that moved like bulldozers.

The company burst through the entryway and galloped up a flight of stairs.

"What's a Flynt?" Ben demanded of Questor as they fled. "I don't remember your telling me anything about Flynts!"

"I probably didn't tell you anything, High Lord," Questor acknowledged, breathing hard now. His robes tangled in his feet and he almost went down. "Drat!" He straightened, moving quickly on. "Flynts are aberrations—a creation of old magic, stone monsters brought to life. Very dangerous! They were sentinels of this fortress once, but I thought they were all destroyed centuries ago. Wizards created them. They don't think, they don't eat, they don't sleep, they barely see or smell—but they hear everything. Their intended purpose was to keep intruders out of Mirwouk, but of course that was a long time ago, so who knows what they think their purpose might be now? They seem rather intent on just smashing things. Ugh!" He slowed momentarily and somehow managed to look genuinely thoughtful. "Odd that I didn't come across them when I was here last."

Ben rolled his eyes and pulled the wizard ahead.

They reached the top of the stairwell and emerged on a parapet roof about the size of a tennis court. Rubble littered the playing surface. There were no referees in sight and only one other way out—a second stairwell at the far end. The company broke for it as one.

When they reached it, they found it blocked with enough timber and stone to build a set of bleachers.

"Wonderful!" Ben groaned.

"I told you I didn't like this!" Abernathy declared with a bark that surprised everyone.

The Flynts emerged from the far stairwell, looked slowly about, and began to lumber toward them. Bunion and Parsnip moved protectively in front of the others.

Now it was Ben's turn to grab Questor. "The kobolds can't stop those things, damn it! Dredge up some magic!"

Questor moved hurriedly forward, robes flying, tall figure swaying as if he might topple over. He muttered something unintelligible, lifted his arms skyward, and brought them down in a grand sweep. Funnel clouds sprang up from out of nowhere, picked up the loose rubble, and hurtled it at the approaching stone monsters. Unfortunately, the funnel clouds also hurtled some of it back at Questor. The rubble bounced harmlessly off the Flynts. It did not bounce harmlessly off Questor; the wizard went down in a heap, unconscious and bleeding.

Ben and the kobolds rushed to pull the wizard back from further harm. The Flynts still lumbered forward, stone blocks and rubble cracking like deadwood beneath their massive feet.

Ben knelt anxiously. "Questor! Get up! We need you!" He slapped the fallen wizard's face desperately, rubbed his wrists, and shook him. Questor didn't move. His owlish face was pale beneath the blood.

Ben leaped back to his feet. Individually, perhaps, the members of the little company were swift and agile enough to evade these stone monsters. Perhaps. But that was before Questor's injury. No one would get away trying to carry out the wizard, and they were certainly not about to leave him. Ben seized the medallion frantically and let go just as quickly. Useless. He was Meeks' creation now, his medallion a worthless imitation. There could be no help from the magic; there could be no summons to the Paladin.

But he had to do something!

"Abernathy!"

The dog's cold nose shoved into his ear, and he jerked away. "High Lord?"

"These things can't see, taste, or smell—but they can hear, right? Hear anything? Anything even close to Mirwouk, maybe?"

"I am given to understand that the Flynts can hear a pin drop at fifty paces, though I often . . ."

"Never mind the editorials!" Ben pulled the dog about to face him, furry features held close, glasses glinting with sunlight. "Can you hit high C?"

Abernathy blinked. "High Lord?"

"High C, damn it—can you howl loud enough to hit high C?" The Flynts were no more than a dozen paces off. "Well, can you?"

"I don't see . . ."

"Yes or no!"

He was shaking his scribe. Abernathy's muzzle drew back, and he barked right in Ben's face. "Yes!"

"Then do it!" Ben screamed.

The whole roof seemed to be shaking. The G'home Gnomes had fastened themselves to Ben once more, crying, "Great High Lord, mighty High Lord" in chorus and wailing like lost souls. The kobolds were crouched in front of him, ready to spring. The Flynts looked like tanks bearing down.

Then Abernathy began to howl.

He hit high C on the first try, a frightening wail that drowned out the G'home Gnomes and expanded the grimaces on the faces of the kobolds into a whole new dimension. The wail lifted and spread, cutting through everything with the tenacity of gastrically induced stress. The Flynts stopped in their tracks and their massive hands came up against the sides of their heads with a crash as they tried in vain to shut out the sound. It came at them relentlessly—Ben would never have believed Abernathy capable of such sustained agony—and all the while, they battered at themselves.

Finally, the pounding proved to be too much, and the Flynts simply shattered and fell apart. Heads, arms, torsos, and legs collapsed into piles of useless rock. The dust rose and settled again, and nothing moved.

Abernathy stopped howling, and there was a moment of strained silence. The scribe straightened and glared at Ben with undisguised fury. "I have *never* been so humiliated, High Lord!" he snarled. "Howling like a dog, indeed! I have debased myself in a way I would not have thought possible!"

Ben cleared his throat. "You saved our lives," he pointed out simply. "That's what you did."

Abernathy started to say something more, stopped, and simply continued to glare voicelessly. Finally he took a deep breath of air, exhaled, straightened some more, sniffed distastefully, and said, "When we get those books of magic back, the first thing you will do with them is find a way to turn *me* back into a human being!"

Ben hastily masked the smile that would have been his undoing. "Agreed. The first thing."

Hurriedly they picked up Questor Thews and carried him back down the stairway and out of Mirwouk. They encountered no further Flynts. Perhaps the two they had escaped had been the last, Ben thought as they hastened back into the trees.

"Still, it *is* odd that Questor didn't see them the first time," he repeated the wizard's observation to no one in particular.

"Odd? Not so odd if you consider the possibility that Meeks put them there *after* he had the books, expressly to prevent anyone from coming back into the fortress!" Abernathy huffed. He would not look at Ben. "Really, High Lord—I would have thought you could figure that one out by yourself!"

Ben endured the admonishment silently. He could have

figured it out by himself, but he hadn't, so what was there to say? What he couldn't figure out now was why Meeks would *bother* placing guards at Mirwouk. After all, the missing books of magic were already in his possession!

He dropped that question into the hopper with all the other unanswered questions and concentrated on helping the others lay Questor on a patch of shaded grass. Parsnip wiped away the dust and blood from the wizard's face and brought him out of his stupor. Questor recovered after a brief period of treatment, Parsnip patched up his injuries, and the little company was back on its feet once more.

"This time we follow Willow's tracks—however many of them there are—until we find her!" Ben declared resolutely.

"*If* we find her," Abernathy muttered.

But no one heard him and off they went again.

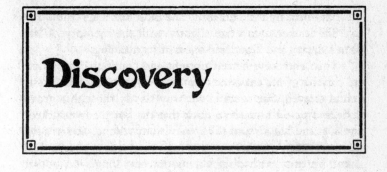

Discovery

The heat of the midday sun settled down across the forests of the Melchor in a suffocating blanket and turned its cooling shadows tepid and dank. Morning breezes died away and the air grew thick and still. Insects hummed their toneless songs, leaves hung limp from their branches, and the warm-blooded life of the woodland lay patient and quiet. There was a slowing of time and purpose.

Willow paused at the base of a giant white oak, the weight of the spun gold bridle tugging relentlessly downward on her shoulders where it lay draped across them. A bright sheen of sweat coated the pale green skin of her face and hands, and her lips parted slightly as she worked harder to catch her breath. She had been walking since sunrise, following the black unicorn as it came and went in wisps of dream and shadow, trailing after as if she were a stray bit of dust drawn on in the wake of its passing. She had traveled the whole of the Melchor about Mirwouk half-a-dozen times over, crossing and recrossing her trail time after time, a senseless journey of whim and chance. She was west of Mirwouk now, scarcely a mile from the aged fortress, but she was barely aware of it, and it would have made no difference to her had she taken the time to think about it. She had long since ceased to care about anything but the subject of her search; all else had become irrelevant.

She must find the unicorn. She must know its truth.

She let her eyes glaze slightly with the memory of last night's dream and wondered anew at its meaning.

Then she drew herself upright and continued on, a frail and tiny bit of life amid the giant trees of the mountain forest, a child strayed. She worked her way slowly through a grove of fir and pine clustered so thick that the boughs interlocked, barely glanced at a stand of Bonnie Blues beyond, and pressed upward along a gentle slope that led to a meadow plateau. She picked her way with careful steps, remembering wearily that she had passed this way before—once, twice, more? She wasn't certain. It didn't matter. She listened to the sound of her heart pounding through her neck and in her ears. It was very loud. It was almost the only sound in the forest. It became the measure of each step she took.

How much farther? she wondered as the heat pressed down. When am I to stop?

She crested the meadowline, paused in the shadow of a long-limbed crimson maple, and closed her eyes against the uncertainty. When she opened them again, the black unicorn stood facing her.

"Oh!" she breathed softly.

The unicorn stood at the center of the meadow, framed in a splash of unclouded sunlight. It was ink black, so perfectly opaque that it might have been sculpted from midnight's shadows. It faced her, head lifted, mane and tail limp in the breezeless air, a statue carved out of ageless ebony. The green eyes regarded her steadily and within their depths called to her. She breathed the sullen heat into her lungs and felt the scorch of the sun's brightness. She listened. The eyes of the unicorn spoke soundlessly, images caught and reflected from dreams remembered and visions lost. She listened, and she knew.

The chase was over. The black unicorn would run from her no longer. It was to this time and place that she had been brought. It only remained for her to discover why.

She came forward tentatively, still half expecting with every step she took that the unicorn would disappear, that it would bolt and run. It did not. It simply stood there—motionless, dreamlike. She slipped the bridle from her shoulders and held it loosely in her hands before her, letting the unicorn see it clearly. Sunlight danced off the traces and fastenings, brilliant flashes that pierced the forest shadows. The unicorn waited. Willow passed from the shade of the crimson maple into the meadow's sunshine, and the sweltering heat enveloped her. Her sea green eyes blinked away a sudden film of moisture, and she shook back her long hair. The unicorn did not move.

She was only a dozen feet from the creature when abruptly she slowed and then stopped. She could not go on. Waves of fear, suspicion, and doubt washed through her, a mingling of whispers that cried out in sudden warning. What was she doing? What was she thinking? The black unicorn was a creature of such ill fortune that no one who had come close to it had been seen again! It was the demon of her dreams! It was the nightmare that had pursued her in her sleep, hunting her as death would!

She felt the weight of the fairy creature's eyes settle on her. She felt its presence as she would a sickness. She struggled to break and run and could not. Desperately, she fought against the emotions that threatened to consume her and banished them. She took deep, long breaths of the sullen midday air and forced herself to look into the creature's emerald eyes. She kept her gaze fixed. There was no hint of sickness or death in those eyes—no hint of demon evil. There was gentleness and warmth—and need.

She came forward another few steps.

Then something new slowed her. There was a flash of intuition that swept her mind momentarily, quick and certain. Ben was near, come in search of . . . of what?

"Ben?" she whispered, waiting.

But there was no one. She was alone with the unicorn. She did not look away from the creature, but she sensed nevertheless that they were alone. She wet her lips and came forward again.

And again she stopped. Her breast heaved. "I cannot touch

you," she murmured to the flawless, impossibly wondrous fairy thing. "I cannot. It will be the end of me if I do."

She knew it was so. She knew it instinctively, the way she had always known. No one could touch a unicorn; no one had that right. It belonged to a realm of beauty that no mortal creature should ever attempt to transcend. It had wandered into Landover, a bit of some rainbow broken off from its dark storm's end arc, and it should never be held by hands such as hers. Memories of legends and songs whispered in snatches of warning. She felt tears start down her cheeks and her breath catch in her throat.

Beautiful thing, I cannot . . .

But she did. Almost before she realized what was happening, she was covering those last few paces in quick, mechanical steps, moving without thinking about what she was doing, reaching out to the midnight creature, and placing the bridle of spun gold gently, carefully about its waiting head. She brushed its silken face with her fingers as she worked, and the touch was electric. She felt the whisper of its mane against the backs of her hands, and the sensation was rife with wonder. Fresh images sprang unbidden into her thoughts, jumbled and not yet understandable, but irresistible nevertheless. She touched the unicorn freely now, reveling in the sensations it caused within her. She could not seem to help herself. She could not stop. She was crying anew, her emotions all uncovered, brought close to the surface of her being. Tears ran down her cheeks as she began to sob uncontrollably.

"I love you," she cried desperately, her hands falling away at last when the bridle was in place. "Oh, I love you so much, you beautiful, wondrous thing!"

The black unicorn's horn shone white with magic as it held her gaze, and there were tears now in its eyes as well. For a single moment, they were joined.

Then the moment was gone, and the world beyond intruded with a rush. A huge, dark shadow passed overhead and settled earthward at the clearing's far edge. In the same instant, a familiar scattering of voices called her name frantically from the clearing's other end. Her dreams took life, their images suddenly, terrifyingly all about. Whispers of the warnings that had brought her to this moment turned abruptly to screams of dismay in her mind.

She felt the black unicorn shudder violently next to her and watched the white magic of its horn flare. But it did not bolt into the woods. Whatever happened next, it would run no further.

So be it. Neither would she.

Woodenly, she turned to discover their fate.

Ben Holiday burst from the trees into the meadow and stopped so abruptly that the others of the little company who followed after stumbled into him in their eagerness to keep up and knocked him forward another few steps. They were all yelling at once, calling out to Willow in warning where she stood at the meadow's center, the black unicorn at her side. The shadow of the winged demon had passed overhead a moment earlier, a monstrous cloud against the sun. It was only the worst of luck that could have brought them all together at this same place and time, but the worst of luck seemed to be the only luck Ben could count on. He had tracked Willow to this meadow after escaping the Flynts, believing the worst to be behind him. Now the demon had found them. He saw again in his mind the River Master's doomed nymphs as the demon burned them to ash and he thought of his promise to the Earth Mother to protect Willow. But he was helpless to do that. How was he going to protect Willow without the medallion?

The demon flew overhead a second time, but it did not attack the sylph or the unicorn or even Ben's little group. Instead, it settled slowly earthward at the clearing's far edge, leathered wings folding in against its body, breath steaming with a hiss. Ben squinted against the sunlight. There was a rider atop the demon. The rider was Meeks.

And Meeks, of course, appeared to everyone watching to be Ben.

Ben heard muttered whispers of surprise and confusion

from those crowded up behind him. He watched himself climb slowly down from the demon; and even he had to admit that Meeks looked exactly like him. His companions quit yelling, momentary indecision settling in. Ben could feel their eyes bore into his back and could sense the clouds of doubt gathering. He had told them who he was and they had believed him, more or less, until now. But actually *seeing* Ben Holiday standing there in that clearing across from them was something else altogether . . .

Then the black unicorn trumpeted, a high, eerie call, and everyone turned. The fairy beast stamped and its nostrils flared, the bridle of spun gold dancing against the sunlight with each toss of its delicate head. Magic flashed in its ridged horn. The unicorn was a thing of impossible beauty and it drew the eyes of all gathered like moths to the light. It shuddered, but held its ground against the weight of their stares. It seemed to be searching for something.

Slowly Willow turned from the unicorn and began to look about as well. Her gaze was curiously empty.

Ben wasn't sure what was happening, but he decided almost instantly not to wait to find out. "Willow!" he called to the sylph, and her eyes fixed on him. "Willow, it's me, Ben!" He came forward a few steps, saw the lack of recognition in her eyes, and stopped. "Listen to me. Listen carefully. I know I don't look like myself. But it *is* me. Meeks is responsible for everything that's happened. He's come back into Landover and stolen the throne. He's changed me into this. Worse, he's made himself look like me. That's not me over there—that's Meeks!"

She turned now to look over at Meeks, saw Ben's face and body, and gave a quick gasp. But she saw the demon as well. She took a step forward, stopped, and stepped slowly back again.

"Willow, it's all right," Meeks called out to her in Ben's voice. "Bring the unicorn to me. Pass me the reins of the bridle."

"No!" Ben yelled frantically. "No, Willow!" He came forward another few steps, stopping quickly as Willow started to back away. "Willow, don't do it. Meeks sent the dreams—all of them. He has the medallion. He has the missing books of magic. Now he wants the unicorn! I don't know why, but you can't let him have it! Please!"

"Willow, be careful of what you see," Meeks warned in a quiet, soothing voice. "The stranger is dangerous, and the magic he wields confuses. Come over to me before he reaches you."

Ben was beside himself. "Look at whom I'm with, for God's sake! Questor, Abernathy, Bunion, Parsnip, Fillip, and Sot!" He turned and beckoned to those behind him. But no one came forward. No one seemed quite sure that they should. Ben felt a hint of desperation creep into his voice as he faced Willow anew. "Why would they be with me if I'm not who I say I am? They know the truth of things!" He wheeled about once more, anger in his voice. "Damn it, Questor, say something to her!"

The wizard hesitated, seemed to consider the advisability of doing what Ben asked, then straightened. "Yes, he speaks the truth. He is the High Lord, Willow," he said finally.

There were muttered hissings and murmurings of agreement from the others, including a few pleas of "Save us, great High Lord, mighty High Lord" from the G'home Gnomes, who were hiding now behind Questor's robes.

Ben turned back. "Willow, come over here quickly! Please! Get away!"

But now Meeks had come forward several paces and he was smiling Ben's most reassuring smile. "Willow, I love you," he told her. "I love you and I want to protect you. Come here to me. What you see from the stranger is all illusion. He has no support from our friends; they are just false images. You can see the truth of things if you look. Do you see me? Am I anyone different from the one I always was? What you are hearing are lies! Remember the dream! You must pick up the reins of the bridle and bring the black unicorn to me to be safe from the dangers that threaten! These illusions pretending friendship are the dangers of your dream! Come to me now and be safe!"

Willow was looking first one way and then the other, confusion evident in her face. Behind her, the black unicorn stamped and snorted delicately, a bit of shadow caught in the sunlight, bound in place by ties no one else could see. Ben was frantic. He had to do something!

"Show me the rune stone!" Willow called out suddenly, head jerking from Ben to Meeks and back again. "Let me see the stone I gave you!"

Ben went cold. The rune stone, the milky-colored talisman that warned of danger when it threatened. "I don't have it!" he called back helplessly. "I lost it when . . ."

"I have it right here!" Meeks announced in triumph, cutting him short. The wizard reached beneath his robes and brought forth the rune stone—or something that appeared to be the rune stone—glowing bright red. He held it up for inspection.

"Ben!" Willow asked softly, some of the hope coming back into her face. "Is it you?" Ben felt his stomach lurch as the girl started away from him.

"One moment!" Questor Thews called suddenly, and everyone turned. "You must have dropped this, High Lord," he advised officiously, coming forward a step or two more, the G'home Gnomes shaken free momentarily from his robes. He held out the rune stone Willow had given Ben—at least, his magic made it *seem* like the stone—and let everyone have a good look. The stone glowed crimson.

Ben had never been more grateful to the wizard in his life. "Thank you, Questor," he breathed quietly.

Willow had stopped again. Slowly, she backed away from them all, the indecision returned. There was fear now in her face as well. "I do not know which of you is Ben," she told them quietly. "Perhaps neither of you."

Her words lingered in the sudden stillness that followed. A frightening tension settled down across the sunlit meadow with its chessboard of frozen figures, each ready to move in a different direction, each poised to strike. Willow pressed back toward the black unicorn, eyes shifting from one set of playing pieces to another, waiting. Behind her, the unicorn had gone still.

I have to do something, Ben told himself once more and wondered frantically what it ought to be.

Then out of the woods strolled Edgewood Dirk. The cat might have been out for an afternoon walk, sauntering with an unconcerned air from the trees, picking its way delicately through the scrub grass and flowers, head and tail held high as it stepped, eyes looking neither right nor left. It paid no attention to any of them. It seemed almost to have stumbled onto things by accident. Dirk walked directly to the center of the clearing, stopped, glanced casually around at those assembled, and sat down.

"Good day," he greeted them.

Meeks let out a shriek that brought them all out of their boots and flung back his cloak. The Ben Holiday disguise shimmered like a reflection in the waters of a pond disturbed by a thrown stone and began to disintegrate. Willow screamed. The wizard's clawed hands lifted and extended, and green fire lanced wickedly toward Edgewood Dirk. But the cat had already begun to change, the small furry body growing, shimmering, and smoothing until it was as crystalline as a diamond. The wizard fire struck it and broke apart, scattering like refracted light into the sunlit air, showering the trees and grass and scorching the earth.

Ben was racing desperately toward Willow by this time, yelling like a madman. But the sylph was already beyond his reach. Eyes frantic, she had pressed herself back against the black unicorn and seized the golden bridle that bound the fairy creature. The unicorn was stamping and rearing, crying out its own high-pitched, eerie call, and darting back and forth in small dashes. Willow clung to the beast as a frightened child would to its mother, grappling with it, being dragged along as it went—away from Ben.

"Willow!" he howled.

Meeks was still after Edgewood Dirk. The shards of flame from his first attack had barely been scattered when the wizard struck once more. Fire gathered and arced from his hands in a massive ball, rolling and tumbling through the air to explode into the cat. Dirk arched and shuddered, and the flaming ball seemed to absorb itself into the crystalline form. Then the fire exploded out again, hurtling itself back toward the wizard in a shower of flaming darts. Meeks threw up his cloak like a shield, and the darts deflected everywhere. Some burned into the hide of the demon crouching behind the wizard and it roared and surged skyward with a rasp of fury.

Smoke and fire burned everywhere, and Ben stumbled on blindly through the haze. Behind him, his companions called out. Overhead, the winged demon blocked the sun, its shadow darkening the meadow like an eclipse. The black unicorn sprang forward with a scream, and Willow flung herself atop it. She might have done so out of instinct or out of need, but the result was the same—she was carried away. The unicorn darted past Ben so quickly he barely saw it. He reached for it, but he was far too slow. He had a brief glimpse of Willow's lithe form clinging to its back, and then both disappeared into the trees.

Then the winged demon attacked. It dropped like a stone toward the meadow, diving from the empty skies, flames bursting from its maw. Ben dropped flat and covered his head. From the corner of one eye, he watched as Dirk shimmered, hunched down against the force of the fire, absorbed it, and thrust it back. Flames hammered into the demon and sent the monster catapulting back. Steam and smoke clogged the meadow air.

Meeks struck again, and Edgewood Dirk repelled the assault. The demon struck, and the cat flung the fire back once more. Ben rose, dropped, rose again, and staggered blindly through the carnage. Shouts and cries reached out to him, and visions floated through the haze before his watering eyes. His hands groped and struggled to hold something, anything—and finally fastened on the medallion.

White heat burned into his palms. For just an instant, he thought he saw the Paladin appear, a faint image somewhere in the distance, a silver, armor-clad figure astride the great white charger.

Then the vision was gone again, a vision that had been impossible in any case. No medallion, no Paladin—Ben knew that. His throat constricted and he choked as the fires of wizard and demon continued to hammer down on Edgewood Dirk and be flung back again. Flowers and grasses burned to black ash. Trees shook and their leaves wilted. The whole world seemed to be in flames.

And finally the meadow itself seemed to explode upward in one vast, heaving cough, steam and fire ripping through everything. Ben felt himself hurtled skyward like a bit of deadwood, flying in a graceless scattering of arms and legs, spinning like a pinwheel.

This is it, he thought just before he tumbled earthward. This is how it all ends.

Then he struck with jarring force and everything went dark.

Cat's Paw

*B*en Holiday came awake again in a deeply shaded forest glade that smelled of moss and wild flowers. Birds sang in the trees, their songs bright and cheerful. A small stream wound through the center of the clearing from the woodlands and disappeared back into them again. There was a stillness that whispered of peace and solitude.

Ben was lying on a patch of grass staring up into a network of branches set against the cloudless sky. A glimpse of the sun peeked through the leaves. He pushed himself carefully upright, aware that his clothes were singed and his hands and arms covered with soot. He took a moment to check himself, feeling about for permanent injuries. There were none—only bumps and bruises. But he looked as if he had rolled through half-a-dozen campfires.

"Feeling better, High Lord?"

He turned at the sound of the familiar voice and found Edgewood Dirk sitting comfortably atop a large, mossy rock, paws tucked carefully away. The cat blinked sleepily and yawned.

"What happened to me?" Ben asked, realizing that this clearly wasn't where he had started out; this wasn't the meadow where he had lost consciousness. "How did I get here?"

Dirk stood up, stretched, and sat down again. "I brought

you. It was quite a trick, actually, but I have gotten rather good at using energy to transport inert objects. It did not seem advisable to leave you lying about in that burned-out meadow."

"What about the others? What about Willow and . . ."

"The sylph is with the black unicorn, I imagine. I wouldn't know exactly where. Your companions were scattered in every which direction. That last explosion sent them all flying. Such magic is best left unused. Too bad Meeks cannot understand that."

Ben blinked away a final rush of dizziness and studied the cat. "He knew who you were, didn't he?"

"He knew *what* I was."

"Oh. How is that, Dirk?"

The cat seemed to consider the question. "Wizards and prism cats have crossed paths a few times before, High Lord."

"And not as friends, I gather?"

"Not usually."

"He seemed frightened of you."

"He is frightened of many things."

"He's not alone in that respect. What happened to him?"

"He lost interest in the fight and flew off on his pet demon. He has gone for the books of magic, I would guess. He believes he requires their power. Then he will be back. He will hunt you all down this time out, I think. You had better prepare yourself."

Ben went cold. Slowly he straightened himself, feeling the kinks in his body loosen. "I have to find the others," he began, trying to think his way through the wall of fear and desperation that quickly settled in. "Damn! How am I supposed to do that?" He started up, slowed as a dizziness swept through him, and dropped back to one knee. "How am I supposed to help them at all, for that matter? I would have been finished back there if not for you. This whole business has gotten completely out of hand. I'm no better off than I was the day Meeks had me thrown out of the castle. I still don't know why it is that no one can recognize me. I still don't have any idea how Meeks got hold of the medallion. I still don't know what he wants with the black unicorn. I don't know one thing more than I ever did about what is going on!"

Dirk yawned anew. "Don't you?"

Ben didn't hear him. "I'll tell you one thing. I can't handle this by myself. I never could. There isn't any point in kidding myself; I have to have help. I'm going to do what I should have done in the first place. I'm going into the mists, medallion or no medallion, and find the fairies. I'll do what I did before. I'll find them and ask them for a magic that will let me stand up to Meeks. They helped me with Nightshade; they'll help me with Meeks. They have to."

"Ah, but that's not true, is it?" Dirk asked softly. "The fairies help only when they choose. You know that, my dear High Lord. You have always known that. You cannot demand their aid; you can only wish for it. The choice of giving or withholding it is always theirs."

"It doesn't matter." Ben shook his head stubbornly. "I'm going into the mists. When I find them, I'll . . ."

"*If* you find them," Dirk interrupted.

Ben paused, then flushed. "It would be nice to have some encouragement from you for a change! What makes you think I *won't* find them?"

Dirk regarded him for a moment, then sniffed the air. All about, the birds continued to sing indifferently. "Because they don't want you to find them, High Lord," the cat said finally. He sighed. "You see, *they* have already found *you*."

There was a long moment of silence as Ben and the cat stared at each other, eyes locked. Ben cleared his throat. "What?"

Dirk's eyes lidded to half-mast. "High Lord, who do you think sent me?"

Ben sat back down slowly, crossed his legs before him, and dropped his hands into his lap. "The fairies sent you?" The cat said nothing. "But why? I mean, why you, Dirk?"

"You mean, why a cat? Why not a dog? Or a lion or a tiger? Or another Paladin, for that matter? Is that what you mean?" Dirk's fur ruffled on the nape of his neck and down the arch of his back. "Well, a cat is all that you need or deserve, my dear High Lord! More, in point of fact! I was sent to arouse your consciousness—to make you think! I was not sent to provide salvation! If you want salvation, you will have to find it within yourself! That is the way it has always been and that is the way it will always be!"

He stood up, jumped down from the rock, and strode deliberately up to an astonished Ben. "I am tired of pussy-footing around with you. I have told you everything you need to know to counteract the magic that has been used against you. I have done everything but shove your nose in the truth of matters, and that I cannot do! That is forbidden! Fairy kind never reveal truth to mortal creatures. But I have kept you safe on your journey when you needed keeping safe, though you haven't needed it nearly so often as you believed. I have watched over you and guided you when I could. Most important of all, I have kept you thinking and that in turn has kept you alive!" He paused. "Well, all that is finished now. Your time for thinking is just about up!"

Ben shook his head quickly. "Dirk, I can't just . . ."

"Let me finish!" the cat snapped. "When in the world will humans learn to start listening to cats?" The green eyes narrowed. "The fairies sent me to help you, High Lord, but they left it to me to choose the means. They did not advise me on what I was to do or say. They did not tell me why it was that they believed I could help. Such is not the way of the fairies— nor is it the way of cats! We do as we choose in any case and live our lives as we must. We play games because that is who we are. Cat games or fairy games, it is all very much the same. Ours, High Lord, is a much different world from your own!"

One paw lifted. "Hear me well, then. No one is entitled to be given answers to the problems that beset them. No one is given life on a silver platter—cat or King! If you wish to know the truth of things, you must find it out for yourself. If you wish to understand what puzzles you, reason it through for yourself. You believe yourself mired in insolvable dilemmas. You believe yourself incapable of breaking free. Your identity is gone, your kingdom stolen. Your enemies beset you, your friends are lost. It is a chain of complications in which the links are joined, Ben Holiday. Cut free a single link, and the chains fall apart! But you are the one who carries the cutters— not me, not anyone else. That is what I have been trying to tell you from day one! Do you understand?"

Ben nodded hastily. "I understand."

The paw lowered again. "I hope so. Now I will say this one more time. The magic you struggle against is magic of deception—a mirror that alters in its reflection truths and makes them half-truths and lies. If you can see past the mirror, you can set yourself free. If you can set yourself free, you can help your friends. But you had better get busy!"

He stretched, turned, walked several paces away, and turned back again. The forest glade was quiet now; even the birds in the trees had gone still. Sunlight continued to shine out of the skies from overhead, casting the dappled shadows of the leaves and branches across the clearing beneath, leaving Ben and Dirk spotted and striped.

"The dark wizard is frightened of you, Ben Holiday," Dirk advised softly. "He knows you to be close to the answers you need to break free, and he will try to destroy you before that can happen. I have given you the means to find the answers that will defeat him. Use those means. You are an intelligent man. You have been a man who has spent his life ordering other men's lives. Man of law, man of power—order now your own!"

He moved soundlessly to the glade's edge, never looking back. "I have enjoyed our time together, High Lord," he called back. "I have enjoyed our travels. But they are over for now. I have other places to be and other appointments to keep. I will think of you. And one day, perhaps, I will see you again."

"Wait, Dirk!" Ben called after, coming suddenly to his feet, fighting against the continuing dizziness.

"I never wait, High Lord," the cat replied, now almost lost in shadow. "Besides, there is nothing more I can do for you. I have done everything I can. Good luck to you."

"Dirk!"

"Remember what I told you. And try listening to cats once in a while, would you?"

"Dirk, damn it!"

"Good-bye."

And with that Edgewood Dirk disappeared into the forest and was gone.

Ben Holiday stared after the cat for a long time following its departure, half expecting that it would return. It didn't, of course, just as he had known all along somewhere deep inside that it wouldn't. When he finally accepted the fact, he quit looking for it and began to panic. He was all alone for the first time since being cast out of Sterling Silver—all alone and in the worst predicament of his life. He was without his identity or his medallion, and he had no idea at all how to regain either. Edgewood Dirk, his protector, had deserted him. Willow had disappeared with the black unicorn, still believing him the stranger he appeared to be. His friends were scattered to heaven-knew-where. Meeks had gone for the books of magic and would return shortly to put an end to him.

And here he sat, waiting for it to happen.

He was stunned. He could not seem to think clearly. He tried to reason, to think what he should do next, but everything seemed to jumble up, the problems and needs fighting for equal time in his thoughts. He rose, his motions mechanical, his eyes dead, and walked to the edge of the little stream. He glanced once more after Dirk, saw only empty forest, and turned back again, a feeling of bleak resignation settling through him. He knelt down beside the stream and splashed water on his soot-blackened face, rubbing it into his eyes. The water was like ice, and it sent a shock through his system. He splashed some more on, throwing it up over his head and shoulders, letting the cold galvanize him.

Then he sat back, the water dripping off his face, his eyes looking down into the stream.

Reason it through, he admonished himself. You have all

the answers. Dirk said you had all the answers. So what in the hell are they?

He resisted an almost overwhelming urge to leap up and charge off into the trees. He forced himself to stay put. Action would have been more immediately gratifying—the sense of doing something, *anything*, better than just sitting around. But running about heedlessly wasn't what the situation called for; thinking was. He had to know what he was doing, had to understand once and for all what had happened.

Links in a chain, Dirk had said. All his problems were links in a chain, all locked together. Cut one, and the chain would fall apart. Okay. He would do that. He would cut that link. But which link should he cut?

He looked down into the waters of the stream, staring at the rippling reflection of his image. A distorted version of Ben Holiday's face glimmered back at him. But it was he, not someone else, not the stranger everyone else saw. What was it that made others see him differently? A mask, Dirk had said—and he was disappearing into it. He stared at himself for a long moment, then looked up again, focusing on a random gathering of wild flowers several yards beyond, seeing them and seeing nothing.

Magic of deception, Dirk had said.

Whose magic? Whose deception?

His own, the River Master had said. The River Master had offered to help, had tried in fact, but in the end couldn't. The magic at work was magic of Ben's own making, the River Master had said—and only he could act to break its hold.

But what magic had he used?

He tried to think it through, but couldn't. Nothing would come. He rocked back on his heels beside the little stream, hunched down in the shadows of the mountain glade and let his mind wander freely for a moment. It all went back to that night in his bedchamber in Sterling Silver when Meeks had appeared before him from out of nowhere. That was when everything had gone wrong and he had lost the medallion. Something grated at the memory, and he grasped futilely at it.

He had lost the medallion, he had lost his identity, he had lost his magic, he had lost his kingdom. A chain of links that needed breaking, he thought. He recalled his shock at finding the medallion gone. He remembered his fear.

A sudden thought struck him, and a memory stirred. The fairies had said something to him once about fear. It had been the only time they had spoken to him, long ago now, back when he had gone into the mists in search of the Io Dust, back when he had first come into Landover and been forced to fight to gain recognition for his right to the throne—just as he was fighting now. What was it they had said? *Fear has many disguises. You must learn to recognize them when next they come for you.*

He frowned. Disguises? Masks? Not much difference between the two, he mused. He had wondered what the words had meant. He found himself wondering again now. At the time, he thought they had referred to his impending encounter with the Iron Mark. But what if they had referred to what was happening to him now—to the fear he was experiencing over the loss of the medallion?

Could the fairies have foreseen that loss so long ago? Or was the warning simply generic, simply . . .

About the magic of this land?

Self-consciously, he reached within his tunic and brought forth the medallion he now wore, the medallion Meeks had given him, its face graven with the dark wizard's harsh visage. It all began here—the questions, the mysteries, a jumble of events that had swept him away from everything sane into this mire of fear and doubt. How could it have happened, he wondered for at least the hundredth time? How could he have lost the medallion without knowing it? How had Meeks gotten the medallion from him when only he could remove it? It didn't make sense! Even if he *had* removed it, why couldn't he *remember* removing it?

Unless he hadn't!

There was a sudden, hollow feeling in the pit of his stomach. Oh, God!

Unless he was still wearing it!

Something had nudged his thinking a step farther than it had gone before. He could almost see the cutters working on his chains. Self-deception, Dirk had said. Magic of his own making, the River Master had said. Damn! He felt his breath begin to come in short, ragged gasps of excitement; he could hear his chest pounding. It made sense. It was the only answer that had ever made sense. Meeks couldn't take the medallion from him unless he removed it himself, but he couldn't remember removing it, and the reason he couldn't remember removing it was because he never had removed it!

Meeks had simply made him think so.

But how?

He tried to think it through a step at a time. His hands were shaking with excitement, the medallion spinning in their grip. He still wore the medallion of the High Lords of Landover; he simply hadn't realized it. Was that possible? His mind raced ahead, exploring the possibilities, whispering to him in a quick, urgent voice. He still wore the medallion! Meeks had simply disguised it somehow, made him think it wasn't the real medallion, just a substitute. That would explain why Meeks hadn't simply finished him off in his bedchamber. Meeks was afraid that the Paladin might still appear—that the disguise was too new, too thin perhaps. That's why the wizard had let him go after giving him the strange warning about not taking off the substitute medallion. He had expected Ben to question that warning sooner or later. He had hoped Ben would take off the medallion and throw it away, thinking he was breaking free. Then Meeks would have had the medallion for good!

His mind spun. The language, he thought suddenly! How could he still communicate in the language of Landover if he wasn't wearing the medallion? Questor had told him long ago that the medallion was the reason he could understand the land's language, could write it, and could speak it! Why hadn't he thought of that before? And Questor—Questor had always wondered how Meeks got the medallion back from failed candidates for the kingship who refused to return it voluntarily. He would have done it something like this! He would have tricked them into taking it off, thinking they had already lost it!

My God! Could all this be possible?

He took a deep breath to steady himself. Could it be anything else? He tacked on a negative answer immediately. It was the only answer that made any sense. The winged demon hadn't broken off the attack on the River Master's nymphs at Elderew because of Dirk; it had flown off because it had seen the medallion held in Ben's hands and been frightened of its power. The demon had recognized the truth when Ben couldn't. Magic had disguised the truth from Ben—magic Meeks had employed that night in his bedchamber—an old magic, Ben thought suddenly. That was what Nightshade had said to Strabo. That was why only the witch and the dragon could recognize it!

But how did the magic work? What was needed to break its spell? Was it this same magic that had changed his identity?

The questions tumbled over one another in their efforts to be answered. Deception—that was the key word, the word Dirk had used repeatedly. Meeks must have used his magic to deceive Ben into believing the medallion he wore was another than his own. And Ben had believed the deception to be the truth. He had let the deception become his own. Damn! He had built his own prison! Meeks must have caused him to dream that he had given up the medallion, and he had convinced himself of its truth!

In which case, shouldn't he be able simply to . . .

He couldn't finish the thought. He was afraid to finish it, afraid he might be wrong. He took another deep breath. It didn't matter that he finish it. It mattered only that he test it. He would *have* to test it to know for sure.

He stared down again into the stream, watching his face shimmer and change with the movement of the water. His mask, he thought—not to him, but to everyone else. He steadied himself, then held the medallion out before him, hands grasping the chain, the visage of Meeks dangling and spinning slowly, reflecting the sunlight in small glimmerings of dull silver. He slowed his breathing deliberately, his heartbeat, and time itself. He focused his gaze on the tarnished image, watching the spinning motion slow, watching until the medallion was almost perfectly still. He shoved the image he was seeing from his mind and substituted in its place a picture from his memory of the Paladin riding out from the gates of Sterling Silver against the sunrise. He looked past the tarnish and the wear and envisioned polished silver. He gave himself over to his vision.

Remember, what you're seeing is all a lie, he told himself. Just a lie.

But nothing happened. The medallion before him continued to reflect the image of Meeks. He fought down a renewed surge of panic and forced himself to remain calm. Something more was needed. Something.

His mind sifted, considering and discarding possibilities. He kept his eyes focused on the medallion. The mountain forest was still about him, the silence complete save for brief snatches of bird songs and the rustle of the wind through the leaves. He was right about this; he knew he was right. Break the first link, and the others would follow. The chain would fall apart. He would become himself again, the power of the Paladin would return, and his magic would be freed. He need only find a key . . .

He caught himself in midthought. Slowly his fingers eased along the length of chain to the medallion itself. Lightly they caressed the tarnished surface, then gathered the talisman into his palms. Its feel was abhorrent to him—but then Meeks would want it that way. His hands closed. He held the medallion, gripped it tightly, felt its surface, its graven image, and envisioned not Meeks, but the Paladin riding out of Sterling Silver, riding out at sunrise, riding to him . . .

Something began to happen. The medallion grew warm to the touch, and there was a barely perceptible change in its feel. He gripped it harder, the image he knew to be hidden there locked firmly in the forefront of his thoughts. He closed his eyes. The image was a beacon of whiteness that became his only light. The medallion burned, but he kept his grip on it. He could sense a shifting in its surface as if something were falling away, a skin being shed. *Yes!* The burning continued, then flared sharply, spread through the whole of his body, lifted away, and dissipated into air.

Coolness returned. Slowly he opened his eyes, then his fingers. He looked down at the medallion that nestled in his palm. It was bright and untarnished. He could see himself mirrored in its surface. The image of the Paladin glimmered back at him.

He permitted himself a huge, almost foolish smile. He had been right after all. The medallion had been his all along.

The chain that had bound him was broken!

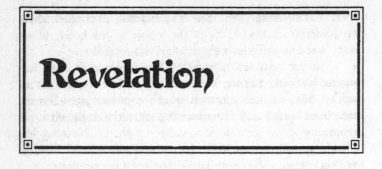

Revelation

*W*illow stirred, consciousness returning as she made the slow, languid slide out of slumber. The sun was warm upon her skin, and tall grasses tickled her face. She blinked, squinted against the sudden brightness, and let her eyes close again. She had dreamed—or had she? She had flown on a cloud, riding wind currents that whipped and buffeted her and bore her over all the world as if she were a bird on wing. She blinked again, feeling the press of the earth against her back. She had been so free.

Then the drifting sensation slipped from her, and a sudden return of memory jarred her completely awake. She sat upright with a start. There had been no dream. There had been only the reality of her flight from Meeks, the winged demon, the others . . .

A shudder passed through her body. She forced her eyes open again, squinting against the sunlight. She sat within a wide clearing in a grove of hardwood trees and scattered pines almost within the shadow of Mirwouk. The walls of the ancient fortress loomed behind her, jagged heights rough against the afternoon sky. Flowers dotted the hillside which spread away below her, their smells filling the still, humid air. The whole of the mountains about her were strangely silent.

Her eyes shifted. A dozen feet away, the black unicorn

stood looking at her, the bridle of spun gold still fastened about its slender head.

"I rode you," she whispered almost soundlessly.

The memory was a jumble of images and feelings that washed over her like ice water and shocked her with their intensity. She had barely known what she was doing when she had pulled herself atop the unicorn's back, terrified by what was happening about her, frantic to escape its horror. Nothing was what it appeared—not Ben, not the stranger who claimed to be Ben, not that cat, nothing. There was fire and destruction all about—such hatred! She had only thought to flee, and something in the touch of the unicorn's body against her own as it had surged past had drawn her after. Hands on the golden bridle, fingers locking in the mane, on the sleek body, and about the slender neck, her own face pressed close . . . The images stirred and vanished, feelings more than pictures, a whisper of need and want.

Her breath came in a small gasp. She had mounted the black unicorn without thinking, and her flight—for that indeed was what it had been—had been magical. There had been no sense of place or time; there had been only an acute sense of being. The unicorn had done more than carry her away from that meadow. The unicorn had carried her away from herself, down inside herself to see all about who and what she was and might be, until the thought of it had left her dazed and filled with wonder. The unicorn had shown her a texture and meaning to life that she would never have believed possible. Just its touch had been enough; nothing more was needed. There were tears in her eyes as she remembered how it had felt. The images were strangely clouded now, but the emotions she had experienced remained sharp and clear. How glorious it had been!

She brushed at the tears and let her gaze meet that of the watching unicorn. It still waited on her. It did not run as it might have, perhaps as it should. It simply waited.

But what was it waiting for? What did it want from her?

Confusion swept through her. The truth of the matter was that she didn't know. She looked into the emerald eyes of the black unicorn and wished the fairy creature could tell her. She needed to know. Here it was, this wondrous being, waiting almost resignedly while she pondered, waiting on her once more—and she didn't have any idea at all what she should do. She felt helpless and afraid. She felt herself a fool.

But she knew she could not afford such feelings, and she blocked them roughly from her mind. Meeks might still hunt them—probably did. That cat, whatever it was, would not delay the wizard long. He would come after her, after the unicorn, after them both. Meeks wanted the black unicorn; the stranger had been right about that. That meant that the stranger might have been right about the dreams as well.

And that, in turn, meant that the stranger might really be Ben.

A twinge of desperate longing raced through her, but she brushed it quickly aside. There was no time to consider the possibility now. The black unicorn was in immediate danger, and she had to do something to help it. It was clearly waiting on her, depending on her, and expecting something from her. She had to find out what.

There was only one way. She knew it instinctively. She would have to touch the unicorn, expose herself to its magic. She would have to open herself to its vision.

She breathed deeply, slowly, trying to steady herself. The sudden fear she experienced made her queasy. She was proposing the unthinkable. No one touched a unicorn and was ever herself again. No one. Oh, yes, she had touched the fairy creature already—a brushing against its body as she slipped the golden bridle in place and a clinging as she rode it to safety from that meadow. But both times she had been barely aware of what she was doing; it had all been something from a brief, wondrous dream that might never have been. What she would do now was entirely different, willful and deliberate, and she would be risking everything she was. The legends were uniform. Unicorns belonged to no one but themselves. Touch one and you were lost.

Yet she was going to do it anyway. The decision had already been made. The black unicorn was more than a legend out of tales a thousand years old, more than the dream that had drawn her on, more even than the reality of its physical being. It was an inescapable want that was an integral and undeniable part of her, a mystery that she must solve. The emerald eyes of the creature reflected her most secret urgings. She could keep nothing of herself hidden. Her own body betrayed her, its need for the unicorn an irresistible force. There was desire in her that surpassed anything she had ever known. The dangers that the black unicorn might pose, imagined or real, paled beside such desire. She had to solve its puzzle, whatever the cost. She had to know its truth.

She went hot and cold and she felt feather light as she rose and started forward. She was trembling, the horror and the anticipation mixing within her in equal measures, driving her reason from her, and leaving only her need.

Oh, Ben, she thought desperately! Why aren't you here?

The black unicorn waited patiently, an ebony statue in the dappled shadows, eyes locked on Willow's. There was a curious sense of its both not and always being mirrored in the sylph— as if it were her most carefully guarded wish, projected into being from her mind.

"I have to know," she whispered to the unicorn as she stood at last before it.

Slowly, her hands came up.

The meadow, once grassy and bright with wild flowers, lay in ruins, a charred, smoking stretch of barren earth amid the forest trees. Questor Thews stood at its edge and peered futilely through the haze. He was covered with dust and ash, his tall, stooped figure more ragtag in appearance than ever, gray robes and colored silks singed and torn, harlequin leather boots scuffed and smudged. That last exchange of magic between Meeks, the demon, and Edgewood Dirk had sent him flying. The wind had been knocked from him, and he'd found himself resting rather precariously in the branches of an aged crimson maple, an object of great delight for the squirrels and birds nesting there. Abernathy, the kobolds, and the gnomes were nowhere to be seen. Ben Holiday, Willow, and the black unicorn had disappeared. Questor had climbed down from that maple and gone searching for them all. He hadn't found a one.

Now his wanderings had brought him back to where he had last seen any of them. And none of them appeared to be here either.

He sighed deeply, his owlish face lined with worry. He wished he knew more of what was going on. He accepted now that the stranger who claimed to be Ben Holiday was in fact who he said he was; the man who appeared to be Ben Holiday was in fact Meeks. The dreams Willow, Ben, and he had experienced had been, in fact, the creations of his half-brother, all part of some bigger plan to gain control over Landover and the magic. But acceptance of all this gained him nothing. He still didn't know what the black unicorn had to do with anything nor did he understand yet what plan Meeks was trying to implement. Worst of all, he didn't have any idea at all how to find any of this out.

He rubbed his bearded chin and sighed again. There had to be a way, of course. He just had to figure it out

"Hmmmmm," he mused thoughtfully. But his thinking produced nothing.

He shrugged. Well, there was nothing more to be accomplished by standing about.

He started to turn away and found himself face to face with Meeks. His half-brother had reverted to his normal form, a tall, craggy figure with grizzled white hair and hard, dead eyes. Dark blue robes cloaked his body like a shroud. He stood less than a dozen yards away, just a step or two back in the trees from the clearing's edge. The black-gloved hand of his one good arm cradled the missing books of magic close against his chest.

Questor Thews felt his stomach lurch.

"I have waited a long time for this moment," Meeks whispered. "I have been very patient."

Dozens of random thoughts rushed through Questor's

mind and were gone, leaving only one. "I am not frightened of you," he said quietly.

His half-brother's face was unreadable. "You should be, Questor. You think yourself a wizard now, but you are an apprentice still. You will never be more than that. I have power you never even dreamed could exist! I have the means to do anything!"

"Except catch the black unicorn, it appears," Questor answered bravely.

The dead eyes flickered briefly with rage. "You understand nothing—not you, not Holiday, not anyone. You play a game you cannot win and you play it poorly. You are a distraction to be removed." The pale, creased face was a death mask. "I have endured exile and a disruption of my plans—all brought about by you and this play-King—and neither of you understands yet what it is that you have done. You are pathetic!"

The dark robes seemed to twitch where the right sleeve hung empty. "Your time in this world and life is just about over, half-brother. You stand alone. That prism cat no longer threatens me. Holiday is helpless and abandoned. The sylph and the black unicorn have nowhere left to run. Your other friends are already mine—all but the dog, and the dog is of no consequence."

Questor felt his heart sink. The others were prisoners—all but Abernathy?

Meeks smiled now, a cold, empty smile. "You were the last possible threat to me, Questor. And now I have you."

Questor stiffened, anger pushing back his fear. "You do not have me yet! Nor will you ever have me!"

The other's laugh was soundless. "Won't I?"

His head inclined slightly, and dozens of shadows slipped from behind the trees all about him. The shadows materialized with the light into small, crooked children with pointed ears, wizened faces, and scaled bodies. Pig snouts sniffed the forest air and serpent tongues slipped between rows of sharpened teeth.

"Demon imps!" Questor exclaimed softly.

"Rather a few too many for you to do much about, wouldn't you say?" His half-brother's words hissed at him with undisguised pleasure. "I don't care to waste my time with you, Questor. I prefer to leave you to them."

The demon imps had completely surrounded Questor, eyes bright and anxious, tongues licking their snouts. Meeks was right. There were too many. Nevertheless, he held his ground. There was no point in trying to run. His only chance was to catch them off guard . . .

They had closed to within half-a-dozen yards, a tight circle of ugly little faces and sharp teeth, when Questor whirled about, hands pinwheeling, and sent them all flying with a burst of magic. Smoke and steam geysered from out of nowhere, flinging them away, and Questor was loping desperately back into the concealing shadows of the forest, leaping over the squirming, momentarily blinded demon imps as if they were mud puddles. Squeals of rage chased after him. The demon imps were up and skittering in pursuit almost instantly. He whirled to face them. Again he sent an explosion of magic into their midst, and again they were scattered. But there were so many! They came at him from everywhere, chittering and squealing, grasping at his robes. He tried to defend himself, but it was too late. They were all over him, pulling at him, pinning his arms to his body. He swayed with the weight of them and toppled over.

Clawed hands fastened to his clothing, then to his throat. He began to choke, unable to breathe. He struggled valiantly, but there were dozens holding him down. Flashes of light danced before his eyes.

He had just a momentary glimpse through the tangle of demon imps of a smiling Meeks standing over him before he blacked out.

Willow's hands were inches from the black unicorn's delicate ebony head when she heard a faint rustling of leaves and brush, the sound of someone approaching through the trees. She drew back quickly from the unicorn, startled, wary.

A moment later, a shaggy head pushed out from the foliage and peered about intently through eyeglasses knocked partially askew by a veil of interlocking pine boughs.

It was Abernathy.

"Willow, is that you?" the scribe asked in disbelief.

He shoved past the remaining branches and stepped into the clearing. His dress clothes were in shreds, the greater part of his tunic torn from his body. His boots were gone completely. His fur was singed and his face looked as if it had been shoved into an ash pit. He was panting heavily, and his tongue licked out at his black nose.

"I have had better days, I want you to know," he declared. "I may have had worse, but I cannot remember when. First, I traipse all over creation in search of you and this . . . this animal for heaven knows what reason, because I surely do not, then we find, not just you and it, but Meeks and his demon as well, then the cat appears and there is a pointless exchange of magic that seems to do little more than fire up a whole section of the forest, and finally we are all scattered to the four winds and no one can find anyone!"

He gulped a chestful of air, gave out a long sigh and glanced about. "Have you seen any of the others?"

Willow shook her head, distracted. "No, none of them." Her thoughts were of the unicorn, of the need that consumed her, of her desire to reach out and touch . . .

"What are you doing here?" Abernathy asked suddenly, the sound of his voice startling her. The scribe saw her consternation. "Is something wrong, Willow? What are you doing with the unicorn? You know how dangerous that creature is. Come away, now. Come over and let me look at you. The High Lord would want . . . "

"Have you seen him?" she demanded sharply, the mention of Ben a lifeline for which she quickly grasped. "Is he close?"

Abernathy shoved his glasses further up his nose. "No, Willow—I haven't seen him. He was lost with the rest of us." He paused. "Are you all right?"

The lifeline disappeared. She nodded without speaking.

She felt the heat of the afternoon sun, the swelter of the day, and the closeness of the air. She was in a prison that threatened to bury her. The sounds of birds and insects faded into silence, the presence of Abernathy lost meaning, and her desire for the black unicorn consumed her anew. She turned from the scribe and began to reach again for the beast.

"Wait!" Abernathy fairly shouted. "What are you doing, girl? Do not touch that creature! Don't you realize what will happen to you?"

"Stay away from me, Abernathy," she replied softly, but hesitated nevertheless.

"Are you as mad as the rest of them?" the dog snapped angrily. "Has everyone gone crazy? Doesn't anyone but me understand what is happening? The dreams are a lie, Willow! Meeks brought us to this place, tricked us into serving his interests, and made fools of us all! That unicorn is probably something that belongs to him! You cannot know what its purpose might be! Do not touch it!"

She glanced quickly back at the dog. "I have to. I need to."

Abernathy started forward, saw the look of warning in the sylph's green eyes, and quickly stopped. "Willow, do not do this! You know the stories, the legends!" His voice dropped to a whisper. "You will be lost, girl!"

She stared silently at him for a long moment, then smiled. "But that is exactly the point, Abernathy. I am already lost."

Her hands came up swiftly and fastened about the neck of the black unicorn.

It was as if a cold fire swept through her. The fire burned from her hands into her arms and down her body. She stiffened against its feel and shuddered heavily. She threw back her head and gasped for breath. She heard Abernathy call out frantically from behind her and then lost track of him. He was there, but no longer visible to her. She could see nothing now but the face of the unicorn before her, a disembodied shape against a backdrop of space. The fire consumed her, mingled with her desire, and turned it into unrestrained passion. She was losing control of herself, beginning to come apart. A moment longer, and she would cease to be herself entirely.

She tried to remove her hands from the fairy creature's neck and found she could not. She was joined to the unicorn. She was one with it.

Then the ridged horn began to glow white with magic, and a jumble of images ripped through her mind. There was a place of empty coldness. There were chains and fire, tapestries of white on which unicorns bounded and leaped, dark-robed wizards, and spells being cast in endless succession. There was Meeks, Ben, and the Paladin.

And finally there was a cry of such terror and longing that it shattered the images as if they had been formed of glass.

Set me free!

The pain of that cry was too much for her to bear. She screamed, and her scream jerked her sharply backward, tearing her free at last of the unicorn. She stumbled and almost fell—would have fallen, had not Abernathy's arms come quickly about her to hold her upright.

"I saw!" she gasped and could speak no more.

But the sound of her scream still echoed through the trees.

Combat

*T*he scream reached Ben Holiday as he knelt alone in the forest beside the tiny stream, restored to himself at last, the medallion of Landover's High Lords a brilliant silver wonder cradled gingerly, unbelievingly within the cup of his hands. The scream rose out of the trees, a thin, high wail of anguish and fear, and lingered like the whistle of the wind through canyon drops in the still mountain air.

Ben's head jerked up, his neck craning. There was no mistaking that cry. It was Willow's.

He leaped to his feet, hands closing possessively over the medallion, eyes searching the forest shadows as if whatever threatened the sylph might be waiting there for him as well. A mix of fear and horror raced through him. What had been done to Willow? He started forward, stopped, whirled about desperately, and realized that he could not trace the direction of the scream. It seemed to come from everywhere at once. Damn! Meeks would hear that scream as surely as he—Meeks and that winged demon. Perhaps Meeks already *had* . . .

He was holding the medallion so tightly that it was cutting into his palms. *Willow!* A vision of the sylph blossomed in his mind, a frail and beautiful creature whose life was his special charge. He recalled again the words of the Earth Mother investing him with responsibility for seeing that she stayed safe and his promise to keep her so. His emotions tore at him and left him ragged and frantic. Truths to which he had not yet given heed flayed his soul.

The truths all reduced to one.

He loved Willow.

He experienced a warm rush of surprise and frantic relief. All this time he had denied his feelings, unable to come to terms with them. He had wanted no one close to him again, not after Annie, his dead wife. Love brought responsibility and the possibility of hurt and loss. He had wanted none of it. But the feelings had remained—as such feelings do—because they had never been his to deny in the first place. The reality of their existence had been forced upon him that first night out in the eastern wastes after fleeing Strabo and Nightshade—revealed in a dream in his dialogue with Edgewood Dirk on the reason for the urgency of his hunt for Willow.

Why do you run so? Why must you hurry so? Why must you find Willow? Dirk had asked.

Because I love her, he had answered.

And so he did—but had not allowed himself until this moment to think on it, to reason on it, and to consider what it meant.

Seconds was all it took to do so now. The thoughts, the reasonings, and the considerations all passed through his mind in a smattering of time that was barely measurable. It was as if everything that had taken so long to reach resolution was compressed down into a single instant.

But that instant was enough.

Ben never hesitated. There was a time when he would have, a time that now seemed a thousand years gone. He released the medallion with its silver-engraved image and let it fall against his chest, the sunlight sending shards of brightness into the dappled forest.

He called the Paladin to him.

Light flared and brightened at the edge of the little glade, chasing the shadows and gloom. Ben's head lifted in recognition, and there was excitement in his eyes. He had thought never to do this again, wished it in fact, prayed it might never be necessary. Now he was anxious for it. A part of him was already beginning to break away.

The Paladin appeared out of the light. His white charger stamped and snorted. His silver armor glittered, its harness and traces creaking. His weapons hung ready. The ghost of another age and life was returned.

Ben felt the medallion begin to burn against his chest, ice and fire first, then something else altogether. He felt himself separating, drawing out of his own body.

Willow! he heard himself scream her name once in the silence of his mind.

It was his last thought. A flare of silver light burst from the medallion and streaked across the glade to where the Paladin waited. He felt himself carried with it to merge with the body of the King's knight-errant. Armor clamped all about, fastening and tightening, closing down. An iron shell encased him, and the memory of who and what he had been was gone. The Paladin's memory became his, a rush of images and thoughts that spanned a thousand other times and places, a thousand other lives—all of a warrior whose battle skills had never been surpassed, a champion who had never been defeated.

Ben Holiday disappeared. He had become the Paladin.

He was aware momentarily of the ragged figure that stood statuelike at the edge of the little stream, bearded and unkempt, a worn and battered shell. He knew it to be Landover's King and dismissed the matter.

Wheeling his white charger about, he surged through the brush and scrub into the forest trees and was gone.

Willow's scream brought Meeks almost instantly. He appeared from the shadow of Mirwouk's crumbling walls astride his winged demon, dark robes flying against the sunlit afternoon skies. The demon plummeted to the hillside with a hiss, settling heavily within a gathering of pines at its far edge. Its leathered wings folded in against its wolf-serpent body, and its nostrils flared with small bursts of fire. Steam rose off its back.

Meeks slid slowly down the scaled neck, hard eyes fixed on the black unicorn as it stamped and snorted frantically some fifty feet away. He cradled in the grasp of his good arm the missing books of magic.

Abernathy pulled a still-shaken Willow protectively behind him. "Stay back from us, wizard!" he ordered bravely.

Meeks ignored him. His eyes were on the unicorn. He came forward a few steps, glanced briefly at Willow and Abernathy, looked again at the unicorn, and then stopped. He seemed to be waiting for something. The unicorn danced and shuddered as if already caught, but still it did not flee.

"Willow, what is happening here?" Abernathy growled urgently.

The sylph could barely stand. She shook her head woozily, her words nearly inaudible. "I saw," she repeated. "The images, the whole . . . of it. But there are . . . so many, I cannot . . ."

She was making no sense at all, still in shock, it appeared. Abernathy helped her over to a patch of flowered grass and sat her gently down. Then he turned back to Meeks.

"She cannot hurt you, wizard!" he called out, drawing the hard eyes instantly. "Why not let her go? The unicorn is yours if you wish it, although I cannot imagine why you would. Heaven knows, it has been a thing of misfortune for all who have encountered it!"

Meeks kept looking at him, but said nothing.

"The others will be here in moments, wizard!" Abernathy declared. "You had best hurry away!"

Meeks smiled coldly. "Come over to me a moment, scribe," he invited softly. "Perhaps we can discuss it."

Abernathy hesitated, glanced briefly back at Willow, took a deep breath, and started across the clearing. He was so frightened that he could barely make himself move. The last thing in the world he wanted to do was walk over there to the wizard and his pet demon, and yet here he was doing just exactly that. He straightened himself bravely, determined to see this thing through. He really hadn't any choice in the matter. He had to do something to help the girl, and this appeared to be the only option open to him. The day was warm and still; it was a wonderful day for just about anything other than this. Abernathy moved as slowly as he could and prayed that the others would arrive before he was turned into the wizard's latest burnt offering.

When he was a dozen paces from Meeks, he stopped. The wizard's craggy face was a mask of cunning and false warmth. "Closer, please," Meeks whispered.

Abernathy knew then that he was doomed. There wasn't going to be any escape for him. He might be able to delay matters for a few moments, but that would be all. Still, even a few moments might help Willow.

He came forward half-a-dozen paces and stopped again. "What shall we discuss?" he demanded.

The cold smile was gone. "Why not the possibility that your friends will be here to help you in the next few moments?"

He gestured briefly with the books, and a ring of twisted little figures appeared from out of the trees surrounding the clearing. The figures were everywhere, encircling them. Ugly, piggish faces with sharp teeth and serpents' tongues snorted and squealed anxiously in the silence. Abernathy felt the hair on the back of his spine arch. A dozen of the little monsters pushed Questor Thews, Bunion, Parsnip, and the G'home Gnomes from out of the trees. All were gagged and securely bound in chains.

Meeks turned. The smile was back. "It appears that your friends will not be much help to you after all. But it was good of you to wait until they could join us."

Abernathy saw his last, faint hope of being rescued disappear.

"Run, Willow!" he shouted.

Then, growling savagely, he launched himself at Meeks. He did it with the somewhat vague notion of catching the wizard off-guard and knocking free those precious books of magic. He almost got away with it. Meeks was so busy orchestrating the arrival of his small army of minions that it never occurred to him the dog might decide to fight back. Abernathy was on top of him almost before he realized what was happening. But the magic Meeks commanded was as quick as thought, and he called it to his use instantly. Green fire surged up from the books of magic, and a screen of flame hammered into Abernathy. The soft-coated Wheaten Terrier tumbled backward head-over-heels and lay still, smoke rising lazily from his singed fur. The screen of fire protecting Meeks and the books of magic flared and died.

The wizard stared back across the clearing to where Willow sat slumped upon the ground and the black unicorn waited.

"At last," he whispered, his voice a slow hiss.

He beckoned curtly to the waiting demon imps and the ring began to tighten.

Silence descended across the little clearing—almost as if nature had put a finger to her lips and said "hush" to the world. There was a moment of time in which everything slowed. Meeks waited impatiently as the circle of demon imps crept forward. His winged demon snorted, nostrils steaming. Willow sat with her head bent, still stunned, her long hair cascading down about her like a veil. The black unicorn moved close, a step at a time only, a shadow out of darkness woefully lost in daylight. Its muzzle drooped and brushed the sylph's arm gently. The white magic of its horn had gone dark.

Then a sudden rush of wind broke over the mountain heights and whistled through the trees. The unicorn's head jerked up, its ears perked forward, and its horn flared brighter than the sun. It heard the sounds that no one else could—sounds for which it had listened for centuries.

Trees, brush, and scrub exploded from the wall of the forest at its northern edge as if torn free by some massive fist. Wind howled through the opening left, and light burst free in a brilliant white flash. Meeks and his winged demon shrank back instinctively, and the demon imps threw themselves down upon the earth squealing.

A rumble of thunder turned to a pounding of hooves, and the Paladin rode out from his twilight existence into battle.

Meeks gave a howl of rage and disbelief. His demon imps were already scattering to the four winds, terror sweeping them away as if they were dried leaves at the end of a broom. The demon imps wanted no part of the Paladin. Meeks turned, the books of magic clutched tightly to his dark robes by the leather-gloved hand. He shrieked something unintelligible to the monster behind him, and the creature surged forward, hissing.

The Paladin swerved slightly, white charger barely slowing as it turned to meet the demon.

Fire burst from the demon's maw, engulfing the approaching horse and rider. But the Paladin broke through the wall of flames and came on, a battle lance lowered into place. The demon breathed its fire once more, and again the flames washed over the knight-errant. Willow's head lifted, and she saw the silver knight and horse disappear in the fire. Sudden realization rushed through her. If the Paladin was here, so was Ben!

Flames pyramided off the clearing's grasses and scorched the sheltering trees. Everything wilted momentarily in a white-hot heat. But then the Paladin was clear of the flames once more, his charger and armor covered with ash and smoking. He was almost on top of the demon now, battle lance set. Too late the demon realized the danger as it spread its wings and tried to lift itself skyward. The Paladin's lance ripped through scales and armored plates and pierced its massive chest. The wolf-serpent screamed and surged back, the battle lance breaking off within it. It tried to rise, a weak, fluttering effort it could not manage. Then its heart gave out, and it fell earthward. It crashed into the scorched grasses, shuddered, and lay still.

The Paladin broke off the attack while the demon was in its death throes, swerving to stay clear of the struggling monster. Then he wheeled back again, drew forth the great broadsword, and spurred his white charger toward Meeks to finish the fight.

But this time Meeks was ready for him.

The hard, craggy old face tightened down in concentration, the wizard's thin lips drawing back until his teeth showed. Whatever magic he yet commanded, he was calling on it now.

Wicked green light flared at a point midway between the approaching knight-errant and the waiting wizard. Meeks cried out and stiffened. His head shot back and the green light exploded in shards.

From out of the fire appeared a line of armored skeletons atop fleshless steeds, half goat, half snake. Willow counted. Three, four, five—there were six altogether. The skeletons held broadswords and maces in their gloveless, bony hands. Helmetless death's-heads smiled in frozen grimace. Riders and carriers both were as black as night.

They turned as one and came at the Paladin in a rush. The Paladin rode to meet them.

Willow watched the battle unfold from close beside the black unicorn. Her senses had returned to her now; her thoughts were clear. She saw the Paladin and the black riders come together in a clash of iron, saw the dust swirl up from the impact, and saw one of the black riders go down in a pile of shattered bones. The fighters wheeled and struck at each other, and the sounds were terrifying. She shrank from the conflict, her thoughts focused not on the Paladin, but on Ben. Where was he? Why wasn't he here? Why wasn't Landover's High Lord close to his champion?

Another black rider went down, the bones of its skeleton body snapping apart, crunching like deadwood beneath the hooves of the Paladin's horse. The Paladin broke away, whirled and struck down a third rider, the great broadsword flashing silver light as it swung through its deadly arc. The remaining riders converged, weapons hammering at him, clanging and sparking off his armor, thrusting him back.

Willow pushed to her knees. The Paladin was in danger of being forced down.

Then small bursts of green fire flared over the bones of the three black riders that had fallen, and six new skeletons rose out of the smoky haze to join their fellows. Willow felt her stomach tighten with cold. They had doubled their strength. There were too many now for the Paladin.

She lurched to her feet, determination giving her strength. Questor, the kobolds, and the gnomes were still bound and helpless. Abernathy was still unconscious. Meeks had disabled them all. There was no one left to help the Paladin but her.

No other left to help Ben.

She knew what she must do. The black unicorn stood quietly next to her, emerald green eyes fixed on her own. There was intelligence there that was unmistakable. She could read in those eyes what she must do, and it mirrored what she already knew in her heart.

She took a deep breath, stretched out her arms, and embraced the unicorn once more.

The magic rushed through her instantly, quick and anxious. The unicorn's delicate body shuddered with release, and the images began. They surged into the watershed of the sylph's mind, jumbling together. Willow jerked back from their intensity, wanted to scream, and fought back against the urge. Her need was less this time, her desire more manageable. She struggled to master it. The images slowed then, straightened into an orderly succession, and came on anew. The mix of pain and anguish that had accompanied them lessened, and their brightness dimmed into something bearable.

She began to recognize what she was seeing. Her fingers caressed the silky, delicate neck of the unicorn as the magic joined them.

A voice cried out.

Fairy-kind! Set me free!

The voice belonged to the unicorn and to nothing. Something of the unicorn was real; something else was not. The images appeared and faded in Willow's mind, and she watched them pass. The black unicorn sought freedom. It had come in search of that freedom. It believed it would find it through . . . *why?* . . . through Ben! The High Lord could set it free because the High Lord commanded the magic of the Paladin, and only the Paladin was strong enough to counteract the magic that bound it, the magic that Meeks wielded—but then there was no High Lord to be found and the unicorn had been left alone in this land, searching, and Willow had come instead, searching too, bearing the golden bridle the wizards had made to snare it when it first broke free long ago. The unicorn was frightened of Willow and the bridle, uncertain of her purpose, and it fled from her until it realized that she was good, that she could help, and that she could take it to the High Lord and set it free. Willow would know the High Lord even in his disguise, when the High Lord himself did not know . . .

The images came quicker now, and Willow fought again to slow them so their meaning would not be lost. Her breath came quickly, as if she had run a great distance, and there was a bright sheen of sweat on her face.

The voice cried out in her mind again.

The High Lord's power was lost to him and therefore lost to me! I could not be set free!

The voice was almost frantic. The images whispered urgently. The dreams that had brought Willow in search of it were a mix of truth and lies, dreams from both wizard and fairies . . . *Fairies! Her dreams were sent by the fairies?* . . . All must come together so that truths could be revealed and the power needed could be summoned—so that Paladin and wizard could meet and the stronger prevail, the stronger that was also the good, and then the books of magic could be, finally and forever, could be and must be . . .

Something intruded, other images, other thoughts imprisoned within the black unicorn for countless centuries. Willow stiffened and her arms locked about the sleek neck. She felt the scream rising within her once more, uncontrollable this time, madness! She saw something new in the images. The black unicorn was not a single life, but many! *Oh, Ben!* she cried soundlessly. There were lives in the images that struggled and could not break free, that yearned for things she could not understand in worlds she could not imagine. She shook with the emotions that ripped through her. Souls imprisoned, lives held fast, magics torn away and used wrongly—*Ben!*

Then there was a sudden image of the missing books of magic, locked within a dark, secret place, a place filled with the smell of something evil. There was an image of fire burning outward from one of those books, burning with the intensity of life being born anew, and from out of that fire and that book leaped the black unicorn, free once more, racing from the dark into the light, searching . . .

The voice cried out one final time.

Destroy the books!

The cry was one of desperation. The cry was almost a shriek. It blocked away the images; it consumed everything with its urgency. The pain it released was intolerable.

Willow's scream finally broke free, rising up against the sounds of battle. The sylph tore away from the black unicorn and stumbled back, almost blacking out with the intensity of what she had experienced. She dropped to her knees, head bent against a wave of nausea and cold. She thought she must die and knew in the same instant she would not. She could sense the black unicorn shuddering uncontrollably beside her.

The words of that final cry were a whisper on her lips.

Destroy the books!

She rose to a half crouch and screamed them out across the battleground of the little clearing.

The words were like tiny wafers of paper caught in a windstorm. The Paladin did not hear them, consumed by the fury of the battle he fought. Meeks did not hear them, the whole of his concentration given over to directing the magic he had called upon to save himself. Questor Thews, Bunion, Parsnip, Fillip, and Sot, abandoned by their demon imp captors, were lying bound and gagged at the clearing's far edge.

Only Abernathy heard.

The dog was semiconscious, and the words seemed to come to him from somewhere out of the darkness of his own thoughts. He blinked hazily, heard the words echo, heard then the sounds of the frightening conflict taking place about him, and forced his eyes all the way open.

The Paladin and the black riders whirled and struck out at each other at the clearing's center, a kaleidoscope of movement and sound. Willow and the black unicorn were small, trapped figures at the clearing's far end. He could see nothing of his other friends.

He panted, his tongue licking out at his nose, and he felt dull, aching pain working its way through his battered body. He remembered what had been done to him and where he was.

Slowly, he twisted himself about so that he could see better. Meeks stood almost next to him. Caught up in the battle between the Paladin and the black riders, the wizard had come forward the half-dozen paces that had separated him from the dog.

The words whispered once more in Abernathy's mind. *Destroy the books!*

The dog tried to get to his feet and found his body would not respond. He sank back. Other thoughts intruded. Destroy the books? Destroy his one chance of ever becoming human again? How could he even consider such a thing?

Another black rider went down, and there was the sound of breaking bones. The Paladin was hemmed in on all sides, armor blackened by ash and rent by sword and axe. He was losing the battle.

Abernathy knew what it would mean for all of them if he did and quit thinking about his own problems. He tried to rise again and found now that he could—but not all the way. His muzzle drew back in a grimace of frustration.

Then Meeks shifted his feet one further time, and suddenly his leg was inches from Abernathy's head. The wizard wore soft shoes; the leg was exposed. Abernathy's grimace turned to a snarl. He had just been given one last chance.

He launched himself headfirst at Meeks, his jaws closed over the wizard's ankle, and he bit down hard. Meeks gave out a shriek of mingled pain and astonishment, his hands flew out, and the books of magic flew up.

Everything happened at once after that. There was a streak of black light that shot across the clearing, past the Paladin and

the skeleton riders, past the clouds of dust and bursts of green
fire. The black unicorn sped quicker than thought. Meeks jerked
his leg frantically, trying to free himself from Abernathy's jaws,
groping at the same time for the airborne books. Abernathy
would not let go. Willow cried out, and Abernathy bit down
harder. Then the black unicorn had reached them. It leaped into
the air, its horn flaring white with the magic, speared the tumbling books, shattered their bindings like glass, and scattered
their pages everywhere.

Down fluttered the loose pages, those with the drawings
of the unicorns mingling with those whose centers were charred
from that inner fire. Meeks screamed and yanked free at last of
Abernathy's jaws. Green fire burst from his outstretched hands
and hammered into the unicorn as it soared, knocking it askew.
The unicorn twisted in midair, and white fire arced from its
ridged horn into the wizard. Back flew Meeks. Green fire exploded into the unicorn, and white fire hammered into Meeks.
The fires raced back and forth between unicorn and wizard, the
level of intensity rising with each new burst.

The Paladin whirled swiftly at the clearing's center,
broadsword arcing in a circle that cut apart the remaining black
riders and scattered their bones. It was a perfunctory task now;
the black riders were already disintegrating. The magic that had
sustained them had gone out of their hollow forms. They crum-
bled instantly and were gone.

Then the Paladin was racing toward the unicorn and the
wizard. But the Paladin could not reach them in time. The fire
had engulfed Meeks, the magic too strong even for him. He
shrieked one final time and exploded into smoke. The black
unicorn was engulfed in the same moment, the fire all about.
Stricken, it arched skyward, leaped into the air and was gone.

The Paladin, too, disappeared. It rode into a sudden burst
of white light, the light washing away ash and dust and healing
silver armor until it shone like new—all in an instant's time—
and knight-errant and light simply faded away.

Abernathy and Willow stared at each other voicelessly
across the charred, empty forest clearing.

• •

Then it happened.

They all saw it—Willow and Abernathy as they crouched upon the scorched hillside, still stunned from the fury of the battle just completed; Questor, the kobolds, and the G'home Gnomes as they struggled futilely to sit upright, still secured by the bonds that the demon imps had used to restrain them; and even Ben Holiday as he stumbled breathlessly from the forest trees after having run all the way from the place of his transformation, not knowing what had brought him, knowing only that he must come. They saw it, and they held their collective breath in wonder.

It began as a wind that disturbed the mountain stillness, just a whisper at first, then a rush of sound like the roar of an ocean. The wind sprang up from the earth upon which the pages of the broken books of magic now lay, stirring dust and ash, whipping at the few tiny shards of green flame that still flickered in the meadow grasses. It lifted skyward in the shape of a funnel, catching up those scattered pages in a snowstorm of white. The pages that were burned became suddenly healed, their ragged edges closing, their yellowed surfaces turning pristine white once more. The pages that were filled with the drawings of the unicorns mixed and joined with them until none was distinguishable from the others. A wall of pages rose up across the skyline, crackling and snapping madly as the wind whipped them through the air.

Then the pages began to change. The drawings began to shimmer and flex, and abruptly the unicorns came alive. No longer frozen in still life, they began to race about the funnel's edge. There were hundreds of them, all white, all in motion, a blur of power and speed. The pages and bindings of the books of magic were gone now; there were only the unicorns. They flew through the air and cried out in ecstasy against the roar of the wind.

Free they seemed to be saying! *Free!*

Then the funnel broke apart and the unicorns scattered, flooding the skies above the mountain clearing in a rush of graceful, delicate bodies—like fireworks exploding in an impossibly beautiful shower. The unicorns spread out across the skyline—buoyed by the magic of their transformation—then soared into the distance. Their cries lingered after them momentarily, then faded into silence.

The mountains had gone still again.

Legend

"*T*here never was any black unicorn," Willow said.

"There was, but it was only a deception," Ben said.

Questor Thews and Abernathy, Bunion and Parsnip, and Fillip and Sot looked at each other in confusion.

They sat within the shade of a great, old oak at the edge of the meadow clearing, the lingering smell of scorched earth a pungent reminder of all that had befallen. The last of the shards of green flame had flickered out, but trailers of smoke and particles of dust and ash still floated weightless through the sun-streaked afternoon air. Abernathy had been dusted off, the others had been freed of their bonds, and the six of them were gathered about Ben and Willow, who were trying to explain what had happened. It wasn't easy because neither of them knew everything yet, so they were piecing the story together as they went.

"It might be easier if we start at the beginning," Ben offered.

He hunched forward, legs crossing before him. He was ragged and dirty, but at least they all recognized him now. Removing his own deception of who and what he was had removed theirs as well.

"A long time ago, the fairies sent the white unicorns into Landover on a journey to certain of the mortal worlds. We

know that much from the histories. The unicorns were the most
recognizable magic the fairies possessed, and they sent them to
those worlds where belief in the magic was in danger of failing
altogether. After all, there has to be *some* belief in the magic—
however small—for any world to survive.

"But the unicorns disappeared. They disappeared because
the wizards of Landover waylaid and imprisoned them. They
wanted the unicorns' magic for their own use. Remember,
Questor, when you told me that the wizards were once a powerful guild that hired out—back before the King sent the Paladin
to dispose of them? Well, I'm betting a major part of that magic
came from the imprisoned unicorns—magic that the wizards
siphoned off. I don't know what magic they possessed to trap
the unicorns in the first place—a deception of some sort, I'd
guess. That seems to be their favorite trick. At any rate, they
caught them up, changed them into drawings, and trapped them
in those books."

"But not whole," Willow said.

"No, not whole," Ben agreed. "This is where it gets interesting. The wizards separated the body from the spirit of
each unicorn in making the transformation. They imprisoned
the body in one book and the spirit in the other! That weakened
the unicorns and made them easier to hold. The body without
the spirit is never as strong. The wizards' magic was potent
enough to imprison each separately; the trick was to prevent
them from joining again."

"Which was the danger Meeks faced when the black unicorn escaped," Willow added.

"Right. Because the black unicorn was the collective *spirit*
of the imprisoned white unicorns!" Ben furrowed his brow.
"You see, so long as the wizards could maintain the strength
of the magic that bound the books, the unicorns could not break
free and the wizards could drain the unicorns' magic as well
and put it to their own use. Even after Landover's King sent
the Paladin to crush the wizards' guild years ago, the books
survived. They were probably kept hidden for a time. Even
later, the wizards still remaining, those now in service to the

King, were careful not to let anyone know the real source of their power. And the books were passed down from wizard to wizard until at last they came to Meeks."

He touched his index finger to his lips. "But—in the meantime—there was a problem with the unicorns. Every so often, they escaped. Something would happen, the wizards would relax their vigilance, and the unicorns would break free. It didn't happen often, of course, because the wizards kept close watch over the books. But now and again, it did. Each time, it was the *spirit* part of the imprisoned unicorns that managed to escape—the magic of the spirit always being stronger than that of the body. The spirit would burn its way free of the pages of the book of magic that bound it and escape. But it lacked a true physical presence. It was only a shadow formed of need and will, a silhouette given momentary substance and life—and not much more." He glanced quickly at Willow for confirmation, and she nodded. "And because it was black in color, being only a shadow, it was generally assumed to be something evil rather than something good. After all, whoever heard of a black unicorn? The wizards, I am certain, spread the story that the black unicorn was an aberration—a dangerous thing, perhaps even a demon. They probably set a few examples to reinforce the belief. That kept everyone away from it while the wizards worked at getting it back again."

"The bridle of spun gold was used for that purpose," Willow interjected, picking up the story. "The wizards employed their magic to create the bridle after the first escape. The bridle was a magic that could draw and hold the black unicorn, giving the wizards time to imprison it anew. It was always caught quickly; it was never free for long. It was sent back again into the books of magic, the burned pages were restored, and all was as it had been. The wizards took no chances. The books were their greatest magic, and they could not risk damage to or loss of them."

She turned to Ben. "That was why the black unicorn was so frightened of me at first. Even in its need, it was terrified. I felt its fear each time I came close and again, later, when I touched it. It believed me to be a tool of the wizards that had imprisoned it. It couldn't know the truth. It was not until the very end that it seemed to understand that I was not in service to Meeks."

"Which brings us to the present," Ben announced, straightening. "Meeks had gained possession of the books of magic in his turn and had used them as had all the wizards before him. But then the old King died and everything started to fall into ruin. The black unicorn hadn't escaped for a very long time—perhaps centuries—and there hadn't been any need for the golden bridle in all those years. I don't think even the wizards before Meeks had paid a whole lot of attention to it for a while because it was apparently before Meeks' time that it was stolen for the first time by Nightshade. Later it was stolen by Strabo and then went back and forth between the two after that. Meeks knew where it was, I suppose, but the books of magic were safely under his control, and the witch and the dragon didn't know the real purpose of the bridle in any case. The trouble started when Meeks went over to my world to recruit a new King for Landover and hid the books of magic in his absence. I suppose he thought he wouldn't be gone long enough for anything to happen to them, but things didn't work out that way. When I didn't come crawling back to give up the medallion and the Iron Mark didn't finish me off, Meeks suddenly found himself trapped over there with the books of magic still hidden over here. The magic that imprisoned the unicorns weakened once more in his absence, and the spirit part—the black unicorn—burned free of the pages of its book and escaped."

"So that was why my half-brother sent the dreams!" Questor exclaimed, new understanding beginning to reflect on his owlish face. "He had to get back across into Landover, recover the missing books, and find the golden bridle—and quickly! If he didn't, the black unicorn might find a way to free all the white unicorns—its physical selves—and the magic would be lost!"

"And that is exactly what it tried to do," Willow confirmed. "Not only this time, but every time it managed to break free. It tried to find the one magic it believed stronger than the magic of the wizards—the Paladin! Always before, it was caught so quickly that it never had any real chance. It knew the Paladin was the King's champion, but it would never even manage to reach the King. This time it was certain it could—except that there was no King to be found. Meeks was quick to act, once he discovered the unicorn had escaped. A dream was used to lure Ben out of Landover before the unicorn could reach him. Then Meeks crossed back with him and altered his appearance so that no one—including the black unicorn—could recognize him."

"I think it might have recognized me if it hadn't been imprisoned for so long," Ben interjected. "The older fairy creatures such as Nightshade and Strabo could recognize me. But the unicorn had forgotten much of its magic while it was bound."

"It might have lost much as well through the wizards' use of it," Willow added.

"Meeks told me that night in my bedchamber, when he used his magic to change me, that I messed up his plans in some way," Ben went on, returning to the matter of his lost identity. "Of course, I didn't have any idea what it was that I had done. I didn't know what he was talking about. The truth was that everything I had done was inadvertent. I didn't know that the books contained stolen magic and that, if he weren't within Landover, the magic might be lost. I was just trying to stay alive."

"A moment, High Lord." Abernathy was shaking his head in confusion. "Meeks sent three dreams—yours to provide him a way back into Landover, Questor Thews' to give him possession of the missing books of magic, and Willow's to regain for him the stolen bridle. The dreams worked as they were intended except for Willow's. She found the bridle, but she failed to bring it back to you as the dream had told her she must. Why so?"

"The fairies," Willow said.

"The fairies," Ben echoed.

"I said that first morning that my dream seemed incomplete, that I felt I was to be shown more," Willow explained. "There were other dreams after that; in each, the unicorn appeared to be less a demon, more a victim. The fairies sent those dreams to guide me in my search and to teach me that my fears were false ones. Gradually, I came to realize that the first dream was somehow a lie, that the black unicorn was not my enemy, that it needed help, and that I must provide that help. After the dragon gave the bridle of spun gold to me, I was persuaded further—by dreams and visions—that I must go in search of the unicorn myself if I were ever to discover the truth of matters."

"The fairies sent Edgewood Dirk to me." Ben sighed. "They wouldn't intervene to help me directly, of course—they never do that for anyone. Answers to our difficulties must always come from within; they expect us to solve our own problems. But Dirk was the catalyst that helped me to do that. Dirk helped me to discover the truth about the medallion. Meeks had instigated the deception that led me to believe I had lost it. Dirk helped me see that *I* was the one fostering that deception, and that if *I* could recognize the truth of things, others could as well—which is exactly what happened."

"Which is why the Paladin was able to reach us in time, apparently," Questor said.

"And why the books of magic were finally destroyed and the unicorns freed," Willow added.

"And why Meeks was defeated," Abernathy finished.

"That's about it," Ben agreed.

"Great High Lord!" exclaimed Fillip fervently.

"Mighty High Lord!" echoed Sot.

Ben groaned. "Please! Enough already!"

He looked imploringly at the others, but they all just grinned.

It was time to leave. No one much cared for the idea of spending another night in the Melchor. It was agreed they would be better off setting up camp in the foothills below.

So they trudged wearily down out of the mountains through the fading daylight, the sun sinking behind the western rim of the valley in a haze of scarlet and gray. As they walked, Willow dropped back next to Ben, and her arm locked gently about his.

"What do you think will become of the unicorns?" she asked after a moment.

Ben shrugged. "They'll probably go back into the mists, and no one will ever see them again."

"You do not think they will go on to the worlds to which they were sent?"

"Out of Landover?" Ben shook his head. "No, not after all they've been through. Not now. They'll go back home where it's safe."

"It isn't safe in your world, is it?"

"Hardly."

"It isn't very safe in Landover, either."

"No."

"Do you think it is any safer in the mists?"

Ben thought about that a moment. "I don't know. Maybe not."

Willow nodded. "Your world has need of unicorns, doesn't it? The magic is forgotten?"

"Pretty much."

"Then maybe it doesn't matter that it isn't safe there. Maybe the need outweighs the danger. Maybe at least one unicorn will decide to go anyway."

"Maybe, but I doubt it."

Willow's head lifted slightly. "You say it, but you do not mean it."

He smiled and did not reply.

They reached the foothills, passed through a broad meadow of red-spotted wildflowers to a stretch of fir, and the kobolds began scouting ahead for a campsite. The air had gone cool, and the approaching twilight gave the land a muted, silvery sheen. Crickets had begun to chirp, and geese flew low across a distant lake. Ben was thinking about home, about Sterling Silver, and the warmth of the life that waited there for him.

"I love you," Willow said suddenly. She didn't look at him, facing straight ahead as she spoke the words.

Ben nodded. He was quiet a moment. "I've been meaning to say something to you about that. You tell me you love me all the time, and I can never say it back to you. I've been thinking lately about why that is, and I guess it's because I'm afraid. It's like taking a chance you don't have to take. It's easier to pass it by."

He paused. "But I don't feel that way right now, right here. I feel altogether different. When you say you love me, I find I want to say it back to you. So I guess I will. I love you, too, Willow. I think I always did."

They walked on, not speaking. He was aware of the increased pressure of her arm about his. The day was still and restful, and everything was at peace.

"The Earth Mother made me promise to look after you, you know," Ben said finally. "That's part of what started me thinking about us. She made me promise to keep you safe. She was most insistent."

He could feel Willow's smile more than see it. "That is because the Earth Mother knows," she said.

He waited for her to say something more, then glanced down. "Knows what?"

"That one day I shall bear your child, High Lord."

Ben took a deep breath and let it out slowly.

"Oh."

Epilogue

*I*t was two days before Christmas.

Southside Chicago was chill and dreary, the snowfall of the previous night turned gray and mushy on walks and streets, the squarish highrise projects and tenements vague shadows in a haze of smoke and mist. Steam rose out of sewer grates in sudden clouds as sleet pelted down. Not much of anything was moving. Cars crawled by like prehistoric beetles, headlights shining their luminous yellow eyes. Pedestrians ducked their heads against the cold, their chins buried in scarves and collars, their hands jammed into coat pockets. Late afternoon watched an early evening's approach in gloomy silence.

The corner of Division and Elm was almost deserted. Two boys with leather jackets, a commuting businessman, and a carefully dressed woman, headed home from shopping, stepped from a bus, and started walking in different directions. A shop owner paused to check the locks on the front door of his plumbing business as he prepared to close up for the day. A factory worker on the seven-to-three shift ducked out of Barney's Pub after two beers and an hour of unwinding to begin the trudge two blocks home to his ailing mother. An old man carrying a load of groceries shuffled along a sidewalk path left in the snow by a trail of icy footprints. A small child engulfed by her snowsuit played with a sled by the steps of her apartment home.

They ignored each other with casual indifference, lost in their own private thoughts.

The white unicorn flew past them like a bit of strayed light. It sped by as if its sole purpose in being was to circle the whole of the world in a single day. It never seemed to touch the ground, its graceful, delicate body gathering and extending in a single fluid motion as it passed. All the beauty in the world— all that was or could ever be—was captured by its movement. It was there and gone in an instant. The watchers caught their breath, blinked once, and the unicorn had disappeared.

There followed a moment of uncertainty. The old man's mouth dropped open. The child put down her sled and stared. The two boys ducked their heads and muttered urgently. The businessman looked at the shop owner and the shop owner looked back. The carefully dressed woman remembered all those magical stories of fairies she still enjoyed reading. The factory worker thought suddenly of Christmas as a child.

Then the moment passed, and they all moved on. Some walked more quickly, some more slowly. They glanced over at the misted, empty street. What was it they had seen? Had it really been a unicorn? No, it couldn't have been. There were no such things as unicorns—not really. And not in cities. Unicorns lived in forests. But they had seen something. Hadn't they seen something? Hadn't they? They walked on, silent, and there was a warmth within each of them at the memory of what they had experienced. There was a feeling of having been a part of something magical.

They took that feeling home with them. Some of them kept it for a time. Some of them passed it on.

A writer since high school, **Terry Brooks** published his first novel, *The Sword of Shannara*, in 1977. It became the first work of fiction ever to appear on *The New York Times* Trade Paperback bestseller list, where it remained for more than five months. He has published numerous bestselling novels since. A practising attorney for many years, Terry Brooks now writes full time and lives with his wife, Judine, in the Pacific Northwest and Hawaii.

To find out more about Terry Brooks and the Magic Kingdom of Landover series visit www.terrybrooks.co.uk

WIZARD AT LARGE

Terry Brooks

Ben Holiday, the High Lord of Landover, is back in his rightful place. The evil wizard Meeks has finally been dealt with, and all seems at peace. But, even in a Magic Kingdom, peace never lasts long . . .

It was all Questor Thews' fault, whether or not the inept Court Wizard would admit it. His bumbling attempt to return Abernathy from the body of a dog to his original human form has resulted in the Court Scribe being transported to Earth, to be replaced by a multi-coloured bottle. Furthermore, Abernathy was wearing the High Lord's medallion at the time, without which his powers are drastically reduced.

When Ben and Willow follow Abernathy to Earth, Questor is left in charge, but in both worlds things quickly go from bad to worse . . .

ARMAGEDDON'S CHILDREN

Terry Brooks

Fifty years from now, our world is unrecognisable. Pollution
and warfare have poisoned the skies, the water and the soil.
Pockets of society still exist, living in highly fortified
strongholds, but even these isolated compounds are not safe.
Armies of demons and once-men assault their defences and,
one by one, they succumb. Civilisation has fallen and
anarchy is the only law.

Logan Tom and Angel Perez are the last two Knights to
stand against the forces of chaos. To them will fall twin
tasks: to find and protect a very old and a very new magic.
Although the odds are stacked against them, Logan and
Angel have the power to halt the destruction of the
Old World.

It will be up to others to usher in the New . . .

THE SWORD OF SHANNARA

Terry Brooks

A tale of mythic proportions, in the grand tradition of
The Lord of the Rings.

Long ago, the world of Shea Ohmsford was torn apart by
the wars of ancient Evil. But in the Vale, the half-human,
half-elfin Shea now lives in peace – until the mysterious,
forbidding figure of Allanon appears, to reveal that the
supposedly long-dead Warlock Lord lives again, and will
destroy the world . . .

Shea, the sole true descendant of Jerle Shannara, must
embark upon an elemental quest to find the sword, the only
weapon powerful enough to keep the creatures of darkness
at bay.

'A marvellous fantasy trip'
Frank Herbert

RUNNING WITH THE DEMON

Terry Brooks

With the epic Shannara series, Terry Brooks turned fantasy fiction on its head. Now he's done it again. Unleashing fantastical creatures and incredible magic into our world, *Running with the Demon* is the first book in a spellbinding new series from a master storyteller.

On the hottest Fourth of July weekend in decades, two men have come to Hopewell, Illinois. One is a demon, a dark servant of the Void, with a terrible secret goal. The other is John Ross, a Knight of the Word, who, while he sleeps, lives in the hell the world will become if he fails to change its course on waking.

At stake is the soul of a fourteen-year-old girl mysteriously linked to both men . . .

And the lives of the people of Hopewell . . .

And, while friends and families picnic in Sinnissippi Park and fireworks explode in celebration of freedom and independence, the fate of mankind itself.